The Alaskan Chronicles

The Provider

The Alaskan Chronicles

The Provider

John Hunt

LODESTONE
BOOKS

Winchester, UK
Washington, USA

First published by Lodestone Books, 2018
Lodestone Books is an imprint of John Hunt Publishing Ltd., No. 3 East St., Alresford,
Hampshire SO24 9EE, UK
office1@jhpbooks.net
www.johnhuntpublishing.com

For distributor details and how to order please visit the 'Ordering' section on our website.

Text copyright: John Hunt 2017

ISBN: 978 1 78535 689 6
978 1 78535 690 2 (ebook)
Library of Congress Control Number: 2017941363

A CIP catalogue record for this book is available from the British Library.

Design: Stuart Davies

Printed and bound by CPI Group (UK) Ltd, Croydon, CR0 4YY, UK
US: Printed and bound by Edwards Brothers Malloy 15200 NBN Way #B, Blue Ridge Summit,
PA 17214, USA

Also by John Hunt

Non fiction

Bringing God Back to Earth

We operate a distinctive and ethical publishing philosophy in
all areas of our business, from our global network of authors to
production and worldwide distribution.

Contents

PROLOGUE   1

PART ONE: SUMMER   5

PART TWO: FALL   101

PART THREE: WINTER   201

PART FOUR: SPRING   233

EPILOGUE   303

Map of the Kenai Peninsula and Anchorage

Main characters

The Richards family
Donald: Father
Mary: Mother
Jim
Bess

The Hardings family
Matthew: Father
Jessie
Sue

Louise Maclaren: Teacher

Bob: Handyman

Paul: Missionary

Nat: Ferry Captain

Theo: Mayor

PROLOGUE

THE NEAR FUTURE

I'm old. I'm tired. A husk, a shell, a frame of creaking bones, memories blowing cold in the attic. There's no sap running through these veins. Sleep comes fitfully – why spend your time unconscious when you have so little of it left? I feel like an old bull moose, energy fading, one winter too many, wolves snapping at its heels, wearing it down, circling, waiting for the kill.

I'm eighty-two this year. A full twenty years older than anyone else in our settlement. It's not normal, in these times, to get to this age. "Normal," now, is different. I guess we've regressed a few thousand years in my lifetime, to the Iron Age – Mrs. Maclaren's history lessons are still with me. I'm wrapped up warm in my bear skins in front of the fire. The fort's earth and stone walls are five feet deep, two-stories high, and keep out the worst of the winter weather, though the cold wind whistles around the corridors. The guards at the door, with their spears, are there to keep me in as much as to keep enemies out.

The Council have agreed to let me write down my story. I don't care what their reasons are. The winters are long, and I've nothing else to do. Gor, my faithful personal servant – and I think, my friend, I hope, knowing what I'm going to ask him to do if I finish this – is free to go out to the woods. He peels off armfuls of birch bark, flattens it with stone slabs, dries it, smooths with oil, and then polishes and trims it into book-sized pages. In the light of the tallow candles I've cut some pens from goose feathers, soaking them in hot water, cleaning out the membrane from the shafts, undercutting the bottom face to form a curve and slitting back a little to create a reservoir to hold the ink, which I've made with blueberries, charcoal, vinegar and oak gall. It's a good ink, the kind that everyone used till the twentieth century, when we

1

started making it with chemicals, and it will last longer.

The twentieth – what a strange century that was. After two World Wars, the Cold War, fascism and communism had been defeated, nationalism was in retreat – we seemed to be on the brink of a golden age of peace and prosperity; of free information, renewable energy, driverless cars, bionic people. I was born in the early years of the twenty-first. Of course, we still had problems, but in what we used to call Alaska you were more likely to die from a lightning strike than be killed by terrorists; to die from eating too much rather than too little. Shops were full of stuff you didn't need, physical work was so rare that people paid to go to gyms to exercise – I don't know if we were happier back then, but it sure did leave us unprepared for what was about to happen. We took what we had for granted. And now, we don't know what we've lost. We're heading back to the dirt rather than the stars. Nature sure has taken its revenge.

But I'm digressing already. I've done what I can here – I played the game, and lost. I hear the warriors around here saying that defeat makes you stronger, but sometimes, I reckon it just means defeat. Those I've loved have gone. My grandchildren, and great-grandchildren are kept from me. Now I just have my dreams. They come back to me at night, dreams of the world that was, of what it might have been. Anyway, what is still to happen, will happen. As an old Aleut friend used to say to me: "Today is all you have."

Will anyone ever read this and tell the stories around the fire at night? We've been through bad times before, maybe we can find our feet again? My fear is that we keep going backwards – but how far? Back to the Stone Age? I remember reading about the last of the Neanderthals, holding out in a cave for a few generations at the very extremity of Europe, when we'd driven all the others to extinction. What went through their heads? Did they know they were the end of their line?

Europe – that rings a bell. I'm sure there must be others,

somewhere, who could tell the story, in places that used to be called Africa, India, China…I remember countries like the Philippines, Indonesia, New Zealand: tribes living a pastoral life on the steppes of Asia. Maybe I'm fooling myself, it's such a long time since I heard those names. But I know there were people living on the earth who weren't dependent on electricity, so it stands to reason that somewhere they could still be living, much as they always had been. Perhaps flourishing in a warmer climate, rather than scratching a living in this frozen corner of the far North. But we have no contact with them. They could be on a different planet.

So this is just my tale, for the record. Without a record, there can be no "history." Without a history, there can be no "people." Without a people, there can be no "individuals."

I *am* an individual. I have my story, my people, *my* history. That's how I see it, and this was my life.

PART ONE

SUMMER

ONE

The quill scratches the bark, the flames flicker in the hearth. I can hear a Great Gray Owl hooting rhythmically outside in the trees – *whoo, whoo, whoo*. Do owls change their language over centuries, like people do? I don't know. There's so much I haven't learned. And so few people now to learn from. Learning…it's so long since I even thought about this. The walls of the fort fade, the years roll back, aches and pains slip away like a snake shedding skin – and I find myself sitting in Mrs. Maclaren's class on a hot Friday afternoon in June: a nervous, over-tall, gangly and gawky teenager.

Mrs. Maclaren was my favorite teacher. She lived in the next road from us, though we didn't meet socially. But when I had a paper round she always left out a couple of dimes for me. She'd been teaching history classes for the 11th grade at Anchorage High for as long as anyone could remember. I enjoyed them. She talked in long, curling sentences that always seemed to be saying something important, explaining how history "worked." She talked about movements, migrations, trends: about soil being degraded, forests cut down, climate changes. She spoke of the Indians coming to Alaska, followed by the Eskimos – I'd always assumed it was the other way around – and of the Vikings in Greenland, when it still had a touch of "green." She talked of the explorers who tried to bend a harsh landscape and a reluctant people to their will – people like the Cossack Zhdanko, and Captain Bering – they were my heroes. I'd look at the map in the evening and trace the places they visited, the names telling their own story: Desolation Point, Goodnews Bay, False Pass, Halibut Cove. I guess even "Anchorage" actually *meant* something, back in those early days.

Mrs. Maclaren was short, bespectacled, her white hair tied back in a bun. Nobody raised their voice against Mrs. Maclaren.

Joss Tinker called her a squaw – behind her back, and she did look part Indian with her light-brown skin and slanted eyes – rumor had it that her Scottish great-grandfather had settled down with a Native woman after he left the Yukon, rich from selling shovels and supplies to the miners. I didn't like Joss, but then, he didn't like me. I talked to Dad about him once, when I came back with a black eye after he'd shoved me aside in the lockers and I'd bumped into the corner of an open door, how he thought he knew everything, but didn't know anything, and didn't care that he didn't, and didn't care who he thumped, either. Dad said that a lot of men were like that, it was why we needed more women in positions of power. That seemed daft to me. Men were leaders, women were followers; at least those were my views at the time, before I really knew any women. Before I met Jessie.

"Spengler describes history in terms of cultures," Mrs. Maclaren said, "one of which is ours, the American/European culture. He says they each have a lifespan of around a thousand years, and ours is coming to an end. Was he just depressed by the First World War? Was he right? An essay, one thousand words, with your thoughts on that."

Joss put up his hand. "What's a culture, Miss?"

They carried on for a while, but it went over my head. Sadie, a couple of desks away, had yawned and was twirling a lock of hair that curled around her ear. The light streaming through the window turned it transparent, like the conch shell I had in my bedroom. I remember wondering, if I could put my ear to hers, whether I'd hear the sea breathing.

"Jim Richards! Wake up, pay attention," Mrs. MacLaren spoke sharply.

Then the school PS system crackled into life – "All teachers to the staff room now please." We'd never heard that before. It surprised everyone into a momentary stillness, then Mrs. Maclaren got up, and with, "Carry on reading the notes on

Decline of the West, class," she left.

About ten minutes later, she was back, the noise subsided, we sat straight at our desks or scuttled back to them. She sounded tense, somehow. "School's closing early today. The buses are at the gate. Something's happened, and you need to get home. We've been contacting those parents who'll be coming to collect you; you can wait here until they arrive. Tell them that the President will be addressing the nation this evening at six o'clock, if they don't already know."

There was a buzz, a babble, a rise of voices, she patted the air in front of her, waving the noise down. "I can't tell you, I don't have any answers. Be calm, go carefully, God bless you."

TWO

Our family were the standard two plus two. I guess people thought of us as a "solid" family, a "happy" one. Dad had a job teaching engineering at the University of Alaska. He was wiry, reserved, someone who made things rather than talked about them. My mom, Mary, had trained as a nurse but gave it up when my sister and I were young. She was plump, hair bushed out in curls; bubbly, mercurial, empathy flowed through her veins – she was always touching, hugging, the warm heart of any room. They were like chalk and cheese, but seemed to rub along well.

My sister, Bess was in ninth grade; at fifteen she was two years younger than me. She had soft, silky brown hair with a rosebud mouth – looked like a TV weather presenter, with the kind of confidence that radiated. If you were in her circle, you were "in." We weren't antagonistic, we didn't fight or anything, we just lived in parallel worlds. Though to be fair, I did overhear her once saying to her friends, "Look, Janice, he may be a jerk, but he's my brother, OK?"

I came home on the yellow bus with her – not that we sat together; she was with her friends at the back, I was up by the driver. I was awkward around girls. And boys, too, for that matter. I couldn't seem to get on the wavelength as far as joshing went, or carry much of a conversation. I was no jock, clumsy at throwing or catching, the last to be selected for the baseball teams. I was good at cross-country, my long legs seemed to eat it up, and I enjoyed getting into the rhythm of it. But we didn't do much of that. If you couldn't measure it on the track, it didn't count.

We lived in Fulton Street, on the edge of a smart area of town; middle class, mostly professionals with families. The houses were set back, half an acre each, with long drives, staggered along the rise to keep the views clear. Manicured lawns ran down to the road, shaded by clumps of hemlock, cedar and birch, everything trimmed to within an inch of its life, cars tucked away in garages. Like a million other suburban streets, it exuded a quiet respectability and pride. It felt like the backbone of America. If it could speak, I guess it would say something along the lines of – "We might have come here as immigrants, but we've tamed the land, we've made it ours, we've built our city on the hill, we're here to stay. And we're going to keep it this way – no need for fences or gates, we're all civilized here. We're prosperous but not showy, stable but not dull. Honest and decent. Other parts of the world might have wars, refugees, but this is a good life, the best there is anywhere, and we vote for it."

Bess skipped past me as we walked up the drive. "Mom, Mom," she began calling out as soon as she got the door open. "What's going on? We got out early."

Mom was on the phone. "I don't know, Brenda," she was explaining to someone, "I haven't heard anything yet. Look, the kids have just arrived, I'll ring you later, honey, OK?"

"I'll go look on Facebook." Bess took off up the stair. "Bess…" Mom started to say, but she was too late. "Oh well, now, Jim, before you get into your gaming, you've got to tidy that room of yours, it's a tip."

Soon it was all humming with noise; the hoover, the dishwasher running, the AC working away, the boiler rumbling in the cellar, *CBS 60 Minutes* on the TV, "This is most unusual," the presenter was saying, "if not unprecedented. We still have no indication of what the President is going to say; the Press Office is keeping a tight lid on it; could it be his resignation?" Our neighbor, Jerry, was mowing his lawn, rush hour traffic roared along Fulton Street, the phone went again, I heard the crunch of tyres on the gravel after a while as Dad arrived home early.

"Kids, your father's home," Mom called out. "Donald, do you

know what's going on?"

"No idea, Mary." The doorbell chimed. "I'll get it."

"Jerry, Marcia, how are you?"

"You've heard about the President, Donald? Sounds like an event. Saw you arriving. Rather than watching it next door, could we come and sit with you? We've brought drinks."

"Of course, great, come on in."

Sitting here now, on these winter nights, the only sounds the scratch of the pen, the crackling of the fire, the Great Gray Owl booming away, mice rustling in the straw, it's those little details that come back to me vividly: the buzz of civilization, of security and convenience, of regulated warmth. The unlimited power dedicated to our comfort, light available at the flick of a switch; hot water at the turn of a tap; communication at the press of a button; food, ready to eat; new clothes and shoes – ready made; the magic of TV – it feels unreal now, a fantasy. I've given up trying to describe it to Gor – he looks at me pityingly.

"People lived in boxes on the wall?"

"Kind of. And there was something called the Internet. You could ask anything of it."

"You mean like the Oracle? How did it do that? You're losing your mind, master," he replied, shaking his shaggy head. He could only have been in his twenties, but he looked more like in his forties. People age faster now.

Am I indeed losing it? I guess that's why I'm putting down this record, to remind myself that this is what life was like, that this is what happened, that it's true. Writing it down – it somehow makes it real again. It's almost as if...if I could understand what happened, I'd know what to do next. As if I could learn something.

We settled on the sofas around the TV. Dad and Jerry were both scrolling through their phones.

"Looks like it might be something to do with the sun," said

Jerry. "But no one seems sure."

At six, the President strode magisterially out to the podium, stared us in the eye, and started talking. From memory, it went like this.

Fellow Americans. I've some important news for you all. In a few hours' time, around midnight, we're expecting to see something happen to the sun. The experts call them Coronal Mass Ejections. But I'll be calling them solar flares. These happen all the time, coming in cycles every few years, and normally cause no problems. But this one, people say, might be huge.

Now the climate people get everything wrong, they're a sad bunch, and they're probably wrong this time. But I've always been honest with you, unlike previous presidents, and I have such a huge respect for you all that I'm telling you this now. If they're right, then you won't be taken by surprise tomorrow morning when you hear about it – we won't actually see anything from here, because we'll be facing away from the sun. If they're wrong, well, you're intelligent people, and you can make up your own minds about where your tax dollars should go.

If it does happen, it'll take a day or two to reach us. Believe me, it will not affect your health, you will feel nothing. It won't hurt or damage you in any way. But people say it's quite possible that the electricity supply will be affected across the country for some days. We do not have the time to build in systems to prevent that. So all solid-state electronics might stop working. That means anything with a circuit board, which includes radios and televisions, cell phones and computers and other electronics. So it could affect cars, fridges, lighting, heating, power lines and landlines.

Fortunately, I'm able to give you this advance warning. Other nations will be following our lead. I'm in regular contact with other presidents. I'll be addressing the nation again at nine a.m. tomorrow morning, when we'll know whether it's happened or not. God bless you all, God bless America.

We listened for another few minutes as other presenters came on, mostly talking about what life might be like without electricity for a while, and what to do about it if it happened. They interviewed a family who had been off-grid for years, and were fine about it. Nearly a million families in the country already lived that way, out of choice. Seemed like it would be a piece of cake.

Then Mom got up – "Come here kids, I want to hug you both," she said, a quiver in her voice.

I hated the fuss, the physical contact, but I put up with it resignedly. Bess looked up at her with her big, brown, doe-like eyes. "Mom, are we going to be all right?"

"Of course we are, dear." Mom stroked her hair. "It'll be fun. Like that Thanksgiving when we had the power cut, and ate sandwiches by candlelight. You remember the games we played?"

Bess rolled her eyes. "Mom, we were kids back then. OK, I'll go along with it, but only if I can have some friends over."

THREE

Anchorage was a church-going community. Pretty well everyone went, at least occasionally. Not that the churches ruled life as much as they used to – the city had grown so fast, and people would come in, move out – much like the air cargo traffic, it was one of the world's biggest airports for that. But there wasn't much "heart" to it. The churches had most of that.

We didn't attend though. Dad didn't talk about religion, other than to say it wasn't for him. He said he was a scientist, he believed in what he could measure, and he believed in people, not the supernatural. Mom was more open. She read the Bible, and I'd seen her praying. Me...I'd no idea. I remember it meant something to me when I was younger, in Sunday School class, but I couldn't remember what.

But Mom had insisted. "This is a time for good neighborliness."

So I went with Mom and Dad later that Friday evening to St. Mary's Episcopal, a few blocks away. Bess was out with friends. The church was packed, people standing around the walls, there must have been several thousand there. I started to count them, multiplying by rows. The minister was a small, roly-poly man, in a smart, greenish suit, brown-framed specs on his pointy nose, jabbing to make his points, like a bird searching for worms. He was just coming to the end of his talk.

"So we're doing our utmost to serve the people of Anchorage in our time of need. In our little church here, Isabel and her sisters have so graciously set up forty volunteer rotas, with half a dozen helpers in each, who will visit areas of the community house by house, bringing material and spiritual food. Like Joseph in the Old Testament, we are creating a central depot and asking everyone to bring what surplus they have so we can distribute it to those in the most need. We can turn this difficulty into something positive, with God's help. I'll take any questions now."

"What if it doesn't happen? Isn't all this unnecessary?" Someone asked.

"I don't think the President would have announced it on TV if he had any doubts," said the minister. "He doesn't take kindly to being made a fool of."

A voice from toward the back of the hall. "I don't know why you think God will help you in this, minister. It's His judgment coming. Revelation 16:8 *"And the fourth angel poured out his vial upon the sun; and power was given unto him to scorch men with fire."* God will look after the believers. We should be praying for grace, for salvation, for God to avert his wrath, not doing the social services job for them."

Like everyone else, I turned to look at him, expecting to see some kind of prophet with long white hair, the way he talked, some guy from Old Testament times, but he seemed an ordinary type.

The minister paused. "There is a role for the Marthas of this world as well as the Marys, my friend. I do believe God is here in this, and will help us. But I believe He wants us to respond in the way Jesus would have done. With compassion, and mercy in our hearts."

The guy wouldn't give up. "I feel called to say something, minister. You don't know Jesus, you haven't taken him into your heart. The Rapture is coming! I call on you all to repent, please, get on your knees to turn the fire away from us. Do it now, before it's too late!" And he turned, elbowing through the crowd to the door.

The minister raised his hands. "Well, our brother has his point of view. Indeed, some of us may agree with him. Some of us have the gift of prophecy and tongues, some of us the more boring ones of service and organization." He shuffled a bit. "But I don't believe this is the end. And the Rapture is not mentioned in the Bible. We do not know when the time will come. Perhaps, though, it's the beginning of the end. And these days will certainly see many more people looking for the path of salvation and righteousness. So churches need to be expanded to contain them. And if we ask for a donation from everyone we help, we might reach our building fund target. In the meantime, it could be a difficult week, but I'm sure if we lose power it'll be restored in a few days. So let's be sensible and follow what the government's asking us to do, and we can see all this as an opportunity to show our faith in action. Thank you all for coming this evening. Let's end with a prayer."

He bowed his head, raised his arms, his voice deepened.

Heavenly Father, protect us in our hour of need. Give us wisdom to discern what's right, fill us with compassion for those who need our help. Guide our leaders, let the Holy Spirit be upon them as they make the decisions for our nation. Be with our loved ones everywhere, and lead us through the coming days. Support all our congregation here, and our service to the community. We ask this in the name of your son, Jesus Christ. Amen. "

The minister wasn't in my kind of world, but his words were comforting. I remember thinking that with so many churches and Christians in Anchorage there would be plenty of help around. And with our strong government, surely nothing could go seriously wrong. There really couldn't be anything to worry about. Not for us, anyway.

FOUR

Hours later, at midnight, way past my bedtime, and we were still watching TV. It was all about the solar flares and what they could mean. Of course, we couldn't see anything in the sky ourselves, it was night here, but on the other side of the world seemed like everyone was outside, watching the sun, through glasses. You could see the black sunspots, scattered all over. The local presenter was talking.

"Well, folks. Amazing things happening here. These people with eclipse-viewing glasses can see the flares. Not all of them, they're mostly outside the range of visual frequencies. I can tell you though, these aren't just "flares," they're vast, it's more like the sun is exploding, throwing off huge fireballs. Each of these individual flares is hundreds and thousands of billions of tons of plasma, the stuff the universe is mostly made of, being ejected, tens of millions of miles across, travelling at millions of miles an hour.

Is this unusual? No, it happens all the time. In fact, back in 1989, the whole of Quebec was shut down for a week! Can you imagine that? No power for a week? Maybe that had something to do with the birth rate the following year! And I'm told there was a huge flare a few years ago, in 2012, but it missed us. The sun's aim is not great. The last big one it managed to hit us with was back in 1859. But guess what? We had no electricity back then. There was only the telegraph to knock out. So it didn't matter. We're hearing that this thing might be a lot bigger, we'll find out and let you know, but the word from the governor's office is that we're going to have a great party. You don't want to miss this, When these solar flares hit the earth's magnetic shield in the early hours of Sunday, it's going to be the most spectacular fireworks ever.

But now on to other news. The Sea Wolves are down thirteen points in their last game..."

Dad was looking stuff up on the Internet. Mom was on facetime to family, but the lines were so overloaded, they kept losing the connection. She managed to get a few minutes of conversation in over several hours of trying. Aunt Beth, in London, England, said that they'd heard about it earlier, when the Prime Minister addressed the nation, same time as the President, and there was some rioting. The news on the Net was that there were a few hundred dead in Manila, wherever that was. But it was getting harder to find information. China had closed down.

"C'mon now, kids," Mom said, "let's get ready, like they say. Jim, you can fill the bath with water. Bess, could you find as many containers as you can. Donald, you've still got those candles and gas burners left over from last time?"

We were sitting around the TV again the next morning, on Saturday, watching the President.

...It's not certain that one of these flares will hit us. But to be on the safe side, to protect our homes and our security, I've declared a state of National Emergency across the whole country. All flights are grounded. Ships are being directed to the nearest port. Now I have tremendous respect for you all, but there are criminal elements in this country, especially in the cities, full of thieves and murderers. Let's not kid ourselves, we all know who they are. So the National Guard has been called out, and a curfew will operate from eight p.m. tonight – the storm, if it happens, will be around midnight. So later this evening, all travel will stop. There will be no panic, and sales of food and water will be restricted per person and family. Looters will be shot on sight. We will offer no mercy to looters. Looters will be treated like terrorists. And borders will be closed. No terrorists will be able to take advantage of this. Your security is my first concern. Priority in services will be given to the military, the police, and hospitals, in that order. All radio and TV channels, until the storm arrives, will be dedicated to providing you with

18

information you need. We'll bunker down, and we'll ride out this storm. As a precautionary measure, the national grid will be shut down until the storm has passed. So from eleven p.m. tomorrow evening, you will have no electricity. It will be restored a couple of hours later.

The President paused, running his hands over his hair, his voice deepening.

Do not be scared by false reports, like those from the Chinese News Agency. Fantastic lies are being told in some quarters. The media is all lies. We will pull through. We'll do more than that. You know I've never shirked a challenge. And this challenge is a huge opportunity for us.

Now here's something I want to share with you people. The grid is in a terrible state. Awful. Most of it is more than a hundred years old! Previous administrations didn't fix the roof when the sun was shining. They preferred spending tax dollars bringing the country down, not investing in oil and coal, sending the work abroad, pretending that we – we – were to blame for climate change. They'll be blaming us for these solar flares next. (He laughed.) *They were too lazy, too corrupt. The grid needs a trillion dollars of repairs. Trillions. So we're going to fix it! It's going to mean massive jobs. Huge. Huge. This is going to be the biggest investment in the history of our great nation. Bigger than the railroads. Bigger than aviation. Bigger than roads.*

You know I've always risen to the occasion. We will all rise to the occasion! Because we are a great people. This is a wonderful opportunity to come out of this even greater, to clean up our streets, upgrade the power, purge America and restore it to its rightful place in the world. I'll be working with you night and day to see this happen. God bless you all.

"What a bullshitter," said Dad. "Though he's right about the grid."

"Seems to me he's right about most things," I muttered. I liked strong leaders. But there was never any point in arguing with Dad, or Mom. Their views were too wet, too set.

We kept on watching, but there was no definite information yet. The news anchor was talking.

Opinion in the scientific community is divided. Most are agreed it will have an impact, but some say it will only affect the half of the earth facing the sun. Others say that the flares we've had before were pinpricks compared to this, and one of those giant balls coming this way would envelop the earth if it hit us directly. Either way, we haven't seen a solar superstorm like this before. Could this be another Carrington Event, likely to happen every century or two, or could it be even bigger, of the kind that might happen only once every thousand years or more? Will it have a localized effect on some power grids, or will it be like the asteroid that ended the rule of the dinosaurs? Exciting days, folks. We'll find out in the early hours of Sunday. They have ninety million miles to cross first...

FIVE

Saturday was a strange day. The Internet connection was still mostly down. It seemed like everyone was trying to talk to everyone else, but no one had anything particularly helpful to say. The news channels just kept repeating non-information. Mom and Dad spent the morning doing the kind of things parents do, sorting out things, checking stores.

"What we have here isn't going to last us long," Dad said, after a while. "I'll drive to the mall to pick up more water and food. Should be fine if the Guard is out."

He came back a couple of hours later, rubbing a big red mark on his cheek.

"I was trying to break up a fight. People were trampling on each other in Walmarts. We were meant to queue and stick to one basket, there were a couple of cops there but I guess they didn't want to shoot their neighbors over a loaf of bread. Glass and flour all over the floor. Same everywhere. All I could get was some lemonade and a few potatoes."

"People are fighting? Here?" I could see the disbelief cross Mom's face. She stood silent for a moment, then, "Never mind, I did a shop last weekend, and the fridge is half-full. We'll get by." Her eyes went to Dad's cheek. "You're going to have a nice bruise there tomorrow, you'd better let me get some cream on that."

I heard some banging from out the back, and went over the fence to say hello.

Mr. Thacker, Bob, lived in a small bungalow that backed onto our garden. He was here when we arrived ten years ago, when Dad got the university job. He'd always kept himself to himself. I didn't know if he had any friends or relatives – but he was always polite, to us at any rate, but not "socially aware," according to my parents. He was shorter than me, usually unshaven, a bit grungy, long white hair tied with a red ribbon in a ponytail, always wearing the same old, faded, blue overalls. He had a sort of ageless look about him – must have been in his seventies, he would never say. But he looked capable. His hands were large, scarred, with misshapen fingers. He never seemed to do anything about the house, which looked more ramshackle as the years went by. He was a veteran, but that was way back in time, and he hadn't had a proper job since – he scraped a living "fixing" things. In his back yard there were a couple of trucks, several rusting cars, old fridges and lawnmowers, half-hidden in weeds. He looked as if he'd been born and bred there, aging along with the plot.

"He brings down the tone of the neighborhood," Mom would mutter.

Still, she liked him, and we got on with him better than his neighbors on the other side, who'd petitioned the council to have his back yard cleaned up.

We generally said "hi" every couple of days. Every weekend I spent a few hours at his place, digging his vegetable patch, washing up, and he gave me the odd dollar, but the great thing – a few years earlier, he'd taught me to shoot a rifle. He wouldn't let me use his Browning BLR or his Winchester M70 but he had two Ruger American bolt action rifles which weighed less and with a smaller kick. It was my all-time favorite thing. The Rugers lost accuracy after a hundred yards or so, but anything under that was easy. After a few months I found there was something magical about willing a small hunk of lead into a bulls-eye. Why go through the cumbersome business of throwing a ball when you could hit the target direct, in an instant?

"You're a natural, Jim," he'd said to me. "Just pop over the fence and pick up the rifle here from the porch any time you like, go practice."

Sometimes, when there weren't too many chores to do, Mom let me go hunting with him. We'd drive for an hour or two and go after small game – squirrels, hares, ptarmigan, that kind of thing. A few times, Mom let me stay with him overnight, out in the bush. I think she was nervous about it, but I always came back happier, and she liked me that way. We'd bivouac, and he'd teach me stuff about lighting fires, how to do it with a lens, or steel, or bow and drill: about following tracks, and being prepared. Boy Scout stuff. I loved it, being out there. He was my best friend. My only one, really, to be honest, if I didn't count those on the war-gaming forums, who I hadn't actually met.

"Hey, kiddo, what's up?"

"Don't rightly know, Bob. I'm nervous. No one seems to know anything. What do you think's going to happen?"

"Don't know myself, kid. That's why I'm doing this."

"What are you doing?"

"I'm fixing this old dump truck. Putting in a new crankshaft, new tires, welding some panels to the back."

"Why? Looks like a clunker from one of those Second World War films, *The Dirty Dozen* or something."

"In case I need to use it."

"What's wrong with your pickup?"

"Nothing at all, Jim, but the starter motor needs electricity. If we've got no electricity, it's not going to last long. With this, I can produce the electrical current from the mechanical power of the engine."

"But why would you need it?"

Getting up, he wiped his hands on a dirty grey rag. For a long moment, he looked at me without speaking, then he said, "Perhaps I'll come over and see your folks tomorrow. I might be around in the morning."

SIX

That night we were all outside, on Jerry and Marcia's lawn, with a group of other neighbors, looking up at the night sky, sunglasses ready, just in case. All along the road and across the other side of the hill, through the trees, we could see lights on, everyone still up, the beams of torches flickering as people gathered. The news all evening had been about the temporary blackout. A minute before eleven p.m. people started chanting "sixty, fifty-nine, fifty-eight..." and ended with a cheery shout on "zero!" Nothing happened. Then, a few seconds late, all the lights went out, and applause resounded around the valley. Around midnight, there were murmurings of approval as the sky started to flame, like the Northern Lights, which we'd seen many times before, but in many more colors. Then it went up a notch, and another one, to gasps of astonishment. Rich purples at the top, down through shimmering greens, yellows and blues, more colors than you can think of. And then it went up another notch, and again. For the first time in my life, I felt my jaw physically drop. I'd seen weird stuff on the Internet, but nothing like this for real. The sky was so bright it was like midday. Streams of fire were flickering along the electrical wires. The ground flared red.

Bess was taking pictures on her mobile. "Awesome!" she shouted. "This is so weird!"

The birds were singing.

"They think it's daytime," Dad said. "Well, I guess one of those fireballs did wrap itself around the earth."

"What a thing, hey?" Jerry called out. "Feel privileged to have seen it."

We stood there, in the middle of the most amazing fireworks display since the world was born till it died down after an hour or so.

"I guess we'll stay out here till the electricity comes back on," said Jerry, shining the torch around. How about you guys?"

"I'm ready to get some z's now," said Dad, "I'll see you in the morning."

I went inside with Dad, and slept late. Around eleven a.m. I finally got up. The room was already hot, the AC wasn't working. Bess was still asleep. Mom and Dad looked as if they'd been up for hours. They were talking in low voices, as if they hadn't wanted to disturb us.

"We should keep the fridge door closed, Mary, to keep the cold in."

"What's the point, Donald? We need the milk for cereal and it's going to go off in a couple of days anyway."

"But if we keep the fridge door closed we could use it tomorrow."

"But why? We need it now."

They heard me on the steps and turned.

"Jim, morning. Wake Bess up, and we'll have some cereal for breakfast."

"I could skip cereal," I offered.

"You're going to have breakfast, young man," Mom replied.

"OK, Mary, let's grab it and shut the door quick."

Bess came jumping down the stairs, her hair flying around. "Dad, my phone isn't working, can you fix it?"

Dad looked exasperated. "Bess, where've you been lately? The power grid went down last night, and it hasn't come back yet. I don't even know if phones will work when it switches on again. We need to keep the food as fresh as we can, so, no trips to the fridge. And there's a curfew coming this evening, so we shouldn't go too far from home."

"But, Dad, I was going to Facetime with Janice this morning," Bess complained.

"Sorry, honey, you'll just have to wait till the power comes back."

Bess pouted. "That's such a drag. I'll just have to go chill with her then. Can you give me a lift?"

"The cars won't start, I've tried them."

"Oh, fine, I'll walk it then."

Dad hesitated. "Look, Bess, we don't know if it's going to be safe out there. It's a long way. What do you think, Mary?"

"I don't want the kids out of sight of one of us in this kind of situation."

The pout became a frown. "Are you locking me down? That's not fair."

"I'm sure Janice's parents will be thinking the same, **Bess.**"

"Oh Mom...don't be ridiculous. It's a power cut, not the end of the world!"

Then there was a knock at the back door. Mom went to answer it.

"Bob, good to see you, come on in. Let me get you a coffee, we've got a gas burner on. Two sugars, wasn't it?"

"Thank you kindly, Mam. I'm sorry to trouble you," he said, "but I think we should talk."

He sat on a stool at the kitchen table, with the four of us, awkwardly cradling his cup.

"I'll get to the point. There's trouble coming."

"Well, we know that, Bob, but what do you mean exactly?" Dad asked.

"There's no power. We don't know for how long. Things are going to get difficult, fast. You've probably not got food for more than a few days. I can help you."

"C'mon, Bob." Dad raised his eyebrows. "You're exaggerating, surely? The government will sort it out. It'll be back to normal in the next day or so."

Bob got up and prowled around. He seemed out of place in Mom's smart kitchen, like something dragged in from the woods.

"You may be right, Mr. Richards. But if you aren't, we could work with each other."

"How?"

"You're a practical guy, Mr. Richards, an engineer. Mrs. Richards knows nursing. I know I haven't been a great neighbor, but I like your kids. And Jim here has potential. If things get bad, it's not a good time to be on your own. I have guns, and I know the bush. I think we could make a team. Teams'll survive better than families."

"Are you for real, Bob?" Mom laughed sunnily. "You've been watching too many survival movies." She grabbed a dishcloth and scrubbed at the countertop, cleaning up non-existent dirt. "And I don't want you scaring the children. The answer is no. But you're always welcome around here at any time."

"Yessum," he said resignedly. "But bear it in mind. I'm gonna be moving out."

"What about the curfew?" Dad objected.

"Just how long do you think that'll last? You think the police and Guard will stick around when their cupboards are being raided and their wives beaten up? It'll be rough then, safer out of the city."

"You've got a really downbeat view, Bob," Mom said accusingly. "You've been living by yourself for too long. This is a friendly community. We'll stick by each other."

"Maybe. But you know what they say about the difference between an Alaskan and a bucket of shit?"

"No."

"The bucket."

"Are you dissing me?" This time Mom's laugh had an edge to it. "You sure know how to appeal to a woman."

Bob was silent for a moment, then he said, "No, I'm calling you a fool...with all due respect. Geez, take a joke," he added, hastily, as Mom bristled. "Anyway," he said, edging towards the door. "Wanted to leave the thought with you. Maybe I'm completely wrong, and I hope I am. But it don't hurt to be prepared. I've seen what happens when food and water runs out. It don't matter where you live, who you are – everyone turns animal." Opening the door, he said, "If you change your mind, I'll still be here for a day or so, got some work to do."

I wondered what he was talking about. But it was none of my business, all down to Mom and Dad.

Not being able to use my cell phone didn't bother me, I rarely used it anyway. But not being able to play *Total War: Rome* – that was a blow. I'd just established the strongest army in the field and could lose my position with a time penalty. I went to my room to put some more stamps into my collection instead. I only had four hundred stamps with birds of the world on them, and there were over ten thousand to go. I'd have to speed up when I got a job. I was looking forward to that – imagining what you could do if you had real money!

I heard Mom curse, which was really unusual.

"Donald, can you get this door open for me? The washing machine's stopped in mid-cycle. I forgot about that when I put it on."

"I think it'll have to wait, Mary, short of taking a crowbar to it. I'm just fixing up kerosene lamps and candles."

It was weird without TV. What did people used to *do* before TV and the Internet? Sleep? Sit around talking?

Still, it was only a day. I expected, we all expected, that it would be over soon. Though in a way, I hoped it wouldn't be – it was different, edgy. But I had no idea that this was it – forever.

SEVEN

On Monday we had cereal again for breakfast. The dishes were stained.

"We should save the water in the tank rather than using it to flush the toilet, or for washing up," Dad said, wiping them down with kitchen roll. "There's no more coming in. Probably the pumps in the water towers are down. We'll only use it for drinking now."

"What are we going to do then?" Bess asked.

"We'll dig a hole outside," Dad replied.

"You mean go to the toilet in the yard? Where people can see you?" Bess looked horrified. "I can't do that. It's gross."

"Bess, there's nothing wrong with it. I don't remember you flushing the toilet when you were a baby." Mom chuckled. "You should try being a nurse, really get to see bottoms then."

"Needs must," replied Dad. "Come on, Jim, let's go dig a hole."

I wished I was more like my dad. Figure out what needed doing, then do it.

I wiped myself down with a towel after the digging. It was hot again. The windows were open for the breeze, the flies were annoying. Dad had been talking to neighbors. No one knew what was really going on; they said there was looting downtown.

"The one time in your life you really want news, you can't get any," Dad commented.

Troops from Fort Richardson now stood at the main intersections. The only traffic on the roads were the emergency services, police and Guards. Around us, along Fulton Street, it was eerily silent. Nobody going to work or school, no deliveries. It seemed like everyone was waiting for something to happen, to be told what to do.

"I'm going to walk a few blocks down to Main Street to see

what's going on." Dad looked at me. "Want to come, Jim?"

"Go carefully," Mom said as we left. "Don't go near any trouble."

It was cooler outside, under the trees that lined the street.

It felt strange, though, walking along the empty street with Dad, I couldn't remember doing that before. I'm not sure I'd ever seen *anyone* walking along the street before.

"Do you think it will be school again tomorrow, Dad?"

"You might get a few days off, Jim. Are you missing it?"

"No, I was wondering if I could go hunting with Bob."

"We'll have to stick together as a family till things are back to normal. When we get back though, you could get a fire going in the yard and we'll start cooking some food from the freezer. It's defrosting. If we cook it, it'll last longer."

"Why aren't there any cars?"

"Everyone's got electronic ignition. You'd need a car that predates that, with a carburetor, back from the 1970s."

"What's a carburetor?"

Dad laughed. "It mixes fuel and air to the right ratio in the engine. Nowadays it's done by fuel injection. But that needs electronics. And those've been short-circuited. I guess you're not going to make an engineer, Jim."

"What do you think I could be?"

"You like biology, don't you? And being outside? Perhaps something to do with botany?"

We'd just passed Mrs. Maclaren's house, one of the smaller ones on the street, a chalet-style place with an all-round verandah, when we heard shouting and a smashing sound. Dad turned around and ran up the drive, with me following. The front door was open.

"What the hell's going on?" Dad shouted, as we ran into the kitchen. "Break it up!"

Mrs. Maclaren was trying to hold onto a gallon container of water and this guy was trying to pull her fingers off it.

"You keep out of this, it's none of your fucking business," he snarled.

"He's stealing my water," shouted Mrs. Maclaren.

I saw Dad tense, and clench his fists. "Leave her alone and get out of here."

"I'm just asking her to share, there's only one of her, I've got a family, it's fair."

"Go through that door," Dad said, pointing. "Don't come back, and we'll forget about this."

Dad wasn't a fighter, but he was broad shouldered and with all the work he'd done tinkering with engines, you could see the muscles in his forearms. I could see the guy's hesitation.

"You're making a mistake getting involved, mister," he said, releasing the container. "I'll be back." He walked through the kitchen, out the back door, slamming it behind him, and disappeared.

Mrs. Maclaren slumped into a chair, shaking. It was a surprise, seeing her by herself, outside the school, so ordinary, so vulnerable. Maybe the adult world wasn't that different from that of the kids.

Dad put his arms around her. "Are you OK?"

"Thank you so much," she whispered, looking at me with recognition in her eyes. "You must be Jim's father?" she said, looking in my direction. "I teach him at school."

"I am indeed. And you must be Mrs. Maclaren. He's told me about your classes, he likes them. Now who was that guy? Do you know him?"

"I've seen him around, he lives a few doors away. But we've never really been introduced. He was asking if I had some spare water, his family didn't have enough. But I just didn't like the way he was asking, and then he just barged in."

"Well, I guess there's nothing we can do about it now, Mrs. Maclaren. I don't think we'll get far troubling the police at the moment with an incident like this, even if we could ring them.

But you can't stay here by yourself. It's not safe. He said he'd be back. There could be others. Why don't you come and stay with us for a day or two? Till this is over?"

"Oh, I couldn't impose on you like that!"

"It's no trouble, really. We've got a spare room. Here, let me help you get your things. Jim, could you go back and wheel over my trolley from the garage. Explain what's happening to your mom. She can make the bed up, and we'll be over before lunch."

I set off at a run. A couple of hours later and we were back home, with Mrs. Maclaren, a suitcase of clothes, a crate of food, and a few gallon-containers of water. Dad introduced Mrs. Maclaren to Mom and Bess.

"Mrs. Richards, this is so kind of you. I hate to be a burden, but I must admit I didn't like the idea of staying on in the house alone. At least it won't be for long."

"It's a real pleasure to have you, Mrs. Maclaren." Mom smiled. "We've got you a room ready, and you're very welcome to stay till things have settled down again. This is my daughter, Bess."

"Very pleased to meet you, Mrs. Maclaren." Bess turned on her full wattage, dimply smile.

"I've seen you around school, Bess," Mrs. Maclaren shook her hand. "I'm taking you for history next term. We'll have to see about you improving your grades." Bess' smile faded.

EIGHT

The rest of the day passed without further incident, though we started hearing occasional gunshots in the distance. We swapped food with Jerry and Marcia in return for water – being just the two of them their tank was lasting longer.

On Tuesday, I accompanied Dad and Jerry down again to St. Mary's. Jerry carried a pistol.

Dad looked surprised. "I didn't know you had one, Jerry."

"Hope I don't have to use it, I've only had a few practice shots, but I'm not leaving the house without it. You should get one, too."

There were two men, also with rifles, in the lobby. Dad recognized one.

"Expecting trouble, Brian?" Dad nodded at the rifle.

"We've already had some, Donald. We're running shifts here to protect the stores, day and night."

"Any chance of food or water?"

"Zilch, I'm afraid. What we have left we're keeping for the sick and elderly. The minister and elders are out distributing it. But it's getting more difficult, several of them have been robbed in the street. I didn't think it would be like this. Maybe Alaskans are just like everyone else, after all. Though I hear we've got twelve thousand dollars in towards the building fund. So that's good. No cloud without a silver lining, eh?"

"So what should we do?"

"You'll just have to ration what you've got, Donald. We all have to. It's been two days now. Can't be long before this gets working again."

"Thanks, Brian. You take care now yourself. See you later."

All through the afternoon we heard gunshots from downtown. They sounded like firecrackers going off, like an all-day Fourth of July.

"Donald, what's going on downtown?" Mom asked.

"I guess once people start shooting, if there's no clamp down, it escalates," Dad replied. "Most people here own a gun."

"I could borrow Bob's, Dad," I said, enthusiastically.

"No way, absolutely not," Mom replied firmly. "We're not getting into any shooting wars."

From my bedroom window I could see several columns of smoke.

Later that evening Dad called an "emergency council". We sat around the kitchen table, along with Mrs. Maclaren and Bob, with mugs of coffee.

"Joe Manning down the road knows someone with a ham radio," Dad opened the meeting. "I wish we had one. He says the messages coming through are confused. No one seems to know when the power is coming back. There's fighting in the cities. The government aren't saying anything, other than to stay where we are. But people are leaving, where they can." He got up and paced around the room. I'd never seen him so uncertain before. "We need to decide what to do. We've emptied the fridge, we've cooked what we could in the freezer, that will last us for a few days, but we're nearly out of water. It's a couple of miles to the nearest creek. I don't fancy getting some without support."

"I've been keeping an ear to the ground," said Bob. "The police and guard are starting to pull out. They're just going home. Downtown, it's everyone for themselves. Nobody's giving a fuck. There are fires starting – arson or not, nobody seems to know. In this weather, people trying to cook, it's easy for them to get out of control. There's no water to put them out. The soldiers are confiscating guns, they'll shoot you rather than talk. But there aren't enough of them out there to keep order. I saw a camel, must've escaped from the zoo, the electric fences are down. There'll be others – polar bears, wolves..."

Bess' face started to crumple. "Wolves? Are they going to come here?"

"Honey," Dad said, "they won't, they'll be running for the hills. Now, you can go to your room if you like. But if you want to sit here with us, you'll need to be brave and not cry."

"I'm going to be leaving later today," Bob told us. "You're welcome to come with me if you want."

"Donald, it can't be that bad, surely," said Mom, sending Dad a worried look. "This is America, it's the 21st century, it'll come right. The government will send supplies in."

"You want to bet your lives on that?" Bob snorted. "I'm not. They'll be looking after themselves."

"But that's ridiculous, there's plenty of food and water in this country, Bob. We don't know what we'll get into if we leave."

"There's millions of cattle down in the plains, Mrs. Richards, and billions of chickens, but how are they going to get here with no transport? Most motors won't start. Petrol pumps don't work. There's probably not more than a day's food and water left in Anchorage, and quarter of a million people to feed. You know how much food that many get through every day? The supermarkets turn their stock over a couple of times a week. How are they gonna replace it? And it'll be the same everywhere."

He stood up in front of the fireplace. "Look, I've got some beans and a bag of oats I can leave you, if you want to stay. I've always kept some in the cupboard, for emergencies. I can survive by myself, live off the land. Don't eat much anyways. If you want, I'd like to help. But we'd have to move. Sooner the better. I'm going to be leaving tonight. The roads could be blocked any time. A few breakdowns, a crash – the traffic lights aren't working. We need to head out to the bush, where we can find fresh water, fish. Trap game. We should get out now, while we can. You've heard the shooting, and it's getting worse. People'll be killing each other."

"Bob, most people aren't like that at all!" Mom exclaimed.

"Not when there's food on the table and cops in the street, sure. But have you ever been without food for a few days? And anyway, you don't need guns to kill. People are using the creeks as toilets, they're dumping waste in them. Others are using them for drinking water. You know about these things, most don't. How long before the city's ill?"

Mom opened her mouth, but then didn't reply. I could see the force of that argument striking home. We were all quiet.

Dad broke the silence. "Where would we head for?"

"Dunno," Bob said slowly. "Guess the interior would be best. Plenty of space. But most people will be heading out that way, to Fairbanks, and beyond. Glenn Highway is likely to be blocked. So I'd go south, to Kenai. A lot of its remote enough, and I know it. Or else along to the Qutekcak villages."

Dad dry washed his face. "I guess if we're going to do this, we need to do it properly," he said. "If we were on the coast, we'd have the sea to support us. But we'd need a boat for that. That's going to be more important than a truck if this is going to carry on for long."

"That's a good point, somewhere on the coast then."

"You mean *steal* a boat?" asked Mom, shocked. "How is this legit? You want us to go to prison?"

Dad hesitated. "Let's call it borrowing. And only if we have to. But I'd feel more comfortable with access to the sea. And anyway, we'll have to break into somewhere to stay."

"Breaking in?" Mom raised her voice. "Donald, what are you talking about? Are you going mad?"

"There are lots of empty holiday cabins around, Mary. We're not going to hurt anybody. And we'll need to be self-sufficient. We'll need all the gear, enough for six, maybe for a week or two. I can't quite get my head around it all yet." He looked at Bob. "I don't think we can be ready tonight. And I'd like to leave it to the last minute in case the power does come back on. But if we start packing now, how about first thing tomorrow?"

Bob hesitated. "OK. I've got some of the necessaries, but probably not enough. Pack now, leave tomorrow."

Mom sighed. "Look, alright, if you insist on this. But I don't like it. I expect the power will be back by then anyway."

"But I don't want to go." Bess pouted. "I want to stay with my friends."

"It's only for a while, Bess," Mom soothed. "Like a holiday."

"I don't want to go on holiday. I'd feel safer here. The wolves are out *there*, not here, Dad said so."

"We have to do this together, Bess," Dad said firmly.

Mrs. Maclaren got up from her chair and spoke for the first time. "It's the five of you. You'll need to count me out, I'd just be a hindrance. I'll stay here, look after the house for you."

"If we go, then you're coming too, Mrs. Maclaren," replied Mom. We're not leaving you here, and that's final."

"But I'd be an extra mouth to feed. And I wouldn't be of any help. All I can do is quilt."

"You can always keep the lessons going with Jim and Bess," Mom replied. "They can catch up with the schoolwork they're behind on."

"Those aren't the kind of lessons we'll need," said Bob. "But I agree with Mrs. Richards. Let's go together. It won't be safe for you to stay."

"If we're going to do this, and be partners in crime, let's at least be on first name terms," said Mom. "Call me Mary, Bob. No more of this Mrs. Richards stuff, OK?"

"OK, if you say so."

Mrs. Maclaren opened her arms in surrender. "All right, thank you, I'll come. And please call me Louise."

"Donald," said Dad.

They shook hands.

"OK folks," Dad summed up, "it's getting late. Let's start, and I'll set the alarm for five tomorrow."

NINE

Bob got the Chevrolet truck started with a crank handle and brought it around onto our drive.

"OK, let's do this," Dad said. "We may as well take all we can. I'll start with the tools in the cellar. Mary, perhaps you could do the bedrooms and anything we could use from the attic? Jim, Bess, all the outerwear you can find, boots – empty the shed. Then we'll get the food. Jim, those survival books of yours, see if they've got any tips on what to take. What was that guy's name, Bear something? Spare batteries, candles, Bob – what do you have?"

"Rifles, ammo, nets, maps, welding equipment. I've got a fifty gallon container of gasoline. And a couple of spare ones. Could you siphon the fuel out of your tanks, Donald? You know how to do it?"

"How long are we going to be gone for?" Bess asked.

"I don't know, Bess," Dad replied. "I hope not long. But best to take as much as we can rather than have to come back for it. Bob, I've got a few hundred dollars in cash – I'll put that under the back seat here."

"What about my computer, can I take that?"

"I don't think there's any point, Bess. And keep clothes to things that are going to be useful."

The truck seemed huge, but after a couple of hours we were running out of space. Bob said that Dad, me and Bess would need to be at the back, in the open, himself with the ladies in the cab, so he'd rigged up spaces for us on top of spare tires.

The activity brought our friends Jerry and Marcia around from next door.

"Donald, what are you doing? Where are you going?" asked Jerry.

"We're heading off for a few days, reckon it'll be safer in the country," Dad explained.

"Have you told the office?"

"No one there to tell, and I'm owed holiday, Jerry."

"You should have talked to us, Donald," Marcia said.

"Marcia, how much food and water do you have?"

"Enough for three days or so," she replied. "But there will be help coming."

"Disasters are not unusual," Jerry added.

"Seems to me that this one is, Jerry. Usually, they're local, regional, whatever. Help soon comes from outside. But where's it going to come from this time? This is national. Hell, seems like it's all over the world. Now, we're almost out of water. I don't want to ask you if we can share yours again. So, we have to go."

"But what food and water there is, that's right here, Donald." Marcia looked upset. "Not out there in the bush."

"Can't see the alternative, Marcia," Dad replied. "And what are you going to do at the weekend, when you've run out, if the power's still out, and the cavalry haven't come? I don't like this, but I don't know what else to do."

More neighbors turned up, intrigued by the activity and talk.

"But it's against the law," said Mrs. Stiglitz. "There's a curfew. You're much safer here. The government will have it under control soon."

"I've heard there's an army convoy of lorries coming from Fairbanks with food and water," added Mrs. Barrack.

"I haven't heard that, Mrs. Barrack. Are you sure? I'd heard that they were running out of food in Fairbanks as well. Where would they be getting more from?" Dad said.

"But it feels like you're deserting us, Donald, you should stay with us. Let's stick together," Jerry persisted. "If we don't, what's going to happen to us?"

"Do you want to come with us, Jerry?" Dad asked.

"What a thought!" exclaimed Marcia. "You think it's safer out there with all those wild animals than here at home?"

Mom came out carrying some boxes of gear. "Marcia, you

know me, I'm not going near any wild animals. Spiders bring me out in a rash. Anything else, I don't want to think about. We'll be careful. Would be lovely if you could come as well, and I'm sure it will all be sorted out soon anyway."

"Want to tell us where you're going, so we can send out a rescue party?"

"Well, we don't have anywhere definite to go to," Mom replied.

"You've all gone crazy as coons." Marcia rolled her eyes in mock horror.

"If Mrs. Maclaren's going with you, who's going to teach her classes? Will you be back for next term?" asked Mrs. Planck.

"I'm sure we'll be back by then, Amelia," Dad said.

"It's the Russians," grunted Mr. Poloski. "I heard they put a bomb in the sun. You shouldn't leave. That's what they want, to get us scared."

"The Russians?" Dad scratched his head. "How could they possibly bomb the sun, and why?"

"No one knows what they can do, Donald, that's why they're so dangerous."

"You can't flee the Judgement that's coming," added Mrs. Palone. "And there's no churches or pastors out in the wilderness. If something goes wrong, you'll die unsaved," she said, looking almost happy about it.

"How much food do you have, Mrs. Palone?" Dad asked.

"We're out, but God and the government will provide. We're praying for them."

"I don't want to go, Mrs. Palone," Bess complained as she came out carrying a box of clothes: "But Mom and Dad are forcing me. Could you say goodbye to Amanda for me?"

"You poor girl! Of course I will. Your parents are making a big mistake, but I expect you'll be back in a few days, do come around and see us then."

"Later," Bess called as she skipped back into the house.

A few of the neighbors started to talk at the same time.

"Hold your horses, folks." Dad's tone was exasperated. He raised his hands. "You know I'm not one for churches anyway. I appreciate your concern, thanks, but we're going, OK? I hope it won't be for long."

"Shall I check the house over while you're gone?"

"Thanks, Jerry." Dad fished in his shirt pocket for his keys.

"Donald," I heard him whisper to Dad, as he handed them over, "I'm disappointed you're doing this. I think we should be looking after each other here. But if you insist on going ahead with it, a word of warning. Are you sure you can trust Thacker? I've heard he's a violent man, ex-con. He could stiff you out there in the wilderness."

"Thanks, Jerry," Dad replied firmly. "I'm sure. Now take care of yourself, OK?"

Dad turned back to the packing, signaling an end to the conversation, and, gradually, the neighbors drifted away, muttering amongst themselves.

It was late in the day when we finished. I walked around the house wondering if there was anything that really mattered that we'd left behind, wondering if I'd miss anything. I overheard Mom and Dad talking, downstairs.

"How long do you think we'll be away, Donald, really? We're leaving photo frames, our files, we *will* be back?"

"Of course we will, honey."

"You know, I've never liked this place that much, to be honest. Actually, I've never really liked Alaska. It's so cold and dark most of the year. And the people...well, I mean, they're friendly, but it's tough for Jim being a bit aspergic. He doesn't relate well to kids his own age, just sits in his room all the time, living in his head, playing those horrible games. And I don't want to see him and Bess growing up as rednecks. When this is over, perhaps we should think of another move, go back to the lower 48. I miss the East Coast."

"I can't see that happening with Jim, Mary, he's a sensible enough kid. But I know what you mean. Perhaps we should head south. Or somewhere in Canada. I could probably get a job in Toronto. I know the department head there."

Mom sighed. "Oh well – I am worried about Jim, though. Bob's too much of an influence. He's starting to talk like him. But we can think again when this is over."

A resentful thought started taking shape at the back of my mind. I didn't want to be a botanist, it sounded boring. Or an engineer. I wanted to be like Bob. He was the one really running the show, looking after us.

Bob and Mrs. Maclaren walked in (I couldn't get my head around calling her Louise).

"I've strapped it all down," Bob was saying.

"What about books?" asked Mrs. Maclaren.

"What the hell? We're not a travelling library," Bob growled.

"No, but what about books that will tell us things we need to know, now we've got no Internet? What about things to read in the evenings?"

"Nothing I need to know that I don't already know," said Bob flatly. "Besides, reading's bad for you. Bad for the eyes, look at you lot, proof solid. And it's bad for the brain. The craziest people I've known, they all got their mad notions out of books. If God had meant us to read, he'd have made us with specs."

Mom chipped in. "No, Louise is right. And we could do with some text books for Jim and Bess, in case we're away for more than a few days. They might even get ahead with some schoolwork."

I walked downstairs, not letting on I'd heard them. We collected a dozen of our own books, and I went back to Mrs. Maclaren's place with her and she picked up around fifty, which we boxed and wheeled back on the trolley. Dad looked at them askance, eyebrows raised, but he stacked them on top. They turned out to be the best investment we made. We should have taken a library.

42

TEN

It never got completely dark in the summer here, and the fires had spread, turning the sky a deep red. The gunfire was almost continuous now. A couple of times I heard cars speeding, wheels squealing as they turned the corner. There was shouting further down the road. I don't think anyone had managed much sleep. At five a.m. on Wednesday the alarm went, and Dad got us up.

"I think we're making the right decision," he said as we loaded our last few bags onto the truck. We'll be safer out of here for a while. Looks like it's only parts of downtown burning at the moment, but if this weather keeps up, if the wind changes, the whole place could go up in flames." A few minutes later and Bob cranked up the engine and we were setting off down the drive. He had his Browning in the cab, and he'd given me a Ruger with the proviso – "Don't use it unless I say so, kiddo."

Mom had looked as if she was about to say something in protest, but kept quiet. She squashed up inside the truck with Mrs. Maclaren between her and Bob. Dad was up at the front, behind the cab, Bess and I were in a nest at the back. The windows were open, so we could hear each other.

"OK," said Bob. "Let's roll. No seat belts on this thing, but we won't be going fast."

The next few moments utterly changed my life. Around the corner there was a dusty pickup blocking the road. Bob pulled to a halt. Four guys got out. I recognized Mrs. Maclaren's neighbor from Tuesday, carrying a pistol. There was another guy I didn't know, and Joss, the guy who bullied me at school, both with baseball bats. And there was Joss's Dad, Mr. Trinker, a big man, must have been six and a half feet, huge beer gut, carrying a rifle.

"Out you get, people. We're taking this," he shouted. I don't think he noticed Bess and me low down in the back of the truck. I quietly loaded a cartridge into the rifle.

Dad stood up. "You can't do this. It's ours."

"Not any more it ain't. We're confiscating it." He laughed; the other guys were smirking. "It's our patriotic duty, as concerned citizens. You've forfeited your rights, you wimps, this belongs to us. Think you can just take all this stuff away? Traitors, that's what you are." He spat.

"But..."

"Not another word from you, mister, or you get it first. Joss, you make a start now," he waved the rifle at the truck.

Joss moved to the passenger door, jerking it open, and grabbed my mother by the arm. Mom fell out of the cab, hitting the ground hard. I saw Bob move down, I guessed to get his rifle. Mr. Trinker saw him do it and fired – the bullet went through the windscreen above Bob's head.

Time seemed to slow. I remember thinking, do I do this? Can I do it? Should I? But I had already picked up the Ruger and half-raised it. It was like I was outside myself, watching as I got to my feet, thumbing the safety catch off. I saw Joss's Dad swinging his rifle around towards me. My finger seemed to curl at snail's pace around the trigger as the barrel came up. I shot from the hip, the gun going off fractionally before his barrel centered on me. The crack sounded abnormally loud. A surprised look spread across his mug. All the everyday sounds seemed to fade from the world, giving way to an empty silence. Slowly, Mr. Trinker slumped, falling forwards, his face in the gravel. And sound came crashing back.

Mom gasped, hands to her face. "Oh God!"

Bess was wailing. Louise held her hands. "Stop this now, Bess!"

Dad jumped down from the flatbed. He turned the guy over. Blood was pooling under him. Joss screamed, "I'm gonna kill you, dork!" and hurled his baseball bat at me.

I ducked in time, quickly loaded another cartridge, and raised the rifle. Bob by now had the Browning up at his shoulder. The other two men looked at both of us, the two rifles pointing at them, shook their heads at each other, grabbed Joss by the arms, and ran.

My mind was blank, I stood there, unable to move. It was a hot, sunny morning, but I was cold, shaking; my mouth so dry my tongue was stuck to the roof of it. I stared at Mr. Trinker, the blood was spreading its dark stain on the ground. What had I done? I wanted, more than I'd ever wanted anything in my life, to wind those seconds back, replay them differently. My brain was working again, desperately insisting it must be possible, surely. This couldn't have happened. The cold trickled down my back, finding its way down to my gut and lodging there. I tasted bile, retched, and then threw up over the side of the truck.

Mom had joined Dad with Mr. Trinker. She was calm now, her professional side taking over. She ripped open his shirt, buttons popping. Mr. Trinker convulsed a couple of times, then blood started pouring out of his mouth, his head flopped to one side. She checked his pulse, and went pale. "He's gone," she said. "What have we done?"

It was the first time I'd seen Bob look worried. He scrubbed at his chin. "Shit. I didn't think you could kill someone with a .22. Must've been the close range." He cast his glance first on me and then at the others. "It was self-defense, we all saw it." He shook his head. "They attacked us."

Mom stood up. "We have to get him to the hospital! We'll have to report this, go to the police station."

Dad paused for a minute. "No," he said firmly. "I don't think we should. We don't even know that it's operating. If we go down there, we'll probably never get back. You hear all that shooting downtown? We'll move on. We can report it when we return. Let's take their weapons, they'll have fingerprints on them. They can be used as evidence."

He picked them up with his handkerchief and laid them in the back of the cab.

"But we can't leave him like this!" Mom shouted. "I have a responsibility here."

"He's dead, isn't he?" Bob said flatly. "Time to make sure we stay alive."

I could see the wheels turning in Dad's head. "Mary, I know it's not what you want to do, and it might look bad for you later. For both of us. But we have to take a decision on whether to get out of here or not, and I think we should go."

"Donald and Bob are right," said Mrs. Maclaren, cuddling Bess.

"Jimmy boy." Dad took me in his arms. "It wasn't your fault. Bess, you go and sit between Mom and Louise in the cab for a while. I'm going to sit in the back here with Jim. Bob, drive on."

Bob engaged gears and rammed the front of the pickup, shoving it out of the way. He spun onto the road, wheels screeching, the truck rocking, and we sped away, dust kicking up. I could see Jerry and Marcia on their lawn, their faces white, mouths hanging open.

Dad gripped my shoulder. "It's OK, Jim."

I said nothing. I wasn't outside myself any more, but I wasn't inside myself either. It was like hovering in nowhere land. Unable to respond, unable to get close to it, to what I'd done. I guess I was in shock.

An uneasy silence settled over us all and after a while it was just the noise of the engine and the gears and the rhythm of the old truck bumping along, lulling us all.

ELEVEN

Half an hour later, still sitting in uneasy, stunned silence, we had left the suburbs behind us. The malls, the drive-ins, the signs, had thinned out, and we were going fast down the Seward Highway. We'd seen a few loaded pickups, Dodges and Chevrolets, a Ford Pinto. But the road was empty now. The scenery was spectacular, majestic – the Chugach National Park and Forest all round us; huge mountains rising directly from the sea, sparkling glaciers and forests of pine, the heart of the playground of Alaska, which people travelled to see from all over the world. But no one was in the mood for it. A few dogs were roaming around, the occasional lodge looked deserted. Power lines were sagging, sometimes broken, with the poles at an angle.

Bess whimpered in Mom's lap. "What are we going to do? Will the police come after us?"

I was kind of numb, surprised by how little I was feeling. Would I have fired again if Joss had come at me with the bat rather than throwing it? I just didn't know.

"I can't do this." Mom was crying softly. "I can't bear it. We can't just keep driving all day, as if nothing's happened. We have to stop and talk, please."

"OK." Dad's voice was strained. "Bob, how about pulling off at Alyeska?"

A mile down the road, Bob slowed as the Alyeska Resort sign appeared. A Caterpillar tractor was parked across the road to the resort, blocking it. A middle-aged man with a rifle stood to one side.

"Move on folks, there's nothing for you here."

"We only wanted to visit, find out what's happening."

"Look, I'm being nice. Try coming through, and I'll shoot. I've got plenty of back-up. You don't want to start a turf war."

"Can you tell us anything about the road ahead, then?" Dad

asked him quietly. "We're aiming to get to Seward."

"I doubt you'll make it. The road's closed at Summit Lake. There's a bunch of hunters in the Lodge there, and they're taking a toll from everyone who comes through. Half of everything you've got. After that, I don't know."

"What do you suggest?"

"If I was you, I'd just find an empty lodge somewhere. Go to ground, and hang out till this is over. There are plenty around."

"Thanks. Do you have any idea how long this is going to go on?"

"No more than you, my friend. But we're prepared to sit this out for a week or two."

"Could we join you?"

"Looks like you've got a lot of stuff back there in the truck, but our committee's taken the decision. No more mouths to feed. We've made our rules, and we don't want strangers with different ideas. Now move on."

"Thanks for the advice, anyway."

A few miles further on, we saw the sign for Portage.

"Let's try again here, Bob." Dad pointed. It was a ghostly kind of place, with some ruined buildings leaning at odd angles and a forest of leafless white trees in the water, making fantastical shapes. Wetlands stretched away, scattered with ducks and swans.

"Now, let's review. What happened back there – it was terrible, but I've been thinking about it, it was probably going to happen anyway. I'm just sorry it was you who had to defend us, Jim. I should've been driving, and then Bob could've had a gun ready. We should've been organized better. We should've left earlier. It was my fault. I'm sorry."

"Not your fault at all," said Louise. "They were the aggressors. I'm glad I was there, so I can be a witness for you. I never liked that Mr. Trinker anyway. He was a horrible man. He threatened me after school once, when I failed Joss, grabbed my jumper. I thought he was going to hit me. I guess it's the bit of Indian in me, but I don't feel much regret. He got what he deserved."

"I was too slow," said Bob. He fixed his gaze on me. "And I won't be calling you kiddo any more, Jim. You did real good. Moved faster than shit through a goose."

"Bob, that's a terrible thing to say! "Mom said sharply. "It's not good, it's appalling. I don't know how we're going to deal with this."

Bob shook his head. "People deal with it, Mary," he said. "They just do. When I was in the army, I killed people, and I didn't have as good a reason as Jim here."

"But Jim's seventeen," exclaimed Mom, "and he's not a soldier."

"A year younger than me back then. But looks to me like we're all going to have to be soldiers now."

Mom began to cry. "Oh God…what are we going to do? Jim could go to prison, and we've left that man in the road."

Dad embraced her, took out his handkerchief and wiped her tears away.

"Be strong, Mary. I know Jim'll need to talk this through."

"No! I don't," I interrupted. "I don't want to talk about it. And I'm *not* sorry. I'm not."

Bess was looking at me as if she had never seen me before, I had no idea what she was thinking.

Dad scrubbed his hand through his greying hair. "I think we *do* need to talk it through – maybe you'll feel more like dealing with that when a bit of time's passed. Right now, though, we're almost out of food and water. Doesn't look like we're going to get help from anyone. And we need to find somewhere to stay, before tonight. Let's look at the map. I think we should find somewhere we can hold out for a week or two if we have to, like that man said. What do you think, Bob?"

"Agreed. We won't get to the coast, and we're on our own. But the basic plan stands."

Mom sighed heavily. "OK, we're on this course, let's make it work. This sun is so hot, let's get some cream on."

Dad handed around the sandwiches as Bob unfolded the map on the bonnet, and, except for Bob and Louise, who ate with gusto, we chewed slowly. My mouth seemed to be numb, too, I couldn't taste anything, it was like forcing cardboard past a closed up throat.

"So," Bob said, "with the Seward Highway blocked to us, I suggest we turn off here, towards Whittier. Then take this road on the right, and here again, up into the hills. Wish we had a larger scale map. We're looking for an isolated, empty cabin or lodge, big enough for the six of us, with water close by, where we can hole up. Let's hit the road."

TWELVE

We drove on, through thinly forested larch and ash, bright green, the lower buckbrush and willow now in full leaf, then we turned right again. We passed a campsite that looked empty, except for a few cars scattered around. We drove in, circled, and no one came out, but the cabins were too small for us; every one looked as if it had been broken into.

"Someone's been here before us," Bob said, "looking for food, I guess."

It didn't feel like a good place. We drove on, the tarmac turned into gravel, the bends sharpening as we gained height. We passed the occasional holiday cottage and stopped to knock. They were empty, but Bob didn't like the position.

"We want somewhere more remote. A place no one's going to stumble across."

The track circled upwards, becoming more rutted, and we jolted through potholes, clinging on at the back.

"This isn't going anywhere, is it?" Mom asked. "Shouldn't we turn back to those cabins?"

"These tracks in front of us are from a car, Mary." Bob pointed. "It's been along here recently. It's too good a track not to lead somewhere."

Pine mostly gave way to birch. A lone eagle floated overhead. A dozen miles along, the trees opened out and we came to a lodge with a great view, right back across to a distant blue corner of the Turnagain Arm, the water and mountains. A guy was outside, chopping wood. He looked to be in his forties, a city type, plump and soft, with a mustache. No suntan yet, handling the ax as if he wasn't sure what to do with it. Dad got out and walked over to him.

"Hi, I'm Donald." He held out his hand. The man took it. "We're looking for a place to stay for a bit and we're figuring there might be a lodge at the end of this track. Do you know?"

"I'm Matthew," the guy replied, casting an eye over the truck. "Matthew Harding. Yes, there's one there. It's another half dozen miles on. There's no one around, and, frankly, neighbors would be welcome. We rented this place for the summer holiday, and thought we'd stay till this is over – there wasn't time to get back to Seattle after the President's announcement. I'm here with my two daughters."

As he said that, one of his daughters came out of the lodge. We all introduced ourselves. Her name was Jessie, sixteen, a year younger than me, slim, long legs, light-blonde hair, high cheekbones. A knockout. My stomach gave a little flip. I looked away as we shook hands.

Matthew ushered us into the cabin. His younger daughter, Sue, was lying on the couch. She was nine, with a ready smile, but not looking at all well.

"She has a temperature," Matthew Harding explained. "Frankly, we would've been out of here by now, but I can't get the car started. I've tried fishing in the lake, where the lodge you're aiming for is, but I kept snagging the line and lost the tackle. We're almost out of food and we were going to walk down to the highway, to see if we can get a lift back to Anchorage. But we can't do it with Sue feeling like this."

Mom was soothing Sue's brow. "It's a fever," she said. "Any other symptoms? Sore throat? Diarrhea?"

"Nothing else."

"I'm a nurse, Mathew. I'll get my bag from the truck." She went out, rummaged around.

"Here's some Tylenol. Keep her hydrated. What are you drinking? You're boiling the water?"

"That's what I was chopping the wood for, but it's hard to get enough. I've never done it before."

The grown-ups chatted for half an hour. Bess and Jessie were getting along famously. I overheard snatches of conversation as

I finished chopping up the woodpile.

"It's been so awful," Bess was saying, "I haven't been able to talk to anyone for days."

"Me neither. I hope you stay at that lodge. Then we can see each other."

Dad left them with some food and we agreed to all meet up the next day.

"He's a complete cheechako," muttered Bob, as he engaged gears and we drove away.

"What's that?" Bess asked.

"A greenhorn," he replied. "We should have given them a lift down to the highway and told them to start walking. They know zip."

Mom turned to him sharply. "Don't say that."

"They'll get in our way, they'll complain, they'll get ill."

"Don't knock them, Bob." Mom looked cross. "You don't know them. Sometimes, you're not a very nice person."

"Three useless, wussy stomachs to feed, as much use as a handbrake on a canoe," he continued. "See how you feel about it when we're all hungry. They'll be the death of us, you see if I'm right. We should ditch them."

"Jessie and me are going to be friends," Bess interrupted. "Why don't you go and live by yourself, Bob? Nobody cares what happens to you."

"Bess, that's not nice either," said Dad. "C'mon now, we're going to stay together, and we'll get along."

"Huh!" Bess replied, unimpressed.

The gravel track got more rutted as we drove and we were soon down to walking pace. An hour later, we cleared a rise to see a lake in front of us, half a mile wide, a couple of miles long, a mountain rising, sheer, from one side. We arrived at a gate with a faded sign over it, "Potter's Place." It was the end of the road. Bob got out his wire cutters and sheared through the rusty padlock chain and we drove along a dirt path to a lodge by the lake. It was built of logs, with a steep wood-tiled roof. It looked as if it hadn't been lived in for years – some tiles were missing and moss had taken over. There were bear boards over the windows – planks of wood with dozens of nails jutting outwards. Weeds were growing everywhere. A birch seedling had taken root in the chimney. There was a derelict looking pickup, a rusty water tank with holes in it. An upturned boat, with a few bits of covering canvas still on it, some planks missing. A jetty running out into the lake, mostly collapsed.

Mom's disappointment sounded in her voice.

"It's hopeless. It's a wreck. We can't live in that. We'll have to drive back."

"No, please," Bess complained. "We've been going all day. I'm hungry, and I have to get my head down. You can fix it up tomorrow."

"Just a bit of tidying up needed, Mary," Bob replied. "It's peachy. Good joints, nice mortice work, storm windows. Great position, in a bay on the lake, high enough above the water, spruce on both sides as shelter for when the wind blows through the valley. It's even got a beach. Whoever built this knew what he was doing. Let's get a fire going inside, smoke out the bugs. And we need to get the first meals in. This lake should have some char and grayling in it. Jim, come with me, and we'll see if we can get some supper. And see those chewed stumps down there by the water? Looks like there might even be beaver here. Perfect."

The evening sun glittered off the water, rippling in a slight breeze, and the lake reflected the mountains and trees all around. As I stood there, taking in the peace, drawing it deep, a blue jay flew off from a rock on the shoreline. The mountains were covered in glaciers, blindingly blue and white. Alder, rowan, birch and the occasional pine swayed gently. After Anchorage, it was unearthly quiet, apart from some ravens cawing in the distance. To me, it felt like we'd come home.

THIRTEEN

Writing this down now, struggling to hold the goose pen with my arthritic fingers, the memories of those days wash over me. They were difficult, but I grew up then. Before, it was as if I knew nothing. It was as if I hadn't been born yet. I thought of myself in terms of how other people saw me, trying to be what they wanted me to be. I would change my voice, my accent, to fit in with whoever I was talking to. Later, there was always the burden of responsibility, the weight of expectation, of carrying people's hopes and fears, of knowing they depended on me to be more single-minded than they were, to take the tough decisions necessary to survive. But in that summer, something changed. I found my "self." I began to feel at home in my own skin. With fewer people around, it was less confusing, fewer pitfalls to negotiate. There was no random noise, no background roar of traffic. Sounds had meaning. There was a reason for everything. At the back of my mind, I thought I'd have to account sometime for killing Mr. Trinker. But – it surprised me – I didn't feel any regrets about it. It was necessary, it was done. I just hoped that I'd never have to see Joss again.

It released something in me. I don't really know how to describe it. When I overheard Mom call me aspergic, I didn't know what it meant. Now, I understand it as having an emotional bit missing. I'd seen people like cars in the street outside: hard, dangerous, to be treated with caution, avoided where possible. But now it looked like they were just flesh and blood, like me. Jelly for a brain, as often wrong as right, and could be pricked like a balloon, snuffed out like a candle. For many years to come, killing people didn't bother me. It was only much later, as the body count piled up, as my own family grew, with children having their children, that I came to understand the bitter-sweet nature of the bonds that tie. It was then that I started remembering, and the faces returned at night: reproachful, angry – the many I'd sent on to the next world, the many that I'd let down. They haunt me.

We soon stopped talking about Anchorage. We had no contact with the outside world, which seemed increasingly distant – as if it had disappeared; as if we'd crossed through a games portal to another world. And it was as if we were never going back.

We got to know the neighbors well – Matthew Harding and daughters Jessie and Sue – they all turned up the next morning. His wife, Alice, had died a few years before from cancer and it was plain from the look on his face when he told us that he was still hurting. Matthew was an accountant with a computer firm in Seattle. He'd always had a hankering to visit Alaska and see the wildlife, try a spot of fishing and hunting, but hadn't caught a fish yet. They hadn't seen any wildlife. They didn't know what around them might be edible.

"I thought I could figure out what to do by googling it, on the phone," he said. "But I'm a bit lost without it. I suppose it was a silly thing to do, coming here, but the three of us haven't really had a proper holiday since Alice died, and I thought it would do us good to be together."

Jessie had never wanted to come on the holiday, so she and Bess had that in common to start with. They were soon as thick as thieves. Even Bess' temper seemed to improve as she became friendly with Jessie; though she missed her own room, and everything that went with it.

Sue recovered from her temperature and her apple-cheeks were regularly creased with smiles and laughter. Although she remembered enough to miss her mom, she had few memories of her as part of the family unit, being only six when she died, and soon became part of our family, rarely leaving Mom and Louise's side. They began by coming over to visit every day (it was a couple of hours walk there and back). Bess stayed a couple of nights with them, but they soon fell into a pattern of staying with us. Matthew couldn't look after himself and the girls, couldn't get the food, but was very willing to help. It made the lodge cramped, the main room was twenty by thirty, but the nights were still warm, and Bob and me were happy to sleep on the verandah.

We all worked hard, from when we rose, to when we fell back into bed: even Bess. We caught some fish in the lake to keep us going.

"We'll have to filter the water from the creek, Jim," Bob said, "but we'll need charcoal for that. For the moment, rig up a tarpaulin on four posts to catch the rainwater, put a hole in the middle, tie a T-shirt across the top, a container underneath."

Matthew cleaned the moss off the roof, replaced tiles, boarded up broken panes.

Bob and Dad scavenged planks and bricks to rebuild the toilet in the outhouse. It smelled horrible and there were always flies, but shoveling ash over it helped, and we got used to it, even to using sphagnum moss to wipe ourselves; it was clear that the toilet paper would soon run out.

Mom organized the inside. Raccoons had been in, burrowing their way in under the walls, there wasn't much left of the stuffing in the chairs, and they'd clawed the ceiling posts. Red squirrels had nested in the roof.

"Well, as we're staying, let's make the most of it," Mom said. "Bess, could you help me scrub it all down before we put the stores away. Louise, if you could clean out the stove. Sue, if you'd like to help, could you use that chair to dust the ceiling. And Jessie, those windows need a good wash. Donald," she raised her voice to call to Dad outside. "I could do with some shelves up here, please."

"This is so strange," Mom said one evening. "I don't think I've ever spent any time before with no radio, TV, Internet, papers, phone, no other people, no strangers – I'm not counting you as that, Matthew."

"Me neither," said Dad. "Not sure if I like it, or if I'm scared by it. I seem at a loose end here, haven't got my work, no students, and it's not a holiday because we're in someone else's place, it doesn't feel right."

"I can't help remembering all the deadlines whooshing by," said Matthew. "Should've got the management accounts out this week."

"I know what you mean," replied Louise. "Right now, I guess I should be teaching Grade 10. I feel guilty. Even when I know they wouldn't be there."

"Do you miss the school?" Mom asked.

Louise smiled. "Yes, I do. I don't know if it does much good, but I've always thought that encouraging learning, thinking, it's just something that's worthwhile doing, even if you never seem to be making any progress."

"I've been out on my own for a few weeks at a stretch," Bob said. "It's fine, if you can live with your own company. Anyway, we're one hell of a lot better off out here than we were in Anchorage. It feels safe here."

Bess stared at him. "That's crazy," she said. "Why would anyone just want to live with their own company or their own family? Why don't grown-ups have friends?"

"It's not that we don't have friends, Bess," Mom replied. "It's just that, well...family becomes more important as you get older."

"That's so dull. I'm not going to get old. And I don't really mind having family, most of the time, but it's friends that matter."

"Bess, I'm glad you've got so many friends," replied Dad. "But friends have to come from families, don't they? So families come first."

"I'm with Bess," Jessie said. "How do you grow up anyway when your parents keep telling you what to do?"

"Most societies have a ritual for it," chipped in Louise.

"My grandmother used to talk to me about the old times. On her mother's side, she was Athabascan. She was sent into the wilderness for a month when she was twelve, before her initiation. I guess she'd have felt comfortable in this place."

Sooner than I would've believed, it was all looking cozy. The window in the main room looked out over the deck, framing the lake, the mountains and glaciers on one side, trees on the other. There was an occasional splash or plop as a fish took an insect on the surface. I watched a bald eagle circling above, slowly drifting out of sight.

FOURTEEN

A couple of days later, and Bess was in one of her bad moods.

"Dad, when are we going home? It's just too weird, staying out here. There's nobody around. I haven't seen anyone for days now."

"Bess is right," said Matthew. "We should really be trying to get back to Seattle. They must have restored power."

Dad shook his head. "If I thought that for a moment, Matthew, we'd be out of here like a shot. But look up at the sky. It's normally littered with planes. I haven't seen one since we got here. And there are no contrails, though we're right under the flight path to Anchorage from the south."

"I hadn't thought of that," Matthew looked worried. "So you reckon the power's still all out everywhere?"

"Got any better thoughts? Seems like it to me. And if it's still out, I don't know as much as Bob does, but we have a roof over our heads, food and water, and I guess we're safer here than trying to get back."

I could see Matthew struggling to come to terms with the idea. "I guess you're right. I mean, a place the size of Anchorage, they'd need to be flying in loads of supplies."

"We've been living from hand to mouth for the last few days, but can we catch enough fish to keep us going?" Dad asked. "And if we can, how do we keep it without a freezer? What do you think, Bob?"

"Should be no problem with the fishing," replied Bob. "And if you look outside, what do you see?"

Mom was standing by the window. "There's the lake," she said. "There are pine trees, glaciers, rocks..."

"And what are glaciers made of?"

"Point taken," replied Dad. "We've got ice."

"Everybody used ice until electricity arrived," said Louise.

"People would build caves or pits to keep the food in, pack the fish around with ice to keep the temperature low."

We dug a cave outside the lodge, and the next day Dad and Matthew trekked the three miles up to the glacier to hack out chunks of ice as large as they could carry.

"We should start catching salmon," Bob said, picking up a bag of nets and poles. "They're not going to stick around here forever."

Bob took Bess, Jessie, Sue and me hiking to the other end of the lake which fed the Portage River.

"Look," said Bob, pointing out over the water, "sure enough, there's a beavers' house."

"Can we catch them?" I asked.

"Sure thing, they're good fatty meat. But easier to get in the winter, when the ice covers the lake, and they've got the most meat on them. We'll leave them for the moment. They can be our reserve supply, if we need it."

We got to the river, and walked down it looking for salmon. There was a slight trail over the rocks. The scene was just like those pictures you see in glossy magazines advertising fisherman's clothes. The sun was blazing hot.

"Wow, this place is so big and empty," Bess said as she struggled to balance the poles on her shoulder. "Why aren't there roads? I can't see a house anywhere. Will we catch a fish? Have you ever caught one, Jess?"

"It'll be my first time, if I do," she replied. "Always up for something different, though. Anyway, it's cool here." She looked at Bob. "What are our chances, Bob?"

"Should get something. It's not the Kenai River, that's where you get the big ones. Most of them around Anchorage are no good for salmon any more, they've been restocked with hatchery trout to keep the tourists happy. Tiddly things. But we're a long way from that here, so this probably hasn't been fished out. It should be OK."

We stood on flat rocks, the river gurgling around them, so clear it was transparent.

"Look, I can see them, real fish!" Sue screeched. "There they are."

The salmon, moving in fleets, shuffled the gravel with their tails to make their spawning craters; those who had spawned were dying or already dead and decomposing, drifting back with the current.

Jessie swept her dip net through the water and caught two of them. They were obviously heavier than she expected, wriggling frantically in the net; she overbalanced, and fell in, coming up gasping and spluttering.

"Christ, it's freezing," she gasped, water streaming off her.

She held out her hand to me, I couldn't really refuse. I pulled her up. It was the second time we'd touched, and this time I managed to hold her gaze.

"Comes straight from the glacier. You'll soon dry off," Bob said, chuckling.

My breath caught as she pulled off her shirt, and rinsed it out. She was lightly tanned all over, even her perfectly rounded breasts. I could feel my face going a deep red.

"I'm going in as well," Bess shouted, stripping down to her undies and jumping in. "Ouch, ouch, Jesus, Jesus," she screamed, "that's cold."

Bob rummaged in his rucksack and handed me a hacksaw. "You can stop gawking, Jim." He winked at me. "Cut a couple of strong poles from that stand of alder over there while Jessie and Bess dry off. These salmon are sockeyes, good eating, we'll string them up on the poles for carrying."

"Ugh, they're so slippery and slimy," Sue said, as she lifted them out of the net, still thrashing around.

"Just break their necks, like this," Bob said, doing just that, "or crack them on the head with a stone. You'll soon get the hang of it."

We got back a couple of hours later, and Bob wasted no time showing us how to gut them.

"When we get more, we'll start preserving them. Then, Mary, they'll need soaking for a couple of days, in a brine solution of water and herbs. Jim, you can make up racks to dry them on. After a couple more days, when they've got a film on them, we'll smoke 'em."

A few days later we had a hundred good salmon. We dug a fire pit, erecting a roof over it, with plenty of headroom, to keep the rain off. We smoked the fish over green alder and oak fires for a couple of days, then wrapped them up in paper and plastic sheeting, packed them into the ice cave, and rolled boulders across the entrance to keep out the wildlife.

The only real problem we had were the mosquitoes. We all suffered, but Sue got the worst of them, and would run in screaming, "Help, help, they're eating me alive!"

"This is nothing," Bob said. "Far worse further north. But we can get a smudge going at the front door, that'll help."

"I'm sure we've got a couple of head nets," Dad said. "I'll dig them out."

Mom was reading a manual, she looked up. "Pesky things. We're going to run out of D.E.E.T. There are lots of plants we could use instead though: lemon grass, rosemary, geranium, wormwood – there are pictures of them here. Let's all go and collect as many as we can find, then we crush them into a pot, stir oil in, and use it as lotion. Says here that the Indians chew alder leaves as well and rub it on bites."

The next few days were cool and breezy, which kept the mosquitos down, and we decided to explore the area. On the Portage River, in the far distance, we could occasionally see the smoke from the fires of a couple of other lodges further downriver, on a different track. One day we spent the morning working our way down to them. Two old guys lived in one and we exchanged pleasantries when we met, but didn't really get to know them. They had no news and weren't communicative, it didn't seem like they wanted more company.

"Bloody queers, best leave them to it," Bob said as we moved on.

Another, a further couple of miles on, seemed to have a single guy living in it; Bob waved, but he didn't wave back.

"Guys living out here alone are usually plumb crazy," Bob said, "best leave him be."

All the time we hiked around we rarely saw anyone – occasionally a hunter or fisherman in the far distance, but the country seemed pretty empty. We were alone. I liked it that way. I wanted to put Anchorage, and everything it represented, way behind me. No more Joss Trinker or his family. The only cloud on the horizon was the idea of having to go back. I brought myself back to the present and smiled. Happiness – I never quite knew what that was, but figured it must be like living in heaven. And this, for me, was it.

FIFTEEN

"Time for you to scale up, Jim. This is for you," Bob said as he handed over his Winchester M70.

"For me? Really? You mean it's mine? Wow!" I stammered out my thanks.

He nodded. "It'll handle anything around here on four legs, or on two. Now we're going to go out every day, whatever the weather. If you can't fire a rifle in the rain, you can't do it in a blizzard when you've got a bear coming at you. Don't rely on the safety catch, it can be tripped loose easily. Keep the chamber empty, with a round to hand."

A few hours later and we were some miles away from the lodge, faced with an impenetrable tangle of hawthorn and alder.

"Here, we'll need to portage, slash our way through this patch, to get over to the next valley. Use this brush ax, its one step up from a machete."

"No, not that way," he said, as I slashed at a branch and it bounced back. "Take it nearer the trunk, lower down. You don't want to be coming through here at night and get a stump in your face." After half an hour I was drenched in sweat and dirt, with a mass of cuts and insect bites.

In the next valley we stopped every now and again to look around, Bob with his spotting scope, me with my binoculars.

"Tough to see animals when you're moving. We'll have to get you one of these." He handed it over to me. "Try it. More like a telescope, sixty times magnification."

"Wow. I still can't see any animals though," I said after a few moments. "There's nothing here."

"They're often still, or browsing. Look for a movement, a change of shade. Try that hill over there. What do you see?"

"Nothing."

"Lame, Jim. Next to that lonesome pine, on the right, about

two miles away?"

"Only a brown rock."

"You see any other brown rocks around?"

"No."

"So it's a bear. Watch for a while, you'll see it move."

"Gosh! It's moved. Shall we go get it?"

"Too far, Jim, and we're downwind of it. And I'd sooner you had more practice before taking on a bear. And see all that thorn we'd have to fight our way through? It would hear us too early. Let's carry on. Looks like good hunting around here, we're at the neck of the peninsula between the two halves of the Chugach National Park. Lots of animals migrating through."

We were walking rapidly along a creek. It was a lovely morning, the wind was still, the spruce black in the shadow, gleaming in the light, willows alive with chattering redpolls. The sun was already high in the sky, the water gurgled over the pebbles in the creek. Jessie would be up by now, washing her face, the water splashing back into the bowl…

Bob shook my shoulder. "Wake up, Jim, what do you see?"

"Sorry, guess I was dreaming." I looked around, scanning the hills again.

"Nothing."

"At your feet, dimwit."

I looked down; we were walking over deer tracks.

"This is a whitetail," Bob said, as we knelt down for a close look. "A buck. See the even walk, the prints a couple of hand widths apart? In a straight line? It's healthy, taking it easy. See these older, fainter prints? The trail's well used, and it's passed this way earlier this morning."

We stood up. "We'll build a hide with saplings, under that rise over there, downwind, should give you a clear shot of a hundred yards or so."

The next day we were back early, before the sun had risen above the hills.

Something was on my mind, had been all the way here. I had to ask, I'd be no use all day otherwise, and I trusted Bob. "Have...have you had girlfriends, Bob? Been married?"

Bob rubbed his thumb down the side of his face. "Figured that was on your mind. She's a class act. Knows what she wants, and is gonna get it." He squinted at me. "You've got the hots for her? She been putting the moves on you yet?"

"Gimme me a break, Bob, you know I'm a loser with girls," I spluttered, blushing.

"No you ain't," he said, thumping me on the shoulder. "You just wanna work up some courage. Anyway – you know what they say about an Alaskan chick?"

I shook my head.

"What's the first thing she does when she wakes up in the morning?"

"I don't know."

"She walks home." He laughed hoarsely.

I thought about that for a minute.

"But why wouldn't she be at home? Oh, I see...that's dirty, Bob."

"OK, I'm not saying Jess is like that, it's just a joke." He looked away from me, to the sun-dappled leaves of an old sugar maple. "I gave up women years ago, Jim. Happened to a lot of guys, after the army. Hard to adjust." He picked up a small stone and weighed it in the palm of his hand before closing his fingers over it.

"Anyway, they're a different species," he said. "Expensive to keep. Ya can't kill 'em, let alone eat 'em, not as amenable as other animals. Now, take your mind off Jessie and start concentrating; we're here. We'll leave some corn on the ground to slow it down."

An hour later he touched me on the shoulder. "Look, isn't that a beauty," he whispered. "It's headed for the corn."

"But it looks like Bambi," I whispered back.

"We all have to eat, Jim," he replied softly. "Now don't screw up here. Stay cool. Aim for the chest if it's head on, or just behind the shoulder if it's broadside to you."

I gently squeezed the trigger. In the still air, I could hear the thunk of the bullet hitting.

"Well done." Bob clapped me on the shoulder. "Your first deer. Through the heart. It's hell tracking them down if they're just wounded."

"I feel bad about it though. Worse than when I killed Mr. Trinker, to be honest. He wanted to hurt us, the deer had no bad intentions."

"There are no intentions out here, Jim – eating, fucking, dying, that's all there is. You've got to eat, fuck if you can, and you'll die anyway. Now let's quit jabbering and get to work."

I took my butchers knife and he showed me how to slice away the heart and liver.

"Don't puncture the gut sack, it'll spoil the meat. Now, here's how to separate the joints."

We left the entrails for the wolves and other animals and birds. Then we hung the carcass up on a tree to let the blood drain out. After an hour or so, we skinned it, wrapping the meat up in canvas to carry home. We washed our bloodied arms in the creek.

"We all need to know how to do this," said Bob, when we got back. "We cut the meat into strips, hang it up for a few days to dry, and turn it into jerky. We scrape the skin and dry it, stretched out on a frame. That'll make better clothing than anything you can buy on Sixth Avenue. Now, Jim, the knives need sharpening." He picked up the whetstone. The surface was worn away, shaping it into a curve. Spitting on it, he described fast circles with the knife, in an oval shape. "Don't pitch the blade too high, or the edge won't last. When it's sharp enough, just touching it to your thumb should bring blood."

SIXTEEN

Thanks to Bob, with the deer and the salmon, we now had enough to eat, though the diet was boring.

"Can't we have something different?" Bess complained, staring at yet another pan full of frying salmon. "What happened to normal food?"

"Bess!" Mom laughed, setting the plates on the table. "At least we have something to eat."

"Can't say I've ever eaten better," Dad added. "Salmon and venison every day – we couldn't afford to live like this in Anchorage."

A couple of days later we shot a mountain goat, and saw a moose, though it was too far away to kill. "Look," Bob said, "see that? The pointed pods of its track? That's how to recognize you're following one of those." He nodded towards the distant animal.

Gradually, as we came across them, he taught me to identify the prints of a coyote, and the trail of a wolverine crashing through the brush. He trained me to know the tracks of caribou, mink, marten, otter, beaver and muskrat: and once we even saw the huge, pancake-like, shallow pads of a lynx.

"You're not likely to ever see one of these, unless you can manage to trap it, but you can always see where it's been. See the distance between the prints? It was running." He grinned. "And where there's lynx, like coyote, it's a sign there's plenty of game around – there'll be other prey you can shoot."

He'd explained some of this to me before when we'd been out hunting, but I sensed an urgency in him to take it to a different level. I had lessons on how to snare ptarmigan with picture wire: how to keep one eye on the ground and another looking ahead to avoid getting caught in a canyon or trapped in thick, black spruce.

He showed me the difference between the tracks of a black bear and a grizzly, whose big toes are on the outside. "If you see a pile of grizzly scat that's steaming," he said, "that's the time to look for a tree to climb, if you can find one. Or play dead, if it's on to you. Lie down on your front with your hands over your neck. Don't curl up into a ball, it'll just roll you over. Black bears climb trees. Grizzlies don't. But they can both move as fast as cats. If a black bear wants to attack, don't play dead, you'll just have to fight it. They can be nastier than the grizzlies. You haven't a chance if you're unarmed, even if it's a small one. So be prepared." He snorted. "The only real insurance you've got, apart from the gun, is to be alongside someone who's slower than you are. So you're safe enough with me."

"I always feel safe with you, Bob."

"Then don't. You need to be able to look after yourself out here. More seriously, Jim, I wouldn't say this in front of the girls, but they start eating you from the bottom up. They're not like the big cats, who start at the head, that's not much use to them. They like the nutritious bits, so they'll be eating your liver and kidneys while you're still alive – it can take a good hour or two. They can amble off when they've had enough, and come back the next day when they want more. Not a good way to go."

"Gee, thanks, Bob, that's really comforting." I forced a laugh.

Bob locked eyes with me. "Think of it as a picnic if you like, Jim, but just remember, everything out here's food for something else. And look, see this spruce here?" He pointed to one we were passing. "See the claw marks? It's a marking post, to let others know he's around." He plucked off a long brown hair from the bark. "It's a big one, look how high the claws reach. It's a heck of a lot bigger than we are." He gave me a long, appraising look. "You need to step up your game. Think like an animal. Be like them. Then you'll be fine, and be able to look after your family."

He sniffed the air. "Can you smell the rain coming? See those clouds rolling in from the Gulf? The ground's nice and wet.

So you're going to make a fire. Look around for dead willow branches, or for spruce trees, there's always these dry twigs underneath. This hard resin here is good for starting fires, but don't use it in the stove, it gives off too much soot. Best of all, see this birch tree here," he took his knife to it, "it's got to be a live one – scrape off a patch of bark like this, doesn't matter what the weather is, you'll find tinder fungus underneath. It's like cork. It'll light from a spark."

It was as if time was short, and he was passing on everything he knew. It felt like learning to read. I began to understand what the words meant, rather than looking at it from the outside. The more I learned about the landscape, the more I was inside it, and it was inside me.

We made a detour to a rise where we could just about see a small stretch of the Seward Highway in the far distance, a dozen or so miles away. "Look at that, the road's jammed solid," Bob said as he checked it in his scope. "We got out by the skin of our teeth."

"Should we go and see if we can do anything to help?"

"Nothing we could do, Jim. What that jam means is that there are going to be thousands of desperate people around, with guns, getting hungrier every day. We've been lucky so far. This has been a holiday. But it's not going to last. And I want us to keep this between ourselves, OK? No point in getting the ladies in a tizzy. Shake on it?"

"OK, Bob."

"It's odd, though," he added, searching the sky, "there don't seem to be many birds around."

I pointed. "There's a flock of starlings over there."

Bob shook his head. "I meant eagles, vultures...anyway... sun's going down fast. I want you to take us to that hill over there, using cover, keeping off skylines – assume we're being hunted ourselves. Then you can try taking us back to the lodge in the dark."

SEVENTEEN

We were about as remote as it was possible to be in the Kenai Peninsula while still having a roof over our heads, but it still surprised me that there were so few people around. A few days later, nearly a fortnight after the Event, and we were ranging a few miles from the Lodge. The morning's rain had stopped, and the sun was steaming our clothes and twinkling on the leaves as they dried out. The insects and mosquitos were back in action.

"There are rabbit warrens around here," Bob was saying. "See all the pellets? Now there's two ways to hunt. One is to shoot, the other is to trap. Better for your prey to come to you, rather than you have to find it. And it saves on ammo. So what we'll do is set up a stone deadfall here for the rabbits, bait it, and check on our way back. The meat on rabbits is too lean to keep us in serious food, but they're great in a stew."

I was whittling away at some sticks, Bob showing me where to put in the notches that would trigger the deadfall when the bait was taken, when he touched my arm, pointing. A small flock of sparrows were scattering out from a bush. "That's twice they've done that, something's coming this way. Here, behind these trees. We'll wait for it."

A mile away, two people were coming around the bend of the canyon.

"Fuck a duck. What've we got here?" Bob looked through his scope. "They don't seem in great shape for this kind of thing. Some jerk with his floozy."

We watched them stumbling towards us. The man in front was tall, large, in his fifties or sixties, a few days stubble on his jowls, dressed in brand new threads – they looked expensive even from a distance. The woman was in her thirties, attractive, dressed as if she was on her way to work, with a short skirt, but evidently struggling. As she got closer we could see her face, legs and arms were a mass of bites and scratches.

We could hear them now. He was irritated.

"Come on, Sarah, for Christ's sake. I'm not carrying you. Keep moving."

We stepped out into their path.

"Finally, some goddam fucking people in this wilderness," he said. "Can you help us?"

"What help do you want?" Bob asked, as we introduced ourselves, shaking hands.

"Fucking mosquitoes," he replied, slapping his face. "Why don't they trouble you? Don't tell me, you're natives. Got no red blood left for them."

"What help do you want?" Bob repeated coldly.

"Look, old timer, I'm not trying to be difficult. We were staying at Moose Park, at the Tern Inn," he said, anger washing his cheeks in a red tide. "We were there for a week, after that solar flare, waiting to get away. Couldn't get a connection. Then those bastards wouldn't share any more. I'm going to have them arrested, put in jail for what they've done. Where are the fucking police when you need them? The local cop was an Indian," his voice dripped scorn. "What do you expect? I need to get to Valdez, pronto. So we set out walking. This bloody damn wilderness goes on forever. No signal anywhere. No airports around here, figured we had to get to the coast, to Whittier, get a boat. We've been walking for days, run out of food, nothing to eat in this God forsaken place. So," he plastered a smile on his face, "great to meet you."

"Here, take this," I gave him our packed lunch. They wolfed it down, tearing at it. No "thank you" was said.

"What happened when you asked the cop to help?" I asked.

"Fuck-all. He wasn't interested. I thought there were meant to be Mounties around here or something."

"That's in Canada, in the Yukon," I replied.

"Whatever. I just want to get out of this."

"How do you expect us to help with that?"

"Look, I'm not asking for much. You must have some kind of transport around here. Just get us to Whittier. Here—" He pulled a roll of notes from his pocket. "I'll pony up for it. A thousand bucks to get us there, with something to eat along the way."

"Are you for real? We don't want your money," Bob replied. "What can we do to help you?"

Giving Bob a sharp, speculative look, he said, "Are you retarded or something? Or do you want more? Look, I have to get to Valdez. I've got important meetings next week. The Secretary of State for Energy is going to be there, the Russian ambassador for Christ's sake. It's about the new pipeline. It's important I'm there. We need to get more oil running."

"Does it matter now?" I asked.

"You really are something, aren't you? Look, Jimmy boy, if that's your name. I'll come clean. I'm a big gun at Exxon. Have you heard of them? Never mind. It doesn't matter. But here's my card." He shoved it at me. "And I can get you a job, a proper job. Right now, all I'm asking is for you to help me get to Whittier. Can you manage that? Look, I'll make it easy for you, I'll bank you five thousand, as an advance."

I looked at Bob. I guess it was more money than either of us had ever seen. He had stepped back. I noticed for the first time that his rifle was cocked.

"Sorry, mister," I said. "I'm not interested in your job, or the pipeline. Don't you realize what's been happening?"

"Oh for Christ's sake! Of course I know. There's been a power cut. So what? Life goes on, and I've got business to do."

"It's more than that, isn't it? There's no power, anywhere."

He laughed. "You think the world's come to an end because the sun's blown some fuses? That it's something we can't fix? There'll be people working on it, right now. Thousands of them. But you wouldn't hear about that in this wilderness, would you? I need to get out of here and join them. Gimme a break, kid. Get real."

"I don't know as much as you," I replied, carefully, "but maybe we need to get used to the idea of living without power."

"Are you with those green lunatics? You just want to roll over and give up? Look, this whole place is just horseshit. Its mosquitos and bogs. Don't know why we haven't nuked it. The only worthwhile thing here's the oil, and that's underground anyway. You can still live on top if you want to."

I felt my anger rising: why should we put up with this guy? He didn't run things any more. "I don't know what a green lunatic is, mister," I replied, "and you've got a big mouth."

"You want me to eat humble pie, is that it? Look, take it all, there's more than that here…" He offered his wallet. "And you can keep the lady, if you like, look after her, she's holding me back."

"Shaddup. I don't give a bag of dicks for your bread. Take a hike," Bob said stonily. "All day, along this valley. You'll come to the Portage River, and a road. Turn right and it'll take you a day to get to Whittier."

"Fuck you too." The guy scowled. "C'mon, woman, they're chucking us out."

She looked at us, tear marks in the dirt on her cheeks.

"You can stay, if you want to," Bob said.

She shook her head, "I want to get out of here as well." We watched them walk down the canyon.

"I think I understand now why I like being out here," Bob said, as we saw them receding into the distance. "It's never been so clear to me before."

"What do you think they were doing?"

"Just away for a dirty weekend, and got caught out. What a shmuck. Thinks the sun shines out of his ass."

"They're not going to survive, are they, Bob?"

"They should get to Whittier OK, beyond that, I don't know. Depends which kind of world we all end up in – theirs, or ours.

He's all wind and piss. Used to run things, and doesn't like it when he can't."

"What's the Valdez thing about?"

"It's the end of the Alaska pipeline. Millions of barrels of oil there. C'mon Jim, you should know this stuff. Didn't they teach you anything at school?"

"Bob, are most people like that? Can you change who you are along the way?"

"Change? Dunno, Jim. Some will, most won't."

"Do you think I could?"

"You? You're OK, Jim. Just need more confidence."

"How do I get that?"

"It's already in you, Jim. Just decide which you want to be like, a bear or a deer. Predator or prey."

"But what if that guy is right, and the power comes back? It's got to, hasn't it? We've broken into someone's house, I've killed a guy. I'll need a lawyer."

Bob started to laugh hoarsely. He carried on till he was bent double with it.

"A lawyer, my God, a lawyer. Shit-a-brick, a lawyer. Do you think there are going to be any of those left standing?"

He straightened up, and looked serious. "Maybe it does come back, Jim, it's only been a couple of weeks. But the time for reckoning what's happened is past. I promise you that. What we've done ain't gonna figure compared to what's been going on."

A thought occurred to me. "Bob, you're not going back, are you?"

"Me? No. I'll stay out here. Always figured I might, one day."

"Could I stay with you?"

"You've got family, Jim," he looked at me seriously. "Don't knock that. You don't know what you miss till you haven't got it."

EIGHTEEN

Louise and Mom were pretty much confined to the Lodge. Louise had a bad hip and couldn't get far over the rough ground. Mom was nervous if there wasn't tarmac or carpet under her feet.

"There are wild animals out there, Bob. I know you can shoot them, but what if you miss? I'm happy to come and look at a view now and again, but that's as far as I want to go, thanks. Now, don't you dare come in off the deck with those boots of yours. With nine of us here, we need to take that bit of extra care to keep it clean. So you can stop making our work more difficult, thank you."

"Yessum, sorry."

Dad was more comfortable working on projects in the Lodge.

"However long we're here for," he said to Bob one day, "I'm not a hunter, and too old to start. I'm about as comfortable with it as you are with computers. I'd just get in your way. But thank you for teaching Jim."

"Teaching? Hadn't thought of it that way," Bob replied. "He's just a fast learner. He's going to be a heck of a lot better hunter than me."

"That's the best kind of teaching, Bob. And you've got the knack of it."

"Can Jess and me come with you?" Bess asked. "I'd like to hunt."

Mom was reluctant. "What about bears?"

"Not as bad as they are in the interior," Bob replied. "There's more food around here." He scratched his chin. "They're unpredictable, though, depends on what mood they're in. It's in the spring you need to be more careful, when they're just out of hibernation, hungry, maybe with cubs, and less to eat. Well, and in the fall, I guess, before the snow comes, when they're trying to fatten up for the winter. And of course, if they didn't fatten up much, they might come out looking for food in the winter as well."

"You should've had a career as an inspirational radio host, Bob," Mom said laughing. "All sweetness and light. Is there any time that *is* safe?"

"Well, no, but we should be OK in the summer, so long as we make enough noise. We've seen a few in the distance, and plenty of scats, but they'll avoid us. Anyway, moose kill more people around here than bears do, especially when they're rutting."

Mom groaned. "You're going from bad to worse, Bob. What should we do?"

"Only thing to do is to learn to live out here, Mary. Learn how to shoot, practice, get good at it. No point in just shutting yourself up in the cabin, then you've got no chance. Anyway, bears are the last thing we need to worry about out here, it's the cold and the water that usually kills you – frostbite, freezing, accidents, a slip of the foot or the chainsaw, starvation, infection, gangrene, fire, gunshot accidents. Hell, a hundred other ways to go. Drowning's how people usually buy it, falling through the ice." He grinned. "Still, on the positive side, if you want some sweetness and light, we're safe from snakebite."

"How come?" Bess asked.

"No snakes in Alaska, too cold. C'mon Bess, let's have a go with the Ruger."

"Here," Bob explained, as we gathered on the beach. "Stand like Jim here. That's it, square up. Check there's no one up front, this bullet can travel a mile. Jim, throw this bottle into the lake, as far as you can. Bess, look through the sight there. Squeeze the front of the trigger, gently does it."

The shot went wide somewhere.

"Have another go," Bob said. "Now, don't flinch this time, just relax, breathe gently, just leave the last bit of your finger on the trigger. Lightly, start to squeeze, focusing on the target. Well done!" As the bullet rippled the water a yard away from the bottle.

"Gosh. Cool! This is great," she exclaimed. "Am I allowed to do this? Don't I have to be eighteen or something?"

"Any age is fine, so long as you know what you're doing."

"How come you haven't shown me how to do this before?"

A few days later and she hit a hare. "Oh, I've hurt it," she squealed.

"Jim, you go and break its neck, could you? Now, Bess, remember, this is the way things are now. We can't get food in the shops, we have to kill it ourselves. It's natural. The Indians say thank you to the animal for letting them kill it. They believe it shows itself to them so that they can do it. Try doing that," Bob said kindly. "Thank the hare for sharing its life with us. Ask its spirit for forgiveness, or ask God. Whatever God you like. It'll help."

Bess and Jessie both got pretty good with a rifle. Dad had never handled a gun before, but he agreed with Bob that he should learn, just in case. At least so we could show a force of strength. We didn't have much ammunition spare though, so once he got the basics right, he didn't keep it up.

Later that day Bob and I were overlooking the Seward Highway again.

"Doesn't look like that jam's moving," Bob said. "I'm glad we're this far away, with any luck no one's going to reach us. We've got some decent canyons in between."

"Shouldn't we tell the others?"

"Why? Your Mom's gonna want to go and help. But we've barely got enough food for ourselves. You can go for a couple of weeks on nothing, if you have to. For a month on very little. But it's around now that people will be thinking of cooking their grandmothers if they've got nothing else."

"Don't be daft, Bob. People don't eat people."

"Why not? It's just meat, a different flavor. I feel closer to the animals I kill than to people."

"But it's not the same."

"Out here, I don't see the difference. And people are surplus, just too many of the buggers, need a cull anyway."

"I'm so grateful you came – I guess we'd just have starved if you hadn't," Matthew said that evening. He had started growing a beard, which made him look much less like an office worker. "I'm hopeless at providing, but I can cook. Bob, any chance of a bread oven?"

"Dad's a brilliant cook," said Sue, "he can make anything you want."

"I'd love some good bread," Bess said. "I'm just going to die if I have to keep on eating fish. I'll be growing fins."

Bob took apart the electric oven and re-welded it into a bread one, which sat in the fire pit. The next day, Matthew was enthusiastic. "It won't last for long," he said, "this modern stuff is too flimsy. But we can get started with it. I'll do sourdough. It uses a natural yeast, a starter, a mix of flour and water, which you get fermenting." He glanced around. "Sue, you can have that job, you can smell the fermentation when it's ready – and keep the fire going."

"It used to be the staple around here," chipped in Louise. "It's why the prospectors were called "sourdoughs.""

"You're right," said Matthew. "I learned about that on my cookery course. We were using one which some old sourdough had started over a century ago...kept it next to his skin to keep warm, and it was still active today."

After a week, once the starter was established, he was cooking a couple of loaves a day, or turning them into hotcakes, sizzling the batter in a skillet.

"I didn't think of you as a cook, but this is real nice," Mom told him as she bit into a warm sourdough venison sandwich, all of us around the table.

"Well, I'm a figures man, really, I like the discipline of

numbers, but I took it up after Alice died, for something to do, to take my mind off things, that's why I went on the course."

"We've something in common there, Matthew," Dad replied, "about the discipline of numbers. I guess we use them in different ways, I use them to make things, you use them as the measure of a business' success."

"Ain't much use around here," Bob grumbled. "Food for the pot, that's all that counts."

Dad nodded toward the corner. "But you can only shoot that rifle because engineers designed and produced it. Centuries of effort went into that. Otherwise you'd still be using a bow and arrow."

"There's something I like about cooking out here," Matthew added. "Everything seems so erratic, so random. In the wild, there's no packaging, the food doesn't come in convenient portions. Cooking seems to bring some discipline into it all, order out of chaos. It's satisfying."

"No way we could live out here without it," said Louise, "not much in the way of fruits and nuts."

"Dunno about convenient portions," Bob muttered, "but decent-sized ones would be nice. I'll have more please."

"A pleasure, Bob," Matthew said as he filled out another sandwich. "We should think about getting out of your hair though, and moving on, get back to Seattle, even if the power isn't back yet."

The corners of Sue's mouth drooped, and Bess looked like she was about to protest.

"No need to on our account," Mom replied, "it's a real pleasure having you here."

I was expecting Bob to say something about the jam on the highway, about how it wasn't safe to travel, but it was Jessie who spoke.

"Dad, you spent months saying we should come on this trip so we could spend some time together. Now we're here, and Sue and I like it, it's different, it's not likely to happen again. And you can afford the time off, so why don't we make the most of it?" She was speaking to Matthew, but she looked at my Dad.

"It's fine by me," he replied.

I couldn't quite figure out why she was saying that. She must be getting on real well with Bess.

NINETEEN

One evening, Bess and Jessie were talking as they washed up the dishes after supper. The rain hissed on the wooden roof tiles, and we could hear it on the water of the lake; thunder rumbled around the mountains, tumbling down the sides, muttering as it moved reluctantly along to the next range.

"I don't mind the hotcakes," Bess was saying. "But it's the munchies I miss. And peanut butter."

"Chicken fried steak, frito pie," said Jessie.

"I'd love a milkshake," Sue chipped in, wistfully.

"*Game of Thrones...*"

"*Teen Wolf...*"

"Oh no, how about *The Vampire Diaries*?"

"*Lizzie McGuire*. Let's watch *Lizzie McGuire*," Sue shouted.

"Yukky, not for us."

"I miss my bike," I volunteered.

"Your bike! That crummy thing. That's just wheels, Jim," Bess said dismissively. "I miss cars, things that can actually get you to places without you getting wet or cold or sweaty."

"I could do with some make-up," Jessie said. "I must look such a fright."

"Oh my God, yes, Jess," Bess answered. "Me too. But what's the point here? There aren't any decent guys in a hundred miles. That makes it even worse."

Matthew looked up from a book he was reading.

"I'd love a coffee, myself, a good triple espresso with a bit of brown sugar to hit the spot. And a nice piece of rich dark organic chocolate to go with it. But look, Mary, I found this, it's yours I think – *Wild Plants of Alaska*."

"I'd forgotten about that one," Mom replied. "It was a Christmas present, years ago, from my sister. I don't think I've ever looked at it."

"We could do things with this, you know," Matthew was getting pretty enthused.

"Yes please!" Bess interrupted.

"There's wild potato around here," he continued. "Maybe I could even make some chips. You can use the roots. Might be too late in the season for that. But there should be plenty of hazelnuts soon, we could try those instead of peanuts. Spice them up a bit. And we need more greens – it's too late for dandelions and nettles, as far as greens go, but there should be fat hen, gooseweed, lovage, wild rhubarb, loads of others. I'm sure we could get a more varied diet going."

Dad looked up from the chainsaw he was working on. "Matthew, I think it's time to appoint you head cook and supply manager. OK with you, Bob? Mary?"

"Fine by me," Bob replied. "Tell me what you need in the way of fish and meat and me and Jim will get it. But I'm not grubbing around in the dirt for roots and plants, no way, that's a woman's job."

"Bob, you do talk trash sometimes," said Mom, affectionately. "You're an unreconstructed, antediluvian dinosaur."

Bob cracked a smile. "You can say that again. One of those big scaly things with claws that ruled the earth for millions of years? Wouldn't have any trouble with bears then, could just say "boo". Sounds good to me. But while we're onto supplies, we need to do something about a wood stack. I don't know how long we're going to be here for, but we'll need a lot to keep the fire going. I can't use an ax, can't raise my arm above the shoulder."

"Can I help with it?" Mom asked.

"No, it's a bullet I took in 'Nam. Smashed the bone. It kind of healed, but it's never worked properly since."

"You should have the hospital look at it when we get back."

"Can't afford that, Mary." Bob laughed. "That's for the rich, not for old soldiers like me. Maybe if Obama had still been there, not that I approve of colored folk in the White House. Stoopid.

He's not even American. But no chance now."

"In the old homesteading tradition," said Louise, you could make free use of empty cabins so long as you left them in better shape than you found them, with a stack of wood. So we could leave a good wood stack as payment for being here."

Dad thought for a moment. "We've got this chainsaw here, but not that much petrol. I think we should keep that mostly for the truck, and for emergencies. Jim, I think this is down to you."

Next day, Bob used a bit of the petrol with the chainsaw to bring an old spruce down.

"Here's how to do it, Jim, never use the tip, it'll kick back, take your eye out."

We planned where it would fall, and after a few moments it came crashing down. I started to chop a big branch off and the ax soon got stuck in a knot.

"Not that way, chucklehead." Bob took the ax from me. "Lightly, at an angle, forty-five degrees, take chunks out, work your way round. And then use a maul to split them. The ax gets stuck when you strike straight down. Never get frustrated," he cautioned. "Work with the grain of the wood. Take your own time."

I grinned at him. "No sweat."

To begin with, I found it difficult. The first day I was always frustrated. The second day I was feeling resentful that it was all down to me. Hell, there were three men here. Why was it down to me to do the laboring? But on the third day, I began to get the hang of it, learning to merge the stroke with the slash, twisting the head sometimes to knock out a heavy piece from the notch. The chips leapt out, covering the ground. I worked on through the days, getting into a routine, keeping up a steady rhythm. I started to enjoy it, planning where each stroke should fall, the precision of it, the thunk of the ax, the pile of logs growing as the sun moved around the sky. I could let my mind drift; images of school, of Anchorage, of Jessie with her shirt off drifted through…a couple of times, out of the corner of my eye, I could see her watching me.

I figured that if I could keep this up for a year or two I might start to build up a bit of muscle. I already felt stronger, my newly-tanned body was taking on some definition and my hands were getting callused.

"You're nailing it," Bob said. "Keep going, we might be here for a while. Here's how to stack them, in the sun, facing west, bark side up, so that the air can circulate and dry it off. There's some corrugated iron over there you can use as cover."

Thinking about that chainsaw now, it cuts to my heart. Dad kept it in great condition, and I did the same, when I inherited it. Many years later, I exchanged it for Gor, along with a can of petrol. I don't think there are many still left now – they'd cost a lot more, though petrol is measured out in spoonfuls, so they're only really of value as status symbols. Like the old decorated swords buried in chieftains' mounds. Still, on the plus side, I guess all seventeen year olds around today are far fitter than I was at their age – scary, many of them; they've been chopping wood since they were old enough to stand.

That evening, we were sitting out on the porch, venison steaks sizzling on the barbie, the grey jays chattering around the woods and edging up to the verandah, looking for scraps.

"Bloody camp robbers," said Bob. "I'd get my gun and shoot them, if I had the energy."

I was dead beat, but feeling good.

"This is such a beautiful spot, I'd like to take a picture of us here," said Louise. "I've got an Instant Print camera – gather around while I go get it."

"I don't know how long we're going to be here for," she said as she brought it back. "But we should have one of us together. I'll put it on a timer, so we can all get in."

I still have that photo, the only one I have. The only one I've seen, actually, for many years. Jessie and Bess are laughing,

Sue's looking solemn, Bob with his unruly white ponytail, Matthew smiling through his newly-growing beard, Louise at the front, Mom and Dad with their arms around each other. All gone now. Myself – well, I looked a bit awkward, but better than I'd thought of myself. The picture is a little worse for wear after all these years, but I keep it in a sealskin wallet for protection. Nowadays, I wear it on a cord around my neck, next to the skin. I want to take it with me when I go.

TWENTY

The mountains rose on one side of the lake. On the other there was a series of hills, split by canyons, with rivers at the bottom, steep sided, but thick with pine and brush.

Bob and I got back late one afternoon and picked up our pace when we heard shouting in the area of the Lodge. Matthew stumbled towards us.

"Sue's missing. We're out looking for her," he shouted.

My guts twisted. Little Sue, alone out here...

"How did it happen? Where did you last see her?" Bob asked.

Matthew was hysterical. "We were all out picking blueberries, got separated. I just don't know where she went to, we all thought she was with someone else."

A few minutes later and we were all gathered outside the Lodge.

"It was a couple of hours ago." Matthew looked scared stupid. "Could...could she have been taken by a bear?"

"No," Bob replied. "Or you would have seen, heard something. You're absolutely sure she's not here? You've checked all the rooms, the outhouse?"

"That was my first thought," Dad replied, "we've been around everywhere. She's not here."

"Fallen asleep?"

"We've checked every cupboard and cranny."

I glanced around, the wilderness seemed to stretch on forever, nothing but hills and forests, rolling on towards the horizon. How were we ever to find her? It hit me – how isolated we were. In Anchorage, even if you got lost, which was hard to do, there were people everywhere, hundreds or thousands to a square mile. Here, it was empty space. But that was the wrong word... every few yards had its obstacles, dangers.

"She's not likely to have gone up the mountain," Bob said.

"So she's lost in these canyons. It's easy to do, and shouting doesn't carry well, hard to tell where it's coming from."

He took the map out. "In two hours she won't have got more than a couple of miles or so as the crow flies, even if she panicked and started running. We'll spread out, and go to these positions." He marked them on the map before barking out orders. "Louise, Mary, you stay here, close to the Lodge, circle around it, spiraling out, keep calling. Matthew, Donald, Jim, Bess, Jessie, head for these points here. We create a circle. Count to five thousand on your way out. Then start zigzagging in back here. Look out for footprints, for any sign of her passing. When you find her, bring her back to the Lodge, and Matthew – you fire a shot twice, to let us know."

"Oh God, I should've been watching her," Matthew said.

Bob slapped him on the back. "We'll find her. The danger is she might've fallen. She could've knocked her head, or gone into water. But at least the weather's warm, there's going to be plenty of light. Let's go."

An hour later, I heard two shots. Back at the lodge, Dad was talking. "She'd lost us, and went off in the wrong direction. When she realized she was lost, she tried to get back, but got into a different canyon. I found her huddled up in a cave."

Mom was hugging her. "It's OK, Sue, you're safe. You're safe, you're back with us now. Let's go and clean you up."

"I didn't mean to get lost, I didn't mean to," Sue wailed, tears streaking down her stained cheeks. Her face and arms were scratched and badly bitten.

Bob turned to Matthew. He shook his head. "This isn't going to work. There are too many of us to look after. I'll take you back to the highway tomorrow."

"Hang on, Bob," Dad cut in. "You've made some good calls for us, but that's not just your decision."

"It's fine in weather like this," Bob waved his arm around. "But if this had happened in a few months, she'd be dead. You want that? You want the responsibility?"

"I know it's different for you and Jim," Dad replied, "but any of the rest of us could easily get lost here."

"We won't let it happen again, will we, Sue," Mom said, her arm still around her.

"Please don't send us away," Sue sobbed.

Matthew met Bob's unforgiving gaze. "Look, I'm sorry we lost her. We're new to this. If you all think we should go, we'll go. But we're not going to be a drain on you, I promise."

I saw Jessie looking at me, a query in her eyes.

"Give them a chance, Bob," I said.

"Bob, don't get so bent," Mom said firmly. "They're not going anywhere. Enough of that."

Bob was silent for a long moment, then he gave an indeterminate grunt, turned on his heel, and walked away.

Jessie was still looking at me. "You go out for a long time with Bob. How do you not get lost?"

I shrugged. "Keep an eye out for features, I guess. Odd trees, rocks, shapes. Remember your angle to the sun. Whether you're going up or down. If we're in new territory, we might slash marks for us to see on the way back. I follow Bob, mostly."

"Bob's right though," Dad said, quietly. "This isn't going to work, is it? We're not suited to this life. We're creatures of streets, straight lines, GPS. I don't know how we're going to learn enough, fast enough, without being able to Google it."

"Matthew was still looking devastated. "Maybe we should just leave, Donald."

"No. That's not an option. We'll figure something out."

Sue was still crying. "There were all these rocks everywhere, and prickly bushes. I just couldn't find my way, I didn't know where to go."

"Sue, I think I can show you how to find the way," said Louise. "Let's go down to the beach."

We all followed, uncertain as to what she was trying to do.

"Now, let's make a map, to show us where we are. This piece of driftwood is the lodge," she said, positioning it on the sand. "And these sticks, those are the trees here." She arranged the sticks. "We'll make these ripples of sand, like this, and that's the lake. Those rocks over there, Sue, bring those over, and they can be this mountain. And here are the canyons..."

I looked across the lake. Nobody had noticed, but two moose were swimming across through the mist that hung around the surface, a male in front, with its huge antlers standing proud, a female behind, an arrowhead of ripples around them. I opened my mouth to say something, but didn't want to interrupt the concentration on the patch of sand. And then the mist closed in, and they were gone.

"And here, these pebbles that we put all around it," Louise was saying, "this is our boundary. We'll need to find some more on the beach here – you see how pretty these are? So, it's like this is our garden, our little private one. And it's just the same as this bigger one, around us. But you stay within this area. Do you understand that?"

"It's a lovely map," Sue replied. "Can we put some flowers in?"

"Of course; we'll go and look for some now, and we can add more later and make the map bigger. And we'll make it as pretty as we can. That's what we're trying to do here, too."

TWENTY-ONE

We soon gave up wearing watches.

"Time is your enemy out here," Bob said. "Make it your friend. Worst thing you can do is rush something, that's when accidents happen."

When the sun was at a certain angle in the sky, it was time for supper. In the evenings we'd barbecue outside, the smell of meat overpowering that of spruce pollen. After we'd cleaned up, we had a couple of hours to ourselves. We'd just hang out, shooting the breeze. We'd play cards or read. The sun didn't set behind the hills till around ten, so we didn't need lamps. Even then, it was generally light enough to read through the night. We actually talked...it seemed like we'd mellowed, and the kind of stuff that was an issue back in Anchorage didn't matter anymore. I remember several occasions with Mom and Dad, sometimes together, sometimes separately, I think they were the first we'd had like "equals", rather than on the "could you hang this washing up for me, Jim," kind of level. We got closer as a family. Bess and me were getting on better. "You're useful to have around, Jim," she complimented me, as I helped her over rocks. "Never really figured that before."

Louise, Bob, the Hardings – we all got to feel more like family.

One evening Mom asked, "What's that you're reading, Louise?"

"It's an old favorite of mine from long ago, *The Swiss Family Robinson*. A family are marooned on an uninhabited island in the Pacific, in the early 1800s, and it's about how they survived. How they made things – a house, a boat. Actually, their situation is in some ways similar to ours. I was wondering if I could pick up any tips to suggest to you."

"What could we possibly learn from them?" asked Bob. "That was centuries ago. Did they even have guns back then?"

"Well, they did, but guns aren't everything. For instance, in the bit I'm reading now, they've tamed some goats. They're getting quite a farmyard together. Makes more sense domesticating animals than having to hunt them all the time."

Bob looked a bit thunderstruck. "Goats. I'll be damned. Why didn't I think of that? We should have got some goats. Keep reading, Louise."

We mostly gave up on remembering which day of the week it was, but Mom kept a calendar, and on a Sunday we'd break into the stores and have a treat, bring out a pudding, a cake, a pot of jam, put a posy of flowers on the table. In the evening, Dad would fish out a bottle of Jack Daniels and we'd sit out at the back, overlooking the lake, Dad offering it around. "Not for me, thanks," said Bob the first time, palms out. "I've been off the giggle juice for a long time."

"I didn't know that, Bob," said Mom, surprised, "though come to think of it, I've never seen you with a drink. How long've you been teetotal?"

"Thirty years now." He paused, looking uncertain as to whether to share more. "It nearly killed me. I was a bum for years, wasted. I woke up in a cell one day, and a minister helped me sort myself out. I lived in his house for a year. I'm not generally in favor of 'em, but he was a good man. A Unitarian. Never been sure what that meant, but they don't have much truck with teaching and stuff."

"What else helped?" asked Dad, looking thoughtful, cleaning his specs.

"To be honest, being out here, in the wild. Makes it easier, not having any booze around. I mean, I could set up a still, make vodka from birch easy enough, but somehow, when I'm out here, it doesn't seem necessary. I mean, why be plastered all the time when you've got this?" He waved his arms around. "I'll put the kettle on for some tea. And Donald, that stuff's too valuable to drink. It's good for frostbite, things like that."

"He's an even better man than I took him for," I heard Louise mutter under her breath after he'd gone inside.

The sun dipped towards the horizon. Chickadees flitted along the beach, going *tsikadee, dee, dee*. The strange, haunting cries of loons echoed around the lake.

"The Indians believe it's their ancestors calling from the spirit world," remarked Louise.

"I could believe that, it's an amazing sound," replied Mom.

"It's down to the shape of the larynx and how you use it," intervened Dad. "Nothing magical about it."

Louise laughed. "You truly have the imagination of an engineer, Donald. But sometimes perhaps it's what you see in things, how you respond to them, that counts more than the thing itself."

"Why's it called a loon?" Sue asked.

"A loon, a loon, it can't hold a tune…" Bess sang.

"It's a Scandinavian word, meaning clumsy," I replied. "They're really primitive birds, the oldest water birds in the world, and they never developed the knack of walking."

"How come you know that?" asked Jessie.

"I know about birds," I replied, blushing. "I mean, only the feathered kind," my tongue seemed to tie itself into knots. What a dork. I didn't want to be like this. And I wasn't going to mention the stamps.

"Nice to hear a song again," Bob said, back with a cup of nettle tea. He started to sing, croakily.

Wi' my dog and gun, through the bloomin' heather,
For game and pleasure I took my way.
I met a maid, she was tall and slender,
Her eyes enticed me some time to stay.

I said "Fair maid, do you know I love you?
Tell me your name and your dwelling, oh so?"

"Oh, excuse my name, but you'll find my dwelling
By the mountain streams where the millcocks crow."

And it's arm in arm we will go together
Through the lofty trees, in the valley below,
Where the lenties sing there so so sweetly
By the mountain streams where the millcocks crow.

"Why, Bob," said Mom, "where did you learn that?"

"From my grandpa. He was Irish, from the old country, knew hundreds of songs by heart. Came over to work on the railways. No family left now. Had a couple of brothers once, but we lost touch. Never had a missus. There're a few other verses, but I've forgotten 'em. I don't know anyone who stills sings the old songs."

"You could teach them to me," said Jessie. "I like singing."

Bob's face lit up. "I'd like that a lot, Jessie. We can do it when we go out hunting or fishing. Get a tune going. We can be like the Potter's Place choir, on tour. It's a good thing to do, keeps the bears away. The one thing they don't like is being taken by surprise."

TWENTY-TWO

In that most amazing of summers, the best of all summers, I fell head over heels for Jessie. How could I not? She was a stunner. Lovely, oval, innocent face, trim figure – at school she would have been beyond my dreams. And she seemed kind, though with a kind of steel inside her that Bess didn't have. And she knew her own mind. OK, she wasn't Miss. America, but she was out of my class. I knew that as sure as I knew anything. But she barely seemed to notice me. She and Bess were a closed bubble.

It was a week later. We were ranging around more comfortably now, fishing, foraging, gathering back at the lodge in the evening. Bob just insisted that we were in pairs, at a minimum, with a rifle between us. Even Mom and Louise came out at times. One day, which still brings a smile to my face as I recall it, Bob and I, Jessie and Bess, were catching salmon down the Portage River.

"Jim," Bob said after a while, "could you and Jessie take these back, then you can get supper started with Matthew. Nice ones here, must be fifteen pounds. Bess and me will stay on to catch some more."

Jessie and I walked back in silence, carrying a pole on our shoulders with several salmon hanging from it. She was in front, moving with the grace of a deer over the rocky ground, and I wondered if she could feel my eyes devouring her figure. It was the first time we'd been alone together. I wondered if I should start a conversation. How did you do that? My mind seemed to have gone blank. I didn't expect she'd be interested in stamps, or war gaming. What did teenagers talk about? The tracks of an animal crossed our path, I thought it might have been mink. But why would she want to know that? And now we were past it, so it was too late to mention it. Should I say something about the weather, about what a lovely day it was in the warm sun, glinting in her hair, the wind blowing strands across her face and rippling the leaves, wispy cirrus high overhead? Perhaps I could bring up the political situation. But what was that, anyway? Where would you start? I wished I wasn't such a goof.

She stopped, put her end of the pole down and stretched, as if needing a break. I did the same.

"Jim, Bess tells me you killed a guy, back in Anchorage."

I started; it was the first time she'd called me by my name. With her next to me now, her hair bobbing around her shoulders, a view of her breasts straining against the red T-shirt she was sporting, tied up so her tanned midriff was bare, I was a bit breathless anyway, had a real boner — my trousers were so baggy, I hoped she couldn't see — and now my heart seemed to stop.

"It...it was an accident, I didn't mean to..." I mumbled.

"Didn't sound like an accident to me," she said. "Bess said you shot him plumb in the middle, with one shot. She's very proud of you, you know."

"She is?" I said, shocked. "I didn't know. It was just something...I didn't mean...you won't tell anyone...?"

"Of course I won't. It's strange here, isn't it?" she said, changing subject, so that my brain spun, trying to catch up. "It could be the end of the world, we're almost alone. Like Adam and Eve...are you gay?"

"What? No, no, not at all!"

"Do you like me?" She stepped closer.

I shuffled my feet. "Of course I do. I—"

"Well then, could we be friends?" She took another step. I was frozen to the spot.

"Us? Me? Well..."

"I don't know where this is going to go, Jim," she interrupted," but here..."

She put her arm around my neck, drew me in, and kissed me on the mouth, soft and sweet, her breasts pushing against me. It wasn't quite the first time I'd kissed a girl, there was the time at some party when I managed to get in because no one realized I hadn't been invited, and a drunk girl came up to me. But I was still a virgin, and I'd never got this close to anyone like her before. Her tongue came in. I stood rooted in surprise.

"We could get to know each other better, if you'd like to," she said. "Looks as if we'll be sharing company for a while."

"I...I haven't had a girlfriend before," I stammered.

"Then it's about time you did."

"But why me?"

"I like you, Jim. You're straightforward. You seem honest. And you were never all over me, like most guys. Actually, I was starting to wonder if you would ever notice I was here at all."

"But, but Jessie..."

"And I love your face," she continued. "OK, it's a bit lopsided," her hands moved over my features, "it's what you might call characterful. And you've got a couple of crooked teeth, and your ears are too big, and you've got a beak for a nose, and your eyes are too close together and never look at me, but I love it when they do, like they are now, and I don't think I'll get tired of it."

Our kisses deepened, our bodies were warm against each other in the sun. Water gurgled in a nearby stream, eddying around the rocks. Flycatchers were whistling *whit whit*.

It was an out of time moment that I never wanted to end. I thought I'd been happy before, but now I was floating up on cloud nine.

That evening Jessie and I walked over to the lake, where Bess was sitting on a rock, fishing. She glanced around. "They're not coming for me like they do for Bob," she said, turning back to focus on her rod. "I haven't caught anything yet."

"I have," Jessie replied, taking my hand.

Bess turned again, her mouth dropping open in what could have been delight or horror. "Gosh, this is soooo wierd. My geek brother making out with my best friend," she exclaimed. "Fantabulous!"

A couple of days later, I picked a moment when Dad was alone and blurted out, "Dad, do you have any condoms?"

"What!"

"Um, you know, protection." My face was hot.

"I know what they are, son, but I didn't know you and Jessie had something going."

"Ur, well, I think so."

He stood up, treating me to a long, searching look. "You've both managed to keep that really quiet. She's a nice girl. Are you treating her right?"

"I wouldn't...I wouldn't do anything she didn't want me to. We've only kissed. This is just in case. Actually, it's her idea," I babbled. "We've been talking about it. She wants to do it." I felt myself blushing.

"Have you done this before?"

"No! I just think...I just think...she might be the one. That this might be...the time."

"Actually, I don't have any, I've been snipped. But we could look out for some." He paused. "I'd like to talk about this with your mom, if you haven't told her yourself, OK?"

I ducked my head, even more embarrassed. "OK."

"Let's do it now, get it over with. I'll go find her, we'll walk over to the beach there."

I was sitting on a rock overlooking the lake, my favorite spot, where you could see the small fry in the clear water, the beetles zipping through the plants, caddisflies trundling across the bottom, and all the way down to the far end of the lake, when Mom and Dad came over.

"Your Dad's told me, Jim, and I've got to say, I don't like it. You're too young."

"Mom!" I could feel the anger rising in me — I wasn't sure where it was coming from. I hadn't contradicted my parents before. "I'm not! And I don't actually need your permission. I'm old enough to fight in the army, and kill people, and I already have. I'm old enough to have a pilot's certificate. So I'm old enough to have sex."

She looked taken aback. "But Jessie's only just old enough at sixteen, Jim, legally. And don't get so thin-skinned about this. We're just concerned about what's best for you."

She hesitated. "Jim, if you feel ready for it, if Jessie does, I'm not going to stand in your way."

Dad looked at Mom, who nodded. "I'm glad for you, Jim," he said quietly. "We'll see if we can get hold of some. But don't even dare *think* about going too far till then, this is not the time for unplanned pregnancies, you understand?"

"Thanks, Dad — I won't let you down."

PART TWO

FALL

TWENTY-THREE

The next day we were all sitting around the table, crammed in – us Richards, the Hardings, Bob, and Louise.

Dad was opening the discussion.

"I'm worried about what's happening in the world outside. We've been here for a month now and there's no way to get news. I keep thinking, do we need to protect ourselves? What's happening with other neighbors? If the government doesn't get the power back, how are things going to develop through the winter? How are we going to make a go of this?"

"Surely they're going to sort things out before winter," Mom replied.

Dad pulled in a long breath, letting it out again in a sigh. "I really do hope so, Mary, but they haven't done it yet. If they had, we'd surely have seen some evidence of it. Some vehicles on the road..."

Bob coughed. "There was a jam on the Highway, at the beginning; it's cleared now, but we haven't seen anyone moving down there for weeks now."

"What?" Mom exclaimed. "Bob, you didn't tell us!"

"What was the point? What could we've done?"

"There must've been something we could've done, Bob," Mom spluttered indignantly. "Oh, I knew I should have stayed in Anchorage. I could have helped."

"Mary, we know each other now. You've got to believe, if it had been a few stranded motorists, we would've gone and done what we could. But how many people are you going to share our food and the lodge with? We're on our own here, so are they."

"But it's just not right, Bob!"

"We made a deal," Bob said harshly, "that we'd look after each other. That's what we're doing. If you want to take care of everyone else, that's fine, I'll move on."

There was a long silence.

"Mary, Bob's right," said Louise. "We have a deal. We shook hands on it."

"But…"

Dad interrupted. "Let's continue. I think we can take it that power, let alone law and order, hasn't been restored yet. I wish I'd figured out about ham radios and brought one along. The guys down the Portage River don't have one either. Honestly, though, I thought we'd have heard something by now. I think we need to venture out, to see what anyone else knows."

Matthew intervened. "Maybe the cities are getting back to normal, and they just haven't got around to contacting people outside yet. Maybe the rest of the country's back on its feet, and it's just in areas like Alaska there's still a problem."

Mom frowned worriedly. "We should think of the risk. Maybe we're better off staying here until someone comes to find us than going looking for trouble. What if we just run into more people like Mr. Trinker?"

I shuddered at the memory. "Mom, first you're saying we should go out and help people, now you're saying we should keep away from them. You need to make up your mind."

She looked at me, surprised. "Well, I just don't think this is right." She got up in a bit of a huff, and filled her cup from the water barrel.

"Donald and Matthew are right." Bob rubbed his chin. "We need to figure out what's happening before the fall snows come. Come September or October, we'll probably be stuck. We won't be able to get anywhere till next spring or summer. And I wasn't reckoning on spending the winter here."

"So if we did have to stay," said Dad, "could we do it? Matthew, you're the storekeeper, what do you think?"

"We've a hundred fine salmon and a load of other fish, three carcasses of deer, several dozen hares and ptarmigan, thanks to Bob and Jim here. They've all been smoked and dried, so they're not going to be fine dining, but they'll see us through for a few months, if needs be, so long as the ice cave's secure. We don't have enough for much longer though. So we'd need a lot more meat and fish. And we don't have much in the way of vegetables or fruit. We need a lot more foraging trips. And if you're really thinking we're going to be here through the winter, we need mega flour, pasta, rice, beans, dried milk, baking powder, cornmeal, as essentials. Then there's cheese, eggs, potatoes, onions, tomatoes...how much more do you want me to list...and of course salt, vinegar and sugar. We do need those. They all last forever, and I can use them to preserve food. If we can't do that, we'll be hand-to-mouth."

"Whoa!" Dad interrupted. "I get the message. That seems about the size of it. So even to get enough food, we have a lot to do."

"Well, it surely looks like we need to scale up the foraging trips," Jessie commented.

"OK. We should go carefully, in groups," said Bob. "Rifles and shotguns. The cranberries are out now, and bears love 'em. And we'll need a lot more firewood as well, the wood stack needs to be the same size as the lodge."

Jessie caught my eye. She seemed to be expecting me to say something. "We'll need more living accommodation," I said.

"You could be right there, Jim," Dad replied. "Though whether we can all fit into this lodge – probably too tight. So we'd have to build another one, or an extension, we'll see."

I glanced back at Jessie. She nodded.

"Jessie and me would like our own place."

There was silence, puzzlement, and then general consternation around the table.

"About time, Jim." Bob clapped his hands. "I thought you'd been up, lately. Glad you're getting lucky. Best keep your trouser snake zipped in though."

Jessie blushed, Mom sputtered, Dad looked disapproving,

Sue seemed not to know what we were talking about,

Matthew looked up in surprise. "What's this? When did this happen?"

"Adults!" exclaimed Bess. "Blind as bats. Never notice anything." She sniggered. "I'm all in favor, I'd have more room, and I don't want to hear them doing whatever they're going to do in bed all night."

We looked at Mom, expecting her to object but she just shrugged. "In for a cent, in for a dollar. This is further than I expected – shacking up. But it's your lives, might as well get on with them now rather than have you and your hormones fretting around us all winter. It does seem strange though, last year you were my little boy and now you're talking about setting up home."

I managed to look Matthew in the eye.

"Is that all right, Mr. Harding?"

He looked at Mom and Dad. Dad nodded.

"It's a lot of extra work," said Dad. "And there's not much time. At least you'll find out pretty quick if you're suited or not. But if it doesn't work out, you stay friends, alright? There's not going to be room for enmity and tantrums here."

"We're not children!" Jessie exclaimed hotly.

"I didn't mean it that way," Dad replied firmly. "Plenty of angry and bitter adults around when they break up. But we could be cooped up here for some time. If you split up, there's nowhere to go to."

"That's not going to happen, Dad," I replied.

Mom added, "Matthew, if you're OK with it…it depends on you."

"Gee. I don't know about this."

Jessie stood up, looking fierce, color flaming in her cheeks. "This is between Jim and me. We don't need your approval."

"Yes you do, Jessie," Mom said firmly. She went over and took Matthew's hand in hers. "Matthew, we haven't known each other for long, but if Jim and Jessie want to be together, I think we should support them."

I went over to Matthew. This was the hardest thing I'd ever done. I could feel my voice cracking. "Thanks, Mom," I said, glancing at her. "I'll look after Jessie, Mr Harding, I promise," I said nervously.

"This is the way of it, folks." Louise smiled. "This is how we used to do it; two families, need blood ties, in the native tradition they're old enough to have been married for years already."

Matthew got up and gave me a hug. His mustache had turned into a soft beard which tickled my neck – he was a few inches shorter. "You're a good boy, Jim, take care of her for me. Call me Matthew, please." He sat back on his chair.

"You know," he continued, his voice breaking, "it was very difficult for me when Alice died. She was ill for a long time. I know I haven't been the father I should've been."

Jessie went over and kissed him on the head, her hand on his shoulder. He raised his to cover it. "It's OK, Dad. And I wasn't a good daughter. I could've helped more."

"Does this mean Jim is my brother now?" Sue chirped up.

"Yes, Sue, if you want me to be," I replied. That didn't seem quite enough for the occasion– I went over and gave her a hug.

"Wish I'd met someone like Jessie when I was younger," said Bob. "I might not have messed up so much."

"Well, after that bombshell," Dad picked up the discussion. "I think we're agreed that we need to do some building."

"All right, I agree with that," Mom replied. "We can make things work here. But we're in someone else's place. We should try and get in touch with the owner, find out who he or she is before we start changing it that much."

I was thinking real hard. I gulped. "We should go to Anchorage tomorrow, find out what's going on," I said determinedly. "Pick up what supplies we can get."

A ghost of a smile hovered on Jessie's face. Dad raised his

eyebrows.

"Yes, let's do that," he replied. "I guess we're all short of some essentials. We've barely used any fuel yet, and I'd like to see how the neighbors are, Jerry and Marcia, and the others. I suggest it's me, Bob and Matthew."

"I'm not sure I'll be much help," said Matthew. "You're the boss, as far as I'm concerned, and I'll do whatever you want, but perhaps Jim would be better. He can shoot, I can't."

"I don't want any more shooting," Mom said tightly, getting to her feet. "And I don't want Jim more involved in this. He's not going."

"Mom, I'm grown up now!" I interrupted hotly. "I need to go."

Mom looked surprised; I guess I rarely chipped in.

"He's the best shot here, Mary, far better than me, to be honest," said Bob.

Mom seemed to struggle with herself. "OK. I don't like it, but you're right." She smiled at me shakily. "I guess I'll always think of you as my little boy, Jim, but I can't deny you're walking taller nowadays. I'd even swear you're a couple of inches higher. We should think about what we need. With more of us now, I could do with more medicine, if you can find any. I didn't think we'd be here this long. I'll make a list. Donald, I need to talk to you about this. And we need sanitary items."

"If you get stuck on that," said Louise, "I could help out, we never had them where I grew up."

"Can I come?" asked Jessie. "Jim and I are together now."

"No, sorry, Jessie," said Dad, as he picked up a rifle from the rack at the door. "It might be dangerous and there's no point in exposing any of us to risk when it's not necessary. Don't worry, the three of us will be fine, and we'll bring Jim back to you. Don't expect us back today though, and don't worry if we're away a night or two. Here, Matthew, you'd better take this gun. Just in case. It's not loaded, get the feel of it, and Bob can show you how to use it this evening."

"While you're gone," said Mom, "we'll make tomorrow a cleaning and wash day. There's a lot of bedding to sort out." She looked through the window at the sky. "Though it's not looking promising for drying. Still...the beds need changing, the stove clearing out, floors sweeping, the kitchen area cleaning, a huge pile of washing to do, the stores need sorting. Matthew, Jessie, Bess, Sue, Louise, I'll need all your help, thanks. Let's get this place spick and span for when they come back."

TWENTY-FOUR

We set off the next morning, a grey day, with dark clouds scurrying across the sky, a hint of rain in the air. It was two months to the day after the Event. Dad was driving, to get some familiarity with the vehicle. After a few miles, as we trundled slowly along the dirt track, throwing up clouds of dust, he stopped.

"OK, Jim, I think you should have a go. You might as well know how to drive this, we're not going to use up petrol just teaching you, so here's where the learning starts. We don't need to worry about three point turns, or the Highway Handbook, but you need to be able to get this truck from A to B."

We swapped places and he showed me how to engage the gears, set off, change gear, steer and brake. I struggled to get the hang of it, lurching along, and when I pressed the accelerator instead of the brake and ran off the road Bob interrupted.

"Donald, if you could take over again, we should get a move on. Jim can practice when there's more space, before he trashes the truck. We could find an empty car park in Anchorage. And we need to be readier with guns than we were last time."

As it turned out, that was the only time I was behind a wheel. Within a few years landslides, fallen trees, frost heaves, vegetation, had all made the roads impassable. Walking pace was the best we generally achieved.

It was late morning before we reached the mess that was Seward Highway. Abandoned old cars and trucks that had been heading out of Anchorage were all over the place, but with no one in sight. To our left, it looked as if the road was blocked, with several cars piled up.

"Where've all the people gone?" I asked.

"Well," Dad replied, "when they got stuck, I guess they would've started walking along the road. That's what I'd have done, or walked back to Anchorage. I doubt many would've struck off into the hills."

We could just get through, pushing the occasional vehicle aside with the truck bumpers. After another few miles, we came to the Alyeska turning. The caterpillar tractor was still there, but now part of a larger barrier. There was no guard, but a car had crashed into the barricade. As we approached some ravens flapped away. Dad went over to take a look.

"You don't want to see this," he said as he walked back. "There's a couple of dead people, been there a while."

"Shall we get through and see what's happened?"

"I don't think so, Bob. I don't like the look of this. Someone should've buried those bodies. It suggests there's no one around. I think we should move on. Let's see if we can find anyone to talk to in Anchorage, find what we need and get back."

We drove on, more nervously now. We saw a couple of humpbacks in the distance, in Turnagain Arm, leisurely ploughing the waves. About half way to Anchorage we came to the small settlement of Indian Valley. We crawled along, windows open, looking for signs of life. Occasionally we passed an abandoned car, but there seemed to be no one around.

"There's something moving in there," I pointed to the Brown Bear Saloon. We stopped. Dad started to get out of the cab when a dog came running out, fast. Behind it another, and another.

"Get that window up!" yelled Dad, scrambling back into the cab. Bob had it half way up as the first dog, a big mastiff, hurled itself against it, snarling, leaving saliva and blood smeared on the outside, some spittle splattering over Bob. I was frozen, just glad it was Bob on that side of the cab – I wasn't sure that I would have got the window up in time. Dad revved the engine and we sped off, with the pack in pursuit. A couple of dozen of them, all shapes and sizes.

"JC!" said Bob. "They've gone savage."

"I'm worried about the others now," said Dad anxiously,

looking at us both. "I'm not sure what to do. Matthew isn't going to be able to fight off a pack like that. The lodge has no defenses. We'll need to get back as quick as we can."

"Should we go back now?" I asked.

Bob hesitated. "Dogs don't range widely by nature. We can do what we want to do in Anchorage. We just won't hang around."

We increased speed and after a few minutes saw the Anchorage skyscrapers, set against the stunning white-topped mountain background. It was clear sky ahead of us, but at our back black clouds were building up, coming in off the sea.

"I've got a rough route worked out," said Dad, looking at the Anchorage map. "We pass a gun store first on 104th Avenue, there's a pharmacy a little further along, and if that hasn't got what we need we'll go to the hospital. Then we want an electrical store, ironmongers, agricultural supplies, food warehouse."

"Hang on." Bob was looking up at the sky. "What's that weird cloud?" We stopped and he got down from the truck and took a look through his scope. His face paled. "Holy Mary Mother of God! Have a look, Donald. I've never seen anything like that before. They're turkey vultures, bald eagles, ravens, must be thousands of 'em. They must've come from all over. That's where the birds've gone."

"I'll drive," said Dad. "You guys have your rifles ready."

We drove on carefully. The hair on my arms stood up when we came across the first dead bodies, but they were everywhere. Some of them had been shot, blood staining the sidewalks and road. I don't mind admitting, I was scared. Dad looked about the same, and Bob had a wild look in his eyes, I wasn't sure if he was ready to run or if it was bringing back memories. The dead were being picked at by ravens and magpies, it was like a scene from a horror movie. The bodies were swollen, some the size of cows, leaking fluids. Birds were everywhere, thousands of gulls and other seabirds.

Dad steered around a corpse and some gulls flew off it,

squawking in protest. "God, it's like that Hitchcock film, *Birds*. They've taken over."

The place was overrun with rats, gnawing on the bodies. I saw a few that were huge, more like cats. A blur of color ran out of a building and I saw a fox, a limb in its mouth. It was quickly followed by another. By the time we reached the gun store, I felt as if I was coming down with a fever...hot and cold at the same time. Sweat covering the small of my back and itching in my hairline.

Things didn't look promising at the gun store. The metal grille at the front had been forced open, the windows smashed, glass spilled across the sidewalk.

"Jesus, I was worried about this," said Bob. "Looks like we're too late."

"What's that smell?" I asked. "Like rotten eggs?"

"It's death, son," Dad said, tight lipped. "Decomposition. Sewage." He nodded towards the store. "I'll keep the engine running. You two go and see if there's anything left. This might be a plague. So don't touch *anything* without your gloves on. Don't go near any bodies."

Bob grunted. "Gotcha."

We jumped down, cocked our rifles and crunched across the glass. Inside the debris strewn store the shelves were stripped bare. A quick survey of the back rooms came up empty.

The pharmacy, our next stop, looked as if it had been gutted, and we drove on to the hospital. There had been fires in this part of town. Whole blocks had been burned down. Some buildings were still smoldering. Apart from the birds, and the occasional dog, rats were the only things moving, and some cats.

We were a few blocks away from our own home. "Better go and have a look," said Dad, breaking the silence. "I feel bad about having left Jerry and Marcia there."

The street was a mess. Some houses had burnt down, all those standing had been looted. There was no one around. Our house, and Jerry's next door, were standing, but with no sign of life. The front doors were off the hinges, the insides had been trashed. Dad went in, he was back out again a few moments later.

"You don't want to go in there," he said, looking ashen-grey, wiping vomit from his mouth. "Jerry's dead, shot. I didn't see Marcia. Pass me that water, Jim."

Dad drove around a body lying in the street. Two dogs were worrying at it. I looked back. The head had no face. My gut roiled and I had to work hard to keep myself from spewing.

The smell at the hospital was the worst. Dad got some cloths, we dipped them in water and wrapped them around our faces. Mom had given him directions to the medical supplies room. We moved as quickly as we could through corridors slippery with filthy water, vomit, feces, God knows what kind of muck. Doors opened onto wards where we could sometimes see bodies still in bed, faces decomposing, tongues hanging out, where they hadn't already been eaten, body fluids dripping down to the floor. Rats were everywhere, and columns of ants along the floors, walls, up on the ceilings. I felt cold inside and I couldn't help it, I puked into a corner, the vomit splashing over my feet. The door to the supply room was open, the shelves had been raided, but there were still plenty of cartons unopened. I guess people didn't know about medicine the way they knew about guns. Dad started going through them. There was a huge crashing noise in the corridor outside. We froze. If I hadn't been rigid with fright, I think I would have run for the window. Bob raised his gun and stepped out. He laughed nervously. "It's just a porcupine. Daft animal's got its head stuck through a hospital trolley." It banged along the corridor, tail thrashing as it tried to escape.

"I've never been so close to peeing my pants," said Dad, his voice shaking. "OK, I've got the rucksacks full, let's get out of here." We picked our way back through the hospital maze. At the entrance, Bob pointed to another wall, which we hadn't noticed on the way in. "Look at that." The word was in rough, six-foot high, white letters, the paint dripping at the bottom:

CHOLERA

TWENTY-FIVE

Bob shuddered. "Jesus. This is a bust. Whoever painted that, I wonder where they are now."

We headed back to the truck, shaken. "All those people who were here a few months ago," I said, my voice coming out as a thin croak. "They can't all have died."

"They haven't," replied Dad, "or we'd have seen a lot more bodies. They've left. Those who've survived must be settled down somewhere, out in the suburbs, cutting themselves off. The townships up Knik Arm – most would've gone north. Maybe there are still people downtown, but I doubt it – it's a cesspit."

Bob pointed up to the right. A few hundred yards away there was a six-story block of apartments. Behind a parapet, at the top, a man was standing with a rifle, not aimed at us, just standing there, watching, lowering binoculars. We waved. He put up his middle finger in reply.

"Let's blow now," said Bob. "This place scares the bejesus out of me. Worse than anything in 'Nam."

"It doesn't look like the locals are keen to talk," Dad replied. "There's nothing we can do to help here. It's so much worse than I thought possible. And we've got those dogs to worry about. This scares me, too, Bob, but there are some things we still need to get."

We picked up our pace, anxious to get out of there. The wind was whipping up, hurling rubbish along the street. We were just opening the cab door when we heard three shots, in quick succession, and ducked behind it. "Pistols," said Bob, listening hard. "Sounds like Berettas, army issue. Some distance away, over towards the prison. Not aimed at us, but let's go."

"Wait a minute, Bob. That builder's depot on the corner, let's assume now we're going to be at the lodge for some time. We need to be able to make things, repair things."

We drove over fast and set to loading sacks of cement, window frames, panes of glass, tarpaulins, ropes, throwing them into the truck. "Burlap sacks, batteries, mattocks, rope, tools, more nails...we'll need all those," Dad was saying. "Bob, cover us."

We found another gun store which had been broken into, but not emptied, and took several rifles and boxes and boxes of ammo. The Alaskan Flour Company had been destroyed, it was a mess, rats everywhere.

"Forget this," Dad pulled us back to the truck as we tried to scrape some up, "it's too full of rat droppings. They've been all over it."

Bramble Electrical Stores had been gutted by fire. The ironmongers had been broken into, but we picked up loads of duct tape, dozens of pairs of gloves, leather oil, cord, everything down to safety pins. "Annie's Stores, let's try that," Dad shouted above the squawk of the birds, "we need thread, needles, canvas..."

"Jesus, Donald, we could get caught here. But OK, while we're at it, snowshoes and trot lines," Bob added.

Anchorage Sports had been trashed, but there were some snowshoes left. Just then we heard some more shots in the distance. We were desperate to leave by now, and Dad took a couple of corners fast.

There was something about the speed we were moving which bought things together in my head – the dogs, the gunshots, hostiles, wild animals – we were never going to be able to shoot dogs fast enough if they were coming straight at us. We needed defenses. I remembered the pictures of Russian forts I'd seen in history books. The Kenai Peninsula alone used to have half a dozen of them. But they had stockades, rows of trimmed trees sharpened at the top. We didn't have the manpower to build those. What could we use?

"Stop!" I yelled suddenly. "Joe's Agricultural Supplies, over there."

"What the hell?" Bob asked.

"Do it now," I shouted.

I jumped out and ran over as the truck slowed down. Yes, they had them! Large drums of high grade wire, the kind the farmers used to protect their crops. I started manhandling one towards the truck, but it was a struggle.

Dad and Bob joined me.

"Jim, what the fuck's got into you?" Dad almost screamed. "We have to get out of here."

"Help me here, Dad, we need fencing. Keep those dogs off. We'll turn the lodge into a fort."

"Not a bad idea, Jim." Bob scratched his head. "Come along then."

While we were at it we took packs of polytunnels and packets of rat poison. The animal feed, grain and oatmeal had all gone. But we found boxes of seeds; we grabbed as many as we could carry.

By the time we'd finished, the truck was as loaded as it had been on the journey out.

"Actually, I'm surprised there was so much left," muttered Dad, at the wheel as we drove down the Parkway.

"It must have all happened real quick," Bob replied. "OK, guys, let's get back fast, while we can still see."

Then the sky went dark, as if a curtain had been pulled across. Thunder crashed around the mountains.

"What about our clothes?" I shouted over the noise. "We've been wading through muck, shouldn't we clean off?"

"Damn. You're dead right, thank you, Jim. Last thing we want to do is carry infection back. 5th Mall is on our route. Let's go get new clothes, if there are any. It's out of the way, could be safer there."

"It'll be all over the cab as well," Bob said. "We'll have to bleach it all down."

"And, um, my problem?" I asked.

"Hell, I forgot that, too. OK, we're passing a couple more pharmacies on the way out, let's see what they've got."

We did some "shopping" in the Mall, especially for boots for everyone, socks, mittens and hats and waterproof wear. In every shop the doors and windows had been smashed, but there were still clothes around – I guess looters hadn't all been thinking forward to winter. We raced around, grabbing what we could, not bothering to check sizes, guns at the ready. Then we moved on to the pharmacies. The first was a gutted shell, the second had been stripped bare. In the third the door had been broken down and there was a jumble of shelf goods on the floor. There were plenty of condoms, boxes of them in the room at the back. "How many should I bring?" I asked.

"Hell, I don't know, son. How much sex are you planning on having in your life?" Dad replied. "After today, I'm not sure of anything. Bring them all. Let's take contraceptive pills as well while we're here. And these boxes. Bound to be of use. But let's go. Go...go..."

It was midnight when we left Anchorage. The headlights weren't working, and we crept along with the help of a torch.

"See anyone following us?" Dad asked.

"All clear," I replied, looking back.

We could see the rain coming towards us like a wall across Turnagain Arm. It was lashing the white-capped waters. When it hit us, it was like standing under a waterfall. Visibility dropped to zero.

"Bob," Dad shouted over the hammering of the drops. "We're not going to make it back in this. Can't see enough. We'll stop at Bird Point."

A mile or two on and we pulled off into a car park overlooking the waters, secluded from the main road. It wasn't raining so hard any longer, but it was still hard to see without lights.

Dad sighed with relief. "Jesus. Well, can't say I'm sorry to leave that place. Hope never to see anything like that again. I don't think we'll be going back there any time soon."

"Never liked it anyway," Bob replied.

"How did you come to live there, Bob?" I asked curiously.

Bob hesitated. "I was in the slammer there, Jim. Had a bad time when I came out of the army. Got into trouble, wrong crowd, caught a nickle, for robbery."

"What's a nickle?"

"Five years. Had no money when I came out to go anywhere, just drank. After that minister got me sober, I started work, repairing stuff. Never had a good enough reason to move out. Still want me around?" He looked at Dad.

Dad looked him straight in the face. "That's the past, Bob, it doesn't matter. You saved us, you know that? I'm eternally obliged to you." He peered into the night. "It's too dark to go straight back, that torch isn't bright enough. So let's strip off, wash in the sea, dump what we've been wearing, clean everything up, dry off back in the cab, get into clean clothes, and then we'll hit the sack under the truck. Not much headroom, won't be the most comfortable night's sleep ever, but it'll have to do. We can at least put a tarpaulin down, some canvas, clothes, keep dry. I think we're safe here, but let's keep the rifles handy. Then we'll get back early tomorrow."

It was warmer in the sheltered waters of Turnagain Arm than out of them; must've been about 60 degrees F. We washed, scrubbed, and changed. I wished Jessie was here, though she wouldn't have appreciated the concrete bed. I was shaping words in my head for her, trying to put the day's images and the screeching of the gulls out of my mind, when I crashed out.

TWENTY-SIX

We got to Potter's Place early, but everyone was up. Jessie and I held each other for a while.

"You're OK?"

"It was horrible, Jessie," I muttered. "Like one of those zombie films. A nightmare, times ten. We're on our own here."

"We've got each other," she whispered. "You kept your promise to come back. I'm going to hold you to that, always, you understand?" She stepped a little away from me, her blue eyes searching my face intently. "Sometimes I struggle to get through to you, I want to make myself clear."

I nodded. I wasn't sure what I could do about it, other than not go anywhere, but I got the message. It felt weird; parents you could take for granted, it was blood, you knew they'd always be there for you. At least for most kids. But to have someone else feel that way about you, it was different. I couldn't quite get my head around it. We weren't family, so what was the connection? What turned friendship into blood ties? Was it the sex, creating new life? Was I really ready for that?

"Now, there's a lot to talk about," Dad said. "Matthew, would love one of those oatcakes, and then let's discuss where to go from here. I think we all need to be part of this."

We spent the morning on it, explaining what we'd seen, answering questions. Jessie was sitting next to me, her body against mine, it was a strange, thrilling feeling, having someone that close. Someone who would just sit by me, because she liked me, loved me. We were barely touching, but it was like there was electricity between us. She took my hand.

"All those people dead!" Sue cried. "Will that happen to us?"

"No, it won't, Sue. We'll make sure it won't," Mom replied. "So long as we all have each other, we'll be OK." She smiled but her voice was determined. "I only watch films with happy endings, and we'll make it turn out that way."

"Sue, there's no way of hiding this from you, the world has changed," Dad added. "But we're going to make things work. We're in a good position here. We can do it, if we stick together. OK?"

"What about my friends?" asked Bess, looking pale. "Do you think they're all dead?"

"I'm sure they got out in time with their families, Bess dear," Mom replied.

"Maybe we should have made more of an effort to bring people with us, Bess," Dad added. "I'm sorry we didn't. It was hard enough to bring you along. But they'll be finding their own way somewhere."

"But how did cholera kill the ones you saw?" Jessie asked.

"Cholera can kill you in a few hours," Mom replied. "The only cure is rehydration, fast, but then, if you haven't got clean water to drink...a lot of people would have died quickly, and it's very infectious. And then with the lack of hygiene... It probably spread like wildfire, and the people upped and left to get away from it. I'm sure that's what happened."

"But couldn't they have taken a vaccine for it?" Matthew queried. "There surely must've been things that could've been done."

"Too late once you've already got it." Mom sighed. "Besides, in a place like Anchorage, where there hasn't been any cholera, they wouldn't have had many vaccines. And if you can't freeze them they've only got a few weeks of shelf life anyway."

"Some things could've been done if law and order hadn't broken down." Dad rubbed his hands over his face. "But then that's why we left. Cholera or not, I guess everyone would've had to get out of Anchorage anyway. For the record, Bob, we're all in your debt."

"No worries." He shrugged.

Sue had tears rolling down her cheeks. Matthew took her

onto his lap.

"We've said before that we're grateful, Donald, but this puts it up to another level altogether."

"Thanks, Matthew. Anyway, the gut issue is what we do now. Let's sweat this. It looks like we're going to be here a while. Doesn't look like there's any help coming. As I see it, we've got four main things to be concerned about. First is getting enough food for the winter. Second is the threat from other people, then there's the wild animals, especially the dogs. I don't know about this stuff. I don't know how to even start thinking about it."

"Bob, Jessie and me can deal with the food, with your help on the foraging," I replied. "People – there are nine of us, we all learn to handle a gun. Even Sue. We'll have this place bristling like a porcupine. We fortify it."

"Jim's right," said Bob. Bears and wolves aren't usually a threat, even in the winter. But then we're a fair way out here. This place would usually be shut up out of season." He stood up and collected one of the guns we'd brought back from Anchorage.

"This is a Remington 870 shotgun, 12-gauge. Best thing for stopping bear. We'll keep it ready by the door here, and I'll show you all how to use it. But the dogs, they're more dangerous at the moment. They'll get desperate as the weather draws in. I guess they've been living off dead bodies so far, but they're going to rot down before the snow arrives. We're cooking fish, meat – any animal within ten miles is going to smell us here.

Dad came to a decision. "OK, we fence ourselves off, and build an extension. We need a bigger fireplace. Or another cabin. And another for Jim and Jessie."

"Should we find a larger place?" asked Matthew.

"There's nothing that looks as promising as this, and it would take too long." Bob looked up from the map. "The weather's changing, we've got maybe a couple of months before the winter sets in. What do you think, Mary?"

Mom nodded. "If we're going to stay here, then we need

to get prepared. Nine people are a lot to feed, clothe and keep clean. We'll all need to help." She looked around.

Dad stood up and paced the room. "First thing's the fence. I don't like the idea of those dog packs."

"Could we make an electric one?" I asked.

"We'd need to adapt a generator, we don't have the time for it," Dad replied. "And it would take a lot of fuel. Or we could get a wind turbine, but I haven't seen any around here. We'll have to do it the old fashioned way."

"What do we use for building?" asked Matthew.

"We drive down to one of those lodges nearer the road, pull it down, use that, it'll be easier than trying to pull down your place, Matthew, which is mostly stone," he finished.

"But, but we can't just pull down someone else's property!" Mom exclaimed.

"If you'd seen Anchorage, Mary," Dad replied, "that's the last thing you'd worry about. The whole place has gone. Nobody's going to worry about the odd cabin. Hell, if we need to, we'll just pay to get it rebuilt. No one's going to complain when it's a question of survival, when all this is over. If this is ever over. If the owners are still alive. If there's still such a thing as money. Will there still be banks, insurance companies? Will our savings still be there? Will it matter? Is there going to be anything left at all? I don't know. I wish I'd read that *Swiss Family Robinson* earlier. Should have got more prepared. We haven't done enough."

Dad looked defeated. Even Mom and Louise were despondent. We sat in gloomy silence.

"It seems like an imposition on you," Matthew said unhappily. "I don't know how we're going to repay this."

"Sorry to interrupt," Bob said, "but I've got to be blunt here. I don't think we'll all get through this."

"Are you saying we're going to die?" Bess was still looking white.

"Just that there are too many people needing support here."

Jessie reached out and held Bessie's hands. "We'll get through this, Bess. It's just going to be different. It'll just be us. We don't need Facebook – that was a dream."

Bess fired up angrily. "I think Bob is suggesting that some of us are a waste of space, and should go kill ourselves."

"Well," Bob said matter-of-factly, "that's not a bad idea, come to think of it."

There was a storm of protest. I looked for the twinkle in Bob's eye, but there wasn't one.

"Look," he said, "Jim can look after himself. Nearly. The rest of you are walking KFCs."

"Bob, you're a horrible man," Sue shouted.

"If you honestly think that, Bob, maybe you really should leave us, strike out on your own," Dad said quietly.

TWENTY-SEVEN

I felt more conflicting emotions than I'd ever had before. I knew Bob, at one level, was right. But I hated what he was saying.

"Bob," I said, "we can do it. It's one winter."

"And then another one," he replied. "And another one, most likely. And more after that."

"There are plenty of people in Alaska living off grid though, Bob," Louise replied.

"Yes, but they used to have enough supplies, and fuel, generators, snow machines. They could get more supplies. They could call in a doctor, or a plane – there are thousands of them in this country. That's how it used to run. We're talking about something different here, a load of greenhorns, without support, who haven't been through a winter before. I haven't even done it myself. It's not going to be the same as in Anchorage. This has been a walk in the park so far."

There was a moment's silence, and then Jessie stood up. "Adults," she said, scornfully. "They get us into this mess, and then they give up. Bess, we're going to change this, are you with me?"

Bess looked up, her eyes brightening. "Sure thing, Jess."

Jessie walked over to the door and picked up a rifle, cocked it, and pointed it at Bob.

"Bob, you leave when we say you can. We're going to make this work."

Everyone's mouths had dropped open. Bob was looking at Jessie, astonished, and then he started laughing. He laughed till there were tears streaming down his face. "My, you're a one, you're the real thing, aren't you?"

Dad frowned. "Jessie, that's not the way. Stop pointing that gun. Bob, I know you don't need us, like we need you, but I'm just praying we can work this out. I think of us all here as one family now. And if we all totally commit to what needs doing to survive this, would you stay? Show us how?"

Bob's laughter slowed. He nodded. "Look, if we're all family, I'm in. And Jess is right. When the going gets tough, the tough get going. All this – it's no surprise. It's been headed this way since the electricity went off. We can give up and cry over it, or we can get to work and do something about it. Which is it to be?"

Dad squared his shoulders. "You're right, Bob, sorry. We'll make this work. We're still all together, that's the main thing. And the rate Jim and Jessie are going, we're getting to be one family anyway. We've got over a month till the snows come. We can get prepared to see the winter out. With nine of us pulling together, we can do it."

He put some cheer into his voice. "Let's break for this morning. We all make notes on the things that need to be done in the next couple of months. We'll meet this evening, draw up lists of what needs doing, sort them, figure out who does what."

"But we're not going to be here forever, are we?" asked Mom. "You surely don't mean that?"

"I've no idea, Mary. But even to get through this winter, we have to do this stuff. Next year, we can think again. Depends on what's happening outside."

"I don't mind being here forever," piped up Sue, as she snuggled up to Mom. "I like it here. Except for the horrible mosquitos."

"Bless you, Sue," said Mom, as she wiped a smudge from her cheek.

"I think we should do one more trip tomorrow," Dad added. "Go down to Whittier. It's only a few hours away. See if it's as bad as Anchorage. There are only a couple of hundred people there, mostly living in one building, from what I remember reading. I haven't been before. Maybe they've been OK. Not so many to feed and water, lots of boats for fishing. I don't think we can spend the next six months trying to figure out what might happen without making an effort to contact neighbors. It's worth a chance."

"There's a three mile single lane through the tunnel," said Bob. "They might've closed it."

"We'll find out," replied Dad. "If so, we'll only have lost a day."

"I'll get some water on for a drink." Louise got up. "I'd just like to say, Donald, that these kind of things have happened before. Communities, societies, civilizations have been destroyed. They've recovered, been rebuilt. I'm sure we can do it again, and I feel privileged to be a part of this."

"Thanks, Louise," Dad replied. "Here, let's shake on it, all of us." He put his hand on the table. Mom was the first to add hers. Everyone else followed. Dad put his other hand down on top of all of them.

"I've never been a religious man, as you know," he said. "But I promise, now, before God, if He's there, that I'll do my best to get us all through this safely."

Later that evening, Jessie and I were on the porch. The sun was below the hills, the sky shading from light blue through azure, violet, purple, indigo to black directly above. I could see the Pole star. The Milky Way was starting to take shape, brighter than I'd ever seen it before.

Jessie twined her fingers in mine. "That was quite something back there. Bob's tough, isn't he?"

"Not as tough as you, though. I guess he knows what needs to be done. Wish I did."

"Are you giving up as well?" Jessie pecked my cheek.

"Me? No...I just wasn't sure what to say. But I'm glad we're more like family. I've always thought of Bob as another Dad anyway. And I thought you were brilliant."

"So if we're family, am I your sister or your lover?"

She leaned over and licked my ear.

"You can be anything you want with me, Jessie."

"I want *you*, Jim…now."

"J…Jessie," I stammered. "Are you a virgin?"

She shook her head. "No, I'm not. I've slept with a couple of boyfriends. But I'm not one of Bob's Alaskan chicks either. It's been a long time without sex." She gave me a hard look. "Do you mind? Are you getting cold feet?"

"Hell, no, feels like it makes it easier for me."

She took my hand and put it on her breast. Under my palm, I felt her nipple hardening. She gasped slightly, her tongue moving over her pearly teeth, licking her upper lip.

"Come then," she said huskily, pulling me up. We took a couple of blankets and walked to the trees. We spread them over the soft pine needles and lay down.

TWENTY-EIGHT

The next morning the sun was still below the mountain when we all woke. We all had a hug first, and it occurred to me suddenly, how easily and wholeheartedly I could do that now. Last night had freed something up in me. Matthew handed over some sourdough sandwiches, Jessie and me kissed; Dad, Bob and I set off as the others went back to bed.

"This is an ancient trail," Dad said as he turned onto tarmac, an hour later. "Whittier's about twenty miles along here. Natives have been using it for thousands of years as a short cut between Port William Sound and Turnagain Arm, carrying their canoes. The trappers did the same, then the gold miners, that's why it's called the Portage Glacier Road. We'll go extra slow through the tunnel, use our flashlights to see the way. It might be blocked."

The river was running low, tumbling over the rocks. The steep sided valley was covered in spruce, aspen and birch, topped with glaciers, glittering in the sun. When we got to the tunnel, it was creepy. We crawled slowly along. After half an hour we could see a spot of light in the far distance, and eventually exited into bright sunshine, driving slowly, carefully, rifles at the ready. The town was nestled in at the head of the bay, surrounded by mountains and glaciers, dazzling and sparkling.

"Welcome to Whittier, pop: 231," Dad quoted the sign. "Anyone here?" he called, glancing around. "Looks deserted," he muttered. "There are some fishing boats there in the harbor, but most seem to have gone. And where are the people? Let's go into Begich Towers, that's where everyone used to live."

I walked through the open doors into the large foyer and called out, but there was no answer. It was like a ghost town. My heart sank, remembering Anchorage.

Outside, Bob fired his rifle into the air. The gunshot ricocheted around the surrounding mountains, prompting a flock of gulls in the harbor to take screaming flight.

"At least there're no scavengers around here," he said, as the echoes died.

"Disappointing," said Dad. "I was hoping we'd find people here. Where the hell have they gone? But you're right. At least there don't seem to be any bodies around, and no rats. We should see if there's anything left lying around that we could use. Let's start with the harbor." We were walking down when a voice called out behind us; "Just hold it right there folks, I've got you covered. Put your guns down."

"Damn, do as he says," Dad muttered.

We turned slowly around. A bearded old man was walking out of The Anchor Inn Hotel, carrying a double barreled shotgun. He looked like the picture on the fish fingers packets; a broad, round, ruddy face, tobacco-stained white beard and sideburns, stocky build. "Who are you, and what do you want? Don't try anything, I can get you all with these barrels."

"We're pleased to meet you." Dad smiled. "We're neighbors, living a couple of dozen miles back towards the Seward Highway, and just came to see if there was anyone around. We don't mean you any harm."

The old man treated us to a measured look. He must have liked what he saw, because he visibly relaxed, and lowered the gun.

"Apologies for the poor welcome. Come on in to the hotel here. We can have the dining room to ourselves. I'm Nathaniel, Nat for short."

We introduced ourselves over coffee. Nat seemed well supplied. "Yes," he elaborated, "I've enough to keep myself going through to the spring. How about you guys?"

"We're fine, thanks," said Dad. "But where is everybody? We were hoping to meet up with like-minded folks."

Nat shrugged. "We heard how things were going elsewhere, especially in Anchorage. Didn't seem like it was going to get better for a while. We're shut off here, by the mountains, not much land for growing anything. Heard it was different in Valdez, the other side of Prince William Sound. It's bigger than us, a few thousand people, but not too big. Got an airport, for when things get better, they'll get relief early on. Main thing is, they've got plenty of oil, it's the end of the Trans-Alaska pipeline. Dozens of storage tanks they can tap into. The community had organized itself there, set up a committee to run the place, and invited us over. Unanimous vote, except for me. They took a dozen boats, those which they could start the motors on, and headed across the Sound – about three days motor-sailing. I opted to stay. Thought about joining them since, sailed over there a month back, but I didn't like what they were getting up to."

"What do you mean?"

"Using soldiers as mercenaries to police the place."

"But wouldn't that be better than here by yourself?" I asked.

"I was born and raised here, been here all my life, and ain't going to leave because of a power cut. Besides, from what I hear, the grass isn't greener anywhere else."

"But how do you hear?"

"Ham radio."

Dad made a frustrated sound. "Wish I'd got hold of one. I'm a mechanical guy, not electrical. What else have you learned? What's happening in the rest of America, the world?"

Nat frowned. "It's patchy, depending on where the ham operators are. I don't think there are any left in Anchorage, for instance. Basically...many places smaller than a town seem to be OK, if they haven't started fighting amongst themselves. Some figure that around half the people have died. Plague, cholera, smallpox, starvation, you name it. We've got off relatively lightly up north; there's food, if you know where to look. Those doing best were already living out in the sticks, off-grid."

"How did it get so bad?"

"The solar storm hit the grid too hard for it to get restarted.

They'd get one bit going, but then the area around it would overload and shut it down again. The coal plants didn't have enough power to restart. They were working on it, but there aren't enough of them to make other than local differences any more. The military has enough backup systems, so we can still fire missiles, the country's "safe," so they said, but they couldn't get the lights working," Nat said drily.

"Washington? The government?"

"Washington's finished. They've got everything – malaria, typhus, dengue fever, as well as cholera and plague, it's the same all the way around down the coast, through to Texas. Everyone who can's fighting their way inland. The government's holed up somewhere, haven't heard a squeak out of them for a month. There are no official channels. There's all kinds of rumors flying around – the government have moved underground, or to Hawaii, no one knows."

"How can people think they've gone to Hawaii?" Dad asked. "That's crazy. How would they get there?"

"How does anybody know anything? You listen to the radio now and you don't know who's crazy and who's real. No way of telling. Weird stuff on there."

"You mean there's no government, at all?" I chipped in.

"Nothing that we can find."

TWENTY-NINE

"I thought there would have been something, surely," Dad said. "What's happening overseas?"

"Basically, cities everywhere are disaster zones. Not enough food, water, plenty of disease. They've all emptied. Third World countries have come through it best. Places like India – hundreds of millions of people who barely used electricity anyway, and with a warm climate, they just keep on doing pretty much what they've always done. Except where the people living in the cities have fled into the country, which can't support them all, then there's fighting. And where there were tensions already, it's got worse. War all over the Middle East. Split by religion, sect, tribe, nationality, we don't hear anything anymore. Borders don't seem to matter. And nothing from China."

"Europe?"

"A mess. Putin's invaded."

"What?"

"Guess he always wanted to, sees a chance to get the Russian Empire back. Did it almost immediately. Not sure how far he's got, they're mostly walking and its hand to hand fighting. No tanks or planes. The Russians have some oil, the Europeans haven't any. But anyway, there's no armies in Europe to fight back, and few guns. The weapons they have are mostly too sophisticated to use, nothing with solid-state electronics survived the solar storm. The Russians have the advantage with older equipment, they've been re-fitting Second World War guns and vehicles."

"England should be safe from the Russians?" Dad asked. "They couldn't cross the Channel? We have family there. My brother. Cousins."

"There are still ham operators functioning, but it's dire. Crowded island, no food. Most of it was imported, they've got no machinery to bring the harvest in. You know how few scythes and sickles there are in the country, and how few people can swing one? And people can't get off the island, not that it's much better on the continent. So it's martial law. London's pretty much deserted, a few people up in the skyscrapers, or in the tunnels, but it's a jungle there. There's still a government, but it's moved a couple of times. Went to York first, I think they're on the Isle of Man now."

"The Royal Family?"

"Last known address up in Balmoral Castle, in Scotland, with a battalion to protect them. But no one's heard about them for a while now."

There was a pause, as we absorbed the news.

Dad put his head in his hands. "My God. This isn't going to end soon, is it?"

"Reckon not. Can't see the grid coming back. The transformers were all destroyed. They were all customized for each substation, so there's no inventory of replacements. There's no electricity for factories to make more of them. I can't see how it could be done now. And there's no government to organize it. Even if there were, the people who might've known how to do it are dead or in hiding."

"It's hard to believe. Just a couple of months ago...I can't take it in."

Nat went over to Dad, and put his arm around him.

"Must come as a shock the first time you hear it, Donald. I've had some time to get used to it."

Bob stood up, looking at the mountains on the other side of the bay. "So it really is everywhere," he said, quietly. "I kind of thought it must be, but it's still hard to believe."

"I know," Nat replied. "I really do. Still," he said shrugging, "this is our new life now. We'll just have to get on with it. Here, I've got another radio kit, and spare batteries, and there are extra antennae on the roof. Let me show you how to set it up. Be good if we could keep in touch, a pleasure to have neighbors again. We can figure out call signs, and we'll be able to talk to each other any time."

We were there for the day. I chopped some wood for Nat while he, Dad and Bob talked. I wondered what had happened to my former games opponents, who I used to play against in the evening. Mostly, I'd never noticed where they came from, if they had let it be known in the first place, but I knew they were from all over the world. How were they getting on? Were they still alive? I'd never know. We'd never met, and never would. I looked around the bay, and the mountains. The world had narrowed overnight to people you could physically see and touch. I shivered.

Dad had brought some goods to barter and pressed them on Nat in return for the radio and the lesson.

"I can't thank you enough," said Dad, as we prepared to leave.

"Thanks are on my side," said Nat, as they shook hands. "I was getting a bit lonely here, to be honest. Was getting the feeling of being the last man alive, kind of thing. Going nuts."

"Do you want to come back with us?" asked Bob. "You look like you'd be an asset."

"Thank you kindly, but no. I've got my sail-boat, couldn't live anywhere away from the sea. Used to be my job, I was captain of the ferry here. We'll talk on the radio, OK? But from what you say, I'm going to lock the gates in the tunnel. It used to be shut at nights anyway and I guess it'll be safer now to keep it closed. Just give me a call if you want to come through again."

"By the way, did an oil guy come through here?" I asked. "A few weeks ago, big, fat, executive type? Aggressive?"

"Him – yes, friend of yours?"

"No, not exactly, we just bumped into him."

"Sure he came. A real pompous ass. Complained like hell about everything, he went on the boats with the others to

Valdez."

"Did he have a woman with him?"

"No, he was by himself. Gave some spiel about surviving the wilderness single-handed – and fighting off bears. Sounded fishy to me. Happy to see him move on. Last I heard, they'd locked him up in Valdez for making trouble."

The sun was below the hills when we got back, the whole sky streaked red and purple. Little brown bats were flickering around the lodge. "Wow, that smells good," Dad said as we walked through the door. "Fish stew?"

"A little experiment," replied Matthew. "We don't have the ingredients for my usual recipes, but we've plenty of herbs, and it's fun to try something different. Could do with getting to the shoreline sometime for mussels, clams. Prawns would be nice. But though I say it myself, this isn't bad."

"But all those people, everywhere," Mom said, as we talked over the meal. She still looked in shock. "I just can't believe what's happened."

"But it has, Mary," Louise replied, clasping her shoulder. "We didn't want it, but we have to live with it and be strong."

Matthew started trembling. "Sorry, I've been struggling to take this in. Hadn't quite believed it yet."

"Focus, people," Bob added. "We've got a situation, we figure out how to deal with it, then we do it. We don't know what's going to happen tomorrow. Let's enjoy this meal."

We pigged out on one of the finest meals I've ever had. "That really hit the spot," Bob muttered.

"Wicked," added Jessie.

THIRTY

"Wierdly, I feel a lot better having talked to Nat," Dad said the next morning over a breakfast of hotcakes and blueberry juice. "At least we know where we stand, now, and there's at least one guy around here we can trust."

"I love it even more here now the mosquitos have gone to heaven," chirped up Sue as everyone laughed.

"OK." Dad clapped his hands. "We've got our lists here of things to do, and I've drawn up a rough schedule to keep us on track. We'll start with the fence. I'll mark out the line, about half an acre – that should be enough? Jim – the postholes and poles for supports. Mary, we'll have two fences I think, a gap between them and we stuff that full of thorns – there are loads of those plants around here. Could you take Louise, Jessie, Sue and Bess with you?"

"But they're prickly," Bess interrupted.

"That's the idea, Bess," Dad replied. "Just think of it as the more prickly it is, the safer we'll be. And we've got plenty of gloves. Jim, can you dig the shit from the outhouse, the fluids should mostly have seeped through. We'll use it for vegetable beds. Matthew, we couldn't get any food in Anchorage, but we've got seed."

"We've got winter vegetables by the look of things – spinach, leeks, kale, parsnips, cabbage, turnips and chard." Matthew was rummaging through the boxes. "That's good. We'll need to be planting before the end of the month."

"Great."

"And berries," added Matthew, "we've missed out on those. Blueberries and raspberries, they might be finished now, but there should be cranberries and dewberries. We could do with barrel loads. If we add the rest of our sugar, boil it – that'll keep us in vitamins through the winter. I can make fruit leather out of them, that lasts for months."

"Anything else?"

"Mushrooms, mega sacksful of them. They're coming into season. If we're careful about baking them, till they're dry enough to snap, they can last for years."

"What can we do about flour?"

"The old-timers used to make it out of cattail roots and acorns," said Louise. "But I don't know how."

"There'll be plenty of acorns soon," said Matthew. "Let's collect some, and the roots, and I'll figure out how to make it. We're going to need more meat though."

Bob stood up, shuffling his feet, I think it was the first time I'd seen him look embarrassed. "Matthew, friend, I owe you an apology. And to everyone here for what I said the other day. I'm sorry. Wish I'd known you before. I've never eaten so well as lately. Let's shake on it."

Matthew beamed broadly through his bushy beard, looking a few inches taller. "That's OK, Bob. Glad to be able to provide something. I don't do a fraction of what you do."

"Right, that's good." Dad stood up and clapped his hands together. "We all have something to contribute. We're going to have to work really hard now, everyone, all commitment. Bob, we'll take a short cut, go down to those other lodges and dismantle one, build a cabin for the Hardings that way, rather than do it from scratch. I think it should be separate, better not to have all our eggs in one basket. Big fire risk, winter's the danger time. Having two places would give us a backup. Can you and Matthew start on that, while Jim and I do the fence? What force can a bear exert per pound of weight?"

"Dunno about that," Bob replied, "but the posts need to be this thick" – and he opened his hands to indicate a foot wide.

The postholes for the fence didn't take long, and then I switched to helping with the Harding's cabin. We'd decided to limit the use of the chainsaw, but short of spending extra weeks on the work we had to. Bob used it to cut down ten-foot sections of pine trees, around two feet in diameter.

"Pass me that's whosowhatsit, Jim – the draw-blade – we need to peel off the bark like this." He drew it down the trunk.

"Why bother doing that? Looks better with the bark on."

"It's full of insects, beetles, the wood'll soon rot if you leave them there. If we're going to do it, let's do it properly."

I worked at it for a couple of days, the glutinous sap sticking all over me, hands getting raw, muscles aching, the scent of resin in the air.

We placed the stripped poles in pairs, upright, and cemented in. Dad and Matthew nailed the planks from the dismantled cabin across, leaving a gap in the middle, which we all filled with earth and any other insulation we could find. Bob made extra windows and doorframes. We beat down the earth inside and put in a raised floor, keeping it off the cold earth, stuffing moss into all the cracks, and covering that with mud. For the extra roofing we added a score of spruce poles at an angle to the ridge, then used the wooden walls from the cabins for the first layer, then a polythene sheet, another layer of poles, then cut out rectangles of moss, half a foot deep, and put it in two layers on top, with poles to hold it down till it grew together.

It took us a month. We sweated and itched, working like demons, all the daylight hours.

Even Bess and Sue chipped in. We didn't have time or the energy to argue. The work was back-breaking. We really needed a crew, but a lot of it ended up down to me; Bob couldn't raise his arm much, Matthew wasn't strong, and Dad didn't seem that well.

By now the sun was setting behind the hills before seven p.m. and it was starting to get dark at eight. The temperature was close on freezing most of the day and there were flurries of snow, and still a lot to get done. We built a shelter for the woodpile and covered walkways made out of corrugated iron between the dwellings, so fire couldn't spread from one to another. We sorted out the stores, building outhouses, one for gas, diesel and kerosene, another for the bulk of what had come on the truck, including all the tools. We added inside shelving in the cabin all around the walls, for what we reckoned to use through the winter. We built an extension to the main cabin, all along one side of it, separated by curtains in the first third, one half which could be pulled back for privacy – and personal washing – and put a bath in. Of the rest, one half was for drying clothes, the other half was lined with corrugated iron, with a fire pit in the center, and a new chimney at the top for the smoke to escape. It had a damper on it, but we were planning to keep this burning as low embers day and night for hot water and cooking. We added another stove and chimney and all helped with making more shutters and draught excluders, filling cracks with mud and securing the polytunnels with wire and ropes.

We were sitting around a brazier on the verandah one evening, its flames mirroring the streaky yellow-red sky. Occasionally we could hear the large smack of a beaver's tail on the water.

"Should be as snug as a bug in a rug," Bob said. "Went better than I thought. Maybe we'll get through this. For this year, anyway."

"Of course we will," Mom replied. "Though I wish there was an alternative. It just doesn't seem right that we're out here by ourselves."

"I can't see one, though, Mary," Dad chipped in. "I've been talking to other people on the radio Nat gave us. Some places have got organized, but mostly its people looking after themselves, like we're doing here.

"Then we'll make the most of it," Mom decided. "Hey, let's think of it as an extra-long holiday, let's make it the best winter we've had."

THIRTY-ONE

We turned our attention to a cabin for me and Jessie. She was standing on a rise a few yards from the Lodge, overlooking the lake, which the wind had turned into a miniature sea, white caps on the waves. The mountains rolled on forever in the distance. Jessie's hair streamed around her face, shirt sculpted to her body.

"You look like a goddess, Jess," I said admiringly.

She grinned, pointing to her feet. "Then the goddess orders her worshipper to build right here."

I spent a couple of days clearing the ground, putting down a floor of gravel and pebbles from the beach. We took the truck down the road and dismantled a cabin from the campsite. Everyone helped putting it up, a snug little place of around twelve feet by ten, supplemented with more cut logs.

"I think I could get used to this," said Dad as he nailed in planks. "Why work all the time to pay the mortgage to live in a house which you can't afford when you can build one for free?"

"It's a strange feeling, isn't it?" Matthew replied, putting nails in on the other side. "We had a large house, back in Seattle, and a huge mortgage. Six bedrooms. I don't know why, there are only the three of us. I had a cushy job, pure gravy. All the stuff we had…I guess when it was just the three of us I overcompensated by buying things. I had three cars, seems crazy now – you can only drive one at a time."

"We had three as well," Dad replied. "Daft, really. One each for Mary and me, and an estate for when we went out as a family. But we could've managed with one."

"Actually, I don't really miss it, except for the hot tub we had out at the back. That was great, any time of year, hot or cold. But I guess the house isn't ours any more, it probably belongs to the bank now. But if the bank doesn't exist any more, whose is it?"

Bob was working on the stove and chimney, putting in a

metal back and sides to help direct the heat. "Guess it won't matter when it collapses. A place like Seattle, the woods'll take over in a few years."

"You know," Matthew added, "nothing I've done in my life prepared me for this. No computers working, no companies needing their accounts doing, all those billions of clicks and transactions going on every day – all gone. I lived on computers, on the Internet, all day long, that's how I met people, talked to them, did business. I could read a balance sheet like Bob here can read tracks. Tell you how healthy the business was, where the problems were, whether to save it or kill it, give you the EBITDA without thinking about it. I looked down on plumbers, bricklayers, carpenters, people who actually went out killing animals were just freaks – sorry Bob – and here we are now with hammers and nails. Everything I've done in my life is irrelevant beside this. I still can't quite believe it."

"Me neither," said Dad. "I thought I'd be helping provide for Jim and Bess by giving them cash for a house deposit or something like that. And here I am, actually helping to build it. With no power tools."

"I wonder what's happened to all that cash?" Matthew looked genuinely puzzled. "All those securities, trillions of dollars. All those IOUs. Quadrillions. I guess it's all just disappeared?"

"I guess there's all that gold in Fort Knox still," Dad replied. "But even if you could get it, what would you do with it?"

"Do you think those days are ever going to come back, Donald? They can't have just gone forever, surely? We'll have companies again, jobs?"

"I honestly don't know, Matthew, but I guess maybe not. From what Nat said in Whittier, and what I've heard on the radio since, it's a different world now. We'll be going back centuries. We'll have to start again. What do you think, Bob?"

"I think if we don't get this stove working soon, Jim and Jessie are going to freeze their butts off in here," Bob replied.

After a couple of weeks it was nearly finished. It wouldn't have the same conveniences as the other two, but we figured we'd mostly just be using it for sleeping.

"We'll leave you to do the rest, Jim," Bob said. "We need to get out and do more foraging. Keep the bed well off the floor. The inside needs lining. You can put those cupboards up. Pegs for clothes. And you could think about a verandah here." He painted on the innocent face he always wore when he was about to cross the line. "Hope she's good enough in the sack for all this."

We were between the lodge and the lake. I looked through the door onto a spectacular view, right across the lake, the wind frilling the water, the pines swaying to and fro. A huge flock of sandpipers swept along the water, shaping and reshaping, flashing dark and light, leaving for the winter. A few months ago and my main excitement was sticking a new stamp into my book. Now Jessie and I were together, and we had our own home.

Soon enough, the day came when the work was finished, at the end of September, a couple of months after we visited Anchorage. The memory of that place, the horror of it, of the dog packs, of what could come in the winter, had driven us on. It felt as if before, in the summer, we had still been playing at it, like a working holiday. Now, we had been working for our lives.

We decorated it with spruce boughs, driftwood and candles. Sue gave us a posy of flowers. Dad nailed up a pair of antlers over the door. Mom gave Jessie a necklace. Matthew cooked a fruit cake in the shape of the cabin. Louise had quilted a bedspread for us. Bob gave me his scope, and another Winchester M70 to Jessie, hanging it up over the door.

"Are you sure, Bob?" I asked.

"You can make better use of the scope than me, Jim," he replied. "Anyway, sometime next year we'll kit ourselves out again."

We didn't get anything from Bess, our relationship had cooled now that I was with Jessie so much. That afternoon, down on the beach, Bess was sitting on her rock, rod in hand. Jessie and me walked down to say hi, hand in hand.

Bess looked up. "Can't you leave me alone? This is my space."

"Your space?" I replied, surprised.

"What else have I got?"

She got up and stalked off.

"What's up with her?" I asked Jessie.

"Jim, you twerp, she feels left out. Thinks I've betrayed her."

"Left out? Well, how do you think I used to feel?"

"That was your choice, Jim. Men!" She sighed. "You can't teach them anything."

"I could think of something," I leered.

"C'mon then, might as well make some use of you, if Bess is going to go sulk. Here, behind these trees."

We lit the stove in the lodge that evening, the crackling sound of spruce merging with the scent of pine from the drying logs, the flames flickering over their rounded contours, and had a party.

"I know it's not like you're married yet," said Mom, embracing Jessie, "but it feels as good as that to me. Welcome to the family." Jessie and me left for our own cabin, and I carried her in over the threshold.

THIRTY-TWO

"Daylight hours are down to a dozen," Bob said. "Let's make a few longer trips while we still can. See if there are any better hunting grounds around here."

The next week, Bob, Jessie and myself were ranging further down the Portage River than we'd been before. Bob was scoping the hills around us.

"There are some promising side valleys here that we should explore," he was saying, when Jessie interrupted.

"Smoke over there, Bob."

A thin, faint column could be seen a few miles away.

"That must be the Begich Boggs visitor center on Portage Lake," said Bob, looking at the map. "Must be someone there. Let's go see."

We moved over to the road and picked up pace. It was strange walking on tarmac again after all the trails and rough ground we'd been walking over. It felt like a ribbon of nothingness: but it was certainly quicker. After an hour or two striding rapidly along we came to it.

The Lake was evidently a popular tourist spot, and a place to set off from for hiking and hunting. There was a large car park, a couple of lone cars in it, and a campervan. The visitor center was impressively big and modern, telescopes set around the perimeter by the water's edge. The smoke was actually coming from a cafe further along which had collapsed into a heap and was smoldering away. "Let's go carefully," said Bob, unhitching his rifle and taking the safety catch off. "Never know what you might find."

We edged closer. "Shit," Bob said, looking at the ground. "I've never seen so many bear tracks in one place."

"Bob, look," I pointed to the side of the building. "There's a raccoon, and another."

"I don't believe it," he ground out. "Whoever's here, they've just been chucking food and waste out of the window."

We could hear the shouting and yelling inside as we got to the front doors. It didn't sound dangerous or panicky: just arguments. A sickly smell hit us as we entered. The place was a tip; rubbish everywhere, furniture overturned, some of it chopped up. The display boards about the area's amenities and wildlife were scribbled over and ripped. A couple of very overweight boys were running around, chasing a dog. They stopped when they saw us.

"Mom," one of them yelled at the top of his voice. "We've got visitors."

An obese lady came waddling down the main stairs. "About bloody time someone got here," she said. "Who the fuck are you?"

"We live a while away," Bob replied, an edge to his voice.

"Who are you? Why are you here? This place stinks."

"We were here on holiday when those sunspots happened," the woman replied. "Stupid idea, but that's Andy, always doing something stupid and dragging us along. Couldn't get the car started the next day, so we've been here ever since."

"Where's Andy?"

"Upstairs. Here, you'd better come see him."

We followed her upstairs, the smell getting stronger. She led us into a room which had obviously been the local park ranger's bedroom. A mountain of a man was collapsed in the bed, stinking of drink and urine.

"Wake up, Andy, we've got visitors."

He pulled himself up, the bed creaking, and looked at us with bloodshot eyes.

"Thank God you've come at last, about damned time." He snorted. "I need help, I'm ill."

Jessie put her rifle down against the wall and went over to him. "I know some first aid," she said. "Let me look at you."

"I need a doctor," he said, "not a fucking girl, go get me a doctor. Get me to a hospital."

"Are you boiling the water you drink?" Jessie asked.

"No, what's wrong with that? It's water, ain't it?" replied the lady.

"Doesn't look like they've been bothering with water," Bob said, his voice as hard as rock. "Just copping the restaurant drinks – he's soused." He nodded his head at the man mountain. "Look, mister, we can't get you to a doctor, or to a hospital. We're leaving now."

"Isn't there something we could do to help, Bob?" I asked.

"Well, what do you want?" he barked at them.

"We have to get back to Anchorage, we've got welfare checks there waiting for us," the guy said.

"You have no idea, do you? There is no Anchorage now," Bob replied, "but looks like you've had enough to feed you here. Was that from the Center stores?"

"There's a restaurant here in the Center, and a Café along the road. But we've eaten most of the stuff they had. We had to chuck out food from the freezers when it went off."

"Then I suggest you walk out," Bob said.

"Walk out? Are you kidding?" the woman screamed. "There are bears around here, hundreds of them."

"That's because you're chucking out the left overs."

"Well what were we supposed to do with them?"

"Bury, or burn."

"We don't have a spade. It's not our job. That's for the Park Rangers to do."

"Hey," Jessie suddenly interrupted; one of the fat boys had taken her rifle and was running away with it, shouting wildly, "Bang! Bang!"

Bob raised his rifle, and cocked it. "That does it," he muttered. "Miss, you're going to get that gun back from your boy, or I'm gonna shoot him."

"Pip, Pip!" She stumbled off screaming. "Give me that."

Eventually, she came back.

"Look, mister," she said as she handed it over, "we can't walk anywhere, so what are we supposed to do? When's the real help coming? I can't manage here any more."

"I wouldn't bank on any," Bob grunted. "Look, we'll do what we can here over the next hour. We'll leave you some grub, something to catch fish with – there's plenty in the lake here. I'll show your boys what to do, if they'll let me. And we'll come back later to see how you're getting on. But you'll need to think about storing wood for when it gets cold."

"Wood? Where would we get that?"

"Look, make an effort," Bob exploded. "You're in the middle of a forest here. Stop jerking us around, no one owes you anything. Chop wood. Store it. Fish. When you're out of food, walk out. Go to Whittier. You could get there tomorrow. Do it before the snows come. We can't help you more than that."

She brushed her hands through her hair; it looked grey now, but there were still traces of henna in it. "I never thought something like this would happen," she moaned, distraught. "What's happened to this country? Where's the government?"

Later, we walked away, relieved to be out in the clean, fresh air.

"Those toilets," I said, "they were just piled up with shit. Why didn't they at least go and crap outside?"

"Hogbeasts. No self-respect. They don't have any."

"But we could teach them some?" Jessie asked. "Shouldn't we do more to help? I mean, it's not like it looks like there are going to be all that many people around next year."

"It's a nice thought, Jessie, because you're a nice person," Bob answered, looking at us both. "But you two have to remember, you'll have to decide who you want to live with. There's no society any more to tell you. No cops, teachers, companies. And if someone hasn't found some self-respect when things are easy, it's a heck of a lot tougher when things are hard."

"Doesn't it worry you though, Bob, that they're just going to die, if we don't help them?" Jessie persisted.

"We've all got to die, Jessie, except for old soldiers like me... I'll just fade away, walk out into the woods one day, like the Indians do. Now c'mon, we're going to have to move quick to get back before dark."

It began raining heavily. We pulled up our hoods, adjusted the packs, and set off at a fast pace. After a while, Bob said, "You know, when I was in 'Nam, I never saw an overweight Charlie. They looked like skinny rats. They lived like them too, in tunnels. Fought like 'em, would never give up. Didn't know when they had no chance. We had our Skyhawks and Chinooks, they had mantraps and poisoned sticks. And they whupped our hides. They're probably doing just fine now, you don't need electricity to grow rice. This is why this country isn't going to survive. Too many like that family. We've lost the will. Look, we'll go back there sometime. But we can't take them in – they'd drag us down, too flaky. Anyway, they can probably live for a couple of months on the fat they're carrying."

THIRTY-THREE

The weather had cleared up, though the mountain tops were now covered in white. It was early evening, the sun had already set, looked like it was going to be a frosty night again. Inside, we were all in the main sitting room, with enough chairs now – we'd raided the other empty cabins along the road. The fire was burning with a nice, steady heat, stacked all around with logs. Three kerosene lamps were lit, enough to read by. The flames flickered and shadows danced around the walls, faces changing in the light. I remember thinking "light" was really "light" here. It was something you had to earn, to work for, to cultivate, that could go out, rather than a constant, even presence at the flick of a switch, like a background noise. We could hear the distinctive whirring of screech owls in the trees around us.

We were all tired but relaxed. Mom was sewing – some of the gloves had got ripped collecting all those thorns but were recoverable. Dad was listening to the ham radio on earphones. Bob was cleaning guns. Jessie was reading a wildlife manual. Bess and Sue were removing stalks from berries – we had mountains of them now – and sorting them into piles – for drink, for jam, for storage. After all the long sunshine hours they were wonderfully sweet. Matthew was figuring out on paper the possible rate of consumption of stores against supply, and time, and when the crossing lines on the graphs got critical. I was sharpening tools on the oil stone, focusing on the whispering hiss they made when drawn across it, trying to get them as crisp as possible.

"I broke my shoelace," I said. "Do we have any others?"

"We're going to have to start making do, Jim," Dad replied. "Mary, do you have any string? That will do just as well."

"This isn't right," Louise said suddenly. "We're falling into the gender trap here. Donald, if we're going to build a new community, I think we should start off right. Men should know how to find shoelaces, and sew. Women should know how to clean guns and work the radio."

Dad thought for a minute. "Seems obvious when you put it like that, Louise. OK, we'll work on that."

Bob laughed. "You speak crazy sometimes, Louise. Next, you'll be saying I should be reading!"

"I do indeed, Bob Thacker. Time for you to start catching up. Never too old to start learning."

"We should've got some chickens," said Bob in a morose tone, a few evenings later – he'd stopped whittling wood and was reading *Swiss Family Robinson*. I think it might have been the first book he'd ever read. Looked like he hadn't got far into it yet, judging by the way the book folded.

"I've never seen a real live chicken," Sue interrupted. "They've got feathers? Like birds?"

"They are birds, Sue," replied Louise. "Domesticated fowl. Easier to keep your meat alive and kicking than have to hunt for it and keep it fresh when it's dead."

"Why do they give us their eggs?"

"We've bred them to do so over centuries, selecting the ones that lay."

"I don't know where they're kept around here, if they are?" added Bess.

"We can find some next year," said Mom.

"Be too late by then, can't see any surviving the winter," replied Bob. "It says here how you can catch wild ones."

And, an hour or so later. "We should've got pigs, too. And a cow. That's what they did."

"Why don't we go and rescue a cow," asked Bess.

"They're probably all dead now," he replied. "Haven't been fed for months – then there's dogs, wolves, bears…"

"Bob, you're so negative," Bess grumbled.

"We should've got our own dogs, too. They'd help keep bears away."

There was another few moments silence.

"Louise, what are you reading?" asked Sue.

"*Pilgrim's Progress.*"

"What's that?"

"It's a kind of novel, a story, written by John Bunyan, in the seventeenth century. For most English speaking people afterwards, for a long time, it was second only to the Bible. They lived their lives by it."

"I've never heard of it."

"It's not read much nowadays, but it used to be important."

"Why not read a modern novel?" Dad asked.

"Good question. Somehow, they don't seem to me so relevant any more. The world they describe's gone, whereas this is as much about the next world as this one. And the themes are more universal, the bigger stuff – survival, salvation, faith."

"Why did he write it?" asked Sue.

Louise hesitated. "Bunyan was in jail four hundred years ago, because of what he believed. People like him, the Pilgrim Fathers, they invaded this country. Everyone here used to read this book. It's about what to do in life, what your priorities are, who you are, where you want to be, where you're going. I wish they'd stayed at home, but I still find it inspiring. It lifts me out from where we are now, shows me a different, maybe better kind of way, even if I can't believe in all of it, in the details."

"Can you read me some?"

"Well, here's the first sentence, from chapter one, if you want it."

"*As I walked through the wilderness of this world, I lighted on a certain place where was a Den, and I laid me down in that place to sleep.*"

"That's us, isn't it? We're in a wilderness, and here's our den."

"Well, yes, but the language and the events aren't something you'd recognize, it's allegorical."

"What does that mean?"

John Hunt

"It's a way of expressing an idea, by shaping it as an event or a story. For instance, he talks about life as a journey. It's a journey of faith, along a path, like up a mountain. The path might be steep, and you stumble and fall, but faith, belief, perseverance, that will keep you going till you get to the top."

"Are we on a path?"

"I think we all are, dear, whether we realize it or not. And in a way, I think we've just started on our journey here, like he did when he left his home town."

"Could I read it?"

Louise hesitated. "Of course you could, but the language is a bit difficult, it's like the language we spoke in America four hundred years ago. It's not quite the same as today. Perhaps I could read it with you, to help you out."

"I'd like that," said Sue.

"You lot are mental," muttered Bob. "Tough enough to figure out what's happening in this world here and now, just outside your door. Why bother inventing different ones?"

Something worried me about the conversation.

"What are we going to read when we've read all our books?"

"It's been worrying me, Jim," Dad replied, looking somber. "I know a bit, but it's mostly theory. I've never built a generator, or a turbine, for instance. That's what we're going to need next year. It's going to be difficult doing it by trial and error."

"We'll have to get back to Anchorage, sometime," Louise added. "Fight our way in, if we have to. A set of Encyclopedia Britannica alone would be like gold dust."

"If there are any books left there," Dad responded. "Anyway, I'm bone tired. See you all in the morning. We should all help to finish off those berries tomorrow, before they go off. But well done guys, I think we've done a good job here. Mary, ready for bed?"

Mom got to her feet. "Goodnight all."

We took our turns in the bathroom. Jessie and I walked over

153

to our place through a light rain, the wind whispering in the trees, arms around each other, kissing all the way. The sleeping bags had been turned inside out to air, she zipped them back together, a double sheet inside, blankets on top. We didn't need a fire.

THIRTY-FOUR

"Societies usually failed not because of the problems they couldn't deal with, but the ones they didn't anticipate," I remember Louise saying in class. And she was right. Our first difficulty, a foretaste of problems to come later, came from an unexpected quarter.

It was a few days later. Bob was out checking his traps. He had a few dozen around in a five-mile radius and usually managed to bring something back for the pot. Matthew and Sue were out foraging for mushrooms, berries and greens. Jessie had the sharpest hearing. She straightened up. "Listen," she said. "Can you hear it?"

By now I'd picked it up, the sound of an engine, the first one we'd heard, apart from our own, since the Event. We dropped our tools, I picked up my rifle and we ran up to the fence. An old Land Rover was coming along the track, looked like it should have been in a museum, apart from the dirt.

Dad opened the gate, we went out and met the driver as he was stepping out of the cab. He was in his twenties, stick-thin, slight, ravaged face, already balding, a goatee beard, unarmed. He leaned heavily on a stick as he hobbled toward us carrying a basket.

"Hello there," he called. "My name's Paul. So nice to meet you."

We introduced ourselves. "I'm Donald, this is Mary, my wife, Louise Maclaren, Jim, my son, Jessie and Bess."

"I'm on a mission to the Kenai peninsula," he said. "I'd heard on the radio that you were in these parts, thought I'd come along and see if I could encourage you to join us."

"A mission? What kind of a mission?" asked Dad.

"To bring people back to the faith," he replied.

"Which faith?"

"The true faith. Believing in God, the only, one, God. Following His commandments in the Bible. We've ignored them for too long and that's why this judgement has come on us. I'd like to explain it better, if you have a bit of time to spare."

Dad hesitated. "I don't think this is for us," he replied. "I think it's best if you move on."

"Do you speak for everyone? We're a democratic society, aren't we? I've come all the way from Fairbanks. I've brought you some fruit here, as a goodwill gesture." He handed over the basket, it was full of figs, dates, raisins, some scrawny apples. My mouth started watering. "Won't you give me the chance to explain what I'm talking about? We're a large group, we could help you. You won't survive here for long by yourselves."

"In all the time we've been here, Donald," Mom intervened, "this is the first visitor we've had. Let's not turn him away like that. Besides, I'm very partial to figs. That's very generous of you, Paul."

"OK," Dad allowed, "as you've come this far. Have you had much luck yet, in your mission?" he asked as we walked over to the lodge.

"We've set up a number of groups along Highway 3," Paul replied, as he limped along. "But Anchorage is a terrible place. A Sodom and Gomorrah. A den of sin and evil. The inmates have taken over the jail and they run the town from there. It's like a fortress. It used to keep people in, now it keeps them out."

"Might have been one of those guys we saw on the rooftop," muttered Dad.

"They capture people from the street, lock them in cells, there are bad rumors about what goes on there," Paul added. "I tried to appeal to them to let me through the prison gates, they said "go away, you're too scrawny to eat." Though their language was less polite than that. I appealed to their better natures, to let some light in. They started shooting at me. I took a ricochet in the arm."

"You poor man. Here, let me look at that," Mom offered, waiting as he rolled up his sleeve for her to see. Examining it carefully, she nodded. "It's infected a little. Come with me, I'll deal with it. We picked up some things in Anchorage that could help."

"So what's your story?" asked Dad, as Mom cleaned and patched the wound.

"I used to be an unbeliever, like you," he started, placing a Bible in front of him. "I lived in darkness, dedicated to the sins of the flesh – to sex, alcohol, heroin. When the Event happened, the lights in the sky overpowered me, went right through me. The Lord spoke to me, telling me to turn away from my path to destruction, back to Him. He directed me to Calvary Chapel. There was a joyful service going on, hands raised in the air in worship."

He paused, his eyes distant. "I've never felt anything like it. I was overwhelmed by feelings of love and peace. This was the true life, the real life, rather than the dark shadows I'd been living in. There's nothing like it on earth, talking with God, knowing him as a Father..." He looked around us all. "Later that evening, Pastor Elizabeth prayed over me, anointing me with the Holy Spirit. Since then I've been baptized, and given a new name. I felt washed clean, saved by the blood of the Lamb. I was a new person, born again. I know that's hackneyed, but I can't think of a better way to describe it. I dedicated myself to spreading the word, to bringing sheep into the fold before this world ends. I'm here to ask you to come with me on this journey. To implore you. This life is not about scratching a living from rocks as the darkness gathers around us. The lights showed a glorious future that's there for us in the presence of God."

"But I haven't been a heroin addict," Dad said. "Maybe I don't need saving as much as you did."

"The Bible says, *For all have sinned, and come short of the glory of God.* Here," he opened his Bible, "it's in Romans 3."

"But why should we believe the Bible?" asked Louise. "It's a collection of old documents, no one knows who wrote them – centuries after the events, which took place in the Stone Age, somewhere on the other side of the world."

"Because these words have power. They're God's words. *All Scripture is given by inspiration of God...*2 Timothy 3."

"But how did Paul know that?" Louise asked levelly. "And which scripture was he referring to? The gospels hadn't been written when Paul sent that letter to Timothy. So what's scripture, exactly?"

"It's true, because it says it is?" added Dad.

"All Scripture is God's Word, Louise," Paul replied, holding up his Bible reverently. "It's quite simple. God loves you and has a plan for you. *God so loved the world that He gave his only Son, that whoever believes in Him shall not perish, but have eternal life.* We are sinful, and separated from God. God sent Jesus to reconcile us to Him. God demonstrates His own love toward us, in that while we were yet sinners, Christ died for us. We are saved by His sacrifice. All we have to do is believe it, and turn from our sins – repent."

"So my ancestors, going back ten thousand years here, and the hundreds of generations before them, they're not saved because they weren't in the right time and place when this unknown guy appears in the Middle East, a couple of thousand years ago?"

"I need a break," Dad interrupted. "Let's get some food. I can hear Matthew and Sue coming back. You're welcome to eat with us, and then we'll carry on."

We should have paid him more attention, in the light of what happened later. We should have taken him more seriously, been more worried. It's odd, thinking back to that visit; the fundamentalists believed the Bible explained what was going to happen. Dad thought it was down to us to make things happen. And he didn't like the direction we'd ended up following – the old ways...but at least if you looked at the birds and the

John Hunt

animals, you knew when winter was coming, when spring was arriving, and then it was a short step to reading signs into how they acted, interpreting their behavior, their entrails. But the fundamentalists had convictions from their sacred words of scripture that it was hard to match. Nature was less certain. We respected life, whereas for the believers this life didn't matter. They had no compulsions about taking it, torturing it. And so they nearly defeated us.

THIRTY-FIVE

"Let's start again. Do you believe God sent the superstorm?" asked Louise, as we started tucking into a venison stew, packed with mushrooms and greens that Matthew and Sue had picked.

"Of course He did. The sun didn't explode by accident. He controls the sun, the stars, the universe, holding it in His hands. He sent the flares to give everyone a last chance to turn back to Him. The clock's ticking down. The Bible already warns us, Luke 21:25-28– *And there will be signs in the sun, in the moon, and in the stars; and on the earth distress of nations, with perplexity, the sea and the waves roaring; men's hearts failing them from fear and the expectation of those things which are coming on the earth, for the powers of the heavens will be shaken.* What could be clearer? The end times are here. The last day is coming. Do not be blind to the signs. As prophesied by Daniel, we are in the times of tribulation, the seven years of grace that God gave us, to enable us to repent, to turn to him. Read Revelation 6, you have a Bible here? I can leave this one with you. Look here," he turned the pages, *Before me was a pale horse. Its rider was named Death and Hades was following close behind him. They were given power over a fourth of the earth to kill by sword, famine and plague, and by the wild beasts of the earth.* Do you not see this happening now?"

"So all those people who've died," asked Mom, "that was His doing?"

"It's because we rejected Him, and brought it on ourselves. We've turned away from His laws."

"I'm sorry," said Matthew, "but I can't see how bombing us back to the Stone Age with solar flares is going to turn us all into believers."

"But don't you see? The greater our suffering, the more likely our repentance. The more we lose, the greater our gain. Of course, the workings of God are a mystery beyond us mortals, but perhaps He's put us into the position of the Israelites in the wilderness. We'd turned away from him, living for idols, for gold. We believed in ourselves, in our own strength. He has brought us to our knees, so we can be raised up again. *To the thirsty God will give water without cost from the spring of the water of life.*"

"You mention laws," said Dad. "You mean the ten commandments?"

"All of them, they're all scripture."

"But there are hundreds of laws in the Old Testament," said Louise. "So eating rabbit, or pork, for instance, makes you unclean?"

"Of course, even pagan Muslims and Hindus know that. The fact that we still do eat it, when we're meant to be a Christian country, just goes to show how far we've fallen from grace."

Louise hesitated, and then spoke, clearly enunciating the words. "How about, *If your brother, or son, or daughter, entice you, saying, Let us go and serve other gods, thou must surely kill him, stone him with stones, that he die.* You really believe we should do that?"

"I don't know that one."

"It's Deuteronomy 13."

"I see you know your Bible, Louise," said Paul, his face hardening.

"I don't know all of it," Louise replied, quietly. "But that one is personal to me. My mother told me that my grandfather quoted it to her mother when he threw her out. He'd made his money, he'd got saved, and he didn't want reminders of his old life around. She was too ashamed to go back to her own people, and she died that winter. There was no help for a cast-off squaw. So he didn't stone her, but he killed her, sure enough. So I do agree with you that words have power. But for evil as much as good. And much of the Bible seems evil to me."

The temperature in the room seemed to drop. I looked at Louise open-mouthed in astonishment. Did people do that kind of thing?

Paul crossed himself. "There are harsh things in the Bible, certainly. That's because it's about the truth of things. And life is harsh. And Hell is a lake of fire. And the word of God does not change. In his infinite wisdom He has brought us back to Old Testament times, to give us a last chance. There's no room for false gods, for other faiths. We've allowed them into our country, and that's brought judgement down on us."

"What about the New Testament – turn the other cheek?"

"Of course, individually we turn the other cheek, to give the aggressor the opportunity to repent. But *vengeance is mine, saith the Lord*, and the day of vengeance has come."

"Have you stoned anyone yet, in Fairbanks?" asked Dad, drily.

Paul hesitated. "No. We do our best to accommodate those who haven't seen the light. But some who couldn't follow the edicts of the Council have been expelled."

"What's the Council?"

"Fairbanks is a godly place," said Paul. "Not like Anchorage. We've two hundred churches to support a population which was thirty thousand. It's around half that now, but thanks be to God, our prayers meant that we've been far less devastated than other places. The churches came together to elect a Council. The Council rules the city, under God."

"Sounds like Calvin's Geneva," said Louise.

"I don't know of a Geneva around here, or a Calvin, and I wouldn't go as far as to say that there're no differences of opinion on the Council. But God has favored the believers. Pastor Elizabeth is the leader."

"How do you run the place?" Dad said.

"The mayor wasn't a believer, he was removed for incompetence, the Police Chief died. The Council's taken over the administrative offices and organizes the work, allocating it to different groups. Its decisions are enforced through the militia."

"A militia?"

"Discipline is necessary for law and order, for handling the dead, reducing disease, to keep food and water coming. We have to live off the land, and there's not enough locally to support the population, so we've commandeered an area of around five hundred square miles, spreading down the Yukon River towards the coast. The militias control the supply of food, there's strict rationing. It means everyone gets enough to eat. Heads of most households are a member of the militia, with a captain for each district."

"Doesn't sound like you're leaving people with alternatives."

"You think people should just be left to die? The old, the sick, the children? We look after them. We take our responsibilities seriously – police, hospitals, schools. There's a price to pay for that. There's no government, no taxes, we have to help each other. Everyone has to play their part."

"What schools?" asked Louise. "Who are the teachers?"

"The youngest child in every family stays at a community school in Fairbanks, where they can be raised properly, by Christian teachers, and taught the Bible."

"Like hostages?" Louise looked appalled.

"Of course not!" His composure was slipping under the questioning and he started to look irritated. "There's no reason for anyone to object. It's not really any different to a private boarding school, except there are no holidays."

"What if they're not Christians?"

"There is no room in our community for non-believers."

"What else do you teach them?

"Well. There's no need to, really, is there, with the Rapture coming. What would be the point? It's only seven years away now."

"What about older children?"

"They have to work, like the rest of us."

"But you're not working!"

"Some have been given the honor of spreading the Word. That's why I'm here, to give you the choice of life."

"Sounds like you've taken over the role of government," said Dad, folding his arms. "Don't you think there'll be consequences for you when they get the power going again and regain control?"

"The government's in the hands of the Antichrist. That's why all this has happened."

"So why has it disappeared?"

"You don't think that the president and government can just disappear, do you? This is the greatest country on earth. That's crazy. This country is blessed by God. We are His anointed people. But as the Bible says, He has let the Antichrist take control. The Antichrist is preparing for his war on Jerusalem, for the last battle of Armageddon. God is watching us to see how we deal with this situation, to prepare ourselves to join Him in the Rapture. Come and join the redeemed."

"Perhaps we should," interrupted Sue. "I don't want to fight God."

"Enough is enough," said Dad. "Speaking for myself, if I was going to believe, it wouldn't be on your kind of terms. I don't think we'll be joining you."

"You should listen to your child here. *From the mouths of babes…* It's not me you'd be joining, but God who you're rejecting. *He who is not with me is against me,* Jesus said. You're making a mistake. I beg you to reconsider over the coming weeks. I've done my duty in warning you, it's you who'll face the consequences. In the meantime, I must continue my mission."

"I don't think we'll be reconsidering," replied Dad, as we walked with him to the Land Rover, "but thanks for the warning."

"Then I cast the dust of this place from my feet," he shouted through the window, as he drove off.

THIRTY-SIX

Bob got back as it was getting dark, with an animal around his shoulders.

"Nothing in the traps today," he puffed, out of breath. "But I shot this Dall sheep. Good meat on this, and we can use the wool."

"We can't eat that," joked Matthew. "It'll make us unclean."

Bob furrowed his brows. "What the...?"

"Deuteronomy. It's in the Bible. Eating animals with cloven hooves makes you unclean. It's not allowed."

"Crazeballs!"

That evening, we sat around talking about it.

"He was mad," said my mother.

"No, he was logical," Louise replied. "If the Bible is God's word, then surely all of it is? And you have to accept all of it, not just the bits you like. But he's dangerous, certainly. The fundamentalists are always the worst, no matter which religion. We could have guessed that this was coming – extreme times breed extreme people."

"But what's wrong with taking the good bits?" asked Mom. "Or the good bits from the scriptures of all religions? Doesn't inspiration come in lots of forms, to people everywhere? Can we live without inspiration?"

"I agree with you, Mary. On one side of my ancestry, the Athabascans had their inspiration – they didn't have writing, but they had their stories, their myths, which they told around the fire at night. You can go back tens of thousands of years, to the cave paintings, and you can see the importance of inspiration. Back then, it was the stories that brought people together."

"But what's the point of a story?" asked Bess. "Isn't it something that isn't true?"

"Told you, didn't I? Reading's a bad idea." Bob gave a dry

chuckle.

"Perhaps it's a deeper truth," Louise replied. "A way of explaining the world. Facts are one thing, truth is another. And even if the explanation changes, we still need a reason for living, for doing things together. You know, back when those cave paintings were done, there were still Neanderthals on the earth. Anthropologists have puzzled over why they died out and our species flourished. The Neanderthals had bigger brains than us, and they were much stronger. What they didn't seem to have was a culture. Something that would bind different groups of them together. Stories, symbols, these are our glue, they give our lives meaning. We can imagine better ways of living them. Especially up here in the north – the world is harsh – Paul was right about that."

"So why in the name of Heaven does someone like Paul think his story is right, and everyone else's is wrong?" asked Jessie. "It's only been around for a couple of thousand years and has splintered into thousands of cults and churches anyway."

"Powerful stories are like two edged swords," replied Louise. "They can equally heal and harm. Bind people together, and make them kill each other. Some stories are just wrong and bad in themselves, those of the Nazis, the colonialists, you can still see it here in Alaska in the white supremacists. But even good stories can be used to bad ends. Anyway, maybe there's something true in what he said. Maybe it *was* a punishment, a warning. We became too arrogant, and it was time for a take-down."

"That's daft, Louise," Dad interjected. "You don't believe in God, do you?"

"Not that one, no. But the odds are something like this was bound to happen sometime. Could have been an asteroid, a virus, a nuclear war, one fact or another. But the truth is, underneath that, we've lost touch with Mother Earth, with how to live on our planet."

"I don't know what you're on about," said Bob. "But these Bible thumpers are getting everywhere. Here, have you heard the one about why God didn't send Jesus to Alaska?"

"No."

"He couldn't find three wise men or a virgin." He burst out laughing.

Mom looked shocked. "That's disrespectful, Bob."

"Maybe. But religions should stick to where they were born, like people. That's what's gone wrong. But, you know, this stuff doesn't work anymore, anyway."

"What do you mean?"

"Well, Jesus couldn't walk on water now, could he?"

"Why not?"

"Got holes in his feet." He brayed like a donkey.

"Let's simmer down," said Dad. "I'm with Bess here. No point in forcing unbelievable stories on people. But I wish now I hadn't started using the ham radio. They must've tracked the direction of the signal. They know we're here now. He sounded like he was warning us to watch our backs toward the end there."

"Wish I'd been here," said Bob. "I'd have shot him."

Mom shook her head. "Don't be silly, Bob. You can't descend to their level."

The change in Bob was sudden. He stood up, his face taking on a tinge of purple, and slapped his hand on the table, making the plates and jugs jump and clatter. "Damn it, Mary, you just don't understand what's going on here, and what's coming down the road. I've seen in 'Nam what happens when people are at war. I've seen what soldiers can do. And that's when they're under orders – the bits of flesh and bone that are left. And these people here, they're not soldiers, they're fanatics. They're the worst. They don't know any levels."

"What he said about the jail in Anchorage, that could be a problem as well," said Dad. "How many prisoners does it hold, a thousand? Two thousand? If they were insulated from the cholera, there could be an army of them. And that jail holds murderers, rapists, pedophiles."

"So we've got one army of criminals on our doorstep, and another of fanatics?" asked Jessie. "We don't have enough guns to fight off that lot. How long do we have?"

"Bu–but we haven't got much that's worth their coming here and fighting over, surely," Mom stammered. "The land's of no consequence, we don't have that much in the way of stores worth getting killed for."

"Look, Mary, you have to start getting real," Bob said, still angry. "I don't like to say this in front of you all here, but we have women. And these guys have been locked up for years. I don't know how to put that in more sensitive words. Even Sue here..."

"Bob, that's enough," Mom barked out, putting her arm around Sue.

"Maybe they'll kill each other off," Jessie chipped in.

"There'll still be too many," Bob said grimly.

"Then we need to make some alliances," Jessie replied.

Sue had tears rolling down her cheeks. "Please don't let them come here...please...?"

"Don't worry, Sue." Dad looked concerned. "We'll all be looking after each other."

Mom still had her arm around Sue. "But maybe everyone will just look after their own patch, even if they *have* been locked up for years."

"Sorry to butt in here," said Louise, "but people are naturally aggressive. You get some groups that really work hard to counter that, the Amish, Buddhists, Quakers, but they're rare in these parts."

"Louise is right," Matthew intervened. "These people, all of them, doesn't sound like they're going to be happy staying where they are. Reminds me of the companies I used to work with. They're like sharks, have to keep moving. They get bigger, or they get eaten. It's the way of things."

"Well, we can hope it works out better, but not much we can do about anything before winter," replied Dad. "But you're right, Jessie, about making alliances. We should look at that next year."

"What's wrong with starting now? Why wait?" I asked.

Dad hesitated for a moment. "OK, you're right. Let's do it now, before the snow gets too deep. I wish we'd picked up an old jeep...the truck'll use up too much petrol, we've used up about ten percent already." He stopped, a thoughtful look dawning on his face.

"Hold on, there were loads of Jeeps over at Whittier. Perhaps we should go back there. I'll give Nat a call."

"And we've all got to learn to shoot," he added. "All of us, OK?"

THIRTY-SEVEN

I woke the next day with my stomach churning, dry mouth, thirsty. Struggling upright, I knew I wasn't going to make it.

Beside me, Jessie stirred. "What's wrong?" she asked, still half asleep.

"I'm going to puke…" I managed and promptly heaved up on the floor. Then I had to make a dash for the outhouse. My bowels loosened before I got there. I pulled my trousers down as a stream of watery poop came out. It looked like the leftover water after rice has been cooked for too long. I staggered in, guts still roiling, covered in sweat but shaking with cold. A few more minutes and it happened again. Eventually, I dragged myself back inside on rubbery legs. Jessie looked up from where she was cleaning the mess, her face worried. "What's wrong, Jim?"

"I feel like shit."

"Come on, let's go see your mom," she said, getting to her feet.

With Jessie's help I hobbled over to the lodge.

Mom looked me over, I could see her concern.

"Jessie, I need a quart of boiled water, fast, and stir in six teaspoons of sugar and half to three quarters of salt."

Then I had to get up and dash to the outhouse again.

When I got back Mom wiped my face with a warm, wet cloth. "You have cholera symptoms," she said bluntly. "Drink this, all of it."

Dad looked shocked. "Is this from when we went to Anchorage?"

"No." Mom shook her head. "Jim would've had the symptoms before this. It acts quickly. You only get it by drinking or eating something that's contaminated. It'll be that fruit. I blame myself. We didn't wash it."

"So, he was bringing us disease rather than salvation," said

Louise.

Jessie paled. "Will Jim be all right?"

"Yes, it's easily fixable, Jessie. He just needs to keep hydrated. He'll be back on his feet in no time."

"But how can you say that when all those people died back in Anchorage?" Jessie asked, almost in tears.

"Sewage, unclean water, they were probably drinking from the river," Mom replied calmly. "Maybe there was no doctor, no one who knew what to do. Don't worry, Jessie, Jim'll be fine. But we need to watch each other for symptoms, and I want to see all of us drinking this."

"I want to nurse him, will you show me how?" Jessie asked determinedly.

"Of course, Jessie dear. But it shows how careful we have to be," she continued. "Washing our hands all the time, especially after we've been to the outhouse, is crucial. That's rule number one now, OK? We'll keep some water simmering for it. Jessie, you'll have to be especially careful. You and Jim are in quarantine now, in your cabin, until he's better. He'll probably be vomiting. Bring that bucket over there. The main thing is to keep giving him this liquid, even if he throws it up. And, Donald, I know it's a hell of a job, but could you add lime to the toilet now, and scrub down the seat with bleach."

Jessie nursed me for a couple of days, in our cabin, keeping me watered, and, when I could hold it down, feeding me soup and some of Matthew's fresh baked bread, washing me down, until I was strong again. I hated being sick. I hated being confined to my bed. But I purely loved the time Jessie and I spent together. Somehow that space drew us even closer.

"Are you still glad you came out here?" I asked her. I put on a woeful face. "Specially now you have to nurse me?"

"Well, Jim, let me think." She frowned. "Back in Seattle I had a big bedroom with a walk-in cupboard, in a lovely big house. I could set the music to play in my room when I was still coming through the front door. There were shops, a great waterfront, bars, football teams, live music every night, loads of friends, hundreds of good looking guys around, money flowing, yachts, trips in the bay. Now what've I got here – I have to figure this out, it's hard to add up so many good things – one broken down kid in a shit hole of a cabin, whose ass I have to wipe. And if I wipe my own I have to clear the flies away first, and it stinks. And there's not even any toilet paper."

She scratched her head. "This is such a complicated thing to answer. It's so difficult. I'm not sure I can decide."

My heart sank. "Do you mean…" She closed my mouth with hers, her hair falling around me. "Jim Richards," Jessie said, smiling. "Sexface, you seem to be getting a stiffie. Would you like me to go down on you?" I grinned like a jackass eating cactus. Seemed like my energy was coming back.

So I missed out on the trip back to Whittier. Dad went with Bob and Matthew and explained what had taken place when he got back.

"We've brought back two Jeep Wranglers. Old ones that can do without electronics. Now, we've got a few weeks before the roads around here get impassable. What I suggest is that we set out in two expeditions, one with Bob and Matthew heading south to Seward, one with me and Jim heading east." He glanced at me. "If you feel up to it now, Jim. We'll play it by ear, but see if we can't link up with some people to talk about co-operating, some kind of informal self-defense league. There aren't many ham operators around here, so we're going into the unknown."

"But how are we going to keep in touch with them later?" asked Mom.

"We can build some radios if they don't have one," Dad replied. "Ones that don't need batteries. It's really just an exploratory mission to see who's around, who we might be able to work with."

"What are your aims?" asked Matthew.

"I'm concerned about next year, that we might not be left alone," Dad replied quietly. "There aren't enough of us to defend ourselves. And even if we were safe, it's not feasible to think that the nine of us could live here forever."

He hesitated. "It's just not going to work, long term. We can't just rely on Mary to be the only one with medical knowledge."

She can teach me," Jessie interrupted.

"That will help," Dad replied. "But we need to be a tribe rather than a family. Society has to come back into the picture some time. I can't see us living with the criminals in Anchorage though, or the fundamentalists in Fairbanks."

"Donald, you're scaring me when you use words like forever," Mom said.

"I don't know, Mary. But we do need to think ahead. Whatever the future's going to be, I reckon we're going to have to make it for ourselves."

"We talked a lot with Nat," he continued. "If things do get rough here over the next year or two, we need an escape route. Because everyone's left Whittier, there's a lot of equipment there we could use. There's plenty of space, the Begich Towers are empty, and the Buckner Building's been deserted for years. Whittier is pretty much cut off, since the opening of the tunnel the old portage trail over the mountains behind it has fallen into disuse. Some of it's still there, but we could block it, if we wanted to. It's a natural bolt hole. Once we collapse the tunnel, anybody coming in with bad intentions would have a difficult hike. And if things get too rough, then there are boats in the harbor we could use to go to sea. I'm just thinking of this as a possibility. I'm worried that if we don't make alliances, get into a larger group, we, and people like us, could be picked off one by one."

"Donald, I know I've spent months saying I hope we're only here for a short time, but are you saying we might leave here now, after all we've done?" asked Mom.

"Possibly." Dad sighed. "I hope not. But we can't control events. This place is serving us well, let's see how we get through this winter, and what the world looks like when the spring comes around. But we do need to make a couple more trips first."

"Would we be coming with you?" asked Sue.

"Of course, darling," Mom replied. "We're family now. We'll always be together."

THIRTY-EIGHT

Over the coming years I got to know the Kenai Peninsula as well as I'd known our local area of Anchorage. The top end was flat and marshy, the bottom half was glaciers and icefields. Half of it was National Forest and Park. Most people lived around the mouth of the Kenai River and up to ten miles upstream, where there was a little agriculture.

The Peninsula had a population of around fifteen thousand people before the Event, mostly working in tourism and outfitting hunters and fishermen. For Alaska, that was real high-density population. Come to think of it, there was probably no place in the world so well stocked with tools for survival. But the hunters and fishermen were no longer there. The dozens of container trucks a day no longer roared up and down the Sterling Highway, bringing food and materials, returning with crates of fish. And the number of people had become a liability.

We set out in the two jeeps one bright, crisp morning, with sacks of dried fish and jerky in case there was any bartering to be done. Big fluffy clouds scurried across a deep azure-blue sky. The fall colors were dazzling, reds, oranges, yellows and greens, mixed up as far as you could see, the glaciers too bright in the sun to look at. Dozens of birds were flying high overhead, in wingtip formation.

"Canada geese," I identified them, "heading south for the winter."

Dad hadn't been able to find out on the radio if the road was open, but when we got to Summit Lake Lodge, where the guy in Alyeska had warned us about the hunters as we fled Anchorage the first time, it looked deserted. After a couple of hours we split, with Bob and Matthew setting off on a minor road through Moose Pass, down to Seward, a population of a couple of thousand. Dad and I carried on the highway to see what was happening in the larger population area.

According to the map, we were coming up to Coopers Landing, at the head of Kenai Lake, a small community of a couple of hundred or so. There was a barrier across the road, made of parked tractors with rolls of barbed wire in front of them. Under the blue and gold flag of Alaska, a bearded man dressed in an army combat uniform put down the stick he'd been whittling and got up with his rifle from his deckchair. We drove up slowly and stopped a few yards away.

I had my rifle at the ready. Dad got down and walked towards him, unarmed. "Hi, are you letting people through?"

"For a price," the man replied. "But frankly, I'd advise against it."

"Can you tell me what's going on down there in the peninsula?" asked Dad.

"It's a mess." He considered, stroking his beard. "The first few weeks weren't too bad. There was some disease. It was controlled. But then more came in from people fleeing Anchorage. That's when we set up this roadblock here. And then things started to get rough around Kenai. Too many people there. The salmon wasn't enough to feed them. And now the salmon run's stopped. They're starving, basically. We've got another barrier ten miles down the road, to stop them coming through to us. There are several guys on that one, just me here because virtually nothing comes through any more from your direction. If you'd come the other way, we'd have opened fire as soon as we saw you."

"So why didn't you shoot at us?"

"Simple. You came up politely, you look well fed, dressed, not desperate, you're not foaming at the mouth. Not like many we've had trying to get through here."

"Are you OK yourselves here? Want to do any trade?"

"If you've got tobacco, or morphine," he replied, "I'll do a deal. Otherwise, we're OK here. We've got the lake and the woods to forage in."

"I can't help you with those items," replied Dad. "But we're concerned what might be coming down from Anchorage and Fairbanks. We'd like to talk about possible alliances. Can we do that?"

The guy hesitated. "Wait here," he said. Then he went behind the tractor, picked up a mountain bike and cycled off.

Half an hour later, he came back with three others, a tall, distinguished looking, white-haired man leading the way. I guessed he was an ex-soldier from the erect way he carried himself, with authority, out of the manual, ramrod back, with a long, blue scar on his face.

"I'm Theo," he said, getting straight to the point. "I'm the mayor here, and these are my colleagues. What do you want?"

Dad introduced us and explained about the news from Anchorage and Fairbanks.

"Doesn't look to me like you're in a good position here," he ended. "All those people down towards Kenai, when they get desperate enough to get out, they'll overwhelm you with numbers. And for the bad guys coming south, this is the only way through. You're caught in the middle, in a no-win situation. There's going to be a nasty face-off."

"You're telling me. So what are you suggesting?"

Dad explained about Whittier. "If things get tough, we could hole up there, set up a community. There's room for a few hundred. With its natural defenses, that's enough to discourage anyone from taking us on. And enough to create some kind of society again, so that we have doctors and schools. And there are boats there for sea fishing. This lake doesn't look big enough to last you long. It's OK to keep ten people going, maybe, but not a hundred."

Theo thought for a while. "We've had all kinds of people coming through here, and mostly we've had to fight them off. But I'm glad you came, Donald. Same kind of stuff's been eating away at me. Let's shake on this. I'll have to buy time for a while, lots of people to convince, it's a big step to take. We won't be able to do it before the winter. But come through, let's start talking it over with others. And we should get our communications sorted, check we've got the call signs right, so we can keep in touch on the radio."

We drove over to the Princess Wilderness Lodge, which served as the community center. Most of the locals gathered around in the evening and Dad talked again. In the morning, we left, after swapping some supplies for tins, soap, needles and thread, feeling we'd made some friends.

THIRTY-NINE

Following advice from Theo, we didn't try going further into the peninsula but went north to a few similar sized communities on the coast. Those of a few dozen, rather than a few thousand, let alone hundreds of thousands, seemed to be the ones who had proved more resilient. Self-sufficiency was more possible. Disease was less of a problem. The more isolated they were, the better they had survived.

We got back home to find Bob and Matthew had made it back a few hours earlier.

"No good," Bob said. "Didn't look like Anchorage, but we couldn't get close enough to tell. There's the big prison across the water, don't know who's running the place. They started shooting as soon as they saw us. We had to reverse out of there fast."

"I want to go and live where there are more people," Bess said that evening. "Its fine for Jessie here, with Jim, they're together all the time. But it's dead boring for me. I've got no one to talk to. How am I going to meet boys? I'll die an old maid here, like Louise."

"Be careful what you wish for, young lady, and don't be rude," Mom replied sharply.

"Me, too," said Sue. "I don't want to be an old maid."

"They're right though," Louise said. "We need to get into a community again." She started singing *I wanna be where the people are.*

"I agree with you," said Dad. "But it depends what kind of community it is."

He was doodling on paper. "Can anyone remember what the constitution says?" he asked.

"Never read it," replied Matthew.

Apparently, only Louise had. "It's a long time since I read

it," she told us, "but I know it's nearly five thousand words long, which isn't long, for a constitution. Short of going back to Anchorage though and raiding the library, I doubt we'll find a copy."

"Do you remember anything about it?"

Louise hesitated. "The individual's right to life is inviolable. As is the right to liberty. Liberty includes personal freedom, political freedom – the right to participate in political decisions, religious freedom, and economic freedom, which means private property and employment. The pursuit of happiness, the common good, and justice – that people should be treated fairly. Equality, diversity, and telling the truth. Then there's something about federalism, separation of powers in the legislative area, and civilian control of the military. That's about as much as I can remember."

"That's helpful," replied Dad. "Certainly puts a perspective on the Anchorage criminals and the Fairbanks fundamentalists. Though I can't see that it's all still relevant."

"Why not?" Mom asked.

"Well, private property, for instance. Who owns what now?"

"Why do you ask about it?" Louise said.

"If we ever do set up something in Whittier, or even if we don't, if we do something else, we need to jot down some principles as to how we're going to organize ourselves. Actually, even if it's just us, I think we should have a clearer structure for making decisions. I don't think it should be basically down to me to persuade you lot. If I went under a bus tomorrow, not that that's likely out here, but you know what I mean, who decides?"

"I think it's a good idea, in principle," replied Matthew. "Are we going to be a democracy?"

"The USA isn't actually a democracy," said Louise. "A democracy is where every citizen participates in every decision. That's what happened in Greece. In America we elect representatives to make the decisions for us. That's a republic."

"I don't think we're going to get into representatives," said Mom. "Let's go for a democracy. So long as my vote counts for three." She laughed.

"I'm not sure of the point of a constitution any more," replied Louise. "You don't see them in nature, and I think we're more likely to end up following custom, and grouping in extended families. But if you want one, the first thing is to decide who's qualified to vote. I think the constitution's a bit vague about this, and in reality, it was down to the individual states to frame their own laws. So slaves couldn't vote in any of them, blacks could in some, women could in some but not others, and I think the voting age was generally put at twenty-five. That's how I remember it."

"No slaves, blacks or women voting. Sounds good to me," said Bob. "What went wrong? Not that I've ever voted anyway. And I'm not going to start now."

"Bob, you and me could get into some serious disagreement some time." Mom smiled to soften her words. "If you break your arm tomorrow, I reckon you'll have to fix it yourself. Obviously, as a woman, I'm not entitled to."

"I'd be happy to go for a democratic approach here," said Dad. "Current voting age is eighteen. That would exclude Jim though."

"He needs to be included," said Bob.

"What about me?" asked Jessie. "If Jim and I don't have a vote, we'll leave."

"Jessie!" Matthew exclaimed. "That's ridiculous."

She had her color up, but was sticking to her guns. "Why? Don't you think we have an equal role to play here? Donald said earlier, we're going back centuries. You think just because you're older, you still get to make all the decisions?"

There was a pause. Bob started humming a tune. Louise raised her eyes at Dad.

"Make it fifteen?" suggested Dad. "After all, everyone's

gonna have to grow up faster. I'll draw something up."

Sue raised her hand. "But that's discriminating against me, that's not fair."

"We have to draw lines somewhere, Sue," Dad replied.

"When you can figure out the details, make it short," suggested Matthew. "If we want to spread it around, get others to agree to it, we can't print it off, we'll have to keep making hand copies."

Later, I bumped into Bess on the way to the outhouse.

"Do you mind what's going on with Jessie and me, Bess?" I asked. "I couldn't help it, I didn't mean to take her away from you."

She looked at me. "I'm pleased for you, Jim, and for Jessie. I think you suit each other. You've got something in you that wasn't there a year ago. I love it. Even though it makes me more on my own. And I still want a different life."

We hugged each other. I'd never felt so close before with my little sister.

FORTY

A couple of weeks later, and I knew as I struggled out of sleep that something was different. It was still dark, but I could feel the cold on my face and my exhaled air turning moist. There was just a little warmth from the embers of the stove, still glowing red. Jessie snuggled into me. "I need warming up," she said.

I kissed her cold nose. We burrowed down and made love with the sleeping bag pulled up over our heads. Afterwards, I got up to put some more logs in and was immediately shivering. "I need warming up now," I said as I got back in, and we did it again, and then went back to sleep.

A couple of hours later, when it was usually getting light, it was still dark outside. "Better go find out what's happening," I said. In the light of the fire, we could see the frost feathering the window with blossoming flowers and patchworks of vine. We warmed water in the pot on the stove and washed, drying each other afterwards. Her nipples hardened as I dried her breasts. So did I. Her breathing quickened. So did mine. We got back into bed.

Half an hour later, it was still dark. "Seriously, Jessie," I said. "We'd better go." After washing again, we put on long underwear for the first time. Trousers, woolen shirts, jumpers, parkas, and went outside. Dad, Bob and Matthew were standing out there, looking at the sky. The wind was gusting strongly, whipping up the fallen leaves in circles. Over to the east there was a huge range of black clouds stretching right across the horizon. The ice was groaning in the lake.

"Looks like a blizzard, a nor'easter," said Bob. "Winter's going down."

"We've had them before, haven't we?" asked Dad. "It can't be too bad?"

"Hard to say," said Bob. "Anchorage is sheltered, and warm.

Hell, it's warmer than Chicago. We're higher up, more exposed, inland, and it could be ten, twenty degrees colder. We'll just need to hunker down, till it blows over. Let's make sure we've everything inside that we need, and we could add more stones to the walkway roofs."

"Come on, lovebirds," Dad said to us. "Let's get to work."

We worked all morning as the storm blew closer. Around midday, when we went in, it must have been gusting up to a hundred miles an hour. Buffeting us, snow driving into our faces, making it hard to see.

We thought we had the lodge windproof and snow proof, but there were still draughts, with little flurries of snow gusting inside. We covered the cracks up with duct tape. The wind buffeted the walls and roof as if it was trying to lift the building off the ground and whip it up into the sky. The stoves were roaring, occasionally backfiring as wind came down the pipes, trying to put them out. We covered the hearth with ash and then moss, to dampen it down and avoid the ashes blowing everywhere. The candles danced in their lanterns, throwing wrestling shadows on the walls.

That was our first taste of what it would be like to all be confined to the lodge. It was tougher than we expected. In the late afternoon Sue called out, "Dad, I can't open the door, I need to go to the outhouse." Matthew went over. "You're right," he said, as he pushed against it. "Must've got jammed."

Bob jumped up. "Shit, should've thought of this, it's the snow piling up outside."

We managed to lever it open a few inches and started scraping snow away, the wind driving the stuff inside, putting out most of the lamps. It was pitch black outside now. "Bring that kerosene lamp over," Bob shouted. "We'll have to rig up a line to the outhouse. One of us could get lost, die out here in the dark, just going for a crap."

"I can't believe we've been this dumb," Bob added later.

"Another couple of hours, and we'd have been locked in. We would've had to break the door down from the inside, and we've left some tools outside as well, they'll be buried."

"At least we figured it out in time," Dad replied. "When the storm's blown over we should do some more work, safety lines outside, better walkways, extend the porch, a drip tray inside here, some more partitioning for privacy. Find a place for every tool, make sure everyone knows where they are."

"We've still got to be more careful," Bob replied. "You only get the one chance out here. Reminds me of the cheechako who dug a really big cesspit for his outhouse. So deep that then he couldn't get out. Forgot to take a ladder with him."

"What happened to him?" Mom asked.

"Bear came along and had him for supper."

We settled down into rhythms. Much of the day was spent collecting compacted snow for water, melting it in the pot, aerating it for taste. Then there was getting wood, feeding the stove, fetching food from the ice store, preparing and cooking it. There was sweeping, cleaning, washing. But there was spare time, particularly in the evenings. The third evening of the storm was typical. Louise had insisted we resume lessons, with the parents' support, and had given us projects to write up, books to read. Jessie was struggling with the principles of the local native Indian language, Athabascan. I'd just finished reading *The History of Alaska* and was helping Bess and Sue with their spelling. Bob was cleaning guns with Louise, showing her how to strip them down. Dad had been teaching Mom how to use the radio and was now bathing some scrapes that he'd got with a salt solution, to the accompaniment of an occasional "ouch!" Matthew was preparing supper, a venison stew with roots and mushrooms. The storm was, if anything, increasing. It was howling around the lodge, like banshees keening and then rising into shrieks that seemed alternately agony and laughter.

Mom took her earphones off and looked up, her face grim.

"What's up?" asked Bob. He had to shout to make himself heard.

"From what I hear, this storm's taken people by surprise. No weather forecasts, and it's early for the year. It's huge, across most of Alaska. Not that people were much prepared anyway, but they weren't ready for this."

"Anything we can do?" asked Matthew.

"When we wake up tomorrow," said Dad, "I think we'll find that we're cut off. Down on the coast people'll still be able to get around, but I don't think we'll be able to get the truck or the jeeps moving. This could be it for the winter, folks."

Over supper, Mom said, "Now, I'd like us to be more cheerful for a moment. We've been incredibly fortunate compared to most. We're all alive and well, and the very fact that we're sitting here comfortably with this storm raging outside just makes me feel very grateful. We've made good friends," (mutters of agreement around the table) "and I want to say thank you to everyone for bringing us here together. I believe God must be watching over us. Also, there's one big thing we've forgotten."

"What's that?" asked Dad. "Did we forget to tie something down outside?"

"Donald, my dear," replied Mom. "I love you, but there are times when you're so wrapped up in work you don't see the wood for the trees. It's Bess's birthday."

Exclamations all round.

"Is it the seventeenth of October?" asked Bess. "I'd no idea."

"We've all been working too hard to keep track," replied Mom. "Matthew, I'd like your birthday dates please, to put on the calendar. Now, Bess, we can't do all the things we used to do, but I've made you this." She handed over a box, with a ribbon bow.

Bess opened it, took off some tissue paper. "Oh, they're so beautiful, thank you," she gasped, holding up a pair of moccasins for us all to see. They were brown, with red cord through eyeholes around the edge, lacing up at the front and embroidered with red and white flowers.

"Louise showed me how to do it," said Mom. "We used one of those deer hides. The flowers are yarrow."

Bob handled one. "These are good, better than anything you can buy in a shop. It's what a lot of people in the Yukon do, make their own moccasins from hide – and mittens, hats, coats – they keep you warmer, don't sweat, last longer, and you can repair them."

"It's not difficult," said Louise. "Easier than quilting. I'll teach you how to do it if you like, Bess."

Bess nodded enthusiastically. "I'd like that!"

"I don't think these boots of mine are going to last through next year," I said. "The leather's coming off here." I pointed to the toe. "I'd like to learn how to make them as well."

"I'll learn with you," Jessie added.

Matthew got up and went to the kitchen. "Here's a little something I put together, Bess." He brought out a cake, with a lit candle at the center. It's a little unorthodox in the ingredients, but happy birthday from us."

We lit some more candles, held hands around the table and sang *Happy Birthday*, to the accompaniment of the wind.

FORTY-ONE

The storm had stopped. Blown itself out. It was hard to get your head around the fact that such ferocity, such malevolence, could appear out of nowhere, feel like it was there forever, and then just disappear. After several days cooped up in the lodge it was a relief to get out. We walked outside, and the world was different. A blinding whiteness, under a cloudless sky, spread all around. The brilliance of it seared the eyes. On the north side, the snow was piled up over the roof. Hummocks of snow showed where the outhouse was. The trees were stripped of leaves. The landscape all around was alien – the drifts had changed shape: new, soft, white curves rather than angular shapes and black rocks. Forests that covered the slopes were now bare and white, the trees sticking out of the snow like burnt skeletons.

"Don't be out for too long without goggles," Bob said. "It can blind you."

Sue came bouncing out of the door, the pompom bobbing on her hat. "Snow, snow," she screeched. "Let's build a snowman."

A thwack of wet snow on my head, and Jessie was laughing. "I'll get you for that," I shouted indignantly, as I rolled up a snowball. She danced away, gathering up more. Sue threw one which just missed me, she squealed in delight, ran to a snowdrift to make more, and fell in up to her neck.

"Help!" she yelped, spitting snow.

We pulled her out, she looked uncertain as to whether to cry or laugh, but split into a peal of giggles. "Let's do it again."

The polytunnels had collapsed. "Not to worry," said Mom. "The seeds underneath should still be OK and the snow will insulate them. We can rescue them in the spring. Jim, Bess, could you do what you can to prop them up for the moment?"

Around the fence, the snow was churned up with tracks. Bob and I spent some time looking them over.

"Look at this, Jim, it's odd," he said. "Both dog and wolf prints here. Looks like the dogs were here first, and the wolves later."

I kneeled down to examine them, studying the differences.

It was so quick – I felt, as much as saw Bob tense. In the thicket to our left came a low growling. Bob started to chamber his rifle, but before he could finish a big dog came hurtling out, at blinding speed, leaping for his throat. I reacted instinctively, getting my arm out in front. There was a stab of pain as its teeth clamped down on my arm like a vice. I heard myself scream as teeth bit into bone. The force of it knocked me over and we rolled around in the snow. I heard Bob shouting and the thunk, thunk, as he brought the rifle butt down on the dog's head again and again and then the crack of the splintering skull.

He pulled me up. "Inside the fence, fast," he shouted, "there might be more of 'em." We ran inside, my arm around Bob's shoulder. The others, hearing the commotion, were running out of the lodge, Jessie loading her rifle.

"Mary, quick," Bob panted, breath steaming in the air. "Jim's hurt."

Inside, Mom cut my sleeve off. "Ow!" I couldn't help yelling as she poured whisky over the wounds. The deep gashes in my arm ran from the elbow to the wrist. Mom worked efficiently, swabbing them out, sterilizing them, bandaging.

"Here, Jim, I'm going to inject you with a vaccine." She picked up a syringe from her bag, filling it from a container.

"What's that?" I asked, nervously.

"It's for rabies. It's very rare in these parts, or used to be, but if you get it, you die. And I don't want to take chances. Donald picked it up in Anchorage."

"You can get it from a dog bite?"

"Or bats, foxes, anything, really. Hold your arm still now."

I couldn't help but be impressed – despite the throbbing agony shooting up my arm, around my shoulders, into my head

– which I felt was going to come off with the pain. I hadn't seen her in action before on anything serious.

"I'd like to learn to do that," Jessie said.

"I'll show you, Jessie," Mom replied. "Jim should be fine, he'll just have some nice scars to remind him of it. We're going to have to be careful with this whisky though, until we can get more sterilizing solutions."

"Mom, what are we going to do when we run out of medicines?"

Her shoulders drooped, and she suddenly looked older.

"Jim, I don't know. We're just going to have to learn how to do without them, or how to make them. Now, that's twice you've needed my help, could you be more careful please?"

"Thanks for that, Jim," Bob said later. "I owe you one. Again. You moved fast, instinctively, sometimes you have to do that, like when you shot that guy. Nourish it. Most people just freeze. Now, the critter looks like a mongrel, a cross between a husky and an Alsatian. It's been starving, you can see its ribs here. My guess would be that the dog packs haven't survived, but we need to be more careful now when we go out. Three at a minimum, always with rifles, and plenty of ammo."

"I don't want to expose us to more danger than necessary, but I'm concerned about the supplies," said Matthew uneasily. "We're getting through them faster than I expected. I don't know if it's the exercise, or we forgot the kids are growing up fast, but I don't think we're going to get through to the spring."

"It's the cold," replied Bob. "You need more fat and protein to keep the energy levels up. A third, or a half more again. We need a moose. That would keep us through the winter. While this weather holds, we should go look for one."

"Is it safe?" Mom asked nervously. "Are you sure?"

"Nothing's ever safe," Bob said flatly. "But animals aren't the real problem, it's the water that kills you. We need experience of moving around in the winter. The most dangerous times are when the rivers are freezing in the fall, and then thawing in the spring. That's when you can't trust the ice. It defrosts from the bottom up. It's real skid stuff. You get open places where the river's fast, then a thin layer of ice, then snow on top of that, you figure it's safe, and fall through. Always got to tap it with a stick, check you get a dull sound. But they should be frozen enough now. Bears are out of the way, they're hibernating. The main thing is not to get lost, not to panic, to watch the weather, to be prepared to bivouac outside if needs be. Never be overconfident."

For the first couple of days, Bob had us all learning how to use snowshoes and poles. "May come a time when we all have to walk out," he said. "We all need to be able to do it." We practiced going slow, fast, uphill and downhill. To begin with, we were all stepping on the frames and falling over, and sliding back when we were going up a slope, until we learned to step up at an angle. After a while, we got the hang of it, though hips and groins were aching and we still walked like ducks. My arm wasn't much of a problem – it throbbed with the exercise, but Mom changed the dressing every day

After that, we were going out every day, usually in threes. Rifles and packs on our backs, with rations, sleeping bags, essential tools. The snow was covered in tracks. "These little dashes, like feathers," Bob would say, "those are ptarmigan feathers, the bird's flapping its wings through the snow to take off."

Sometimes we'd disturb them and they would suddenly break out and take off frantically, their wings knocking the snow from bushes and trees as they flew off with their clackety clacking noise. Jessie brought one down with a quick shot, but though we floundered in the deep snow for ages, we couldn't find where it had fallen through.

"This is where we need a hunting dog," Bob said. "We'll have to tame one, find some puppies or something. Makes no sense, not having a dog."

The spruce trees were bowed over with snow so heavily that just a touch, a breath of air, would be enough for the whole burden to fall. Occasionally there would be a crack as a whole branch broke off with a thump as it cratered the ground. Apart from that, and the occasional raven cawing, and our heavy breathing, it was utterly quiet. The sunlight was a rich red, like it would be in the evening further south, because it never rose much, just circling around the low margin of the sky. The whole short day was a sunrise or sunset, with the purples, reds, yellows lighting up the snow and ice and the glaciers in a dazzling pastel of colors. When a breeze came up it would lift the ice crystals in clouds into the air, rainbows sparkling through them. "Snowbows," Bob called them.

One evening there was the most spectacular Northern Lights display. The weaving curtains of green and blue shimmering up and down, rippling side to side across the entire sky. Streaks of red and yellow blinking on and off. It lit the valley around the lodge as the ice in the lake creaked and groaned under the deepening grip of winter, like giants in chains.

"How can anyone not believe in the old gods?" asked Louise, as we stood on the porch, in the middle of the eternal war between ice and light.

FORTY-TWO

Though the going was slower than in the summer, in the snow, we could travel further. We crossed rivers which had been barriers to us before. One day Bob, Dad and myself, each with large packs and rifles, went back to the Begich Boggs visitor center. Jessie was guarding the lodge – Bob was uneasy about its safety without one good rifle there. The center had been burned to the ground and there was no sign of the overweight family.

"Hell," Bob said, shuffling through the embers, "there are some charred bones here, but I don't know enough about this stuff...Donald, are these human?"

"I wouldn't know," Dad replied, holding one up. "Could be a fibula? Shall we take some back to ask Mary? She'd know."

"I guess not. No point. They died or they moved on, or some of them did. That's all we're going to figure out, all we need to know."

Another time, we were over a ridge, trekking through a valley we hadn't been in before, through large spruce, twenty, forty meters high. The massive branches dropped almost vertically.

"These spruce are sheltered here, that's why they're growing so big," Bob explained. "Up north they can be hundreds of years old but still just a few feet high."

"I can see tracks, Bob. A moose?"

We snowshoed our way over. "It's recent," he said. "It's a big bull moose, the print's about nine inches long, same as my boot. You see how crisp it still is around the edges? It's new, it hasn't hardened yet. And it's still fluffy in the middle. Can't be more than a few hours old."

"Wow, look here," he added later, as we followed the tracks. "That's some antler. Shed recently – double-shoveled, looks like over forty points. Its pair will be around here somewhere. And see this?" He pointed to a spruce – "You can see where it's stripped the bark, rubbing to get the antler off. They do the same in the summer, scraping to get the skin off the antlers when the bone hardens."

A bit further on we saw a pile of black stools, in nuggets. "Definitely recent," Bob said. "Still warm. Feel it. It's like this in the winter because they're browsing on wood, so it's full of fiber." He held it up for us to see. "In the spring, when they're eating grass and green stuff, it's more sloppy, like a cow's turd."

An hour or so later, when the sun was dropping behind the mountains, Bob stopped again. "There it is," he said. "Must be a thousand pounds."

I looked through my own binoculars. It was a mile away, browsing. It still had its other antler, making it look very lopsided. Occasionally it rubbed in an irritated fashion against a tree, trying to shake it off.

"They love willow," said Bob. "You can see where he's pruned it right down. And you can see how awkward those antlers are around trees. If you're ever in trouble with a moose, that's the thing to do, get behind a tree. Keep it between you, and if you're lucky it'll give up after a while. Now – it'll smell us if we get any closer from here. We'll have to circle around, get downwind."

"Shouldn't we get back?" asked Dad. "It'll be dark in an hour or two."

"Weather's dicey, but can't miss this opportunity," replied Bob, scratching ice off his stubble. "Might not get another one like it this time of year. And we won't get back before dark anyhow. We'll be fine camping out here."

We detoured around, shuffling through the snow. It was hard going, clambering over snow covered rocks with our heads down, trying not to make any noise, worried about getting caught in the crevices. Dad started to cough hoarsely, and retched.

"Damn, sorry," he whispered, "I'll go back."

"Quietly," Bob replied with a finger to his lips. An hour or so later, shuffling slowly along, then crawling through the snow on our bellies, and the two of us were getting close, about two hundred and fifty yards away. The moose raised its head, sniffing the air, and we froze. It moved on a few yards and carried on browsing, stripping the bark from the alders.

"They hear real good," Bob whispered. I don't think we'll get any closer, Jim. Your shot. Can you manage it from here?"

"Easy-peasy," I lied.

I kneeled and brought the Winchester to my shoulder. It was a tricky shot in the fading light, with a few branches in the way, a breeze drifting snow down from the mountains towards us. I could just make out the upper front quarter of the moose. It might not work, but another minute and it could have shifted position, and the light would have faded too much, and the breeze could have strengthened...I focused; stilled my breathing, took my glove off – and my fingers immediately stiffened in the cold. I willed the shot, allowing for a fall of a few inches in flight and gently squeezed the trigger. The noise ricocheted around the valley. At first, I thought I must have missed. Then it slumped to its haunches and keeled over.

"Uh-huh," said Bob, "straight through the heart again. Goddam, Jim, that's great. Fucking brilliant. This will feed us for months."

I felt proud, exhilarated. My first moose. And that was the most difficult shot I'd made so far. When we came up to it, it looked like it was asleep in the snow. Sadness washed over me. It was such a huge, magnificent animal. I put my hand on its head, still warm. "Thank you for coming to us and giving your life. We respect you as our brother, we honor your spirit, may it walk in peace." I didn't really know if it meant anything, but I felt better about killing it.

It was getting dark.

"Jim, we'll have to camp here. I'll make a start, could you go bring your Dad over, he's not sounding too good. Not going to be enough light to do the meat, we'll deal with it in the morning."

Bob had got a fire going by the time I got back with Dad.

"That's a heck of a lot of meat," Dad looked on admiringly. "Matthew's going to be happy. Maybe there is a God looking out for us after all."

"You can thank Jim for it, I don't think I could've made that shot." Bob grinned. "Could you clear the snow around here, and – Jim, let's put up an A frame here, spruce boughs on top, then cover it in snow. Hear that?"

When I stood still, I could just hear the mournful, eerie sound of wolves howling.

"Are they a danger to us?" asked Dad.

"Nada, or they'd be here already. Sounds like a decent sized pack, about ten miles away. They're probably not as hungry as they will be later. But we'll take it in turns on watches to keep the fire alight, or in the morning we'll find they've taken the moose."

"Bob," Dad said, as we chewed some of the moose meat we'd roasted over the fire, "it's been great to be out with you and Jim. A new kind of experience for me. I was just wondering, I don't want to ask too many liberties of you, but you could keep an eye out for Bess as well?"

"Bess?" Bob looked up in surprise. "She'll be fine, just her hormones firing. Needs a guy. You're not suggesting it's me?" He laughed.

Dad smiled, wryly. "No, I just think she hasn't found a way of dealing with being out here yet."

"Shape up or ship out, that's the way of it, Donald," Bob replied. "But she's going to be OK. She's a good kid. Just needs a bit of sense knocking into her. Time will take care of it."

We went to sleep in our triple-layered, arctic-proof sleeping bags to the noise of crackling logs and the wolves' song rising and falling in the distance.

FORTY-THREE

We were up hours before sunrise, Bob had a kettle on over the fire for tea and sourdough pancakes. "Shouldn't be cooking on the campsite in bear country, but with the three of us we'll be OK." We had them smeared with honey, around the fire, warming ourselves up as the frost melted from our eyebrows, chewing jerky, appreciating the warmth of the tea sliding down. With the firelight, the full moon and the stars, there was plenty of light to work by. The three of us managed to haul the moose over onto its back. One of its frozen legs came swinging over and the hoof caught me a glancing blow across my cheek.

"Could've clubbed you badly there," said Bob. "Got to watch out for that kind of thing. Your Mom's not going to appreciate you knocking yourself up again. Here, you start with the knife."

Even with my razor sharp, foot long, Bowie knife, it was tough opening the stomach. When I managed it, a burst of steam came out along with the guts.

"Wow, these guts must weigh as much as the last deer I killed," I exclaimed, as I pulled them out, putting the heart and kidneys into separate sacks.

"Careful not to get any hair or dirt on the meat," said Bob. "It'll spoil it. Separate it into legs, ribs, haunches and head. I'll go make a travois, plenty of spruce and alder around here, I'll use that. We'll leave the guts for the wolves. Everyone around here has to eat."

Dad and I finished the skinning with fleshing knives. It was hard work; they rapidly blunted on the frozen hide. My arm was working fine by now, just twinges. Bob had cut down springy saplings and made a travois in the form of an isosceles triangle, lashed together with crosspieces, using spruce roots for the rope – withes – they were close to the surface and didn't take much digging up.

We wrapped the meat in canvas, the organs went into a flour sack, tied it all onto the travois, and brushed off as much as we could of the frozen blood and guts. By the time we were ready to leave, the sun had risen, skirted the horizon, and set again. With the strongest spruce ropes attached to the frame, we took it in turns pulling it across the snow. It wasn't too difficult. The saplings scratched through the ice, the frost crystals broke underneath our feet, sparkling blue and yellow as we scrunched through the shimmering carpet – like swimming through plankton studded seas. The low-hung, huge, white moon that seemed to take up half the sky cast our shadows further ahead than we could see, giving plenty of light to find our way back. It was eerie, trekking at night, but I'd never felt so safe. I felt confident and strong. One shot, one bullet in the right place, and we had food for the winter. I was getting familiar enough with the stars – tracking their regular pattern across the sky – particularly on a night like this, with the Pole Star right overhead, to know the way without the help of the compass. And, more obviously, our track out was still clear, breaking up our shadows as they fell on the sparkling ice covering the snow.

Occasionally we crossed other tracks, animals leaving the mark of their passing and their smells to follow, for those who could. Once or twice I saw the gleam of eyes from the trees. I felt privileged to be living in the same space as the owner of those eyes, though with such inadequate sensory equipment. Over one horizon we could see Mars, flaming red, and after a few hours we could see the lodge on the other horizon, miles away, a pinpoint of red in the black wilderness. As we got nearer the dot turned into an ember, got larger, and then the outlines of a window took shape. We began hollering as we came close, everyone running out to greet us, and helping get the meat inside.

"Wow," said Matthew, his eyes lighting up, a broad grin on his bushy face as he finished skilleting some hotcakes. "Congratulations, gentlemen. Honor to the hunters. Now, how would you like it – Steak? Stew? Meatloaf? Burger? Ribs? Roast? Soup? Meatballs? Fried? Fricasseed? Ladies and gentlemen, place your orders. We are open for business."

PART THREE

WINTER

FORTY-FOUR

Soon, it was colder again. The thermometer was down to minus 25. The door hinges were heavy with frost and it was creeping up the windowpanes so thickly you couldn't see through them. Every few minutes we could hear the groaning of the ice in the lake as it thickened.

Bob, Jessie and I were on our way back from checking the traps, carrying two marten. "Look," Jessie said. "I think that's Dad and Bess."

I looked through the scope. A mile away, two figures were heading for the lodge. Matthew seemed to be struggling, leaning on Bess.

"C'mon," said Bob, putting his binoculars back in the pack. "Let's go help."

Matthew looked frozen, his teeth chattering. We helped him back.

"Strip him down," Bob said, as we got through the door. "Clothes up to dry – no, not directly above the stove, Donald, they could fall down and catch fire."

"Let me check your hands and feet for frostbite, Matthew," Mom said. She took his socks off, rubbed his toes. "They seem OK, you weren't out for long. But we all need to be more careful. I don't want to be amputating fingers and toes out here."

Matthew started to stutter as he warmed up. "I'm s...s... sorry, guess I'm not very fit. Could do with some antifreeze in me on a day like this. We just went out to see if there were still any cranberries left. The book says they can last past Christmas."

"Here, I'll get you another jumper," said Mom.

"Not that one, Mary," Bob said as she brought it back. "It's synthetic, a lemon. The problem here, Matthew, is that you'd started to sweat, and then your sweat started freezing to your skin."

John Hunt

"You'd better tell us, Bob," said Dad. "We're not used to being outside in this kind of weather. I just used to go from the house to the office in a car, with the heating on."

Bob got up, and started taking off his clothes.

"My fault, I should've guessed that, and explained all this before. There's a way of dressing for the winter, OK? The key thing is lots of layers, and keep 'em loose, to use air as insulation. Keep to natural fabrics. They work best."

"Sounds logical," said Jessie.

"Now, first, long underwear, like I'm wearing here. I keep mine on at night. If it gets colder, wool socks and booties, sweaters, parkas, put sleeping bags inside each other. When you go outside, socks, two pairs. First cotton, then wool. If they're tight, your feet will freeze off, and you'll be hobbling on stumps for the rest of your life. Then jeans, flannel shirts. Then snow pants, then jackets, scarf, then parkas, always with a hood, over a wool cap. Wolverine ruffs are best, the ends of the hair don't frost up like others do. The beavers in the lake, they'd do fine. We'll have to get ourselves a couple now. Remember, warm air rises, so you want to cover your neck and your head, that's where a lot of the body heat's lost."

"Like the hat says to the scarf, you hang around, while I go on ahead." Sue laughed.

"Right on, Sue. Now, though the clothing has to be loose," he continued, "you don't want gaps at the edges for the cold to get through. Think like you're on Mars, wearing a spacesuit. In the right clothes, an Eskimo can fall into the sea and stay dry. And the main problem is the wind. When it gets properly cold, 50 and more below, breathe through a veil or you'll get frostbite in your lungs. If you're outside you need to cover your face. A wool scarf will just ice up. A mask, with goggles…the skin always needs to be covered."

"Oh my God," said Bess. "This is so icky, Bob. You want us to dress like animals?"

"We *are* animals, Bess," Louise replied. "Bob's right. We need to be fit for the weather, like they are."

"Mukluks are best when the snow's dry," he continued. "They may look fancy, but they're moose hide, with layers of felt, and what works for the moose will work for you. If it's wet, though, they're no good. Never wear tight boots. Two pairs of gloves, cotton first, then moose-hide mitts. When you're outside, watch each other for frostbite, like Mary says. It's easy not to realize you're getting it. The skin goes white and hard, or black. Don't try warming it up, carry a dressing in your pocket, slap it on, and get back here as fast as you can. But frostbite means you've been stupid, not brave.

"Once you're inside, first thing, always hang everything up to dry, only not directly over the stove. If they're damp when you go out again, you'll freeze. Any questions? No? Now remember, it'll get colder up here than it ever was down in Anchorage. Be prepared."

"It's like living in the old times," said Louise.

"Exactly. We have to start thinking like they did. Don't rush at anything, don't build up a sweat. And learn to improvise. If you need lip salve, for instance, wax from your ears is as good as anything you could buy in a shop."

"Yuk," said Bess. "That's tacky. I don't even have any make-up, and now you want us to use earwax? What next. Snot? Piss?"

"Good point, Bess. Piss is really useful when you have skin stuck to metal. Back when I was in…"

"That's enough, Bob, thank you," interrupted Mom, firmly. "We're closing this subject now." Sue was looking on wide-eyed.

"Hey, Bess," Jessie added. "It's not so bad, just that it doesn't come out of a tube."

"I don't think we'll be going out the next few days, though," Dad said. "I was on the radio this morning, there's this one guy who seems to know about the weather, says there's a deeper cold front following this one."

"Jessie, I think we'll have to move back to the lodge till it gets warmer," I said later that night. "Look at this, the sleeping bag's frozen to the wall on my side."

"Whatever you say," she mumbled. "I'm cold."

I was up several times in the night putting more logs on the fire. One time I woke thinking there was something strange in the room. It was the stove, glowing red-hot. Sparks were jumping from the open damper on the door. "Hell, Jesus!" I exclaimed. The stovepipe was glowing red. It looked like it was going to explode. The chimney was roaring. I grabbed the glove, opened the door and threw the bubbling bucket of water on top into it. Steam hissed out and the room filled with smoke and the stink of burning tar. Black creosote ran down the pipe.

"Damn, hell!"

The temperature in the room immediately plummeted. By the time we'd got some clothes on, we were shivering with the cold, teeth rattling. We ran the few steps to the lodge, our breath freezing to ice, the cold clawing into our veins, and stumbled in.

Bob wasn't sympathetic. "Should've been knocking the stovepipe to bring the creosote down, but don't do it when the fire's alight, you'll crack the pipe."

The next day the temperature was down to minus 35. "This isn't so bad," he said. "Up in the Yukon it's often thirty, fifty degrees colder."

The sound of a shot came from outside. We jumped up. Then another one.

"What's that? Bob?"

He was still sitting, unperturbed. "Trees cracking in the cold."

"Why did people ever come here? How long's this going to carry on for?" Bess asked.

"We don't know, Bess," Dad replied, stoking the fire. "It's just weather. We'll survive."

"What's the point of just surviving? Same shit, different day? I want my life back. I hate this. It's crap."

"People will live anywhere they can," said Louise, wrapped up in furs in front of the fire. "Even here. Life will always go anywhere it's possible."

"Bess, it's OK," Jessie said. "I know it looks like shit, but we'll get through the winter, and it'll get better."

"OK for you." Bess snorted. "You can fuck all night. You're in too deep to say "hi" to me. What do you expect *me* to do?"

Mom looked as if she was about to say something but I waved her down.

Jessie looked upset, but knelt down and took Bess' hands. "Bess, we'll find someone for you next year, OK? Not a lanky geek like Jim here, but someone you'd like."

"If we get that far," Bess muttered, still far from happy.

Bob and I checked our cabin. He was up the ladder looking at the roof. "Lucky, Jim, we'll need to patch this before you can use it. But at least it didn't set the whole roof alight. We'll need tarpaulin, moss, a couple of poles, let's get to work. Don't make a boo-boo like that again."

The next day it was minus 40. The wind was careening around, the sky ragged grey, snow streaming off the tops of the mountains. Going out hunting or doing work was impossible, even with masks and goggles on – with all the mittens you needed to keep your hands warm it was too hard to handle tools, let alone shoot a rifle.

Some jobs still had to be done; though doing anything outside was a pain. One chore that was unavoidable was to get wood.

"Get the birch logs rather than the spruce when you go out, Jim," Bob said. "They burn hotter." We had to keep shoveling snow off the porch to avoid being blocked in. And we shoveled up more snow around the lodge as insulation. Stepping outside was like drowning in a frosted lake, the cold searing the lungs. Thumbs would get cold first and it would creep down the wrist. Any spot that wasn't always wrapped up, it stung. After a minute, eyelashes and nostrils gummed together with ice. At least the outhouse no longer smelled – everything immediately froze solid.

Which led to other problems.

Bess came raging through the door. "I can't crap in the loo. It's made an icycle, sticks up my bum when I sit down. What the hell's going on?"

"Damn," Bob replied. "We should have thought of that. You need to spread the shit around before it freezes, even before you wipe yourself."

"Oh my God," Bess muttered.

"Jim," Bob continued, "a job for you. A shit one." He laughed. "You'll have to take a hammer and chisel to it. Make sure you strip down and clean up when you come in, because you're going to be covered in the stuff, and it will stink when it thaws out."

There were a few hours of grey light every day, but the sun never rose above the hills. Most of the time it was pitch black, cold and windy, and we gave up going to the outhouse. We started using pails inside; the place soon stank of shit and urine, wet clothes, sour skin, defrosting meat and fish. We were getting lethargic, with not enough body fat, and grimy, using hot wash cloths rather than stripping for a bath. We got scratchy. We slept a lot, partly to conserve energy, partly because we'd lost the will to do anything else. But we never rested well...it was more like dozing...off and on. We usually ended up sleeping around the stoves for warmth, and every half hour someone had to get up to stoke the fires, or shovel snow away from the door, letting the cold in. When the stoves weren't roaring, our breath would rise and freeze to the roof, forming a blanket of frost which would then melt as the fire was stoked again, dripping down onto us. We were too hot, and sweaty – or too cold, and frozen. It was a miserable time.

FORTY-FIVE

Matthew was clearing the breakfast table, Bob was cleaning his rifle, the rest of us were doing odd jobs without enthusiasm. Despondency hung in the air like the mist over the lake.

"Mom, we're out of toothpaste," Bess complained. "Do we have more?"

"I don't know, Bess, Mom replied, disinterestedly. "Matthew?"

"It's not one of those things that got picked up in Anchorage, Bess. We'll have to manage without."

"But how am I supposed to brush my teeth?"

Mom thought for a moment. "There are a lot of things we're going to have to manage without, Bess, and mostly, it really doesn't matter. Salt or baking soda will do just as well. Or even just dry brushing your teeth. We're not eating much sugar, so the fluoride in the toothpaste doesn't matter."

"Oh, this is so gross," she pronounced.

Later, I saw her switching her phone on and off.

"What are you doing that for? You know there's no signal," I said.

"What's the point of being here like this, with no phone?" she grumbled, still pressing the button. "This isn't a life. It's all so cheesy. I want to go home. I don't want to stay in this armpit."

"This is home now, Bess."

"No, it isn't, it never will be. I hate it here. I hate it!"

Dad looked up. "That's enough, Bess. Pull yourself together. You're feeling the blues."

"I won't, I won't," she wailed, her lips trembling. "I hate you, too. You brought us here."

Sue started crying. "I don't hate it here."

"Well I do!"

"Look, Bess…" I said, ready to try reason.

Bess turned on me furiously. "I hate you, too! You've taken

my only friend away."

I stood up. "That's mush, Bess, grow up," I said angrily.

"Stop it everyone," Mom shouted. "Enough."

Bess rounded on Mom. "You love this, Mom, you've got us all trapped here. I hate it! It's driving me up the wall."

Mom actually laughed...and laughed, with a note of hysteria.

"What's up, Mary?" Dad asked, perplexed.

"Got to laugh or cry, Donald," she replied. "We're all here, we're safe, we have shelter, water, food...now, Bess, what's eating you? Is it the time of month?"

"None of your business," Bess almost snarled. "It's all just horrible. I'm dirty. Look at my hair, it's stringy. I've probably got nits."

"It's tough here right now, Mary," you've got to admit, Matthew replied. "Feel like I'm going bonkers myself. The cold...the dark...crowded in here..."

Sue was really sobbing. Jessie was trying to say something. Voices were getting louder. I got up and started to shout, "Shut up everyone," when an earsplitting crack echoed around the confined space. Our heads snapped around to Bob, standing there with his rifle, gun smoke drifting from the nozzle. There was a shocked silence.

After a moment, Dad smiled. "Hey, Bob, you've just gone and put a hole in the roof."

"Cabin fever," Bob said. "It happens when you're cooped up for a long time together. Sends people mad. Or they kill each other. A lot of guys just top themselves out here in the winter."

We looked at each other. "It's not that bad here," Louise said, after a moment. "Think of the Eskimos, they used to spend this time confined to an igloo. We've got far more space here."

"Yes," Dad said. "Let's lighten up. It's difficult, I know, but what can we do? We don't want a meltdown here."

There was another few moments' silence.

"Bess," Jessie said. "We should wash our hair, and then cut it.

I've done Sue's before, I'm sure I could do yours. Fancy a bob? What d'you think? And then you could try mine. It's too long anyway."

"That's a great idea, Jessie," said Mom. "You could do mine as well."

"Sweet. Could I have a bob, too?" asked Sue.

"You bet. Let's start getting some water on the stove, we must have some decent scissors somewhere?"

"Jim," Jessie said, "you look rubbish, too. I don't know if that's just a fuzz you've got, or meant to be a beard, but I'm going to shave you, if you can't do it yourself."

"Tell you what." Dad got up. "This place's been getting into a mess lately. Worse than your rooms back home, kids. Jim, could you give me a hand? We could do with some more storage space. And shelves, and pegs. With all of us in here in this weather, we're just piling things up. Getting harder to find what we need. I spent ages yesterday searching for a screwdriver. We've been getting into a state."

"I'll help. And we need to get outside," Bob added. "We'll start tomorrow. Just for a couple of hours, in parties, one group at a time. The wind's dropped. And we could do with building an arctic entry. Stop so much cold coming in when we open the door."

Matthew looked up. "Mary, I was just wondering, isn't it Turkey Day soon? Last Thursday of the month?"

"Oh!" Mom put her hand to her mouth. "I've been forgetting to check the calendar." She dug it out of the drawer. "Yes, it's next week, six days' time. Let's do something for it."

Matthew opened the cupboard. "I'll start preparing, we haven't got turkey of course, but ptarmigan would do. I think we've the right sort of herbs here, and we've got cranberries, how about salmon pate to start with?"

"To be honest," said Louise, looking more like an Indian than ever, with her hair longer, in a ponytail. "I've been feeling a bit of a spare part here lately. Would you let me organize Thanksgiving? It's not a tradition native to these parts, but we need an occasion, I'd be happy to do it."

"Great if you could, Louise," Dad replied. "Just let us know what you want us to do for it, if anything."

We started to pull together again. Leaving the lodge the next day helped, there was more headspace outside and being outdoors helped you appreciate indoors. We got better at dealing with the cold. After a few days, the temperature dropped back to minus ten.

"We'll be able to get out more," Bob said. "Those clouds mean a depression, warmer weather, it'll start snowing again soon. In clear sky the warmth just disappears upwards. Now, who wants to come on a beaver hunt?"

Bob, Jessie and I walked over the ice to the beaver house, carrying some long, cottonwood saplings. A thin trail of heat was rising from it, as if someone was burning a fire inside.

"I reckon their stick pile's down here," Bob said, prodding through the snow. "They use it as a store room through the winter. We need to dig down to the lake ice and then make a hole through it, a few feet in diameter. So get digging."

Jessie and I dug through with ice picks. It was hard going. A stench rose up as we broke through, methane bubbles popping on the surface. Bob attached a wire snare to the end of the pole.

"The idea is that the beaver comes to chew the end of the stick and gets his head caught in the snare. He can only swim forwards, so that will tighten the noose. We leave it here, dig a couple more holes, and come back tomorrow."

The next day, one trap hadn't been touched. On the second, the bait had been nibbled around, but the snare was still intact. The third pole was really heavy. We couldn't pull it out of the ice.

"It's getting stuck beneath the ice," said Bob. "Start digging, guys. Don't fall in – if you get lost under the ice here, you won't be coming back up."

Half an hour or so later and we pulled up a large beaver, male, over three foot long, about thirty pounds. It had frozen solid.

"We'll have to hang it inside to thaw it out," Bob said. Lots of good meat on this, and it's fatty. Fat is what we need in the winter, not your lean meat – it's why Eskimos do so well on seals. We can trim our hoods with the fur, it's going to help."

The lower temperatures now felt tropical. We were back in touch with the world, and with each other. We slept better and went back to using the outhouse. The emotional level simmered down; Bess and I got to be friends again. The three of us were out collecting wood a few days later when Bess said, "I'm sorry about what I said back there, Jim. I don't really hate you."

I stopped in my tracks. I couldn't remember Bess talking to me like this before. Maybe this is what "family" meant. I liked the feeling that grew inside me. "Bess," I said slowly, "I guess I *have* taken your best friend away from you. You've got every right to feel pissed."

"No, that's not right, Jim," said Jessie. "I'm still your best friend, Bess, it's just that I'm Jim's as well, in a different kind of way. But I feel closer to you because of it. We're sisters, rather than just friends."

Bess put her arm around Jessie's shoulders. "God, I'm so glad we all met up. Can you imagine what life would have been like, stuck here with just Jim? Hell, I'd have died."

I gripped her arm. "Bess, I'll look after you, but you've got to pull yourself together, get real, stop talking about Anchorage as if it was still there, OK?"

She gave a nervous laugh. "Jim, you've changed. All these years you've been boring me, and now you're scaring me. Where have you been hiding all these years?"

We hugged.

"Bess is going to come with us tomorrow, Bob," I said as we

went back inside, with armfuls of logs.

"The three of you go," Bob replied, massaging his leg, "I've got twinges on the hinges. You'll be fine."

From then on the three of us often went out together, each with our rifle. I think, actually, that we got closer than we had been before. We'd seen the precipice and decided to walk away from it. It made us stronger.

FORTY-SIX

On Thanksgiving Day we gathered in the lodge, the smell of sizzling hotcakes drawing us in. We'd spent the previous day cleaning and preparing.

"Wow, isn't this beautiful? I love it!" Sue ran around the place.

The room was decorated with boughs of spruce and holly. Paper chains hung across the ceiling. On the table there was the most extraordinary candelabra, two feet across, two feet high, a whirl of branches in a bed of pine cones, leaves and acorns, with a dozen lighted candles.

"Bob's been working on this for the last few days," Louise said. Jessie went up to him and kissed him on the cheek.

"It's lovely, Bob, thank you."

For the first time, I saw Bob blush. "Just bits of driftwood," he mumbled.

"Now, it's a nice day, not too cold," Louise said, as we sat around the table eating the hotcakes drizzled with blueberry jam. "When I was a child, my mother's family used to go in mourning today, remembering the times that their lands were taken over by the white people. Thanksgiving Day for them was a time of bad memories. We're also in mourning today, because we've been overtaken by disaster. We have bad memories. The future's uncertain. But here we are, today, and have a lot to be thankful for. We've survived, we've met each other, we have new friends. So today I'd like us to focus on that. There are only a few hours of daylight, so we're going to use those for a treasure hunt outside. We'll have dinner this afternoon."

"A treasure hunt!" Sue squealed, jumping up and down. "I love treasure hunts."

"There are a few clues you'll need to work out," Louise continued. "Here's an envelope for each of you. Everything's within the perimeter of the fence, you don't need to go beyond that."

I took mine. The first part said;
Birch is good, but spruce is better.
High is dry, lower is wetter.
East is cold, west is warmer.
Search for the shoe
To find your next clue.

The wood stack? I found the shoe, high up on the west side amongst the spruce logs, the next clue inside. There were a dozen clues to follow. The treasure was in a hollowed out oak, wrapped in greaseproof paper. I opened it and gasped, it was a ring, looked like a diamond set in a gold circle.

I was the first to finish. The others were wondering around, Louise giving occasional "hot" or "cold" hints. I took her to one side.

"Dang, Louise, who's is this?

"It was my mothers. She gave it to me, I'm giving it to you."

"I can't take it, it's too much."

"I don't want it any more, Jim. And anyway, you don't have to keep it, you can give it to Jessie."

"But..."

"I mean it, Jim. It's not my business. But if you're serious, do it. You don't have to do it now, just take it, see how things go, and we'll keep it a secret between ourselves. I've got some nephews and nieces somewhere, but I know I'm not likely to see them again. I'd love it if you could use it."

An hour or so later and we were all back in the lodge.

"That was wonderful, Louise," Mom said. "You must've spent ages on it. So what've we all got?"

Bob held up a framed print showing all of us on the porch outside – it was the picture Louise had taken in the summer.

"I'm just choked," he said, struggling to get the words out. "The last picture of me I saw, it was a police mugshot. I've never seen one of me with other people." He ran his hand across his face. "How can I give you something in return?"

"You're very welcome, Bob," Louise replied. "And you already do, give back, I mean – not just to me, to all of us. We've much to thank you for," she ended quietly.

Matthew held up a rack of kitchen tools, hand carved.

"These are just so great," he said, a big grin splitting his face. "I don't know where you got them from, Louise."

"Bob carved them. I hope they'll come in useful."

Dad had a picture of Bess and me. Mom, a beaded pouch.

"For your first aid things, rather than carrying them around in those plastic boxes," Louise said.

"Oh my gosh!" Bess was stunned. "These jewels, Louise, it's too much!"

"They look valuable, Louise," Mom said. "Are you sure?"

"I don't know what they're worth, they've come down the family on my grandfather's side. He was wealthy, so they might be valuable, but what's the point of that today?" She smiled at Bess. "Keep them if you like them, Bess. I'd be grateful. You'll be doing me a favor."

Bess started laughing, and laughing.

"Bess, what's up?" Mom asked anxiously.

"I was just thinking, Mom, about when you said we could play games like we did at that Thanksgiving, when we were kids. And here we are, doing it again. Things haven't changed that much, have they? And maybe it's not so bad after all."

"I so love this, thank you," Sue said and went over to Louise to hug her. It was a traditional native Alaskan doll, in costume, with gold seams in the dress.

"Louise, are you sure?" asked Jessie. She was holding up a native Alaskan headdress. It was incredibly intricately worked, with hundreds of colored beads that fringed the face and hung down over the shoulders.

Louise got up, went over to Jessie and arranged it on her

head. "It's been in our family for generations. I wore it when I got married. I've got no one to pass it on to, and no point in it piling up dust. I've got too much stuff, that's why I'm giving it away. I'd be honored if you would take it, Jessie."

"But how did you know it was going to come in useful, Louise?" asked Mom. "Why bring it?"

"I just reckoned there might be the possibility of not going back to that house, Mary. So I brought along what mattered to me. My mother used to say that if you can't carry what you value with you, you've got too much stuff."

"I wish I'd done that," Mom replied.

"Louise," Matthew looked troubled, "I'm ashamed to say, I didn't know you'd been married. What happened?"

Louise laughed. "I'm too much of an old crow to have ever been young? Yes, I was a maiden once, Matthew, and a mother. My husband and baby were killed in a car crash."

I was stunned. It had never occurred to me that Louise had ever been anything other than a rather old lady. I looked closely at her face, imagining it without the wrinkles – yes, she must have been beautiful once.

"I'm so sorry, Louise," Mom said. "It must still hurt?"

"I didn't actually know my husband that well to begin with, my brother found him for me – we didn't exactly go in for courtship where I grew up. Choices were limited." She smiled wanly. "But we got to love each other. I've never really got over it. But I say a prayer every morning, it helps."

"A prayer to God?" Dad asked.

"Depends on which God you mean, Donald. I don't believe in the Christian one who sent his son Jesus down to earth to save us. Back in those days, gods were always coming down to earth and sleeping with women or men or swans and producing semi-divine humans, going back to heaven, and so on. If I was going to be a pagan, like that, I'd sooner believe in the gods of my tribe, those of mountain, water, the gods of nature. But that's just my opinion. In my tradition, every tribe has their own gods, and you respect them. I respect the belief of Christians. And an intelligence behind everything, a spirit, that the universe is conscious in some way, rather than just matter, I believe in that, yes. And that in some way I'll be with my husband and child again. It's why I could never remarry."

"I don't mean to attack your beliefs," Dad said. "But that's just not true, Louise, there's no evidence for it."

"You're a good man, Donald," Louise replied. "But you know what they say; when an engineer wants to know about life he asks a biologist, and when he needs to explain his evidence he asks a chemist, and a chemist has to ask a physicist, who has to say that there is no evidence, that we don't know what matter is, and can't find most of it, so he has to ask God. And maybe there's no purpose or meaning to anything. But people have believed in Spirit of some kind since we came down from the trees. Now that we don't believe in anything, except possessions, where has that got us? Look at what's happened over the last year...we're going to have to believe in something if we're going to hang together. Something to hold us."

"Could you tell us one of your prayers?" asked Sue.

Louise thought for a moment. "Well, here's one of my favorites, Sue.

I give you this one thought to keep: I am with you still – I do not sleep. I am a thousand winds that blow, I am the diamond glints on snow, I am the sunlight on ripened grain, I am the gentle autumn rain.

When you awaken in the morning's hush, I am the swift, uplifting rush of quiet birds in circled flight. I am the soft stars that shine at night.

Do not think of me as gone – I am with you still – in each new dawn."

FORTY-SEVEN

We ran around the Lodge in a silly dance contest, seeing who could do the weirdest things with their limbs, all falling over occasionally onto the floor. Sue was declared the winner. After a while Matthew called out, "Dinner's up!"

We sorted ourselves out around the table. Matthew had even arranged name cards along with the place mats. The candles flickered away.

"Smoked salmon starter, with dill and onion," he began. "No lemon juice, I'm afraid, but I've made this herb sauce."

"This is wonderful," Louise said between mouthfuls. "I've never had better."

The main course was ptarmigan braised in deer stock, with side helpings of greens and small new potatoes. "How did you make this mustard?"

"It's basically wild celery and a bit of left-over Dijon."

"Where did the potatoes come from, Dad?" asked Jessie.

"I found a few small, wild ones. Not many, I saved them up for this."

The pudding was a fruit pie, crammed with blueberries, raspberries, cranberries.

"Thank you so much, Matthew," Mom said, as we were finishing. "Do you know? This is the best Thanksgiving Day I can remember."

After we had cleared up, Louise spoke again.

"Now, I know the last few months have been hell in many ways. And they still are for most of the world. We've probably lost friends and family. But we're here and have good reasons to be thankful for that. So as this is Thanksgiving Day, I'd like to suggest something. I have sheets of paper here and pencils. I'd like everyone to write something down. Something positive. Do share it, be as honest as you can. It could be your favorite memory from childhood. Or what good thing's happened in your life this year. Or something nice you can say about the person sitting next to you. It doesn't really matter what it is. Try and keep it to one sentence, half a dozen words. That's difficult, I know, but I want us to focus on what good has happened. Shall we break for half an hour, so you can think about it?"

"I don't need to think about it," said Bess. "I've made a new best friend."

"And I've found a family," added Sue. "I don't know where they were before, but they're here now."

Matthew laughed. "Well, I guess I'd have to support my daughter in that one. It's been meeting you guys. I've felt adrift out here and I miss my work, the structure it gave me. But you've helped me a lot. I wouldn't say I've got used to it, but I hate to think what would've happened if we hadn't met."

"I've never really learned to write," said Bob. "Didn't pay much attention at school. But this has been the best year of my life, and I'd like to thank you all for that."

Mom got up, went over to him and kissed him on the head. "That's so nice, Bob, thank you."

"Me and Jim have met," said Jessie. "And we're going to stay together. That's the best thing that's ever happened to me."

I thought for a while. "I'd like to thank you all. This is the first year I've really felt alive."

"You've grown up, Jim," Dad said. "I'm sorry about the circumstances, but it's been great to see."

Mom sniffled a tear. "I'm just so thankful we've all met and are here. I don't understand why all this has happened, but I love you all. "

"How did you two meet?" asked Matthew, curiously.

"I had to go to the medical unit when I injured my fingers in a lathe," Dad said, holding up his left hand and pointing to the scar. "Mary was the nurse on duty. She was so unfussed by the blood and careful with the bandaging. I remember thinking to myself that she cared about people in the kind of way I cared about engines. I knew she'd look after me, and she always has."

"Oh, Donald, don't be silly, you've got this the wrong way around," Mom replied, blushing a little. "You've been looking after me."

"Seems to me you've done a great job of looking after each other and brought up two fine children in the process," said Louise. "As have you, Matthew."

"Thanks, Louise." Mom hugged her. "And it's been so great having you here. Now, there's one thing you could all do for me. I'm not one for war, or nationalism, but I'd like to hear the national anthem one more time, the Star-Spangled Banner."

"What's that?" asked Sue.

"It was a poem, called *The Defence of Fort M'Henry*," Louise replied. "It was written the morning after a critical battle for the fort in Baltimore, which the British were trying to take. If they'd succeeded it could've split the country in two. We used to sing it at school every day when I was a child, but it's not so much in fashion nowadays. For old times' sake, I'd like to hear it as well. I can't remember the words though. Does anyone?"

"I can sing it," volunteered Jessie," I had to in front of School Assembly once."

And she did it well, with feeling. I knew by now she had a good voice, but I still got a real kick out of it. I was glued to the seat.

"That was beautiful, Jessie," Mom said. "Have you been taught to sing?"

"No, but I did go to piano lessons for a few years. My teacher encouraged me to sing along with her."

"I used to tinkle the ivories a bit when I was in the army," Bob added. "Just bar songs. I miss it."

"You know, I don't think we've got a single instrument here," Dad said thoughtfully. "We should find some next year. I'm not musical myself, but it would be great if you kids could pick up something."

"You mean make our *own* music?" asked Bess.

"Not much point in ones that we can't repair or replace," Louise commented. "We couldn't get new strings for a violin, for instance. But we should look at the native ones, drums and pipes. How about thinking of some aims for next year?"

"I'd like to play a pipe," said Sue.

"If we could get some skates, I'd like that," Bess chipped in. "It always looked so elegant. I'd like to skate faster than any of the boys I might meet, so they can chase me."

"Skiing is going to be important," I said. "I can do it a bit, but I'd like to get good at it. And I'd like to be able to carve."

"I can help you with that," Bob replied.

"I'd like to play the harmonica," Jessie added.

"I've got something for Donald and I to do," Mom added. "We've been slow on the uptake here, but we're going to get used to the outdoors. We're going to go for hikes, with backpacks and rifles, like Bob, Jim and Jessie do, and brave the bears. OK, Donald?"

Dad laughed. "OK, Mary, we'll do it together."

"And I'd like to learn to shoot," Louise responded. "Right, we have some targets, let's get good at what we want to do."

FORTY-EIGHT

Thanksgiving Day passed and we took up our usual routines. With all the physical work and the cold and ice, we seemed to be always banging ourselves, slipping, making mistakes when we were tired. There was a steady stream of minor injuries. I stripped skin when picking up my gun by its frozen barrel, having left it outside in the porch overnight. Bob got quite steamed up with me over such a small thing.

"Now what would you've done if you were out on your own? You've got to use your gourd more, Jim, you only get the one chance. It's the little things that kill you. If that went sceptic, you're dead. You're not as dim as this."

I was in the doghouse with him for a few days after that.

But we survived over the next few months, even flourished, and very happily in my case. Christmas came and went without problems. There were four or five hours of daylight, when we tried to get out. We gradually became acclimatized to the lower temperatures. We walked around our trails, checking traps, compacting the snow down with each trip. As the trails hardened, snow banks built up around them and animals also used them. Jessie and I got the stove going again, finding the knack of leaving the right amount of embers in it so it only needed topping up a couple of times a night. We had long evenings together in the lodge, when we would variously work on projects – Dad was building non-battery crystal radios while Mom talked with other ham operators. Bess would still grumble, but loved her jewels, and Jessie and Louise worked with her in making necklaces and anklets; sewing them into deerskin. "You look like an Indian princess, now," Louise said. "Now how about a decorated waistcoat, and we need something to go around your forehead."

With the lake frozen, we used an iron rod and chisel to make a hole and fished there with occasional success.

"Cover the hole with a board and put snow on top to slow down the freezing for next time," Bob instructed. "And take a stool with you. Sit on the ice too long and you'll get polaroids." He chuckled. "Hey, have you heard the story of the drunk Alaskan who goes ice fishing...no? He saws a hole, and this big voice booms out "You'll find no fish there." He looks around. "God, is that you?" he asks. "No," the voice replies, "I'm the manager of the ice rink."" He roared out laughing.

But one thing happened which I find it still difficult to think about.

Bob, Jessie and me were tracking another moose, a big bull. We'd been following it for a couple of hours. It had circled around in the direction of the cabins we'd seen a few months earlier. Banks of ice fog were rolling down the mountainside, making the tops invisible, the wind was whistling around the canyons. The day was greying, and the further down the canyon we went the colder it got. It was like walking down into a clammy freezer. The clouds were thick with snow.

"I'm worried, Bob. We should get back. I think we've lost the trail."

"A bit longer, Jim, we're getting close. Just taking a short cut. He'll be on that rise over there."

But we got stuck in impenetrable thickets of alder, twenty foot high tangles of knotted, twisted black wood. It was oppressive, gloomy.

"You're always telling me to follow my instinct, Bob, and we're shit out of luck here."

"OK," said Bob. "This isn't going to work. Best not to push ourselves into problems. Look, as we're here, let's go check out that cabin we saw earlier, that single guy. We're not going to get back tonight anyway and it's on our way. If he's still there, we can find out what he knows. If not, we can camp there, use the stove, see if he's left anything useful."

It was getting dark when we got there. There were no lights burning. We hollered, but nobody came out. We walked up to the door. There was a snow-covered hump in front of it.

Bob started sweeping the snow off. It was a corpse! The skin was blue, covered in ice crystals. The eyes had gone and much of the emaciated face.

"The voles've been at him," said Bob, pointing. "You can see their droppings here, and the tunnels they've made through the snow to get to him."

"Oh, that's so awful!" Jessie paled. "The poor guy. What happened?"

"Starved to death, I reckon," said Bob. "Look, we can't get back now, we'll have to sleep in here, unless you'd prefer to bivouac outside."

We opened the door, and it was a shambles. Animals had been in and the smell was overpowering.

"I'm sleeping outside," said Jessie. "The bag's warm enough."

"OK, Jessie. Let's camp over there, out of the wind," Bob agreed. We'll get a fire going, make some tea. There's some sticks of dried fish in my pack. You make a start, I'll check the cabin."

He made a torch with a ball of resin wrapped with wire around a cleft stick; a few minutes later he was back. "We're in luck," he said. "A semi-automatic, .223, it's light caliber but you can get thirty rounds into this clip. This'll be good for Louise. Two boxes of ammo. Some useful tools, and a handgun. I think it's a Magnum. Could come in useful at close quarters. We'll take them back with us – will be heavy, but we can manage between the three of us."

The next morning, we talked about what to do. The sky was overcast. The world a grey, monochrome sludge. There had been a few inches of snow but nothing to slow us down. I shivered.

"It's only a little out of our way to the other cabin," Bob said. "I reckon we should detour for it, see what's going on, and then we should be back by the evening. We just need to avoid the side of the river, that's where any bad ice is going to be. So we'll circle around a bit."

We got there, and again hollered out when we were still way back. There was no answer. "Looks empty, no smoke, let's see if there's anything we can take," said Bob, cocking his rifle. "Have your rifle ready, in case a grizzly's made its den there for the winter."

We were coming up to the front steps when the door swung open and I had a brief impression of a ragged skeleton standing there, a few feet away, with a shotgun. He was screaming something as he fired at Bob. I was shouting, "No! No!" as I shot him, the force hurling him inside and across the room.

Bob was on the ground, Jessie cradling his head, her tears falling onto his face. I checked his pulse. He was dead. It couldn't be! But the bullet had taken him in the chest, half of it was torn away. There was blood everywhere, on his clothes, on my hands. I moved like a robot. There might be someone else inside. I went in. The guy was spread-eagled on the floor, no one else. The stove was cold, the cupboards empty, apart from piles of old, yellowing magazines, Playboys. Water dripped from the roof, pooling on the floor.

"Son of a bitch!" I screamed. I wanted to mash him into pulp, but there wasn't much of him to mash. He was all bones, with a few wisps of hair on his head. His skin was discolored. He'd lost most of his teeth. His clothes were tattered rags. He smelled terrible.

I came back out. Bob looked peaceful, slightly surprised, his eyes staring. "Bob, Bob." I took over from Jessie, cradling his head. With the fire gone from his face, the quirk of his mouth straightened out, no sarcastic look in his eyes, he just looked like a tired old man. "He was like a father to me, Jessie," I said after a while. "This is so unfair. He's the last person who should have died here. He's kept us all alive. I don't know what I'm going to do without him. Jessie hugged me. "What're we going to do?"

I felt something break inside me. Something strange was happening in my chest, throat, eyes…for the first time in my life, I sobbed.

"And I've killed again."

"You couldn't have done anything else, Jim." Jessie said, tears streaming down her face. "I'm so sorry. I wish it had been me who'd shot him. I would've done it for you."

"Twice, Jessie, twice. I've killed two people. I'm a real murderer now."

"Jim, you're not! It was self-defense. He killed Bob first. There was nothing else you could do."

"Oh God, is this what it's going to be like? It was just too quick, Jessie. I want to talk to him. I want to tell him I love him."

"Jim, listen to me." She was looking at me fiercely. "We are going to get through this, OK? Bob didn't die for you to go feeling sorry for yourself," she muttered, her chest heaving. "But it's done. Now…come on, let's start clearing up."

FORTY-NINE

We carried Bob inside, he seemed to weigh nothing. I took the guns, the ammo and the tools, closed the door, and we spent the rest of the day trekking back to the lodge. As soon as we came in, everyone could see something bad had happened. We explained.

"I can't believe it," Dad said, looking white. "I thought he was invincible. And he was right, as usual, we didn't all make it through the winter. It just doesn't seem fair that it was him."

"I was so nasty to him," Bess sobbed. Louise hugged her. "He knew your heart, Bess."

"That guy who killed him, he probably wasn't a bad man," said Mom later. "From what you say, he was starving to death. That brings on convulsions, hallucinations, it's like being on LSD, but worse – he probably had no real idea of what he was doing. But I feel terrible about the things I've said to Bob. I'd never really even thanked him for what he's done for us."

"What I don't understand," said Dad, "is how come these guys didn't do more to help each other? They were only a couple of miles apart."

"Maybe they tried," said Louise, "but neither could actually help much, because they didn't know how to in this new world. And after all, they were only ten or so miles away from us, and we didn't help."

"You think we should've helped them?" railed Dad. I'd rarely seen him so angry. "Dammit, Louise, Bob was right all along. We just refused to see it. We can't make everyone our responsibility. We've got enough to do with looking after ourselves here."

"You're sounding like Bob. If that's really what you and everyone else thinks," she replied sadly, "then we all die separately."

"Never mind all this ethical worrying," Matthew said. "This is a disaster. Bob was the lynchpin here, he knew how to survive in this damned wilderness. We're sunk without him. We'll end up like those starving guys."

"We can figure out how to recover from this later," said Mom. "I'm sure we can. But for the moment, how are we going to bury him?"

"We should bring him back here and put him in a grave," said Dad.

"Why don't we dig a grave back there?" asked Jessie.

"So do we have two graves down there then," asked Mom, "one for him and one for the guy who shot him? Or do we only bury him, and not the guy who was out of his mind with starvation?"

"We can't dig graves around here, in this ground, with a spade, it's frozen solid," Matthew commented.

"So should we just leave the bodies there?" Bess asked. "Nature will take care of it. That's what you guys keep saying, isn't it? Work with nature?"

Louise interrupted. "It's generally accepted that when a valued member of the tribe dies, or indeed any member, that some kind of ceremony is in order. Otherwise there's nothing to bind the tribe together. If we just leave them, without anything – there are animals who show more respect than that."

I jerked myself up and interrupted. "This is what we're going to do. He's inside the cabin, I've taken out anything we might need. His killer is inside there as well. We'll take the body from the other cabin into it. Then we'll burn it, like a funeral pyre, like the Vikings used to do. Down to the ground. I would've done it yesterday, except I thought you might want to be there for it. You can't stop me on this. He was my friend. I think it's what he would've wanted. Anybody who wants to come with me, we're leaving tomorrow morning. I don't want to talk about this anymore." Dad raised his eyebrows, but no one objected, and I walked out.

The next day, luckily, the weather was brighter.

"This is the first time we've all been out together," I said. "We'll probably be back tonight, but we'll take rations for three days. Louise, your hip isn't going to make it, you can travel on the sled, we'll have two pulling. We'll take another sled for the gear. Jessie, could you check that everyone's dressed well enough. I don't want us coming back with frostbite. Particularly Louise, as she won't be moving. Now, let's get things together."

We all trekked over to the cabin in a somber mood. It was hard going, so we split into two parties, myself and Jessie up ahead, with the others following at their own pace. Jessie and I collected the other body on the sled and started piling up burning material inside the killer's cabin. By the time the others arrived, we were ready to go.

His hands were frozen rigid, but I put his favorite wood-carving chisel into one, and a piece of jerky in the other. I set fire to the pile of straw and wood in the cabin and stepped out. The flames soon took hold. Within moments they were licking up the walls, reflected in the snow. Soon, it was a furnace, the wind lashing the flames, whipping the sparks high into the air and we had to step back some yards. The structure collapsed in a roar of fire, and then started dying down. After a while, just the embers were left, glowing in the grey desolation all around. The temperature dropped down to the minus fifteen of the surroundings.

It was zero dark thirty. We had to help Louise back on the sled. It took us hours to get back, trudging through the snow; Dad and Matthew, Jessie and myself, taking it in turns on the ropes. I did most of the work; it helped, but my mind still churned over. The path ahead looked bleaker. I was going to have to be responsible. Was I ready for it? The grown-ups – Dad, Mom, Matthew, Louise – I loved them all. But they couldn't manage out here by themselves. Bob had always been right. There was room in this new world for sentiment, for love, but not for weakness. In a moment of clarity, I knew I had to step up to the plate, or we were all going to die.

The sky was blazing white with stars, the Milky Way streaming across the heavens, a pathway to other worlds. I pulled like an automaton, homing for the lodge without thinking about it, the constellation of Ursa Major, the Great Bear, angled to my left. All those suns, so far away, with their own planets, billions of them. Memories of a science lesson at school came back to me, along the lines of "Throw a pea into the Atlantic Ocean, and that's the size of Earth in the solar system. Then make the solar system the size of a pea, throw it in again, and that's the solar system in our galaxy. Then make our galaxy the size of a pea, and throw it in again. That's our galaxy in the universe."

And on this microscopic speck of dust, with billions of people on it, one had just disappeared, returned to ash. And it hurt me. The last time I'd been on a night trek, after killing the moose, I remembered feeling so happy about it. Now, after another single shot, I'd never felt so bad.

We were such a small huddle of a group, struggling through the frozen snow, completely isolated, not much different from the humans who first came into Alaska from Siberia several hundred generations earlier. They probably had better clothes, but we had the same transport, the same thoughts, the same loves and hates, the same uncertainties. And as the world wheeled through the heavens, the clock of time seemed to tick back, forwards, back again, and I thought that nothing ever really changes. This was the future, repeating the past; a tiny group, carrying its old and infirm, in a hostile universe, heading into the unknown.

PART FOUR

SPRING

FIFTY

Bob's death, and my second killing, put some iron into my soul, which even Jessie couldn't remove. Our relationship changed subtly. She was still the center of my life, but I had a larger purpose now, into which she fitted. I think she understood that, and it made us stronger rather than weaker. Killing Mr. Trinker had seemed like an accident, like something I'd have to account for, but could just about explain. This had been different. I could still explain it, but now I thought that the explanation didn't matter. I'd do it again, as often as was necessary.

When I was out now, I looked at the world through Bob's eyes. It really was as if he was still with me, and I didn't bother using the compass anymore. There were a myriad ways of finding your direction, from remembering landmarks, the lie of the hills, the way the wind and sun shaped the trees, the movement of water, the direction of snowmelt, snowdrifts and shadows, the orientation of the anthills, the position of lichen and moss on the trees – it was becoming second nature to me. Besides, I felt Bob walking alongside me, his occasional sarcastic barbs opening my eyes to the life around.

I didn't see "wilderness" anymore, in the sense of human absence, but I did see the "wild." It wasn't empty of life, it was full, as full as it could possibly be. But it was life at the margins. Every living thing on the surface, above it, beneath it, had its own mechanisms for survival, had evolved for that purpose, treading the finest of lines between life and death. There was no "comfort zone" in this world. It was hard, and the weaker went to the wall. There was no welfare out here, no support services. You had to fight for life. It was a zero-sum game. For one animal to live, others had to die. That was the DNA of nature. There was never any Garden of Eden. We had to relearn how to live.

And people were weak. Even Mom and Dad – we were all

weak. I loved them, more than ever – I don't think I really knew what that meant back in Anchorage – but I became more aware of the grey in Dad's hair, of how he sometimes lost his specs, the slight tremor in his right hand, his bad cough. Of the way Mom tried to conceal her unhappiness in this wilderness country by being cheerful and raising everyone's morale, of Matthew's uncertainty in this different landscape, and Bess's fear.

Here, on the one hand, life had no intrinsic value. On the other hand, it was everything. We had to find again our place in this web. I moved from thinking, "this is beautiful, but I'm scared of being prey," to thinking "this is my world, I'm part of it, it's part of me, and I'm the predator." This was the real world now, of bears and wolves, grunts and screams, cold and hunger, exhilaration and despair. We had to be sharp every day, every minute, senses alert, thinking ahead, there weren't any second chances.

I struggled to remember the boy I'd been – hesitant, obedient, shy, collecting stamps. It was like looking down the wrong end of a telescope, at someone in the distant past. Still "me," but at the other end of a long tunnel of time. We never openly discussed it, but I sensed a shift in the dynamics of all our relationships from then on. It was tacitly understood between us now that things weren't going to be easy, there was no going back to the old days, and we each needed to be all-rounders, as far as we could. We shared the cleaning, the sewing, the hundred tasks that needed doing every day. But we also gravitated into the things we were best at. Dad, for instance, could shoot, but had little sense out in the open of what to do, where to go. Matthew could fire a rifle, but couldn't hit the proverbial barn door. Mom could shoot, in theory, but we all felt safer if she wasn't trying to. So I became, by default, the provider, along with Jessie.

We generally went out hunting together now; she wasn't as good as me with the rifle – I was feeling more confident all the time – but she had an eye for it as well. We were both increasingly fit – Jessie had been good on the track, back at school. She was faster than me, if she put her mind to it, and we were both out all the time, ranging about rather than sitting at a desk. What with checking out the traps in a ten-mile radius every couple of days, we soon came to know every ridge, ravine, river and hummock like the back of our hands. In February, the sun began to return, with amazing sunsets. By now the squirrels and jays around the lodge were almost tame and would take nuts from Sue's hand, which thrilled her. She had the knack of standing totally still for minutes at a time while they picked from her hand, even settling on her shoulder.

The following month the rivers were still frozen, the waterfalls were solid ice, but the air was softer, the glaciers sparkling blue in the light. Almost imperceptibly at first, the sun got a little warmer, the days a little longer. The winter underwear was put away and we could hang the laundry outside to dry. In April we were getting up to fourteen hours of sunshine a day, when it wasn't raining, and the snow started to melt. It was break-up time. It began at the tips of the stalactites all around the lodge roof, with a single drip once every few minutes. The ground turned into impassable mush, which we couldn't get through even on show shoes, except on our hard packed trails. The lake began steaming in the low-lying sun. There were still heavy frosts, but the ice began to shift in the rivers, leaving pools of water on top, till you couldn't see where to step in case you fell into deep open water. Along the cracks, the slab edges pushed over each other, till they looked like miniature versions of Antarctica, with jagged slopes and peaks. The volume of water increased and soon – now a dirty brown rather than the gin-clear of winter – it was roaring down the valleys and you could hear the grinding of the boulders being swept along the bottom. The Portage River became impassable, with icebergs the size of cars tumbling over and over as they were carried in the torrent down to the sea. The hillsides were a riot of shades of green, the dark green of the pines turning to light green, yellow at the tips. We hunted down one side of it nearly as far as Whittier. We had to change from our light, dry, warm, mukluks into thigh-high waterproof boots that we'd brought from Anchorage. We had the polytunnels back up and some vegetable shoots were poking out of the ground, promising a change in our diet of mostly fish and meat.

A couple of times we visited the cabin which we'd burned, with the three bodies inside. There were just charred timbers left. There was a gap somewhere, we were missing something. What could I say in his memory? I found a nice, flat, granite slab and started chipping with chisel and hammer.

BOB, FRIEND AND MENTOR, LIES HERE. MAY HIS SPIRIT
LIVE FOREVER

"He'll always be with us," said Jessie, reading my thoughts, as she cooked some fish we'd caught that morning over the fire.

"It's not the same though," I told her morosely as I finished digging out the words from the stone. It had taken me three days, while we camped out there.

"No, it's not. But I'm starting to think like Louise, even like your Mom. He's out there somewhere, watching us. We'll survive, like he wanted us to. And we always have his memory in us…that's all we have, that any of us have."

"What use is a memory? It's his help we need."

Jessie came over, took my face in her hands and kissed me on the lips. "Don't go getting weak on me, Jim. Memories make us. You remember what you told me about how Indians would make cairns or fires in the desert, so they could look back and check they were travelling in a straight line? Those are our memories. We're going to make our own now. I know what we can do. We're going to get there. And you're going to believe in yourself."

We placed the slab on top of a cairn of stones. Jessie collected some spruce branches for the fire as I thought about him, wondering whether there really was a world beyond this one, and if so, whether it was the Christian idea of heaven, which I couldn't understand, nobody ever seemed to try and explain it – where was it? Why? What did people do there? Valhalla made more sense than that. I couldn't imagine Bob being happy in heaven – maybe he'd gone to the spirit world of the native Indians or been reincarnated in a new baby, as many believed in these parts. Out here, in the bush, it was easier to believe like the Indians – everything was dying, decomposing, growing again. Every atom stayed the same, just recombining in new earth, beetles, trees and people. Bob's ashes would feed the grass, which would be grazed by deer, which we would shoot and eat, so we were all part of everything, forever.

We were lying on grass in a clearing of cottonwoods, where the snow had melted away. Jessie had her arm around me. Not far from us two cranes were courting: musically chortling, bowing, skipping, leaping. I thought they looked like the civilized couple, compared to us, going through their elegant rituals. I started stroking her breasts. She pulled off her shirt and then her pants and we made love, frantically. Death, love, life.

FIFTY-ONE

Or might he come back as a bear? I wondered about that. Particularly as the first adult male bears started to come out of hibernation. He'd always seemed like a bear to me, a bit reclusive, solitary, unpredictable, but fierce and loyal.

A few days later, we were woken by a commotion. There was the sound of growling and rifle shots, growing to a crescendo, a roaring, as if the hounds of hell were around us, and shouting. I jumped out of bed, my heart pumping, grabbed my rifle and ran outside our cabin, heedless of the stones underfoot, putting a round in. Then I heard the deep-throated boom of the Remington 870. I turned the corner of the lodge and Matthew and Bess were ahead, the smoke of the gunshots still in the air, a big grizzly slumped, tangled in the barbed wire. It was huge, looked like as big as a moose, several times the size of any of us. It had pulled down about thirty feet of fence. Half a dozen posts had been splintered off or pulled out of the ground. Another half dozen leaning drunkenly.

"Bess killed it," Matthew said, looking astonished, shaking, the reaction setting in. "I heard it trying to get through the fence. It was trying to climb it. I wounded it and it went mad. Bess came out after me, and she shot it. She shot it real good. "

I looked at Bess, she was trembling. "I didn't want to do it. Gosh, my shoulder really hurts."

"Bess, thank you." I put my rifle down and hugged her. "I don't know what to say. You got one before I did. Well done. That was an amazing thing to do. Especially choosing the shotgun. Really quick thinking. You'll probably come up with big bruises on your shoulder."

She looked at me curiously, and I realized I was naked.

Jessie had joined us, carrying a rifle, she'd taken the time to put my shirt on.

"Wow, Bess. You killed this bear? It's ginormous! You're a hero."

Louise, Sue, Mom and Dad were out a moment later.

"Look at those teeth," Sue gasped. The canines were as long as my fingers.

"Why's it so scraggy? Is it diseased?" Mom asked.

"He's shedding his winter coat," I replied, "you can see the new, dark one growing out underneath. It's one heck of a big one. Scares me just being close to it here. Jessie, could you get an ax, clippers, spade? We'll need to get it off the fence and then replace those posts. Thank God we had the fence there. At least it was slowed down for long enough."

"And you'd better go and get some clothes on first, Jim," Mom replied sharply. "You're scraggier than that bear is."

When I got back, dressed, a few moments later, everyone was still standing in a circle, a few yards away, all too nervous to get close. "Get a grip," I said to myself, and walked up to it. Tentatively, I put my hand on its head. The fur was deep and bristly. It was clearly dead, eyes staring, but still seemed to exude power and strength.

"This isn't the same thing as a deer," I said to Matthew, later. "How do we deal with them?"

"In one of the cabins we raided I found this old copy of *Hunters Pocket Guide to Field Dressing*," he replied, looking up from the book he was reading. "There's more fat on a bear than a deer. When we've taken off the head and paws, we suspend it from its hind legs a few feet off the ground, cut off the fat in pieces and keep it for lard. I can use that. We cut off the muscles that run along the spine from the bottom of the rib cage to the hind legs for steaks, and dice the rest. If we work on it together, it'll be easier."

We peeled off the rib meat and cut it away from shoulder, hip joints and limbs. Over the following days we dried the meat on racks, packed it into bags, and as the ice cave was now warming, we trekked to the glacier where we dug a deep hole, packed it in with ice and built a cairn of boulders on top to keep it secure as a reserve supply.

With the skin, we had to move quickly, before it started to decompose. We first scraped off the remaining flesh and fat with a fleshing blade, being careful not to scratch or puncture the hide. We boiled the brain in water till it was like soup. Then we washed the skin, bored holes around the edge and stretched it onto a drying rack for about a week. Then we scraped the hair off, washed it again, squeezed it dry and rubbed the brain oil over every inch of it. We let it soak in for a couple of days, then stretched it on the rack again, running a heavy stick over it for a couple of hours to get it nice and soft. When it was good and pliable, we sewed up the edges to make a bag, inverted it over a frame with a fire underneath, and smoked it for half an hour or so, then turned it inside out and did the other side. Hunter style, we put the head up on a peg in the lodge, with a sign underneath: "Killed by Bess Harding, age 15".

She was so proud of that, often standing in front of it, saying things like, "It's so huge! Look at it. I can't believe I did that."

Louise made her a necklace of the claws. "Oh my God, this is so much my favorite thing ever!"

I think something changed in her that day as well. I guess she reckoned she'd earned a role, a place at the table. There was less of the drama queen. The mutterings about how awful everything was died down. She wore the necklace every day. Years later, she was known by the natives as "Bear Woman." There were strong taboos against women killing bears, or eating bear meat. The fact that she had done it, without harm, meant she was a powerful spirit, not to be crossed.

That first skin took a long time, but we were getting the hang of it. When it was done, Louise showed me how to make waistcoats out of it. I'm wearing one of them now, as I write this.

There was another day, shortly after that, when Jessie shot

a whitetail. I was unpacking the knives from the rucksack, and Jessie, looking at the paintbrush a few feet away, said, "Hang on, Jim, what's this? It's her baby. Oh God, I've killed her mother!"

The fawn couldn't have been more than a couple of days old, only a few pounds, spindly legs. Silky skin, reddish brown, covered in hundreds of white spots.

"We'll take it back, Jessie, nothing else we can do. Perhaps Sue could look after it." I tied her legs together with a scarf and we carried her back. After a few struggles she lay quietly in my arms.

"Oh, it's so beautiful," Sue said, after we carried it back to the lodge. "Can I touch it?"

When I untied her, she wobbled on her spindly legs and then nosed around the room. Sue stroked her and she nuzzled her hand, licking it.

"She wants feeding," Louise said.

Matthew got a little non-fat powdered milk we had left in the stores, boiled up some oatmeal, added sugar, and gave it to Sue with a rag.

"Dip the rag into this," he said, "and let her suck it."

After sucking it all up, the calf followed Sue around the room till she went to bed, when it lay down by her side. But the next morning, it was still and cold.

Sue was distraught. She cried all day.

"It wasn't meant to be, Sue," said Louise. "It had lost her real mother. Let's give it a nice burial in the garden, and make a headstone for it."

One evening we were talking around the fire.

"We're still snowed in up here," Dad said. "But I've been talking with Theo, he says the Seward Highway is clear around them now. They're having problems with people trying to get out of Kenai, fighting them for food. Armed bands wandering around. I wonder what it's like down on the coast."

"I thought our batteries had all run down in the cold?" Mom

asked.

"They have," Dad replied. "But I've managed to get through on this crystal radio I've built. There are far fewer operators around now though, I guess most have run out of power. Or they didn't last the winter."

"We should go see if anything's moving on the highway. Jessie and me could get there and back in a day. Or maybe we should go as far as Alyeska? That would take two or three days."

"That would worry me, Jim. If we do that, I think it should be more of us, going in the truck, when we can get that out through the snow. Which might be only a few days away, if this weather stays. As it is, I'd come with you to the highway, but I'd slow you down, I can't keep up with you two anymore."

"Sure you could, Dad," I replied. "But I'd feel safer if you were here."

"Do be careful, please," Mom said. "I know I'm just being a silly old woman, but I remember what Bob said about taking things slowly, not taking unnecessary risks, because you only get one chance out here."

"We will Mom," I replied. "But you know how it is, don't worry if we're not back tomorrow." And I remember thinking back then, that I really had better be careful. If they didn't have me or Bob, I wasn't sure that they'd survive for long.

"I'll pack you some grub," said Matthew. "Jerky, biscuits, juice, OK?"

FIFTY-TWO

Jessie and I left first thing the next day, wearing backpacks, and with three rifles between us. I had the Winchester strapped to the pack for moose and bear and carried the Ruger for the opportunistic shot at small game. I also now carried the Magnum which we had taken from the cabin, as extra protection. It all added up to a fair bit of weight, along with the tools, and a year ago I would have complained about that, but it had become second nature to me, no more trouble than the heavy parka. Jessie had her Winchester. The sun was shining, our hearts were light. Around the lodge, the snow was still piled high. Drifts covered the track, it would be a while before we could take the truck or a jeep out. But as we descended, it thinned out. Where it had melted there were sheets of wild flowers growing in the warming earth, the different yellows of cinquefoil and violet, the purples of iris and fireweed, the air alive with the hum of insects and bees.

By around midday we were getting close to the highway. Then I froze, and held Jessie still. Over the last few months I'd started to sense movement in the landscape before I registered what I was seeing. Off in the distance, to the right, a couple of miles away, there were several forms moving. At first, I couldn't tell what they were, my mind was so attuned to looking for animals they seemed like an alien presence, unknowable. And then I realized, they were people. The first living outsiders we'd seen for six months.

"Over here, Jessie."

We scrambled uphill to take cover behind some rocks and I looked at them more closely through the scope. Then I handed it to Jessie.

"Two men and two women, one of them supporting another. They look in a bad way, shuffling along, stumbling. And they're not dressed for outdoors."

"What shall we do?" Jessie asked.

"We study them till they get here, looks like they're going to pass within a hundred yards of us. We'll check there's no one else around, see if they're armed. Then talk to them. I'll get up and do the talking, you cover me."

It must have taken them an hour to get to us, they were so slow. But they seemed harmless. When they were opposite, a few yards away, I stood up. "Hi, folks."

The reaction wasn't one I'd intended. One of the women started running away, the other collapsed. One of the men sank to his knees, the other looked wildly around.

I hadn't realized I looked so threatening. I probably looked like a hunter to them – tanned, heavily armed, dressed for camouflage. Well, I guess I was. I slowly put my rifle down on the ground, took my hat off and laid it alongside, kept my arms away from my sides.

"I don't want to hurt you, I just want to talk." The woman who was running stopped and took a few steps back. I walked towards them. "It's OK, Jessie, you can come down."

The man still standing asked, "Who are you?" His speech was slurred, his jaw didn't seem to work properly. Gaunt, ashen-faced, with a long, straggly beard, he looked like he'd been in a cell for the last year. They all did. A couple were emaciated, in rags, blue and shaking in the cold.

"We live around here," I replied, as Jessie joined me. "My name's Jim, and this is Jessie. Who are you?"

"I'm Ethan, and this is Noah, Emma and Abby," he replied, indicating them. "We've walked from Anchorage."

"Why don't we sit down in the shade over here," I pointed to a tree, "and you can tell me about it. Would you like some tea? Give me a couple of minutes and I'll get a fire going."

"We'd be very grateful for that," he replied.

As we sat down and waited for the fire to boil a pan I'd

suspended over some twigs, the story came tumbling out.

"...and they were all roaring drunk, we managed to creep out. That was three days ago. A couple of months after they caught us. We've found some berries, drunk water from streams. There were five of us, but one fell through the ice – we hadn't realized it was thin. We couldn't get her out. She died so quick. It was terrible."

"Here," Jessie said, "we've got some food. Do take it. We've plenty."

"Slowly, slowly," I said, as they scarfed it down. "Bad for your stomachs if they're shrunk and you eat it too quick."

"They're animals, these convicts," Ethan was saying. "There's little food in Anchorage, no meat anyway, so they're eating people."

Jessie paled. "No way!"

"It's worse than that," Noah went on. "They keep them in the prison cells, sometimes just take a limb at a time, cauterize the wound with tar. You can hear the screams all day and night."

I stood up and walked around, trying to escape the gloom that seemed to envelop these poor people talking of horror under the midday sun.

"How many of them are there?"

"About two hundred, hard to tell exactly."

"Why aren't you walking along the road?" I asked, already knowing the answer. "It would be quicker."

"Because they could be looking for us along the road, we felt safer inland."

"You could stay with us," I said. "There's a spare cabin a few miles away, we could look after you."

He shook his head. "They'll find you, you know. It's not far enough away here. They're raiding places all around Anchorage for food, doesn't matter whether it's animal meat or human. Children or old people. And everyone's raped. The leader, Brutus, a serial killer, he's the worst. He enjoys torturing people. Sometimes they put them in with wild animals in the yard, for fun. In front of the lady here, I don't even want to start describing some of the things they do. We'll keep walking."

"You don't look in good enough shape to get far." I shook my head. It's a long way to get anywhere, Ethan, and it's not going to be any different when you get there."

He glanced back in a hunted fashion, to check there was no one following. "I don't believe that, I can't. There's got to be somewhere where people are living normally. But thanks for the offer. Really appreciate it. This is nowhere far enough away. If I was you, I'd start running as well."

"OK, though we're staying put. Anything else we can do for you?"

"Do you know what's happened down in California? I've got family there."

"I'm sorry. Seems like everywhere's a mess."

"My God. What's going to come of us all?"

"We're going to be alright, Ethan. We'll make it work."

"Really? When I thought about the world ending, I always assumed it would be with a bang, you know? I'd never have figured it would be because we couldn't switch the lights on."

"But a century or two back we didn't have lights, we just have to live like they did – they managed."

"I guess you're right, but this was so sudden...it's not the lights that's the problem, it's the people. Seems like the worse you are, the stronger you are. I've never been particularly religious, but it's Satan who rules here now, not God. How do you fight evil like that?"

After they had rested, we parted.

"Something to think about," I said.

"What are we going to do, Jim?"

"I don't know, Jessie, we'll talk back at the lodge. What a bummer. One thing for sure, we're going to have to fight, and the killing hasn't ended, it's barely started."

When we walked back into the lodge, I could sense immediately that something was wrong.

"Dad, are you OK?" Jessie ran over to Matthew, lying on a bed. Mom was bent over him, feeling his leg.

"We had an accident," Dad explained. "Me and Matthew were fixing some loose titles up on the roof. A rung of the ladder broke under Matthew and he slipped down. Fell awkwardly on some rocks and broke his leg."

Matthew tried to make light of it. "Oops! That was so stupid, so sorry," he groaned. He was grey and in pain.

"Wasn't your fault," I replied. "We should have fixed that ladder better. That was careless of us."

"I can't tell definitely without an x-ray," Mom said. "But it looks as if it's a clean break in the fibula, between the knee and the ankle. It could have been a lot worse. Matthew, you need to keep the leg raised like this, on the pillows. You'll just need to rest it for some time. I'll put ice on it every hour to reduce the pain and the swelling. Donald, could you and Jim go and find or make some splints for me to strap around the leg. And we'll need crutches for Matthew for when he starts to walk again. That's a few weeks away."

Dad and I left to get what she wanted. I couldn't help feeling relieved that it was Matthew who had fallen down the ladder rather than me. Who would then be the provider? Who would bring in the meat? We really were only a step away from disaster. One accident, and we were finished. Dad was right. We had to be part of a larger group, with room for specialisms, for different kinds of knowledge and skills.

"Dad," I said once we were out of earshot, "I need to tell you about the people Jessie and I met." His face grew grim as I spelled it out.

"Don't tell your Mom about this, it'll worry her silly," he said. "I'll talk with Theo, we'll need to meet up. I guess we're stuck here for a few weeks till we can get a jeep out. Still, at least the snow means they can't get to us yet."

FIFTY-THREE

Our birthdays were fairly evenly spread through the year and we got into the habit of letting the birthday person decide what they wanted to do that day. On mine, the third week in April, when I put my head outside the cabin, the day was cold, but crystal clear; you could see for miles, and I knew what I wanted.

"I'd like to go for a walk with Jessie," I said over a quick breakfast. "Not to bring back game, this time, just to get to the highest point we can."

We set off with our backpacks, full with rations, rifles, emergency supplies and snowshoes, heading uphill. I was feeling jacked up, it was so good to be out. We hadn't gone far when I heard a bird song which was new to me, a musical chattering, dying off at the end, coming from a clump of hazel and willow. We crept closer.

"I love that," I said, handing over the binoculars to Jessie. "A warbler, I think it's a Wilson's warbler, with that bright yellow and black cap. First time I've heard it."

"And how did that little thing survive the winter?"

"It couldn't. It flew down to Central America instead, probably just got back."

"You're kidding! It's no bigger than my thumb."

"Well, it's done it. Makes our job look easy, doesn't it? If a bird like that can commute five thousand miles... Now, I just want to get a good view of where we are, of where we've been over the last few months."

We walked fast, cruising speed, almost running, shaking off the lethargy of winter, steadily climbing, rarely stopping to look at tracks, ignoring the tempting sounds of partridge and squirrel and the sheep droppings. Huge rockfalls covered the mountainside, waterfalls poured over granite lips. After a few hours we were well above the tree line and we sometimes had to stop to put on our snowshoes to cross over blinding white drifts. The air got cooler, the tracks less common.

I suddenly stopped. "Several fresh wolf tracks here," I pointed out to Jessie.

"Look," she replied.

On the far hillside there was a group of them, loping along with tails down. I got out Bob's scope from the rucksack. "Five of them, a big male in front, a female, three youngsters."

"A family." Jessie nodded thoughtfully. "Your Dad was right, Jim, families come first. There are no friends out here."

We skirted a glacier, the dirty grey ice soaring above our heads, carved into bright blue fissures and canyons by the wind and rain. We jumped from rock to rock across the streams that tumbled musically down from it. By early afternoon we were about as high as we could get, short of having to cross the glacier itself.

A pair of sea eagles flew below us, swooping around the sky, heading for a clash at high speed, tangling their claws, spinning over and over, tumbling through the sky, locked together, separating at the last minute, when it seemed as if they were just going to crash to earth.

"Are they fighting?" Jessie asked.

"No, courting."

"I don't remember you coming after me like that, Jim."

"Next time, I'll try harder."

The views around us were glorious. We could see across to Prince William Sound in the east, across Turnagain Arm to Lake Clark wilderness in the west. To the north and south there were the mountain ranges and glaciers of Kenai and Chugach. Far below us I could just make out, through the scope, the smoke rising from the lodge. In the far, far distance, to the north, I could see the Denali range and the distinctive twenty-thousand-plus-foot peak of Denali itself, sacred to the Indians, spearing the sky.

"Wow, that's incredible, what is it?" said Jessie.

"It's Denali, means the mighty one, it sure is. Tallest mountain on earth, if you take it from the land base. It's about a hundred miles away."

"Wasn't it called McKinley?"

"Some bureaucrat called it that, after the guy who became president – neither of them had ever seen it."

I felt a sense of destiny up there, a foretaste of what was to come.

"This is our territory, Jessie," I told her. "This is what we're going to have to take."

"Take? You mean as in conquer?" Jessie looked up in surprise.

"Control," I replied. "You can see it – it's all one territory, bounded by these mountains. It's, what, a thousand square miles? But that's not much when you can see it all in one go. If we're going to be safe, this area needs to be safe."

"But it's huge," she replied. "How do you expect to control it?"

"I don't know. But it's a natural basin, a ring of mountains around the sea… I just feel…we can squabble around here forever, fighting between lodges, between small groups, killing each other off bit by bit or we can rule it."

"Are you sure you're different from the others?"

"I don't know, Jessie. I hope so, with your help. I know that nothing good had happened to me before I met you. And I know that we either live in fear from one month to another, wondering who's going to turn up next, or we take charge of what's going to happen, as far as we can, create a good society."

"I'll be with you on that, Jim."

I didn't understand then the significance of the ten-billion barrels of oil sitting in the storage tanks at Valdez. And how one action leads to another. And how centuries of history – millennia – can be telescoped into decades if the will, knowledge and resources are there; and similarly, how equally fast society can disintegrate if they're not.

We opened the lunch Matthew had prepared for us. "Look at this, where did your dad get this from?"

It was a bar of chocolate, with a note that simply read: "With my blessing."

Jessie kissed me with cold lips. "Well, if there's all this territory to take, we'd better start getting back before we freeze or we'll become part of the scenery."

We came back more slowly, talking about what we were going to do, and went skinny dipping in the river, gasping in the cold. It was getting dark when we reached home. Sue had prepared a birthday supper, following Matthew's instructions.

"Eskimo ice-cream," she said proudly, as she brought in the tray. "Dad gave me a recipe, bear fat whipped into a cream, with chopped venison and berries."

"Um, well," I had to say as I spooned it down hesitantly. "I guess the Eskimos like it. Thanks Sue."

"You know how the Eskimos used to survive through the winter, when they couldn't get outside for weeks or months on end?" asked Louise. "They would take a sealskin, fill it with everything they could – guts, birds, scraps – sew it up, tie it by the head to the top of the igloo, let it ferment, open the anus, and drink the juice that trickled out."

"Lovely, I'm sure," said Jessie, "but I'm not feeling that hungry."

"Not one of your better recipes, Matthew," Bess agreed.

"Sue, it was great," Mom said. "Maybe a bit ambitious for a first time, your dad and me will help you out on this. It's brilliant that you're starting to cook."

We chatted comfortably across the candles. When it was over, Dad stood up.

"Jim, I'd just like to say something. Your Mom and I had thought that for your eighteenth we'd get you a car, but," his mouth twitched, "even if we could get one out here, there's nowhere to drive it. We've put our heads together, but really can't think of anything we have that would do justice to the occasion.

None of us expected a year ago that we'd be in this situation. Now this is a kind of awkward thing to say, but I'd like to say it. It's not just that you're eighteen, but you've become a man now over these months, and I'm very proud of you. We both are."

Mom nodded.

"And I'd just like to offer you respect and responsibility. I'd like you to think of yourself as an equal partner with your mom and I. If anything, you seem to be better suited to this life than we are. So from here on, we decide things together. OK?"

I gulped and nodded. "Thanks, Dad, and Mom. Are you sure?"

"Jim," Louise interrupted brusquely, "I haven't known you as long as your Mom and Dad. But so long as you don't do anything stupid...fall into a crevasse, shoot yourself in the foot, you're going to be a leader. For thousands of years, the best hunters have been the leaders, and that time has come round again. You'll need to take on responsibilities. It's not an enviable position, but someone has to do it. Better get used to the idea."

FIFTY-FOUR

A few days later, we were in May. Back in Anchorage, I'd never really noticed the seasons. OK, it was hot or cold, dry or wet, but here, it was Life. Spring was coming on in leaps and bounds, as if the life-force had been released from its icy bars and was desperate to reclaim the land; fighting for every inch of sunlight, to grow, set seed, to reproduce. The cottonwood buds were unfolding, the hillsides were a misty green. This evening though, the rain was lashing down outside; Louise and Mom were sewing. Jessie was cleaning the guns we'd fired earlier in the day. Matthew had been able to get up, with his leg in splints, and was grilling char over the fire, sitting on a stool, makeshift wooden crutches by his side. Beth and Sue were trying their hand at making baskets from willow which we'd dried and then rehydrated in water. I was bringing in more logs. We were getting into good routines, everyone pulling their weight in different ways. But I guess we all knew it couldn't last. And, indeed, then it all changed.

Dad took off his earphones. "I've been speaking with Theo and some of the others we met last fall," he said. "He's suggesting a conference, a parley, tomorrow, where the Hope Highway meets the Seward Highway. The roads are passable now. The leaders from a number of different communities will be coming."

"What's the agenda?" asked Matthew.

"He wouldn't say. He was just fairly insistent that we should all meet."

"Who's going from here?"

"Just me and Jim, I think," Dad replied. "He seemed to want to keep the numbers down."

"Is it safe, to leave here, Dad?"

He nodded. "He says it is, I think we have to trust him on that."

"I'm glad we're getting to meet some new people," Mom said.

"It'll be good for us, seems so long since we had other company."

"Jessie, could you make up some grub for us to take," I said as I rose from the table. "I'll clear some snow up to the gate. Dad, perhaps you could get the snow chains on while I do that."

Dad and I set off early the next morning in one of the jeeps, with a rifle each. The going at first was difficult, with the wheels spinning on the snow, and we got stuck in drifts a couple of times and had to dig our way out. But as we got lower it turned to mush. By around midday, when the sun was at its highest, we got to the Seward Highway and turned left towards Coopers Landing. We passed the occasional abandoned truck or jeep but got to the junction with Hope Highway without incident, and without seeing anybody. The others had already arrived. There were a dozen vehicles there, and a few dozen people, mostly men, most carrying a rifle. It was strange, seeing so many people: like a recluse must feel having to go to a meeting in a city. And everyone seemed changed, somehow. A bit like how it must feel meeting relatives after a few years and being surprised by how much older they looked, how much the kids had grown. They didn't look as tailored as they might have done a year ago. Most had ragged beards and clothes were shabby, some starting to fall apart. They looked more like survivors of the Civil War than upright American citizens. I guess we looked the same.

A light rain was falling. Clouds were banked up on the horizon. There was a warehouse at the junction, gutted by fire, with no walls, but the roof looked secure. We gathered around inside. I'd never shaken so many hands before. Many of them clearly knew each other and were chatting like old friends. A lady called Makayla was at the heart of it; middle aged, competent-looking, colored.

"Pleased to meet you, Donald, Jim. I've got some coffee here in the thermos. Would you like a cup?"

"Coffee! Gold dust," Dad replied. "I haven't had any for months." We spent an hour exchanging stories, about how we'd got through the winter. After a while, Theo got up at the front, looking as smart as ever.

"Thank you all for coming," he began. "I asked for this meeting because what I want to say needs to be kept off the airwaves. I've been talking with the mayors of the communities represented here. We've had a kind of unofficial, ad hoc committee going between five of us. The point of this meeting is to bring more into the conversation."

"I don't know how much you all know about what's been happening over the last few months around the planet. A lot of radio contacts have dropped out, but I've still got some, and been talking most days with someone. The world's changed. In the USA, no one seems to know what's happened to the government. Best bet is they've gone underground, to nuclear fallout shelters. India and China had large populations which weren't dependent on electricity or coal and oil, and they've come out relatively strongly. But in the rest of the world government's patchy, where it exists at all.

In this country, it's been a rough winter. People have been dying like flies. Most weren't prepared for anything like this, living without electricity, without medicine, services. Disease has taken off many, some've starved to death, some frozen. The population is probably a fraction of what it was a year ago and many of those left are in a bad way. The cities have mostly emptied. Where people have done best, it's in small towns in the Midwest."

He sipped from a bottle of water.

"I'm not going to beat around the bush. The situation's intense. Now you all know that law and order have broken down around here completely. Here's the low-down. Anchorage is controlled from the jail there. I'm sure there were some prisoners who shouldn't really have been there, who are basically good people, but the hardened criminals have taken over. They're psychos. They're raiding communities up and down the Matanuska and

Sisitna valleys. They take their food. If they can't give them enough, they take the people. And I don't know how else to say this, but they rape them, keep them in cells, and then they eat them."

FIFTY-FIVE

There were shouts of dissent around the group.

"Surely not!"

"No one's that evil."

"Cannibalism's not that unusual in history, when things are desperate."

"How d'you know all this? We hear all kinds of rumors."

"It's straight from the tap. And I swear down on this. A few people have got out. They're traumatized, been through hell, but credible witnesses. We've taken a few in, though a couple died of their wounds in the winter. Now the real reason I wanted to call this meeting, and not have this on the radio where they might hear it, is that I have one contact inside the prison. He says there's a running civil war between the Anchorage criminals and the Council of fundamentalists who control Fairbanks. It's reached a stalemate, with the George Parks Highway being blocked off between Cantwell and McKinley Park. Both sides've put up fortified defenses. The road's been ripped up. There's a no man's land of several miles between them, and a small army on each side."

"Can't we just talk to them?"

"They'll shoot you sooner than talk."

"What are you saying here?"

"With their route to the north blocked, the criminals have decided to come south. I believe they're planning to come down the Seward Highway next week."

People visibly paled. There were murmurs of horror.

"What about the army at Fort Richardson?" someone asked.

"Ah. Here's where the news gets really bad," said Theo. "If it was just the criminals, I'd suggest we band together and fight them here. But law and order's broken down in Fort Richardson, like everywhere else. Disease decimated the soldiers, like it did the population of Anchorage. Many of those left tried to get home. Some of them've joined the criminals. The upshot is that the criminals have armored Humvees, with machine guns and rocket launchers. I'm not yanking your chains here. We can't fight that on this road, wouldn't have a prayer. We've got enough problems already with people from Kenai trying to get out. We need to get onto different territory, which we could use to our advantage."

"How are the Council fighting them then?" someone else asked.

"They have their own armored vehicles from Fort Wainright," Theo replied. "That's basically why they're in a stalemate in the pass. Neither of them can get through the other."

A woman at the front piped up. "This is terrible news, Theo. You've got us all really worried. But what do you suggest we do? You must have something in mind."

He nodded. "I've been wondering where we could go. Kenai is too full. They're fighting for food along the coast, and are not going to welcome more people. Donald here left Anchorage with his family last year and they've been living in a lodge some distance off the Seward Highway. We've been in touch. He's a man of foresight. I figure he guessed something like this might happen. He came to me last fall with a proposal that the mayors here have been considering for some time, which I now want to run by you all – which is that we should all move over to Whittier. The road gets there through a tunnel, as you probably know, which can easily be blocked off. Not much would get over the mountains. There's empty buildings there which would fit us all in. It's a port, so we'd have access to the sea."

"But that means abandoning our homes," a woman objected.

"I'd welcome hearing any alternatives," replied Theo.

A tall, bearded man spoke up. "I've stockpiled several years' worth of food, Theo. So my first question is, how would I move it all? And second, would it still be mine?"

"I can't see how it would work apart from sharing, Dick, we'd all be in the same building. We live together, or die separately."

"Why should I be the one to share more, because I've taken the precaution of saving?"

"Well, the way I see it, think of us as being on a cruise ship. We get wrecked, and stranded on a desert island. Now do first class passengers get better food, because they've paid more? Or do we take care of women and children first? Seems to me that's the position we're in."

"Well, I don't like it. Sounds like socialism to me. I'll take my chances, stand and fight. Anyone who wants to stand with me, welcome."

"Of course, anyone who wants to stay, fine. Those who leave, we'll have to figure out some ground rules."

"But even if we go, Theo, they could follow us. Some of those Humvees can climb up most anything," another pointed out.

I tentatively raised my hand. It was the first time I'd spoken to so many people. "I know the Portage Pass. Humvees couldn't get through the bogs around the lake, and they'd roll over when they got to the ridge. And besides, we could use IEDs."

"What are those?" someone asked.

"Improvised Explosive Devices," Theo explained. "You're right, Jim, terrorists make them the world over. I'm sure we can."

There was quiet for a minute, then a buzz of conversation.

Theo waited for a while. "Could I have a show of hands? Is there anyone who thinks we should stay where we are and wait for the criminals here?" Nobody raised their hand.

"Anyone who agrees we should move to Whittier?" A few hands went up. Then more and more, till eventually they were mostly up.

"We're agreed, then," said Theo. "I know this is a big decision for all of us. But we haven't got long. We'll send an advance party in the next day or so, to get things ready. Now, I think we need a smaller group, a committee, to make the arrangements, to sort things out, there's a huge amount to do. I suggest that's our current committee, Makayla for Coopers Landing, Jeremy there from Sunrise, Benji from Seward, and Anna from Hope. Donald." He turned to Dad. "This was your initiative, I hope you can join us."

Dad hesitated. He was looking pale. "If my son, Jim, can as well."

I looked at him, shocked, but my heart swelling with pride. He nodded at me.

"That's ridiculous," someone said. "I'm not suggesting he's a wimp or anything, but he's a kid."

"He's killed two men in self-defense already, Dad replied quietly. "So he's not a kid any more. He saved our family. And he's probably the best shot here. He's the provider. He comes up with the ideas. And if we have to fight, he knows the ground we'll be fighting on better than anyone. I don't think age matters much in this situation. If you want me, he's part of the deal."

Makayla spoke up. "If this was the kind of committee we're used to here, Theo, dealing with planning issues and so on, I'd say it was a nonsense. But from what you say, we need people to lead us who can fight. I can't do that, so I'd be happy to step down in favor of Jim."

Theo paused. "I don't think that's necessary, Makayla. And we'll need all kinds of skills. OK then, so that makes seven of us, rather than five. We'll see how it goes. Now I suggest the committee stay and talk, the rest split and start getting ready to move. You'll probably have to do more persuading, but I've got to stress, this is a one-shot thing. When we've shut the tunnel, that's it. Anyone who hasn't come, is on the other side of the mountain. And let's keep radio silence on this, that's really important. Any questions?"

A heavily-bearded man chimed in. "Can't we have more time to think about this? We've been in our home for thirty years. My wife's not going to be happy about moving out at this kind of notice."

"I understand that," Theo replied. "But this is all the time we have. We move out now, or get rolled over."

I raised my hand again. "Anyone here been a soldier? A miner? Knows where we can get hold of explosives? A chemist?"

Nobody was putting their hand up. "I don't think so, Jim, but that's a good point," Theo said, as he looked around. "We'll find out. Donald, I'll talk to Nat, in Whittier, today, and some of us will be around at your place in the morning. Thank you for coming folks, let's move."

FIFTY-SIX

It was late evening when Dad and I got back. We talked for hours. "I can't believe this, that people can be that evil," said Mom, tears running down her face. "It can't be true."

"It is, Mom," and I told her about meeting Ethan.

"Oh, no, what's going to happen to us. How can we possibly stop them?"

Bess stood up. "If I can kill a bear, I can kill a man, lots of them," she said, bravely. "I'm not scared."

"That's the spirit, Bess," Jessie replied. "I bet we can shoot better than they can."

"But it sounds like there are so many of them," Mom stumbled the words out.

"Mary, that's why we need to join up with more people," said Dad.

"But can we trust them?"

"I have good vibes about this. I'm impressed by Theo. I think these are the right people."

"It feels like we're going to war," Mom replied. "It's not what I wanted."

"I know. But we have to play the cards we've been dealt."

I got up and kissed Mom on the forehead. "This has to be done, Mom. Time for us kids to look after you."

"I'll be sorry to be leaving here," said Louise. "I never thought I'd say this, but it's felt like home."

"Me, too," said Dad. "But I don't think there's another way. Hopefully, we can come back to it. Let's sleep now, we'll pack tomorrow."

"Bob could always see ahead to the way things were going," I said to Jessie later, in bed.

"Then be like him, Jim. We'll have to look after our parents, you realize that?"

"Yes. Bess is coming along well, isn't she? Turning into a right little warrior."

"Nothing like the prospect of rape and death to focus the mind," she muttered, stroking me.

"This could be our last night here, Jessie."

"Then let's make the most of it," and she got on top.

It was a bit colder next morning and had snowed again overnight, but not enough to trouble us. It was just damp, our breath hanging in the air, fog hanging low on the mountain. We were loading the truck with all our possessions and stores when Theo and half a dozen other men and a couple of women arrived in jeeps.

"Donald," Theo said as he stepped down from the vehicle, "you know Makayla, Jeremy, Benji and Anna from yesterday. Jeremy's a guide by trade, Benji's a plumber, Anna ran the goods store." We shook hands all round.

"Nicely set-up place you've got here," Makayla said. "The fence is for bears?"

"Mostly for dogs and wolves," Dad replied, "but it's worked for bears as well."

"You got through the winter here, by yourselves? Just you lot?" Benji asked. He was a competent looking older guy, long, grey-streaked beard, seemed as if he'd been living off-grid for a lot longer than the last year.

"Mostly, with the help of a neighbor we had back in Anchorage," Dad replied. "But he was killed a few months ago."

"Sorry to hear that," Anna chipped in. She looked to be in her thirties, self-possessed. "We've lost so many good people."

"We have," Dad replied. "It's strange, having to start up again, with new friends and neighbors. But welcome, come in."

"I've spoken with Nat," Theo said, as we sat around with nettle tea. We were all crammed in around the table. "I told him as little as I could, just enough to get him to unlock the tunnel. But I don't think we'll be able to keep this move a secret for long.

It's bound to leak out. A few cussed folk are refusing to come, but they know where we're going. We can't not use the radio indefinitely, so they'll be able to track the source. There are a few in our group with military experience, but it's very limited. Mostly grunts. I'm the only one with serving experience as an officer."

"I didn't know that," Dad interrupted.

"Lieutenant colonel in the 75th Rangers. Afghanistan, Iraq...I retired back here, close to my home, I grew up in Anchorage. I'd guess we have a couple of dozen who'd be prepared to shoot and kill. We've sent one party with plenty of firepower, led by Andrew Bovotsky, used to be a miner, down to Soldotna, to see if they can find any explosives – there's a road building company down there. Donald, you're an engineer, and you've met Nat. I think it'd help if you could get to Whittier by this evening. We need to get heat working, generators, places to store food, defences. The more time we have to prepare, the better. There'll be another dozen coming through tomorrow to help with the labor. They're just packing up their homes first. Can you manage that?"

"This evening! OK."

"Jim," Theo continued, "perhaps you could come with us now. You know the ground, I'd like to reconnoiter it with you."

"So you're taking over, just like that?" asked Louise.

"Well, not quite just like that," Theo replied, looking at her. I'm the mayor of the largest community involved here and the leaders of the others have agreed that I should run this transition. Are you comfortable with that?"

"Not entirely, but I appreciate in these times we have to take short cuts. So, yes."

"I'd be happy to talk about this with you again, Louise, but for the moment we need to move fast."

"I'm glad you've come, and that we've met," said Mom. "It's like a door opening for me, meeting decent people again. Real neighbors. I've missed that so much."

"Donald's told me you're a nurse, Mary, and I just can't tell you how valuable that's going to be. We don't have any doctors in our group. I'm sure we could have saved some lives over the winter if we'd known what to do. A lot of people died simply because they had no support, no medicine, and couldn't contact anyone. And yourself, Louise," he continued, nodding to her, "we have a couple of dozen kids who'll need teaching. Matthew." He turned to him. "Donald's told me how well you've been doing here, feeding everyone. In Whittier, we're going to have up to a couple of hundred to feed. With no electricity in the apartments, it's going to have to be done centrally. We'll need a big kitchen. So I'm very glad we've met up with you guys."

I packed a bag rapidly, and turned to Jessie, standing quietly, twirling a lock of hair as she stared at nothing in particular. "Jessie, I have to go. Do you want to come with me?"

"I'd better stay to help pack. I'll see you tonight," she whispered in my ear, as we kissed.

"Say goodbye to the place for me," I whispered back.

FIFTY-SEVEN

We left almost straightaway, back to the Portage Glacier Road. A couple of hours later, we reached the tunnel. Nat had opened it and we drove through.

"Hullo everyone," he said as we shook hands. "Really good to see you. It's been a long and lonely winter. Theo said you'd be coming. I've started to get things ready. Want some food? I've got an omelette frying, I can rustle up more."

"You've got chickens?" I asked.

"No, but the birds are nesting. I go foraging. Here, let me show you people around."

"I'll leave you to it," said Theo. "Me and Jim are going to head up to the ridge, to have a look around."

"How well can you shoot with that?" Theo asked, as we got back into the jeep and drove up the Portage Pass Trail. I was carrying my Winchester .30.

"At two hundred yards on a still day, I can put a bullet through a moose's eye," I replied.

Theo whistled. "Not bad. Now I guess these two guys you killed, it was an immediate thing, right up, close range, you didn't have to think about it?"

"That's right," I replied. "How did you know?"

"It's one thing to fight for your life, spur of the moment, adrenaline flowing. It's another to shoot at a distance, in cold blood. When your opponent doesn't even know you're there. You need to calm your breathing, slow down your pulse, focus. Allow for wind and weather. Focus again. Aim to kill. Think you could do that?"

I thought about Bob, about the family, about Jess. "No problem."

"You're sure?"

"You betcha."

"Even if it meant shooting someone in the back, who was running away?"

I hesitated. "Yes. We're outnumbered. They could be back with reinforcements."

"OK, I want you to have this, practice with it for the next few days."

He reached across the back and passed me a rifle, one I'd never seen before. It lay perfectly balanced in my hands, metal gleaming in the sunlight, exuding power and threat. Compared to the Winchester, it was something else again. Holding it, I felt like Thor with his hammer, invincible. Thinking back, I can't remember what happened to it, I ran out of bullets many years ago. It's probably now propping up a hen coop somewhere.

"It's an M24. Standard army issue. Very reliable, any conditions. It's the one the army snipers use, though you can detach the sight. The magazine takes five rounds. I've got a case in the back. You'll need to lie down to shoot it. See how close you can get to a bulls eye. It's accurate to a couple of inches, at a thousand yards. We're going to need a sniper."

"OK, thank you, sir."

"Call me Theo."

Clearly, since the tunnel had been built back in the Second World War, the Portage Passage Trail had fallen into disuse. After a few miles the gravel track, overgrown as it was, simply petered out. We left the jeep and started hiking to the top of the ridge. Theo made easy conversation. I found myself telling him about how we left Anchorage, and about Bob.

"He sounds like a guy it's a shame to have lost. We're going to need more like him. You and Jessie are an item?"

"We're going to get married, though I haven't asked her yet."

"Then we should think about holding a potlatch for you."

"What's that?"

"A tribal ceremony, a feast, where people give things away. It used to be practiced all along the Pacific Northwest. It kept goods circulating and prevented individuals from getting too rich. The missionaries got it banned in the nineteenth century, because it stopped the natives from becoming Christians. Never figured out why, I thought that was what the gospels were about. But I'm no minister. Looks to me, though, like we might need to get back to some of those old traditions."

"You sound like Louise. She keeps talking about the old times. But people weren't civilized then, were they?"

"You think we are now? Did Anchorage look civilized to you? I'd like to get better acquainted with Louise, from the little I saw of her this morning. Is she by herself?"

"She told us that she was married once, but her husband and child died many years ago and she's never wanted to remarry."

"Sorry to hear that. My wife died as well, four years ago. I had two boys in the army. One was serving in Europe and is in Washington now. The other..." his voice trailed off..."I'd sooner not talk about it. I haven't seen the grandchildren for a couple of years now."

"I'm sorry, it hadn't occurred to me, about your family...I guess we've been really lucky, our family, still being together. Dad has a brother in England, had a brother, I don't know now..."

"Count your blessings, Jim, though in my experience luck is usually what you make of it.

Anyway, perhaps I could talk with Louise a bit more. She seems to have her head screwed on right. Remember, Jim, the Indians have been living here for ten thousand years. Us whites have barely been here a couple of hundred, and right now, I wouldn't bet on our being here in another hundred."

At the top of the ridge we could see for miles around: the Portage Lake glimmering below, surrounded by the mountains and glaciers of Chugach.

Theo scanned it through the binoculars, and then handed them to me.

"Now, tell me, Jim, if the enemy was coming for us, along the road there, where and how would you stop them?"

I didn't have a clue. Then I started thinking about it as if it were a war game on the computer. The landscape in front of me was the screen. There were significant elements there, factors in the game – the road, tunnel, mountains, boat, lake, bogs, rocks, things you had to take into account, which you could play with. I imagined units of men, with vehicles. There were other elements as well, like the weather, time of year, how many resources – supplies, weapons, skills – we'd managed to accumulate. I visualized them, shuffled them around in my head.

After a while, Theo interrupted my thoughts. "Have to come to a decision, Jim…if they were coming now, we're losing valuable time here while you make up your mind."

"They'll try the tunnel first," I finally said, "and find that blocked. If we had dynamite, I'd leave a few guys at this end of the tunnel, wait for them to go in and then blow up this end, shooting any guards they left to cover their backs. But that probably wouldn't work, because if I was them, I'd have come with at least a couple of dozen guys and plenty of empty spaces to take prisoners back, so that means a number of vehicles. So I'd send one vehicle forward, with just the driver, to check out the tunnel first. So if that were to happen, and we don't have dynamite anyway, we'd need to fight them when they've left the Humvees and are on foot. So they'd come around the lake here, aiming for this trail. They'd have to walk. Unless they could use that cruise boat on the other side. So I'd sink that first, in case they got it going, to slow them down. We don't know which side of the lake they'd come. If they went looking for a boat first, then the other side is shorter, but there's a glacier to cross. So maybe they'd come around this side, but we couldn't be certain and we wouldn't want to give ourselves away by moving. If they came now, that area below us looks really boggy and it would slow us down trying to get through it. I think I'd wait here, positioning ourselves around those rocks there, and create an ambush. Hit them while they're still in the bog, in open territory, just before they got to hard ground."

"Not bad," he said. "So how—"

I interrupted him, wholly focused on the issue. "And we'd have to know they were coming. So I'd hide a couple of people back at the Seward Highway, as sentries, with a two-way radio, to give us advance warning. I'm not sure the radio range would reach to Whittier, so perhaps another couple of sentries at the top of the lake, and another couple about here, in a jeep, who could radio it on to us. Then that would give us time to drive up here and position ourselves before they arrived, if we were ready to move immediately. And I'd prepare the positions in advance."

"Pretty good!" He laughed. "Where did you learn strategy from?"

"Playing *Catan*."

"What the hell's that?"

"It's an online war game," I replied. "I used to play those kind of games every night with people I met on the Internet.

He laughed again. "Probably as good as anything they teach you in Staff School."

"Do you think they're going to come?"

"I'd be surprised if they didn't. Compared to those militant crackpots up in Fairbanks, God's Army, they'll see us as easy pickings. They'll know how many we are, and our supplies."

"Are you sure they'd come this way?"

"It's the only route through, Jim, if the tunnel's closed, isn't it? They've got to come over this pass."

"No, pardon, but you're wrong. If I was them, I'd come by sea. OK, it's ten times the distance, but I'd figure, if I was them, that we might be expecting them to come. They'll know that we know that they know we're here, if you see what I mean. Must be a boat they could use in Anchorage. It would take them a lot longer, maybe a few days, but we wouldn't be expecting that.

If they arrived at night, without lights, came quietly into the harbor, we wouldn't know much about it till it was all over."

Theo paused and nodded. "I hadn't thought of that. You're right. Will bear it in mind."

"Who's your source in Anchorage?"

"The source is in a dangerous spot, Jim, I haven't told anyone. It's my ace in the hole. Need to know basis. Safer that way."

He thought for a while. "But look, it's also not a good idea if I'm the only one who knows. You'll promise to keep it to yourself? Not even tell Jessie?"

"Sure thing."

"OK. I won't tell you the real name, but their code name is Zenith."

FIFTY-EIGHT

Over the next couple of days a steady stream of jeeps and trucks came off the Seward Highway from points west, and down the Portage Glacier Road. There were heavy frost heaves on it, and if the road menders weren't coming around anymore it wouldn't last many years. There were about two hundred people, along with dogs, cats, even assorted livestock – some chickens, mules, goats, a couple of cows – that hadn't been killed yet for food. It was about the same number that had left Whittier in the Fall. We took over Begich Towers, where the previous population had lived – a fourteen-story block of two and three bedroom apartments, a hundred and fifty of them. It had been built in the 1950s as the headquarters of the US Army Corps Engineers, the biggest building in Alaska at the time. There was a similar sized building, Buckner, which had been empty for a couple of decades and was pretty dilapidated, but looked like being recoverable if needed.

Of course, the elevators no longer worked, so apartments were allocated on a need basis – the most frail at the bottom, fittest at the top, gradations in between. Three bedroom apartments for the larger families, two for the others, one for singles and couples.

"You and Jessie take a single," Dad said, "two singles for Matthew and Louise, Bess and Sue – OK for you to share? They're short of singles here."

Apart from that, furnishings and fittings were pretty standard throughout. There were common rooms, and even carpets on the corridor floors – it was odd walking on them again. I thought Bob wouldn't have liked it, couldn't see him fitting in. I heard a few people grumble that they'd swapped a house for a couple of rooms, and if they couldn't pay for something better, but nothing serious. They were given short shrift – what use was money?

It felt strange, being with all these people, I guess like someone who's never been to a city before suddenly turning up in New York. I missed the lodge desperately, my thoughts often turning to the lake, our cabin, the places on the beach where we'd made love. But it felt so much safer, being together with all these people. Maybe it was an unhealthy, communist kind of thought, but I couldn't help wondering why society didn't work that way more generally. There was no hustling for space, the accommodation was the same for everyone, it didn't matter how much money people had enjoyed before, or not. Maybe the Indians weren't so primitive after all. Bucks no longer had any value anyway, except as toilet paper or kindling. What could we pay for more bullets, and where could we get them from?

The room for Jessie and me was small, but comfortable.

"Wow, the nicest mattress I've seen for a while," she said, as she bounced on it.

"I've got to go and help Dad sort out arrangements," I said.

"Look, Jim." She reached up and grabbed my collar, pulling me down. "You can get as busy as you want. But I come first, do you understand that?"

"Of course I do, Jessie."

"I don't think you understand it enough. I think you need a lesson. Let's christen the mattress." She kissed me, and started taking my pants off.

When everyone had arrived, we crammed into the largest of the common rooms one evening, standing room only. Theo addressed the gathering.

"Welcome to Whittier everyone. Now, I won't go over the reasons again as to why we're here, you know that. I can only say that it's providential we've found this place, which fits us exactly, and I've spoken with the people in Valdez, who used to live here, and they're happy with what we're doing. Now, we've a lot to organize over the next few days. Not least, how we're going to run ourselves. Currently, we've got a committee.

I know that a committee's like a horse with four back legs, and with seven it's even worse, and I'm not suggesting that this is going to be permanent or that I should be its spokesman. But we've an immediate threat to face, and I suggest we continue on this basis till it's passed. I don't know whether that will be next week, or next month, but by the fall it'll be clear, because we'll either have lost to them, or we'll still be here, and the snows and mountains will start cutting us off from the outside. At which point, if not earlier, I suggest we hold elections for a new committee and chairman.

"How's the committee going to be elected? What powers will it have?"

"I don't know yet, to be honest. I've been in touch with some other communities, like in Valdez, and they're all doing things a bit differently. I suggest we set up a steering group to look at some kind of constitution for us and how we're going to operate, which will also then be put to the vote. I think Donald here, whose brainwave this move was, has already given some thought to that. Does anyone have any disagreements with what I've said so far? Please raise your hand if you do. Don't be afraid to do so."

He stopped, looked around. No hands went up.

"No? Remarkable. I'd like to add that I'm happy to talk to anyone about this at any time. But not over the next few days. We're going to have to dedicate those to protecting ourselves, our families, from unprovoked, vicious assault from criminals, including some ex-soldiers, armed with military weapons. You all know me, and my record. For that reason, I offer myself as your military leader during this period of danger. Does anyone have any objections to that?"

He looked around. "No again? OK."

"What I ask for in this period," he continued, "is your total co-operation. More than that, your obedience. I need to be able to pick who fights, and where. We'll only beat these people if we're better organized, more disciplined, quicker, cleverer. And we need to stack the decks in our favor. Are we agreed?

"OK. Now, let's start. The committee will be meeting now to draw up policies, how we distribute food, how we prepare it, how we get more, work lists and rotas. The better we can work together, the stronger we'll be. Thank you all for coming this evening. We'll have some information – and food – for you in the morning. In the meantime, anyone who can handle a rifle, who's prepared to shoot to defend ourselves, I'd like you to come back here in half an hour. Gender and age don't matter. Just so long as you're a good shot. Could you bring any weapons you have with you, any two-way radios, anything else you think could come in useful. Oh, and watches. Thanks."

Theo, Makayla, Jeremy, Benji and Anna, Dad, Mom and myself went up to a smaller room.

"I'd like to start on military preparations," began Theo. "I want Jim here to ride shotgun for me. Jeremy and Anna, I'd like you two to arrange the food supply, control the stores, manage the preparation, cooking, distribution and cleaning. Divide the work between you. Donald and Benji – infrastructure. We need the heating working, enough water, containers to carry it, pens for the livestock. We'll save time and energy in the long term being all in one building together, rather than having to keep dozens going. But food is going to be critical, sharing it out fairly. Mary – you're here because I think you're the most senior on the medical side. We'll need a surgery, a makeshift hospital, be able to treat gun wounds. Makayla, could you be available to answer questions from anyone at any time – we'll need a central office on the ground floor. Jim, you and me are going to be on defense. OK?"

After some discussion, they left, and the potential soldiers started turning up, three dozen of them. We introduced ourselves, talked about our experience, made an inventory of weapons and communications. Theo divided them – thirty men and six women, including Jessie and Bess – into two teams.

"Now, we'll need watches, if you've given up using them. We'll need to co-ordinate timings. Check we're all on the same time."

Some others came as well, Sue among them, but Theo turned them down. "Sorry, Sue, you're on the young side, and we'll need some defense back in this place. You can play a part there. We should fortify the ground floor, not make it too easy for anyone to get in." He gave instructions about sentries and shift changes.

"Now, this could begin at any time. The key is going to be having surprise on our side, not on theirs. They're coming to rape, murder, imprison our folks, do terrible things to them. There's no point in just giving them a bloody nose. We send them all to the farm. Or they'll come back in more force, better prepared. No prisoners. If you're uncomfortable with that, excuse yourself. This is life or death for all of us."

FIFTY-NINE

Andrew Bovotsky turned out to be one of the biggest guys I've seen, a real hench, six and a half feet tall, bald headed, bearded. He had managed to get hold of some dynamite.

"Hi, Jim, good to meet you. Theo's told me about you. A bit young for this, aren't you?" He smiled, to take the edge of, handing over a big box as he enveloped my hand in his. "It's not much, and it might be a bit dodgy."

"Hi, Andrew," I replied, wincing in his huge grip. "Love those tattoos."

He grinned, showing a couple of gold teeth and flexed his huge biceps to show off his Popeye forearm.

"Can we use it to block the tunnel properly?" Theo asked.

"Give me a few hours and we can do that, and have something spare for the far end if we need it."

The next day we set up the sentry positions, one at the Seward Highway, another on a promontory overlooking the sea, stocking them with food and water. Then we organized rotas. I started carrying a two-way radio receiver in my belt at all times, cell phones already a distant memory. We practiced receiving a call, then I set off the fire alarm in Begich Towers and we timed how long it took the three dozen of us to gather and drive up to the ridge. Once there, we spent the rest of the day digging a couple of dozen fox holes across a hundred yard stretch, ten feet apart, a hundred yards away from the trail, and rearranging rocks so that we could see but not be seen. We worked carefully to make sure it all looked completely natural.

"Theo," I reported at the end of the day, "the firing positions are ready."

"OK, now we wait," he replied. "While we do, let's start fortifying this place. There's no one living on the ground floor, let's brick in the windows, leaving loopholes to fire through.

Ramps to stop trucks getting too close. Sniper positions on the roof. I don't know how we'll stop a boat getting here though, let's hope they're not as bright as you, and come by road. And let's get some shooting practice in. I want to see all soldiers down in the park, all afternoon."

The sun now cleared the mountains all day and most of the night. Leaves were unfolding, the skeletons of trees were now a blaze of light green, translucent in the sunlight. You could feel the pulse of life in full gear, the birds returned, the young calling. In the Begich Building, it was organized chaos. Mom, Dad and Matthew were totally wrapped up their work. There was always a queue to see Mom, people who hadn't seen a nurse or doctor for a year.

"Jim, I'm too busy to talk right now, could you open these boxes for me? It's so nice to be able to help around here. Jane, you've got the hang of the syringe now, could you give Mr. Jablosky here an injection, same as you did with his wife?"

Dad was engineer in charge of the defense construction. Matthew was hobbling around on his crutches organizing a couple of meals a day for two hundred people.

"Jim, this is hopeless, we need bigger pans, we need vats, big ones, could you do something? Talk to Theo?"

Sue had playmates, Bess was in seventh heaven, chatting to new friends non-stop, making up for the months of isolation.

"There are *guys* here, Jim, not just girls," she said to me once, in passing. "Real guys! Unbelievable! They're all asking me about this necklace. I'm so glad we came."

Jessie – what can I say? Those first days I was a bit worried, to be honest, about the competition, worried that the previous months had been a dream, and she would go off with someone better looking. But she gave no sign of it. She made me believe I could do this, that it was possible.

"Harder, harder," she gasped as we were making love the next night. "We're not doing this again till you've killed every one of those fuckers, you understand me? Oh! Oh! That's it, come...come..."

The bleeper on my radio from the sentries on the Seward Highway, fifteen miles away, went off the next morning. Andrew Bovotsky was on duty at the time – I'd thought that we needed really responsible people there. He had Gill with him; a middle aged, competent lady, a bird watcher, who I figured would be used to spending lots of time patiently looking through binoculars.

"Two Humvees and four trucks coming your way, Jim," he said. "Can't see how many guys, maybe two dozen, maybe three dozen. Once they're past us, me and Gill will follow and come see what we can do to help."

I gulped, feeling cold all the way down to my stomach. This was it.

"Thanks, Andrew. Don't get so close though that you distract them from coming. Let them get right up to us, you'll have to stay well back."

"Understood. All the best, Jim, we'll be thinking of you."

I punched the nearest fire alarm, a few yards away. The klaxon went off in the building. I had just enough time to quickly hug Mom and Dad.

"Jim, I love you..." Mom said, her voice breaking.

"You, too, Mom. Don't worry." It sounded a bit daft even as I said it, my heart pounding with fear, excitement, anticipation.

"Take care," Matthew shouted as Jessie, Bess and I ran past the kitchens, "and give them hell!"

Moments later, three dozen of us had scrambled into jeeps and trucks and were driving fast up the Passage Trail. We left the vehicles below the rise and hurried to our prepared places, wading through paintbrush and forget-me-nots. The ground was scattered with blue and purple and yellow, with insects buzzing around. Little pipits hopped away in front of us, taking off again as we drew closer. The sky was a clear blue, dotted with small, fluffy clouds blowing in from the Gulf of Alaska. A perfect day for dying, I thought. It all seemed unreal. I had to pinch myself.

"Don't leave me hanging there, will you, Theo?" I asked jokingly.

"You'll be fine, Jim," he replied, looking me straight in the eye. "Now, we'll go higher, watch your back, and go to where we're needed. Just don't get uptight about it, let it happen, let them come to you, keep waiting, like we said. OK? You all right with this?"

"I'm fine."

"All the best."

We shook hands, Jessie and I hugged each other.

"Come back to me, Jim."

I'll always come back, I promise," and she was gone, walking away with Theo and a dozen others, heading for the top of the hill.

I was in charge of the rest, the shooters I'd selected as the most solid. We all hunkered down into our holes, covering ourselves with moss and bracken till we were invisible from anyone more than a few feet away. We'd already smeared ourselves with mosquito repellent, though it wasn't really necessary, a steady breeze was keeping them down. I signaled Theo to show we were ready and he withdrew into hiding with his force.

"Complete quiet now," I called out. "I know we've been through this before, but here it is again. Keep yourselves right down, don't show yourselves, cover any bare skin, no itching. When they're within a mile or so, I'll give a raven call, and another one at half a mile. After that, keep absolutely still. Stay hidden. Don't look up. We want them to come past us. We want to wipe these guys out, not spook them. Don't raise your heads till I fire the first shot. When I do, aim first for the guy directly opposite you."

I looked through the binoculars, careful that they wouldn't reflect the light. The convoy came around the bend and stopped at the tunnel. As I thought, they had sent one driver through; soon he was back with them. They set off on foot around the lake. They had about a three-mile walk. The minutes crawled by. I didn't mind that – it gave us time to settle down, calm ourselves. I could see Andrew and Gill arriving in their jeep at the bend, but they quickly reversed and stayed out of sight. The moss a few inches from my eyes was a miniature world of fronds, little leaves spiraling around the stems, tiny flowers, crusty lichen on the stones, every shade of green, red, brown, yellow, orange. Little ants and beetles hastened purposefully through their jungle, on their way to wherever it was ants and beetles went to, doing their thing, like the millions of generations before them. As the criminals came closer, I counted them, twenty-nine. They were an ugly looking lot, scary. My heart sank. Any one of them could have beaten up half a dozen of us in a fight. Some were stripped to the waist, heavily muscled after years of exercise in their cells, tattooed, with bandoliers of cartridges, pistols, machetes, coils of rope, assault rifles, even one machine gun. The instinct to jump up and run for it was, for a moment, almost overwhelming. I pushed it away, praying that no one else gave in to their own version of terror. It seemed almost impossible that no one would. But it stayed quiet. I turned my attention back to the approaching men. They were undisciplined: scattered over a couple of hundred yards, talking, joking, slapping away the clouds of mosquitoes that were down in the bog as they ploughed through it, no scouts out ahead. Just a bunch of careless clowns, I told myself.

I gave the first raven call, then the second. I was at the far right hand side of our line, closest to Whittier. The oncoming mob walked along without noticing us hidden amongst the rocks. As the first of the group went past me, I raised the M24 and shot him through the head. I saw it exploding with the force of the bullet, bits of brain and skull flying out. He went down like a stone. The relief was immediate. They died like any other flesh and blood mammal, and they seemed far easier to kill, because they didn't live here, not out here in the bush, they were creatures of rooms and tarmac. I was squeezing the trigger on the second as a storm of bullets came from the rocks along to my left. There were more of them than us, they were more heavily armored, but they could barely see us, were lower down, and had nowhere to hide. They were sitting ducks. And we were hunters. They dropped like flies. Some got off a few rounds before they went down and bullets sang off the rocks, chipping off splinters, but I didn't hear anyone hurt on our side. Half a dozen at the rear, who hadn't reached the firing zone yet, started running back. Four of them took bullets and fell. Two survived and kept on weaving, zig zagging, running for their lives back to the lake. I could see the "plock" of bullets in the water of the bog as we missed them. I brought the M24 around, steadied it on its stand, and focused. Measured my breathing, watched their movements, timed my response, and shot them in the back, at six hundred yards, six hundred and fifty.

It was a massacre. I rested my forehead on the gunstock. I could feel myself starting to tremble, but my hands were still. I felt fine. Like I was born to do this. A year ago I was playing this on a screen and now there were bodies lying all around. Mostly dead, but some with limbs twitching, a couple crying out in pain. Somehow, a couple of vultures were already circling overhead.

Jessie must have hurtled down the slope. I'd barely stood up before she had her arms around me. "My God, Jim, you did it, you did it!"

"Good work, everyone," said Theo as he came down with the others. "I've never seen an ambush better done. You didn't leave us anything to do."

He walked over and put a bullet through the foreheads of those who were still alive.

"Not in accordance with the Geneva Convention," he said. "But we're not in a world where that applies anymore."

People were chattering excitedly, embracing each other, shaking hands, a couple were whooping, euphoric, others were crying with relief.

"Where's Mason?" Someone asked.

We went quiet. I hadn't checked that we were all OK. Theo and I ran to his position. His head had been thrown back, a bullet through the eye. He was still alive, but his face and skull were a mess, the grey of his brain showing.

"Mason, can you hear me?" asked Theo.

He burbled and nodded.

Theo took me aside and whispered, "We can't save him, Jim. Possibly if we had a field ambulance and an operating theatre and surgeons back in Whittier, but not like this. There's no chance."

He called out to the others who had followed us. "Let's have some privacy here please."

Then, as abruptly sober, they turned to go. "Anna, could you arrange for the bodies to be stripped of weapons and then set up two work parties. We need a big grave, and we need to hide the Humvees and trucks. Thanks."

He regarded me solemnly. "Looks like he was just unlucky, Jim. It was a ricochet off the rock there. He paused, still giving me that grim look. "So, what do you want to do?"

I gaped, stuttered, "I...I don't know."

We knelt down by his head. "Mason, it's going to be all right," Theo said. "I'm just going to make you more comfortable." With one hand, he pinched his nose and with the other covered his mouth. Mason struggled, kicked, and then it was over.

"But..."

"I'm sorry, Jim, this was the best way. He would only have suffered, and died anyway." We got up, sadly.

By now the others were driving the trucks around the lake, up a track through a valley on the other side, as far they could go to cover them in rocks.

Andrew and Gill turned up. Andrew looked thoughtfully at the heap of bodies for a long time, and at the pile of weapons.

"Theo was right about you, Jim." He held out his massive hand to shake. "You done well here. Wouldn't have thought it...all those guys...a nasty bunch. Wouldn't have liked to have tangled with them myself. Scum of the earth...and you being a kid and all...can't quite believe it still. But any support you want, you have it from me."

SIXTY

I wish I'd known then what I know now. We could have started off so much better, faster. We hadn't thought things through well enough – the key things – how was power going to be distributed? How should it be exercised? How were we going to develop a strong enough social contract? What was the glue, other than survival and self-interest, that was going to bind us? How were we going to encourage rational thinking rather than leave everyone prey to fanaticism, bigotry and superstition?

It took years, decades, for all the implications of all this to sink through. And by the time we started to take the issues seriously, it was too late.

But it started off well enough. That evening, Theo stood up at the front addressing us all.

"We've lost Mason, and we all mourn with his family. Phil, the pastor in Hope community, will be conducting a service for him tomorrow. We will remember him. He gave his life for us. I don't expect he'll be the last.

For what it's worth, I've spoken with my contact in the prison. I don't think the criminals will be troubling us again this year. They don't know why their group didn't return, and it's been a blow to them. We've managed to kill a bunch of the worst. They're uncoordinated, divided. Some are afraid. But I suggest we build a permanent hide near the Seward Highway, where we can see the approaches, with a generator and landline between us, so we always have a few hours' notice of threats.

Now, let's wrap this up. We've got a lot to do here to get ready for next winter. We need to build up our livestock. Start sea fishing. Hunt moose. Get generators working. We can siphon off the petrol from the abandoned cars on the highway and there are a couple of petrol stations along there which I think are untouched. We can jury rig pumps and get that out before someone else does. Find enough oil for the boilers or convert them to wood burning. We need a larger communal kitchen and eating area. It'd be good to have the equivalent of a doctor's surgery or hospital, and a school. We need to figure out what skills we have collectively, and how best to use them. We'll have to agree some rules, and how to enforce them. How do we share food, let alone medicine, when we haven't enough? There'll be disputes, that's inevitable, we need means of resolving them. We should prepare to defend ourselves next year, whether that's from the criminals in Anchorage, from armed bands down in Kenai, from fundamentalists in Fairbanks, whoever. We should explore alliances with other communities around Prince William Sound – Valdez, Cordova."

He paused for a moment, looking around the room, where everyone was hanging on his words.

"We're all going to be on a steep learning curve here and should be open to getting some things wrong, to correction, to new ideas. We'll have to agree a policy on who's going to be in this community, what to do if people want to leave or if new people want to join. After last winter, I expect there'll be many who don't want to survive another one by themselves. What's our criteria for joining going to be? Or do we just welcome everyone? Across the board? The whole question of private property's going to be difficult – we've come from our own homes, with our own possessions, and now we have to share most of the things that are going to keep us alive...food, water, heating, the very roof over our heads. Even that isn't ours, we're here courtesy of others. There will have to be some allocation of jobs and recognition of them being well or poorly done – I think we'd all agree that there's no point in trying to pay people salaries. Money has no value any longer, even if we could get hold of it. In some ways, we'll be going back thousands of years, starting again."

Theo glanced around the assembly and shrugged. "Any

questions, so far?"

"Are we going to be free and equal? How's it going to work?" Asked Makayla .

"I think that's the minimum," Theo replied. "But I don't have the answers."

"Jesus said something about giving each according to their need, from each according to their ability," someone piped up.

"Actually, that was Karl Marx," Louise replied. "And it's not a bad idea."

I raised a tentative hand. "How about we just agree to all work to the best of our abilities, and the committee decide who isn't pulling their weight, and if they're not, ask them to leave?"

Theo paused. "Thank you, Jim. We'll have to talk this through in more depth, draw up some rules, a constitution. Donald here has started on it. Now, folks, as I said, I don't pretend to have the answers, I'm as new to this as you are. And, like all of you, I have my sadness, my regrets, over what's happened in the last year. I miss my home, I miss family. I'm sure that's the case for all of us. It's going to be a strange new world here.

"But I propose that for the meantime we elect the existing committee to continue running this place, with myself as leader. Or do you want something different? Do we want to do this by secret ballot or can we do it on a show of hands? Whatever you think."

There was no immediate response, just some low level conversations going on, but then Louise stood up.

"Theo, I think I can speak for most here. We applaud your leadership, and that of the committee. The victory today was an inspiration to all of us. It showed we can survive, and even flourish, if we keep together, work together, and are committed to each other. We're happy to go with the flow here. I think a vote of hands would be enough."

"Thank you, Louise," replied Theo. "Any objections, no? OK, a show of hands then. Who agrees that we keep the current arrangements?"

Every hand went up.

"Thank you, everyone, for your support. My first decision, then, is to appoint Jim here as my deputy."

There were mutterings of disapproval.

"But he's an outsider, Theo, we should have someone more representative. How about Andrew? He's a fighter."

"I've run it by him, and he's fine with it."

"But, Theo, he doesn't look like he's out of high school yet," someone piped up.

A young, handsome looking man chipped in, "With all due respect, sir, all credit to Jim, but there are plenty of us who can shoot, and with more experience."

"I understand that, but I think he has the eye for it. And he has actually *done* it. Maybe there's been luck, circumstance, sure, but who else here has done the same? And, yes, he is young, seventeen, actually, eighteen now, I think. But then I'm seventy-three, so you can take our average age as forty-five, which is more respectable." He smiled. "And Alexander the Great was only twenty when he led the Greeks against the Persians and created the world's greatest empire. Now, I'm not making any comparisons between Jim and him of course. More seriously, though, we're in an unusual situation here. I think we need some youth at the top rather than all grey hairs. And the plan to ambush the criminals was Jim's idea, he chose the spot, and led it. Twenty-nine of them killed, with one death on our side. This thing with the criminals isn't over, and even when it is, we're going to face similar challenges. It looks like the government's abandoned us. Most of us here voted for them, but they've spurned us. We have to assume they're buried away somewhere, looking after themselves, and it's down to us to organize ourselves, provide for our families. Self-defense is going to have to be our priority. We can only create a genuine community here for the long term, where we can flourish, and bring our kids up in safety, if we have security. And it's not physical strength that matters here, it's tactics."

A couple drifted out of the door, shaking their heads, but a chorus of approving noises began building around the room, startling some crows from the window ledge.

"Thank you all. The committee will start work tomorrow. For the moment, that's enough of the serious side. Matthew has excelled himself this evening on the food front, Jeremy's brought along a stock of birch wine, which he made this spring, Anna's got a group together – with instruments – let's have a party."

SIXTY-ONE

I woke early the next morning with something of a hangover, that birch wine had a kick to it. As Jeremy had said, "plenty of trees around here, people, unlimited supply." Though I'm not sure he'd started to worry yet about sugar supplies. Anyway, I didn't remember much of the evening, other than Jessie dragging me away towards the end of it. I looked over at her, breathing quietly, long hair splayed over the pillow, and smiled at the memory of the night. Despite the mouse crawling around inside my skull, there was a surging contentment in my heart. The people yesterday had been so friendly, the bed was so comfortable, the world seemed a good place, never better.

Crawling out from the sheets without disturbing her, I went over to the window, overlooking the harbor. This high up, we had a great view. A small, lonely figure was clambering over some boats. It looked like Dad. I slipped on some clothes and ran down, taking the stairs in leaps.

No one else seemed to be around yet. The sun sparkled over the ruffled waters, the boats were bobbing gently in the stiff breeze, straining at their lines, like dogs on a leash, eager to be out after a year of inactivity. Halyards slapped against the masts, in the harbor entrance terns were diving for fish. The tide had been going out, leaving the smell of mud, seaweed and all the generally shoreline fishy things I couldn't identify yet. Dad saw me coming, and waved me over.

"Hi, Jim. I was wondering which of these we could use best to get out to sea, do some more serious fishing. This motorsailer looks a good bet, wouldn't have to use the engine, but it's there in case it's needed, and it starts fine with a crank handle. I'll have a word with Nat."

"Dad, thanks for standing up for me the other day like that, but I don't think I can do this. All these people are so much older

291

than me."

"None of us think we can do anything much till we start doing it, Jim," he replied. "When I was your age, I hadn't thought about being married, and kids had never crossed my mind."

"But then you went on and got a job? And met Mom? You had skills, you could look after yourself?"

He swung over the railing, and we walked along the pontoon, feeling it rocking gently under our feet. It wasn't wide enough for two people to walk along separately, side by side, but he put his arm around me, so we could fit on it together. Out in the bay a sea lion poked his massive head out of the water and looked at us curiously.

"Nice boats still left here," he said. "Reckon there were a hundred last year, before they went to Valdez. How many do you think got used more than a dozen times a year?"

"I don't know, most of them?"

"About one in ten. The rest are just toys, sitting there, depreciating. And how many of those skippers really knew what they were doing?"

"Half of them?"

"About one in ten."

"What's your point, Dad?"

"I'm not saying this just because I'm your father, Jim. I can see your weaknesses, better than I can see my own, that's usually the way of things. You don't relate well to other people, though Jessie will help in that. But you have a strength in you, a focus, to do what needs to be done. That kind of detachment you have, it might not have helped you in the old life, but it's going to in the new one. You're one in a hundred, one in a thousand. And that's what this community needs. And that's what Bob saw in you. I'm ashamed to say that he saw it before I did. And Theo sees it in you as well, that's why he wants you as his deputy."

"But..." I stammered. "If you see all this, why don't *you* be his deputy?"

"I can *see* it, but I can't *do* it, Jim. I don't have the skills to be a fighter, a leader. That's what's going to be needed around here. And other people can see that...it's why you got the support. I just want you to promise me one thing – that you'll never start to enjoy the killing."

"I promise, Dad, it just feels necessary."

"I'm not saying all this is going to be easy for you. You'll have a lot on your plate. You'll have to keep growing fast."

We moved on a while, his arm still around me.

"I feel like we've just started to get to know each other over the last year. I'm glad we had it, you know...that life in Anchorage, seems like a parallel universe now. I don't see those days coming back. Just look at these boats here – how would we build one of these now? You know how tough it is to make fiberglass, or any composite material? Let alone engines. How are we going to do it without factories and supply chains? These boats are going to be incredibly valuable, but how do we even patch them when they spring a leak?"

"Perhaps we'll have to learn to build in wood," I replied.

"Sure, but who's going to teach us? There will've been a few traditional boat-builders around, but where are they now? And how would we make new sails? I don't think you can grow flax or hemp this far north."

"So what do we do, Dad?"

"We're going to have to learn again from scratch. How to make things. And fast. Each year, each month, the stores of what we've living on, everything from tins of food to bullets – these are going to get scarcer. Especially knowledge. That's what we're really going to be short of."

"We can do it, Dad. We'll work on it together. You can teach us how to make things. We've got time."

"Not as much as you think, Jim. There will be others like the convicts. It'll be the tough bastards who've survived. And there'll be people who won't want to help. I don't know what's coming down the pike, but I reckon you're going to have to face things that I can't imagine." He shook his head, waves lapped the sides of the pontoon as the wind strengthened, splashes wetting my feet.

"These are desperate times," he continued. "We're like a flock of sheep here, needing shepherds to protect us from the wolves. And you have it in you to be a shepherd."

"But...what if the sheep don't want a shepherd?"

"They will when they hear the wolves. Afterwards, who knows? But I don't see that coming any time soon."

"But Dad..."

"Religion got drummed out of me by your grandparents, son. You never really knew them, they were harsh people. But I had to learn stuff, and still remember some of it. Psalm 23 –

Even though I walk through the darkest valley,
I will fear no evil, for you are with me;
Your rod and your staff, they comfort me.

That's the kind of help we're going to need here. People need to look up to something, someone, to help them get through.

It's been a privilege watching you grow up this year. I'm getting too old anyway, to do what you can do, Jim."

"Dad, c'mon, that's rubbish."

"I was diagnosed with cancer last year, before all this happened. Too much smoking when I was younger, I guess. I've no idea where I am with it now, but I'm not feeling great."

SIXTY-TWO

My heart gave a flip. I looked at him, troubled. "I've been blind, I hadn't realized. That's why you've been coughing so much. Does...does Mom know?"

"It's one reason why she didn't want to leave Anchorage. You can't get scans out here...but I don't mind, really. I just want to see you and Bess as safe as can be."

"How long have you known?"

"I started getting pains a couple of years ago, but the doctors took a while to find the cause."

"Dad, how serious is it?"

"That's what I don't know, son. We'll just have to see how it goes. It's one reason why we had to go to the hospital, in Anchorage – we took all the morphine we could. Actually, I feel bad about that, I've already used more than my fair share."

I felt as if the bottom of the world had dropped out. I couldn't lose both Bob and Dad...so soon?

"I'm scared of all this, Dad."

Dad took me by the shoulders. "Jim, I guess we're all scared, underneath. That's OK. But it doesn't really matter, you know."

There was little warmth in the sun yet, and now a cloud was crossing it. The wind was picking up, the flapping of the ropes against the masts sounding like a Greek chorus, echoing around the bay.

"Look at it one way, you know, and we've been really fortunate. Most of the people your Mom and me have known... our families...even if any of them have survived, I don't see how we're going to meet up again. I just hope that some of them are still out there.

You know something – I've even started to pray. I think, maybe, I've been getting it all wrong. I've been talking to Louise a lot while you've been out hunting, and she might be right. I

295

spoke to the pastor from Hope yesterday, about maybe getting baptized."

"What! Dad, that's just not you? You don't believe in God? It's not real. You've always said so!"

"Well, maybe I should. I'm not sure what's real anymore. Is maths real? I used to think so. Hope, love, even faith – are they "real"? Look, Jim, I'm not saying I'm ever going to agree with the details, but maybe it's something like the AA believing in a Higher Power. No one's sure what it is, but it works, you're more likely to keep off the booze if you can believe in something bigger than yourself. So does it matter whether it's *real* or not?" He made quote marks in the air.

We walked on. "Einstein believed in something like that, some kind of intelligence. There are these tiny particles, you know, at the bottom of everything, that only appear when you look for them, and when you don't, they're not there. Maybe the whole universe is like that? It needs an observer. It's an *act* of creation, and behind it is a creator of some kind, with a purpose. It's what all the religions say, at heart. And what was good enough for Einstein, I guess it's good enough for me."

"That doesn't sound like a good enough reason for you, Dad."

Dad smiled. "But haven't I always been interested in what works? I guess, for me, it's fifty/fifty."

"But you've always been going on about evidence, and fifty/fifty is just a toss of the coin. How can you get baptized, if you aren't convinced?"

He laughed. "Good questions, Jim. I guess I find Louise's idea of a kind of transcendent cosmic spirit makes more sense to me than God appearing in the form of one man for a few years. If I was looking at monotheism logically, I guess I'd be a Muslim. But as Louise says, you should respect the traditions you were born into. I don't want the Christianity of my grandparents, but I think I understand them more now. The Depression was tough for them. Anyway, what tips the scales for me is that your Mom would like it, it's a little something I can do for her. Not much else I can do. Isn't that good enough?"

"Is this because of the cancer?"

"It makes a difference, sure, if your Mom is going to live more easily afterwards, knowing I've been baptized. But it's not the main reason. I think I can honestly say that.

"We all have to go, Jim, it's the only thing we can be sure of. I'm not scared of dying, just hope it's not too painful. Living – that's different, that's scary now. This year has changed my thinking, Jim. It all seems senseless. If I look back, it's desperately sad. All those people, our friends, family, everything that we've lost. I feel bad about Jerry and Marcia, I should've tried harder to persuade them to come with us. We were lucky, we've got this far, thanks to Bob. But it's not just the people, not just my job, the university, our house, it's like…it's like everything's gone. In months. The structures of society, the knowledge, the books, the news, the museums, the technology, what we got up in the morning thinking we were going to do, went to bed going over what we'd achieved during the day, it's all crumbled. And if I look ahead, it's bleak. Everything that made life work for us – you can't reassemble it overnight without a power supply. And we could get that going again, sometime, but it's still going to take us decades, centuries, to get back to where we were. And in the meantime, I think we're going to have to believe in something that's bigger than ourselves, something worthwhile, to get us through."

We turned around at the end of the pontoon.

"Dad, what am I going to do?"

"Just live the best you can, Jim. Do well by other people. Be honest with them. Encourage them. You'll need help. Particularly Jessie's – a man and wife…no better support structure's been invented. Make friends, alliances. Theo'll help, but he's no spring chicken. I'll do what I can – we should get some workshops going. You'll need engineers, chemists, carpenters, agriculturalists, vets.

People will need to retrain. You'll need generators, hundreds of them."

"But there's oil in Valdez, we could use that?"

"Maybe. Maybe there's enough there for a generation. Does oil go off in storage? I don't know. But I doubt they're just going to give it to you. So you'll need to have something to trade. And a means of getting it."

We walked on for a while.

"Dad, is this going to work?"

"Of course, Jim, life will carry on. I hope it works out as well for you and Jessie as it can do. That's all I can say. I'm not going to sugar coat it for you. Looking back, I think we were always running too close to the edge. We weren't thinking ahead, putting in fat for the lean times, it was all too short term. And some good things will come of all this, already have done. After all, you and Jessie wouldn't have met if we'd stayed back in Anchorage, and Mom and I wouldn't have agreed to your setting up home together if circumstances hadn't been a little—" He winced. "Unusual".

SIXTY-THREE

Jessie and I were sitting out on the harbor wall, arms around each other, legs swinging over the edge, looking over the boats that were still tied up at the pontoons. Along the beach, Sue was playing with friends in the water, despite the chill – it was probably warmer in the water than outside it. Shrieks and splashing noises echoed around the bay. It was so long since I'd heard children laughing. Theo and Louise were walking around the headland, talking, heads together. Further up, on the ridge, where what was now being called "The Battle of Portage Pass" had taken place, the huge, golden-red sun was setting, its rays lighting up the glaciers on each side as if they were fire rather than ice. They flickered off Jessie's eyes, her skin, she looked fantastic. Overhead, the snickering laughter of a bald eagle.

In the distance, I could see a boat sailing in from a fishing trip, a flock of gulls diving around it. I could just make out the couple of figures on board.

"That looks like Bess, the one chucking guts overboard. Is that her? Is that Bobby with her?"

Jess laughed. I loved her musical laugh, I can still hear it in my head. "Bobby was yesterday, that's Billy. She's trying them out, one every couple of days."

"What? She's not giving any of them a chance?"

"You might not believe this, Jim, but sometimes you just know. And she has time to make up."

We were quiet for a while.

"It's just over a year since this all started," said Jessie, turning to me, her new ponytail swinging. "Hard to believe so much has changed in such a short time."

"Yes. I'm not sorry about it though," I replied, weighing it up. "Even with all the dying...we've met...it's brought us together."

"I'm not sorry either," she said. "I'm glad."

"I'm still not sure why you wanted to go with *me* though," I said. "Was it because there wasn't anyone else around?"

"Jim, my last boyfriend was captain of the football team, but a Mommy's boy. He would have ended up selling insurance in his Dad's firm, except he's probably dead now. He wouldn't have survived out here for a month – would've ended up with a knife in his back. And I didn't know this about you when I first got interested, but you can track animals in the dark, shoot them through the eye, build huts, wipe out bandits, and you're going to lead a community...so start taking yourself seriously."

"So if I couldn't do all that stuff, would you still love me?"

You're such an idiot sometimes." She laughed, her eyes dancing in the sunset. "I like that about you, it's your best quality. I can wrap you around my little finger."

"I'm very happy to be wrapped around you," I replied, taking her finger in my mouth and sucking it. "Shall we go back and do some wrapping?"

She punched me lightly on the shoulder. "Jim Richards, you have a one track mind. Like mine, I guess. Anyway, on that subject, there's something I need to tell you."

"What's that?"

She hesitated. "I'm pregnant," she said, shyly.

"What? You're up the duff? I thought you were on the pill!"

"I was, but I came off it."

"Why?"

"I was talking about it with Louise. There was something she said...it was about how just surviving wasn't enough. We had to put down roots, grow communities, and build families. Look to the future."

"But, Christ, Jessie, we've got a war on here."

"She talked about that as well. She said war's normal. Always has been. It's only the last few generations who've never really been in one. You can't stop having kids just because some stupid men want to strut their stuff. Are you saying you don't want me to have it?"

"No, of course not! It's just...I don't feel ready for it, Jessie. Last year – I hadn't even ever had a girlfriend."

"Last year you hadn't killed anyone either. What's the number now...six? Seven? I saw you shooting in that fight, you were picking those guys off like ducks in a gallery."

"But that was different. We had to do it. We had no choice."

She hesitated. "We have to do this as well, if we're going to live for real, rather than just hunting or being hunted. And if we're going to start, why not now?"

"Do Mom and Dad know?"

"Your Mom does. She gave me the pregnancy test. She had a kit that you brought back from Anchorage. I don't know if your Dad does. I haven't told my Dad, but I think he'd like being a grandfather. Anyway, it's not their business, it's ours."

What a year it had been. I felt it rolling up behind me, like a carpet, leading inevitably to this moment, happiness surging through me.

I took a few deep breaths. "I love you, Jessie, and I love the family we're going to have. Jessie...would you marry me?" I scrabbled around in my pockets and came up empty and momentarily stumped. Then I remembered and pulled out my gloves, feeling the solid lump at the bottom of the left hand one. Pushing my fingers inside, I drew out and held up the ring Louise had given me.

"Jesus, Jim, where did you get that from? Are you trying to make an honest woman out of me?" Jessie's eyes were huge. "Anyway, you need to get onto your knees to ask me that. Do it properly," she insisted, laughing.

I knelt on the cobbled wall. It was slimy with moss and seaweed, but what the hell.

"Sorry. Jessie Harding," I said, my voice sounding very serious, "would you think about the possibility, would you...

would you do me the honor of…hell, will you marry me?"

"Jim Richards, I would love to. The answer is 'yes.'"

EPILOGUE

That was the story of the first year after the Event, sixty-five years ago, as seen through my eyes. Of the many battles I've won in my life, that, the first, was the easiest, and the most complete. Later, it got more difficult, as enemies grew wary of me, even feared me.

I was going to jump forward now, or I'm never going to finish this. Forward by five to ten years, to describe the beginnings of the Northern Free State: of how a family became a community, how a community became a country. But the fort is in turmoil. Gor has rushed in, worry all over his seamed face. "Master, the aliens have come. They've come for slaves!"

It took me a while to understand what he was talking about. Apparently, we have a visitor, just arrived in Anchorage, or what remains of it – you'd barely know it had been there nowadays. Exploding petrol stations, chemical depots and raging fires played havoc in the first couple of years. The houses, parks and roads have all reverted to almost impenetrable woodland, fertilized by bones. The few buildings left, rising above the sea of green, are covered in vegetation; lichen, ivy and bearded creeper have taken over the skyscrapers still standing, now homes for falcons and wildcats, foxes and bats. It's a giant cemetery, with ghosts haunting the ruins at night, eerie winds whistling around empty corridors, screams of prey being taken, the occasional rumble of floors collapsing and cladding falling off the buildings. No one from the settlements would venture in; it's a place for outcasts and outlaws, for anyone beyond the pale.

But a boat has arrived, a huge, Chinese junk, from Japan. It carries not just a visitor, but an ambassador. Short, with slit eyes, like the remaining Inuit here. Speaking good English. And the ambassador is a woman! It's a long time since we've seen any women in positions of authority. She has a couple of hundred soldiers at her back. And they have weaponry that we lost the skill of using decades ago – they even have cannon.

And to cross the vast Pacific – that's extraordinary. We don't have anything that can do more than coastal hops, and wouldn't know how to get to Japan even if we had the boats to get there.

The news has put me into a tremble. I'll ask Gor to open a can of peaches – I've been left with my own supplies and have hoarded a few tins. They're seventy years past the sell-by date, but are mostly still fine, and with no teeth there's not much I can eat nowadays anyway.

I sense a change in the attitude of the guards. Gor says the Council don't know how to respond to the Japanese ambassador. Scarcely surprising – they were probably unaware of the country's existence. She's offering sugar, salt and other goods in exchange for strong, young boys and girls. So long as they're white – apparently, the fairer the skin, the higher the premium as slaves, as status symbols, especially in the African Empire, where many of them are shipped on to. From what she says, that's the most advanced society nowadays, much more so than the new Republic of America, in the Midwest, run by Trump 111. That's recently spread to the Pacific coast, which has pushed their slaving expeditions further north. I am called to appear before the Council tomorrow. I will have to put this parchment aside for the moment, to collect my thoughts.

LODESTONE BOOKS

Lodestone Books

YOUNG ADULT FICTION

Lodestone Books is a new imprint, which offers a broad spectrum of subjects in YA/NA literature. Compelling reading, the Teen/Young/New Adult reader is sure to find something edgy, enticing and innovative. From dystopian societies, through a whole range of fantasy, horror, science fiction and paranormal fiction, all the way to the other end of the sphere, historical drama, steam-punk adventure, and everything in between (including crime, coming of age and contemporary romance). Whatever your preference you will discover it here. If you have enjoyed this book, why not tell other readers by posting a review on your preferred book site. Recent bestsellers from Lodestone Books are:

AlphaNumeric
Nicolas Forzy
When dyslexic teenager Stu accidentally transports himself into a world populated by living numbers and letters, his arrival triggers a prophecy that pulls two rival communities into war.
Paperback: 978-1-78279-506-3 ebook: 978-1-78279-505-6

Shanti and the Magic Mandala
F.T. Camargo
In this award-winning YA novel, six teenagers from around the world gather for a frantic chase across Peru, in search of a sacred object that can stop The Black Magicians' final plan.
Paperback: 978-1-78279-500-1 ebook: 978-1-78279-499-8

Time Sphere
A timepathway book
M.C. Morison
When a teenage priestess in Ancient Egypt connects with a schoolboy on a visit to the British Museum, they each come under threat as they search for Time's Key.
Paperback: 978-1-78279-330-4 ebook: 978-1-78279-329-8

Bird Without Wings
FAEBLES
Cally Pepper
Sixteen year old Scarlett has had more than her fair share of problems, but nothing prepares her for the day she discovers she's growing wings...
Paperback: 978-1-78099-902-9 ebook: 978-1-78099-901-2

Briar Blackwood's Grimmest of Fairytales
Timothy Roderick
After discovering she is the fabled Sleeping Beauty, a brooding goth-girl races against time to undo her deadly fate.
Paperback: 978-1-78279-922-1 ebook: 978-1-78279-923-8

Escape from the Past
The Duke's Wrath
Annette Oppenlander
Trying out an experimental computer game, a fifteen-year-old boy unwittingly time-travels to medieval Germany where he

must not only survive but figure out a way home.
Paperback: 978-1-84694-973-9 ebook: 978-1-78535-002-3

Holding On and Letting Go
K.A. Coleman

When her little brother died, Emerson's life came crashing down around her. Now she's back home and her friends want to help, but can Emerson fight to re-enter the world she abandoned?
Paperback: 978-1-78279-577-3 ebook: 978-1-78279-576-6

Midnight Meanders
Annika Jensen

As William journeys through his own mind, revelations are made, relationships are broken and restored, and a faith that once seemed extinct is renewed.
Paperback: 978-1-78279-412-7 ebook: 978-1-78279-411-0

Reggie & Me
The First Book in the Dani Moore Trilogy
Marie Yates

The first book in the Dani Moore Trilogy, *Reggie & Me* explores a teenager's search for normalcy in the aftermath of rape.
Paperback: 978-1-78279-723-4 ebook: 978-1-78279-722-7

Unconditional
Kelly Lawrence

She's in love with a boy from the wrong side of town...
Paperback: 978-1-78279-394-6 ebook: 978-1-78279-393-9

Readers of ebooks can buy or view any of these bestsellers by clicking on the live link in the title. Most titles are published in paperback and as an ebook. Paperbacks are available in traditional bookshops. Both print and ebook formats are available online.

Find more titles and sign up to our readers' newsletter at http://www.johnhuntpublishing.com/children-and-young-adult

Follow us on Facebook at https://www.facebook.com/JHPChildren

and Twitter at https://twitter.com/JHPChildren